# Bloodcurse

# Bloodcurse

BOOK 5 IN THE BLOODBORN SERIES

## SYDNEY WINWARD

This is a work of fiction. Names, characters, places, and incidents are either the product of the author's imagination or are used fictitiously, and any resemblance to actual persons living or dead, business establishments, events, or locales, is entirely coincidental.

Bloodcurse

*The Bloodborn Series, Book Five*

*To all of those who don't quite fit the mold of your society.*
*Sometimes you just have to forge your own path!*

**Books by Sydney Winward**

**The Bloodborn Series**
*Bloodborn*
*Bloodbond*
*Bloodscourge*
*Bloodbane*
*Bloodcurse*

**Sunlight and Shadows Series**
*A Breath of Sunlight*
*A Taste of Shadows*
*A Glimpse of Music*

**Lord Death Series**
*A Waltz with Lord Death*

**Novellas**
*Through Wylder Meadows*
*Root Brew Float*
*Yours, Sterling*
*On Silver Wings*
*Bloodmoon*

# CHAPTER 1

Another settlement...infected.

Kirsa Frey lifted her protective eyewear to gain a better perspective on the destruction that had befallen Vrahsea. She made sure to keep her mask covering her nose and mouth to protect herself from the spores floating lazily through the air. The Rotting Blight. That's what they called it. Deadly. Highly contagious. And it had already wiped out most of the dwarven race.

She swore under her breath as she placed careful footfall after careful footfall along the body-strewn path. Blank, dwarven eyes stared up at her while spores ate away at their rotting flesh. Her eyes scanned the caves, searching for survivors, and as she passed each rotting body, she counted.

One...two...two hundred and thirty...three hundred and five...

The deeper she traveled within the settlement, the thicker the spores that suffocated the air. She double checked the air flowing in and out of her mask. She was safe for now, but if the mask slipped even an inch…

A shudder ran through her at the thought. She'd seen firsthand what the Rotting Blight was capable of. The supposed tormenting pain following exposure to the disease was not something she'd wish on her worst enemy.

"Help…me…" a voice moaned.

Kirsa's eyes widened when she realized someone had survived the Blight. She sprinted over fallen bodies, kicked open a door someone had unsuccessfully attempted to bar closed, and then she found him—a dwarf nearing three hundred years old judging by the gray sprinkled in his long beard and the muted gold in his irises. The stench hit her first, and she panicked when she thought her mask ceased working but relaxed only slightly when she found it intact.

The male's leg looked torn apart, as if shredded by a wild beast. Red blood became black rot that slowly worked its way up his torso and ate a chunk of the side of his face.

"The…chieftain's…daughter…" he addressed her with wheezing breaths, one eye wide while the other threatened to fall from its socket. "Help…me…"

Instead of replying immediately, she reached into the bag strapped around her shoulder and pulled out a vial filled with bluish liquid. A simple clear tear escaped the man's eye, and he hung his head in defeat.

"We both know you are too far gone," she murmured, her voice muffled through her mask as she unstopped the vial and held it to his lips. He drank it willingly, only the smallest amount dribbling past his parched lips. "Where did the outbreak begin?"

"The...baby..." he said. "The mother...she hid it...when she returned...to the settlement. We should have checked... We always...check."

The baby he spoke of must have contracted the disease from outside the settlement, or even from a visitor who didn't know they were infected until it was too late.

His muscles relaxed, and the pain in his eyes drifted away with the spores circling overhead like vultures, waiting to kill their next victim. The blue serum quickly worked through his body until he finally smiled, the pain seeming to have disappeared. Then at last, his head drooped, the light fading from his eyes as his life slipped away. She didn't dare touch him, not even to close his eyes in death.

Her posture slumped as she subtracted the numbers she'd counted in this settlement from the total number of remaining living dwarves. Four hundred and twenty-two. No more remained of their dying race. For years, they'd sought out a cure with no luck. The only thing they hadn't done yet was seek outside help, as proud of a race as they were. Kirsa, herself, would have asked for help long ago, but the chieftain forbade it. Her mother's pride was far greater than anyone she'd ever known.

Not wanting to spend a second longer than necessary in this death trap, she hurried toward the exit and drew on the entrance of the cave with flammable rock salt, and then she sparked the substance to life. The rock wall burst into flame for mere seconds before leaving a scorched symbol behind, a mark to warn all others to steer clear of the infected caves.

Knowing dawn would soon approach, she placed the same symbols on several more entrances and departed as quickly as she came.

Nearly every inch of her was covered, protecting her from the sun. The faintest ray of sunlight on the skin could turn a dwarf to stone, making the precaution of wearing extra clothing necessary.

Just as dawn made an entrance, she returned to her own settlement in Vrork where two guards waited for her at the Mountain entrance. Elric and Adrietta wore masks with weapons strapped to their chests. She understood the standard procedure all too well and followed the female guard into the next room where she proceeded to undress until she stood completely naked, every inch of her exposed. Adrietta inspected her for any sign of the infection, including inside her mouth, before the female nodded in approval and ushered her behind a changing screen where a new set of clothes awaited. She changed quickly, glad to be covered again. No matter how many times she ventured outside the Mountain, she'd never felt comfortable being scrutinized in her nakedness.

The guard returned to her post while Kirsa breathed in the fresh Mountain air. The scent of rich earth greeted her as she stepped into a large cavern, glowing green crystals lighting her way.

Home. This was home.

And she was terrified of the Rotting Blight taking it away.

She passed grim-looking dwarves who'd already lost so much, even family members of their own. They looked at her with hope, but her expression remained impassive as to not show them the truth of their situation.

Dwarves would likely go extinct, and sooner rather than later.

As she'd expected, she found her mother, Chieftain Mathilde, in the infirmary, her lips pressed together so tightly they looked nonexistent. She wore a circlet around her head, golden dwarven symbols weaved together with a single ruby placed in the middle of her forehead.

Her mother tore her gaze away from the sick and dying, and her expression became graver upon seeing Kirsa.

"What news do you have?" her mother asked.

Kirsa shook her head and frowned. "Three hundred and five dead from the Blight. Theirs was the last settlement aside from our own."

Not one to hold in her anger, her mother struck out at the wall with an enclosed fist, rattling jars filled with ointment and medicine. Several nurses glanced their way, but they quickly averted their attention when they laid eyes upon the chieftain.

"That was half our population, gone in the blink of an eye. What caused the outbreak?"

"Not following standard procedures upon returning to the settlement. Someone brought it in. They didn't catch it."

Her mother lashed out at the wall a second time, startling the nurses yet again, who suddenly found the need to work at the opposite end of the infirmary.

"We're losing our greatest minds to this Blight," her mother snarled. "We need to increase the testing. Where is a blasted elf when we need one?"

Kirsa shook her head slowly, not wishing to anger her mother further. "We can't experiment on an elf. You know we can't. We would all but resign ourselves to war, and we have no strength in numbers. They will wipe us out with ease."

"Not if they can't cross our border."

That much was true. No one but a dwarf could enter the invisible border surrounding the Mountain, not unless they were invited. It warded against vampire materialization, elven magic, and enchanted weapons. And the dwarves never invited anyone inside unless they were a test subject.

"Dracula hasn't declared war despite the vampires we've taken," Kirsa pointed out. "Elven blood and vampire blood are one of the same." The blood of both races coursed with healing and immortality, unlike their own.

"Yes, but it's not *working*."

They fell silent as they watched the nurses inject patients in stasis with their daily dose of serum to help slow down the effects of the Blight and eliminate the possibility of contagiousness. In a carefully controlled environment, the Blight couldn't spread.

"How is he doing?" Kirsa asked finally as she approached the bedside of her younger brother, Tille. She trailed the back of her fingers down his cheek, willing him to open his eyes, but he didn't. Rather, he lay still with his chin etched with what looked like black vein-like markings from the Blight. The etchings covered the rest of his body as well, festering beneath the clothing he wore. If he opened his eyes, Tille would have had bright golden eyes that matched her own, his chestnut brown hair the exact same shade as hers. The two of them looked remarkably similar.

"He's stable," her mother answered, a hardness taking root in her eyes. "But I fear we can only restrain the Blight for so long." She glanced up, the worried expression of a mother replaced by a tough and unforgiving chieftain. "We need another vampire. Immediately. You're still friends with the emperor's daughter?"

Trying to hide her grimace as she thought of her human friend, Kirsa nodded. "Yes."

"Good. They have vampires visiting the big city now and again. Find one and bring it back. Take shelter in the palace when the sun is out."

Bile rose to her throat as she remembered the screams as vampire after vampire had succumbed to death in the dwarves' futile efforts to find a cure. So much innocent blood spilled, all for nothing. She had no hope that the next vampire would be any different. Just more innocent blood spilled on her watch.

"I won't disappoint you," she said, finally pushing the horrid memories from her mind. Her people were nearly extinct, and she'd do whatever it took to lead them back to prosperity, even if it meant bathing in a whole river of innocent blood.

Her mother nodded her head in dismissal. Kirsa placed a gentle kiss on her brother's forehead and left the infirmary. Her feet were laden with fatigue as she collected her belongings and equipped herself with an arsenal of weapons, but if she stopped to rest, more of her people might die. She would either rest when her people were cured, or rest in death. She saw no other option.

With determination set in her eyes, she adorned herself in sun-proof clothing, left the settlement, and started in the direction of Ironfell. Whatever unlucky vampire happened to cross her path…it was as good as hers.

# CHAPTER 2

Ichor Knell never slept. At least not within the heart of the city. Lively music and rambunctious laughter filled the atmosphere as if trying to dispel the shadowy darkness lurking in the corner. The gloom remained—a smoky haze of despair lingering in the late-night breeze.

Luca Dragomir swallowed a large gulp of his sangrose, and then another before *thunking* his tankard down on the table, which received him more than a few looks to where he brooded in the darkest corner of the tavern. One of those stares glared at him and turned away haughtily, a female he'd courted years ago. He remembered the courtship well.

Danika first sparked his interest at a blood moon celebration, and they'd courted for only a few weeks until he broke her heart. In fact, he counted at least three females he'd courted in the past in this very tavern, a long trail of broken hearts he felt no desire to mend. If he'd been three hundred instead of thirty-nine, no one would have blinked an eye at his courtship endeavors. But it seemed one more was one too many, earning him the title of Ichor Knell Heartbreaker.

He watched several drunken females dance along to the music nearest the hearth, flickering embers glowing against their dark silhouettes. In another life, he might have attempted to woo one of them.

"Another round?" the barmaid asked. He didn't need to nod before she refilled his tankard, leaning closer to him as she too-obviously leveled her bosom to his line of sight. Scented oil leaked from her in coiling, suffocating waves. He turned his head away from her, letting his displeasure show. What he wanted was to be left alone with his drink, and not even a pretty face could tempt him away.

The barmaid leaned even closer. He bared his fangs and hissed as a warning. His status as an unmated Dragomir placed too many unwanted suitors in his path.

She seemed to get the hint, as she quickly scurried away and left him to his own devices. He began to nurse his drink while his eyes once more glazed over. He felt detached from his surroundings, as if the word existed around him and he wasn't a part of it.

Numb. He felt numb.

The silver ring insignia of two intertwined wyverns on his left pinky caught a glimmer of candlelight, and he stared at the foul thing as if it had personally offended him. The ring marked him as a Dragomir vampire and created expectations he couldn't uphold.

Someone slammed their palms on the tabletop, and Luca didn't even flinch as his tankard rattled against the vibration. His friend, Gavril, slid onto the seat beside him while laughing amusedly, and Skender followed after. The trio, people called them, at least they did now that there were three of them and instead of four. While Luca had black hair and violet eyes, Gavril had blond hair and blue eyes, and Skender red hair and brown eyes. They looked completely different from one another, yet inseparable and always noticeable in a crowd.

Skender snatched Luca's drink away before he could take another sip, a growl following the unwelcome intrusion. "You've had one too many of these tonight, my friend," Skender said, downing the rest of the drink in his stead. He wiped the thick red liquid dripping from the corner of his mouth. "You know what happens when vampires get too drunk."

"Aye," Gavril said with one eyebrow raised. Luca still didn't know where his accent was from, and he didn't divulge the information either. "Dey vake up in da morning, tethered to mates dey don't vant."

"I'm not drunk," Luca finally muttered, though his eyes burned from the liquor mixture. Vampires concocted their own types of alcohol that their bodies could handle, those infused with human blood. Any other liquor wouldn't have worked otherwise.

Gavril and Skender shared a look, and Luca found he didn't like the understanding passing between them.

"She's gone, Luca," Skender said, patting him on the shoulder. "It's been seven years since Laurel ended it. No use pining over her still. She's taken."

"I don't know what you're talking about." Luca stared emptily at the table, worn and scarred over decades of use. "Now if you'll kindly allow me to get back to my night…"

He attempted to stand, but Gavril pushed him back down. "Ve're vorried about you. Come on zee fishing trip with us. Get her off your mind once and for all."

A fishing trip… Getting away sounded nice, but not only for a few days, or even a summer. He needed to get away for much, much longer. Ichor Knell was draining the life out of him, and he felt as if he could do nothing but stand by and watch it happen.

He rubbed his pained eyes, unsure whether the ache stemmed from the excess liquor or the lack of sleep. Both, he decided. His head pounded. Heat seared his face. And a gaping hole festered in his chest right where his heart should be.

Shaking his head, he reached for the empty tankard and dribbled the dregs into his mouth. "I'm headed home." He stood and swayed on his feet, blinking back the vertigo crawling through his head.

"Good luck," Skender said at last.

"Ve'll keep your seat varm," Gavril joked. His friend's words might have brought a smile to his face if he didn't feel like a thousand horses had trampled him into the ground during a stampede.

With a nod, he left the tavern and the music, the laughter, and the company behind. His mind remained blank as he returned to the castle, though it didn't feel much like home lately. He felt like a stranger walking the halls, a ghost of his former self, a shell of his past.

"At the tavern again?" a stern voice behind him asked.

Turning around with a bleak expression, Luca took in his father, Lucian, standing with his arms crossed over his chest, and his mother, Bridgette, several paces behind him, her hands clasped in front of her. As always, his mother was transparent, more so than his father. She looked close to tears, her eyebrows drawn together with worry, which indicated his parents only recently fought with one another.

His gaze returned to his father, and their interaction years earlier immediately broke through his weakened barriers, as his emotional void could no longer hold the memory back.

*"He's dead," Luca had said with tears strangling his voice. He didn't usually reach out to his father for comfort, but he needed it so badly. However, his father didn't answer as he sifted through vials of medicine in the infirmary filled with other patients who had been injured in the war.*

*"I watched those blood hunters kill him," he continued, despite clearly not having his father's attention. "And I couldn't stop it."*

*Finally, his father lifted his head to meet Luca's gaze. "What was that? Never mind, I have vampires to see to. One of them won't stop screaming, but nothing is wrong with her body. I'll see if I can calm her down."*

*His father left, and the last remaining string in Luca's heart snapped.*

That had been the last time he hadn't been completely broken. Such a long time for the darkness to grasp hold of him with its smokey, tendril claws.

"I've paid your tabs night after night," his father continued, his shoulder-length black hair glinting under the candlelight. "I've let you do as you please, but it ends tonight."

Luca continued to stare blankly at his father, preparing himself for what was to come. It seemed fitting for his father to come to him now instead of months, or even years earlier. He was the youngest child, yet the most overlooked. At thirty-nine years old, he was still considered young for a vampire, looking to be in his twenties, and his appearance wouldn't change much for the duration of his life. It had been a long time since he'd viewed his own portrait, as he couldn't see his own reflection as a vampire, and he didn't want to get another one painted just to see how haggard and lonely he looked.

"Your mother and I have decided to cut you off. You may continue to live in the castle, but now you will work for your keep."

"I'm sorry," his mother whispered. "I'm so sorry."

It didn't surprise Luca in the slightest. When his life had spiraled continuously downward for years, he expected the pattern to continue. His own parents didn't care anymore. Not when he was broken. Shattered. Empty.

"Fair enough," he replied as he turned away from them and continued down the hallway.

"That's it?" his father scoffed. "No pushback?"

"No."

He wanted more than anything for his parents to rush after him, to tell him they loved him despite their decision. But they didn't. They never did.

Ichor Knell was no longer his home. Even if his parents would still allow him to live within the castle, he wanted nothing more to do with this city. Not the culture nor the people. Especially not the people.

When he reached his room, he startled at the female lying in his bed, sleeping. He couldn't remember her name, but through the haze of fog in his brain, he vaguely recalled kissing her. A lot.

But nothing ever went past kissing, as he would have hated getting stuck with her, or anyone else he somewhat liked, as a mate. It seemed he would add one more name to the Ichor Knell Heartbreaker list, if only he could recall it.

His gaze passed over the mess of parchment, scrolls, and books scattered about the desk and floor. Mostly about his interest in learning new languages and cultures. He could read, write, and speak a variety of different languages. But tonight, it held no interest for him.

The female remained asleep as he packed a bag with only a few of his belongings. A full flask of vampire liquor. A change of clothes. A book written in the Old Language. He knew he should leave the ancient tome. But his father would be furious if he took it.

And he wanted his father to be furious just one last time. He hoped they would never cross paths again.

His eyes remained glazed as he left the castle without bidding farewell to a single soul. And when he found himself in front of Oriel Covaci's estate, he froze, a lump forming in his throat. Candlelight flickered softly through one of the windows, the drapes pulled back to reveal four smiling, happy vampires inside. His gaze lingered on one vampire, a beautiful blonde female with blue eyes the color of crystal waters, sunshine on her very breath. Laurel sat close to her mate, Zachariah Degore, her head resting familiarly on his shoulder as she chuckled at whatever Oriel said.

His gaze roamed over the satin petals of the pink flower tucked neatly in her hair, and then it lingered on her lips, the memories of each kiss they'd shared attacking his mind like the claws of a feral bear. He always made sure to avoid the places she spent her time, and it had worked. At least until now. Something unseen squeezed his heart, a fierce ache rising in his chest.

"I should not have come," he whispered to himself. He wanted to walk away, but his feet seemed to be nailed to the ground, not allowing him to move even an inch.

Oriel suddenly became stiff, visible through the window, and his gaze darted outside to meet Luca's, even in the darkness. Being six times older than him, it failed to surprise him that Oriel had picked up on Luca's quiet words, even with a barrier of bricks between them.

Wearing a scowl, Oriel turned to his mate and Luca's sister, Cosette, and said something he couldn't hear, not even with enhanced vampire hearing. Immediately, Cosette jumped to her feet and threw the front door open. Her face broke into a wide smile, which faltered all too quickly upon noticing Luca's pack.

"Are you going somewhere?" she asked, her voice dangerously quiet in the darkness of the front garden.

It was as if a dam broke inside of him after seeing his dear sister, the only family member he could be his true self around. Cosette had always been his best friend, but lately…

"Where have you been?" he asked in a wet tone, his chin quivering. He knew it wasn't fair to put this on her, especially with her now six-year-old adopted son needing so much of her attention. He adored Leif himself, but they haven't been coming around anymore.

"Right here," Cosette said, taking a step toward him. "I haven't gone anywhere."

He shook his head and gestured to the expansive estate, to the beautiful gardens, to the male still inside, sitting across from their two guests  . Each of them sat with rigid postures, as if listening to their every word.

"I feel like I can't see you anymore," he despaired. "Not since *him*."

Not since she had mated with Oriel, who was Laurel's brother.

Tears now trailed down Cosette's cheeks, empathetic to the wavering emotions building inside him. It didn't help that he was likely a bit cup-shotten despite how he had insisted he wasn't to his friends.

"But Oriel is my mate."

"I know," he sighed, running a hand down his face. "I know."

She took yet another step toward him, nearly close enough to touch. "Luca, what—"

He moved out of her reach, knowing he would break down completely if he allowed her to pull him into her arms. "I have nothing here, Cosette. Nothing. You've been the only thing keeping me here, and now I don't even have you." He swiped at his cheeks, moisture collecting there from his burning eyes. "I'm happy for you, I really am. But I'm miserable here. I came to say goodbye. I don't know if or when I'll ever be back."

Tears escaped mercilessly from her eyes, and she clamped her hands to her mouth as if attempting to keep her emotions at bay, but she soon began weeping. Each sob pained him more than the last. He wished to comfort her, to wrap her within his embrace, but he stopped in his tracks when he noticed Oriel move from the window to the front door. The pained look in Oriel's eyes reflected what Luca felt beneath the layers of alcohol he'd consumed.

Although he didn't move closer, Luca detested that Oriel's presence was taking yet another moment away from time with his sister.

Intimidated by Oriel standing in the doorway, he turned without another word, but he took only two steps before Cosette closed her fingers around his, her eyes pleading.

"I need you, Luca," she sobbed, grasping onto his hand as if to keep him grounded. She was also six times older than him and therefore much stronger and could physically force him to stay if she tried. "Stay. I beg you."

"Stay for what?" He didn't need to explain his strained relationship with their parents, as she understood all too well. Not to mention his broken heart over Laurel, which seemed to ache fiercer by the day.

Her grip tightened on him. "For me."

He swallowed and forced himself to turn away to avoid looking at her sorrowful expression. He needed to leave now.

Otherwise, he feared he would lose the strength altogether. "Like I said," he whispered huskily. "I never get to see you anymore. It will be as if nothing has changed."

At last, Cosette's grip slackened as her weeping returned with a vengeance. He hated to leave like this, but the only alternative was to leave without saying goodbye at all. Although he had no qualms about doing it to the rest of his family, he couldn't do it to Cosette.

"I'm sorry," he said, trying his best to ignore the burning behind his eyes as his heartache intertwined with his lack of sleep. "Tell Leif..."

His words trailed off, not knowing, exactly, what he wanted to say to his nephew. So, he instead clamped his mouth shut and walked away from the estate and left his teary sister behind. Even when the estate disappeared from view, he still heard the conversation transpiring in his absence.

"Cosette—" Oriel said softly.

"Why?" she spat in a tone he recognized as pure anger. "The incident with Laurel happened seven years ago. Why can't you forgive Luca? I thought he didn't visit me because he was busy, but it's because of *you*."

He flinched at his sister's words, not wanting to be the wedge between her and her mate. But still, he kept walking.

"He can come and go as he pleases," Oriel replied defensively.

"Can he? As I recall, glaring every time you see him isn't exactly inviting."

Luca picked up his pace to put enough distance between him and the others to no longer hear their conversation.

When at last their argument became muffled, his posture relaxed, but only slightly, because as he stared at the long road ahead, he realized he had no idea where he was going. But he didn't care. As long as he continued placing one foot in front of the other, he'd find himself farther away from the darkness that clung to him in the vampire city and closer to a place he wanted to be, one that might dispel the shadows suffocating him from the inside out.

# CHAPTER 3

Traveling outside Vrork always felt like stepping into an alternate world. Mountainscapes shrank into what she considered miniscule hills, people grew to tower above her, and the cultures never ceased to shock her. In her settlement, dwarves spent most of their days tinkering with new discoveries, though nowadays, they spent that same time trying to find a cure for the Blight. In other races' cities, there were so many more people. More activity. More laughter. And their clothing styles were…atrocious.

Kirsa grimaced as she watched a pair of human ladies twirling their colorful umbrellas and walking in small steps as if their skirts didn't provide ample room to move, let alone run in the case of an emergency. She glanced down at her own attire—thick red pants airy enough to protect her against the heat and warm enough to shelter her from the Mountain cold, tucked into her calf-length brown boots. She wore her waist-length cape with its hood up but the mask cloth off when clouds protected her from the afternoon sunlight. Long gloves hugged the entire length of her arm, once again to protect her from sunlight.

People stared as she passed, a combination of wonder and curiosity in their expressions. Dwarves didn't venture from their territory often and seeing someone walking about a foot shorter than them was bound to be shocking.

*I'm not that short,* she said to herself as she enviously eyed a tall woman on the opposite side of the street. *Perhaps short for a human, but I'm rather tall for a dwarf.*

But the stares she received said otherwise.

Ignoring the gawking humans, she followed the road leading to the white and gray palace looming in the distance. She'd visited several times since the Crusader war years ago, if only to see the friend she'd met during the frightening time. The war had been another threat to her people, forcing them to flee to their settlements and rarely leave. They couldn't afford to lose more lives, especially not to war.

Guards stared her down suspiciously as she approached the front of the castle, their postures becoming rigid as if she might use one of the weapons strapped to her back.

"State your business," a guard said, his eyes a bit too far apart, even for a human.

Hearing the human tongue startled her for several moments, and she only just remembered to switch from the dwarven tongue before opening her mouth.

"I'm here to see Princess Chloe." The words sounded foreign to her ears, and she almost didn't recognize her own voice. "I would like an immediate audience with her."

"As would anyone wanting to get a glimpse of the future bride," the second guard snickered. "Move along, runt. We have better things to do."

She wasn't sure what took her aback more—that the guards had better things to do than stand in one spot all day, or that Chloe was engaged to be married. When did the betrothal happen?

She started to argue, but a familiar voice cut across her. "Oh, don't mind them. Please come inside, Kirsa. Before the sun catches up to you."

Being too short to see the face that belonged to the voice over the soldiers' heads, she craned her neck to the side and her smile grew wide as she took in a feminine figure wearing a blue gown, a crown weaved into her light brown hair. The guards didn't stop her as she flew into Chloe's arms, embracing the friend she hadn't seen for far too long now.

"Look at you!" Chloe exclaimed, holding her at arm's length. "You've grown."

Rolling her eyes, she stepped out of arm's reach. "Ha-ha. That jest gets funnier each time you say it."

Chloe smirked, her mischievous side shining brightly despite the dim room. "I do enjoy gloating that I am several inches taller than you. Come, we must speak in my room. Away from prying ears..." She glanced toward the guards, who stood straighter than they had a minute earlier. Kirsa eyed them warily, wondering if either were a vampire. She carefully watched each servant and each noble in the hallways on their way through the palace, searching for tell-tale signs of vampirism. However, none of them gave any indication.

When they reached Chloe's room, she shut the door behind her, and her shoulders drooped simultaneously while her eyes lost their previous spark.

"I'm to be married in a month," Chloe croaked, and as if on cue, enormous tears trailed down her cheeks like a gushing waterfall.

"Married?" Of all the things to worry about, marriage seemed like a rather insignificant obstacle in Kirsa's opinion. She would much rather have the weight of marriage on her shoulders than the survival of an entire race.

Chloe nodded, dabbing at her unceasing tears with a handkerchief. "I don't know anything about the man other than he's a prince. My father is worried he'll die without an heir, and he's forcing me into a marriage to produce a grandson."

Kirsa tried to find empathy, she really did, but the number *four hundred and twenty-two* flashed in her mind, reminding her why she'd come to Ironfell in the first place.

"You are fortunate," she said quietly as she walked onto the balcony and looked out at the grove of pink blossom trees below. They were in full bloom as if reflecting the prosperity of Ironfell. If they resided in Vrork instead, they would shrivel and die, gnarled as the black earth sucked its essence dry. "I would give anything for the opportunity to marry and bear children. But I don't have the luxury of time."

"I apologize," Chloe said quietly as she joined her on the balcony. "I forget the burdens you carry."

"Yes, but it doesn't make your burdens any smaller." She forced a smile to her face and turned to her friend. "Can you arrange a meeting with this prince before the wedding? You might find you actually like him."

With a nod, Chloe plucked a single blossom from the tree and twirled it between her fingers. "I will try. But more importantly, why are you here? I don't assume you're here to witness the nuptials."

"I swore you to secrecy about the state of the dwarves," Kirsa reminded. "All I'm asking now is to seek shelter inside the palace while I'm in Ironfell."

"But why?"

"The less you know, the better."

Chloe's mouth turned downward as she stared at her for the longest time before she finally nodded. "I trust you."

An idea flew by so quickly that she had to grasp a hold of it before she dismissed it entirely. Time was not a luxury she could afford, and even if she had to put her friend at risk to achieve a greater goal, she would do it.

Raising an eyebrow, she asked, "How much do you trust me?"

Nightfall approached, and with it, a sense of eager anticipation. Kirsa placed iron knives in her belt and strapped a crossbow to her back, one already set with a dwarven-crafted bolt. Once released, the steel bolt would embed itself into the target, becoming a thick barb once inside the body that could not be pulled out easily without causing plenty of damage. A steel bolt wouldn't do much harm against a vampire, but the liquid iron waiting dormant inside the bolt would. Only with her own authorization in the dwarven tongue would the liquid release from the vial and into the vampire's bloodstream. Either painfully slow or quick enough to kill the creature before it killed her first.

She shuddered at the thought of killing yet another vampire. She wanted to avoid it at most costs, but not at the cost of her people. Her people came first. Always.

"Ready?" she asked when she met the princess near the back palace doors, ones not guarded day in and day out. Chloe wore a dark cloak, the hood casting her face in shadow.

"I'm still unsure," Chloe chuckled nervously as she wrung her hands. "I'd feel much more comfortable if you told me why you want me to traverse the woods alone at night."

"You won't be alone," she reassured with a smile not quite genuine enough to convince herself. "I'll be with you the entire time, you just won't see me, remember?"

As if to prove her point, she held her breath, and her body camouflaged itself with its surroundings. Her arms blended in with the gray bricks, her head with the decorative pot of flowers sitting on the small, circular table behind her. The camouflage only worked as long as she held her breath, which was for only a few minutes at a time.

When she released her breath, her body came back into view. Chloe's eyes widened, and she held her arms a little closer to herself as if witnessing the feat made her even more nervous. She eyed Kirsa's crossbow, and then her row of knives.

"I forgot you can do that," Chloe said, now tugging anxiously at the hood of her cloak. "Promise you'll stay near?"

She nodded.

"Good. Now let's hurry and get this over with."

Chloe quickly let herself out the door and stepped into the night. Kirsa made to follow after, but she only took a couple of strides before a voice spoke behind her.

"Miss Frey?" a maid asked, approaching with a respectful dip of her head. "It seems we were unable to make up your usual room, seeing as we ran into a bit of a…rodent problem. It's hiding in the chambers, and we can't get it out. But we've made up a room just down the hallway instead. I hope it meets your expectations."

"I don't care which room I stay in," she replied tensely, shifting from one foot to the other. "It could have a hundred rats inside. It doesn't matter."

Anxious to begin the vampire hunt, she turned toward the open door and froze in her tracks, her eyes widening when she faced the empty doorway with no trace of the princess within sight.

"By the Mountain," she swore under her breath.

And she started to run.

# CHAPTER 4

A desert.

That's what Luca decided his throat felt like. Parched. Dry. Thirsty. Although he'd never seen a desert before, Oriel Covaci had threatened to strand him in one often enough that he'd imagined what it might feel like to trudge through thick layers of shriveled sand in a hasty attempt to find shade before the sun broke over the horizon. In his imagination, he never found shade, and the sun scorched him, eating away at his skin until nothing of him remained but wisps of flesh.

He lifted his canteen of sangrose to his mouth, but to his dismay, found it empty, without a single drop left. He'd traveled aimlessly for days, not knowing where he was going, nor caring where he ended up.

Emptiness filled him from the inside out, his mind dry like the desert he often imagined. Cut off… His parents had cut him off. That didn't matter as much as the fact that they had never done such a thing to any of his other nine siblings. They'd even supported Cosette for two hundred and thirty years before she'd mated with Oriel.

A flash of anger coursed through him as he lashed out at a tree with his foot. His eyes widened in shock as the tree groaned under his strength. What surprised him was he *felt* something. An emotion. He hadn't felt anything in so long that it shocked him.

But as quick as it had come, it disappeared into the night, despite how he desperately tried to cling to it. He wanted to feel again, even if anger coursed inside his blood rather than a more pleasant emotion.

He ran a hand down his face as the numbness returned with a vengeance. His parents must truly detest him if they were willing to cut him off. He'd never meant to take it this far. All he'd wanted was their help. Their love. Their support.

And now he had none of it.

Temptation ate away at him to simply fall onto his back and stare up at the sky until the sun rose and burned him away to a crisp, to no longer exist in a world that didn't want him, didn't need him.

But his instincts kicked in, nonetheless. His eyes flashed red as the scent of human wafted past his nostrils. He needed to feed if only to satiate his dry, burning throat. His eyes focused, his ears alert as he followed the scent on deft feet, silent while he crept through the underbrush in the darkness of night.

Leaves broke overhead to reveal a glimmering moon. Shadows swayed as a light breeze moved through the boughs, a whisper moving on its breath. And then footsteps. Faint.

Taking a deep breath through his nose, he isolated a single human scent. The human was alone, which meant vampire law allowed him to hunt them.

Luca crouched low as his hunting instincts took over, leading him forward like a lion ready to pounce on its prey. He moved fluidly, the dense forest obeying his every whim from the whisper of a breeze carrying the human's scent toward him to the branches bending soundlessly when he prowled past.

And then he saw her.

The human wandered quickly and nervously, glancing over her shoulder at every turn in the bend. Her cloak clouded her face in a mask of shadow, making him unable to see her features. But it didn't matter. A meal was a meal, despite the face beneath the hood.

His fangs sprouted from his gums, and she must have heard the sound because her gaze darted in his direction, her wide eyes barely visible beneath her hood. She scrambled backward, but she wasn't fast enough to escape as he leaped from the shadows and pounced on top of her, pinning her flat against the ground. He aimed his fangs toward her neck, but he froze when her hood fell away to reveal a terrified young woman, her fearful eyes two pools of shimmering moonlight.

But not just any young woman.

Even in the darkness, he swore she looked like the human emperor's daughter.

Slowly, he lowered the hand ready to snap her neck a moment before. He retracted his fangs, and his eyes faded from a deep red to a light violet. Surely, he was mistaken about her identity.

She gasped, her breathing returning rapidly to her lungs as she clawed her way to her feet and sprinted away from him, clearly anxious to put as much distance between the two of them as possible. He followed stealthily, not to attack again but because his curiosity urged him forward.

Looking behind her shoulder every few seconds in her escape, she sprinted straight into the city, through a winding garden full of pink, red, and white blooms, and then she ran into someone else.

He withdrew into the shadows as he watched a pair of arms grasp a hold of the woman's shoulders while she wept, though a large, towering flowerpot obscured his view of the second person.

"How could you?" the woman cried, her tears unceasing.

"I'm so sorry, Princess. I'm so sorry."

Immediately, his face paled as he shrank deeper into the shadows as he realized where, exactly, he hid. The palace loomed overhead, and the gardens were far too ornate to be anything but royal property.

So, it had been her. He had almost killed the emperor's daughter.

"You sent me out as vampire bait?" she continued to sob, and even from this distance, he smelled the hint of salty tears on her cheeks.

"You weren't supposed to get hurt," the other voice said, but he couldn't see the face from this angle, though it was distinctively female. "I was supposed to be there. You were supposed to wait for me."

"I thought you were following behind." The princess sniffed again, creating a deep pit of regret inside him. Again, the emotion surprised him. "He didn't hurt me. I wonder if he recognized who I was."

Guilt smashed into him. Killing the crown princess would likely have put humans to war against vampires. He was a fool.

His appetite fled from him, replaced by insurmountable shame. All he managed was to make situations worse. He'd left Ichor Knell and his miserable self followed. What would it take to leave that person behind altogether?

Not wanting to get caught in the royal gardens, he quietly melted into the shadows and camped out in the woods throughout the rest of the night and well into the next day. Guilt continued to eat him raw until he could no longer stand it. When dusk fell, he snuck back into the gardens, following the scent he remembered from the following night, which led him to a terrace. Judging by the strong scent of the princess embedded into the climbing roses, he guessed she used the terrace often.

He took a deep breath and stretched his hearing to encompass all sides of him before he started to ascend. The rose thorns pricked his palms as he climbed, but he did his best to ignore the sharp, inconvenient pain.

Finally, he reached the lip of the balcony, peeking his head over just enough to catch a glimpse of the princess. The doors leading to her room were wide open, revealing the young woman in a long green gown, her hair plaited down her back. She paced back and forth, skirts swishing around her legs as she read the letter in her hands. Her eyebrows were drawn in deep concentration.

Confident she was alone, he pulled himself up just a bit more and placed his arms casually on the railing. "You shouldn't travel in the woods alone at night," he called out. The princess spun around to face him, her eyes widening with fear the size of a mountain.

"Stay back," she whispered hoarsely, unsheathing a dagger from a jewel-embedded scabbard. She held it threateningly between them, and for a moment, he wondered if she planned to use it on him.

He studied her for a moment like she did him. She was the very definition of grace and poise, much like Laurel back in Ichor Knell. But something lived within her eyes—a fierceness, an untamed wildness—Laurel had never possessed. Although she was beautiful and regal and absolutely woo-worthy, emptiness remained inside of him, refusing to disperse no matter how much he willed it.

"You have nothing to fear from me," he finally said, resting his chin on his arms in a show of benevolence. "I came to apologize for last night. I'm only beginning to realize if I had killed you, I might have started a war between humans and vampires. You're the emperor's daughter."

She nodded, taking a single step closer as her fear visibly melted from her expression, though she never sheathed the dagger. "It's foolish to travel anywhere by myself, especially at night. I know vampire law. I was simply…helping a friend. Or at least trying to."

His thoughts drifted back to the conversation between the princess and the second female. He wondered if she was the friend she spoke of.

Slowly, he shifted his weight to lean more fully on the balcony, but he remained on the other side of it to avoid scaring her. "That's a good-looking dagger," he commented, gesturing to the jeweled weapon.

"Yes, it is…" A sigh escaped her as she turned it over in her hands. "A gift from my betrothed. I'm to be married in a month."

Another wave of remorse washed through him as he realized he not only nearly killed the crown princess, but he almost prevented this marriage from happening. However, a part of him liked feeling the guilt, because at least it was something other than the dark emotional void living within. He didn't want to leave the balcony, not if she could evoke more emotions from the dry, withered ocean inside him.

"An arranged marriage, I'm guessing," he said, judging by her forlorn expression. "We don't have many of those in Ichor Knell."

"I've heard vampires are a loving, passionate people. At least to other vampires," she amended as if thinking about when he'd nearly killed her. "Is it true?"

"When vampires find a mate, yes."

An ache filled him at the thought of Laurel. Seeing her with Zachariah killed him, shriveled him to dust. But she obviously seemed happy. Now he just needed to find it within himself to be happy for her. It was no easy task.

The sound of a door opening inside her room startled both of them, and to his surprise, the princess stepped closer to shoo him away with her hands.

"Go," she whispered. "If someone catches you here, it won't end well for you."

Luca nodded and started to climb down from the balcony, but she leaned over the side, her words halting him in his tracks.

"You will return, won't you?" she asked quietly, a daring hope shining in her eyes. "I've never had a vampire friend before."

"Nor should you."

"Please?" she asked again.

He hesitated, knowing his father would quite literally kill him if he ever found out he nearly fed on the princess, let alone spent time with her as a friend. But then he reminded himself his father had cut him off, practically disowned him while estranging him from the rest of the family. He answered to no one, especially not his father.

"Fine," he said quietly. "If we are to be friends, you must call me Luca."

"Then you must call me Chloe."

Noises coming from within the room drove him deeper into the shadows, but as he caught one last glimpse of his new friend, an unfamiliar warmth touched his heart, one he hadn't felt in a while. Happiness. It was only a flicker, but he cherished it, nonetheless.

Over the next week, Luca visited his new friend every night when the sun descended behind the Dohr mountains. Like clockwork, Chloe waited for him on the balcony, usually jesting about a guard or telling him an amusing story. He listened intently, remembering stories of his own back when he'd participated in family events. Although he didn't miss Ichor Knell one bit, he missed Cosette. But as long as the guard dog she called a mate prevented him from visiting her, he had no reason to stay in the vampire city.

"And then the wine spilled all over her lap," Chloe laughed.

"No!" He grinned from ear to ear, enjoying her story as he balanced on the railing of the balcony with his legs crossed. Tonight, his heart felt lighter than it had in such a long time, as if Chloe's friendship helped push away the darkness.

His friend laughed again, plucking apart a rose and throwing the petals over the side of the balcony. The petals twirled like the skirts of a dancer leaping across a stage. "I'm telling you I've never seen anyone more embarrassed in my life."

"I would have liked to see—"

"Chloe?" a voice called from within the room. His head darted toward the sound, and shock jolted through him as he remembered the voice from the night he'd almost killed the princess.

"Hide," Chloe ordered, but he didn't need any warning. He hopped down from the ledge and allowed his vampiristic transformation to wash over him, his feet turning into small black paws, his body into a furry red coat. As a fox, he easily hid behind a flowerpot and peeked his head around the corner just enough to watch the speaker walk out onto the balcony to join Chloe.

His heart caught in his chest, like his hair snagging tightly on a branch that wouldn't come loose, but only managed to become more tangled. The female stood at a height shorter than Chloe, each of her movements careful and calculated. She walked on the tip of her toes as if ready to flee in the opposite direction at any moment. Although he'd never seen one before in his life, he recognized her for what she was.

A dwarf.

His heart finally unsnagged and melted into a puddle as his gaze roamed over her heart-shaped face and across the bridge of her adorable nose. He couldn't tear his gaze away from her golden eyes. They looked like small drops of sunlight, framed by long, dark lashes the same color as her chestnut brown hair. The clothing she wore was like nothing he'd ever seen either. Long, flowing pants tucked into a pair of boots, though her top was more revealing. It strapped over one shoulder, loosely falling over her upper arm and leaving her other shoulder bare, and nearly half of her stomach was visible to reveal a small and slender waist.

Not able to take his gaze off her mystifying eyes for long, he watched from his hiding spot, hardly able to keep from showing himself and demanding her name.

"You're back," Chloe said casually, but her rigid posture was anything but relaxed.

"I thought I'd find one by now," the dwarf replied tiredly, loosening her braid little by little until her hair fell around her shoulders. He froze, startled by the searing heat rising to his chest. Another emotion, but one he couldn't pick apart in time before the dwarf continued, "They were easier to catch several years ago."

"That was before the war."

He crept forward just enough to get a better glimpse of the two females, but then his canine eyebrows furrowed. War? Were they talking about the Crusader war between vampires and blood hunters?

Chloe's rigid posture softened into concern, and she lightly touched the dwarf's arm. "Get some rest. You need it."

The dwarf shook her head. "I will rest when I'm either dead or watching my people prosper. There is no time to rest."

As quickly as she'd come, she disappeared, and Luca couldn't stop himself as he followed after her. He transformed back into his vampire form, hurried step after hurried step as a desperate need to meet her surfaced inside him.

And then Chloe blocked his path.

"Who was that?" he marveled, still staring after the spot where he'd seen the dwarven female last.

She smirked, amusement shining in her eyes. "Taken a fancy to my friend, have you? She needs a male admirer now and again."

"Introduce me. I beg you."

"No."

The word was simple, but it held an air of finality that crushed his heart to pieces. He hadn't taken a true interest in any female since Laurel, but at the moment, his old flame was on the very back of his mind. How could he think of anyone else when the dwarf's golden eyes burned so brightly in his mind?

He took another step toward her door, but when he tried to step into the room, blistering heat burned his skin. He hissed and jumped backward, cradling his arm to his chest. The wound throbbed, a painful reminder that he couldn't enter a room without permission. He'd never felt so desperate to enter a room before.

"Luca." Her tone sounded forceful enough for him to tear his gaze away from the door and meet the seriousness in her expression. With lips drawn tight together, she said, "I will never introduce you to her. Never."

"But why?" A vampire whine escaped his throat before he managed to stop it. "Is she already mated?"

"*Married*," she corrected, making him realize he knew nothing about dwarven culture. Was it similar to human culture then? "And no, she's not. But I advise you to keep your distance."

An ache settled in his chest, and he welcomed the feeling of his thawing emotions. But he much preferred the heat the dwarf inspired in his heart over anything else. "Give me a reason."

Chloe sighed and touched his hand gently, the way a friend would console another friend. "Her name is Kirsa Frey. She's the eldest daughter of the dwarven chief. And she's a vampire killer."

His face paled as every pleasant emotion he'd felt in the past several minutes washed away, the stream far too fast for him to catch up and retrieve them.

*A vampire killer...*

Flickers of fire rained down upon his memory, screams filling his ears. For a moment, his strength left him as he relived those memories. A blood hunter bound his wrists together with cuffs made of vodryx metal and dragged him bloodied and bruised to a stake. No matter how much he writhed, no matter how much he fought, he was no match for the blood hunter without his vampire strength, the vodryx draining every ounce of energy he possessed. Only several feet away from him, another blood hunter tied his friend to the stake and lit it on fire. Luca fought fang and nail to save Tavian, to rescue him from the fire, but the blood hunter pounced on top of him and smashed his face into the ground, forcing him to watch the flames tear through the kindling and forge their way to his friend, who screamed and wailed from the pain. Luca joined the wailing with mournful cries until Tavian became silent in death. Everything happened so fast afterward when the shimmering red ward dropped, and other vampires swooped in to save those not yet lost. But he never tore his eyes away from Tavian's burning body.

He'd never been the same since, drowning himself in liquor until he felt nothing at all. During times like these, he preferred the numbness to the throbbing ache.

"I should..." He swallowed the rising terror in his throat and backed up a step, and then another. "I should go."

"Wait, Luca—"

But he didn't stay long enough to hear the rest of her words. He hopped down from the balcony and fled from the fire, the smoke, the screams, and he didn't stop until he reached the safety of the forest where nothing was ablaze. He fell onto his hands and knees and clutched his head, begging for the screaming to stop. When he scrambled for his pack, his hands brushed against his liquor, and he hastily opened the flask. But not even a drop escaped to help dull the terror. Nothing at all.

"Please," he begged, sobbing into the damp earth. "Don't kill him. I'll do anything."

But it was too late because Tavian was already dead.

# CHAPTER 5

irsa stood anxiously on her toes throughout the day, her hand clasping and unclasping around the steel arrow she kept hidden in the waist of her pants. She didn't need a crossbow to jam it into a vampire, but she certainly preferred one.

She shifted her weight from one foot to the other as she carefully watched the front entrance doors of the palace, where a half dozen guards waited with perspiration dripping down their faces. Although they stood stone still, the drop of a needle might have startled them into fleeing from the castle entirely.

"Will you hold still?" Chloe muttered, just loud enough for her parents not to overhear. The emperor and empress looked regal in their finery and their crowns, also watching the doors intensely. But they possessed an eerie calm, a refined poise that stemmed from years of practice.

"How can I?" she replied in an equally quiet voice, glancing once again across shiny marble floors to the entrance of the palace. "A vampire is about to walk through those doors."

"A vampire you won't want to meddle with. The vampires who come to collect are a millennia old. They aren't like the decades-old vampires you usually capture."

She didn't get the chance to reply when the doors opened to let someone in. She immediately tensed when a male with shoulder-length black hair and violet eyes stepped inside. He wore black pants and a brocade vest, with a light purple shirt beneath and a darker purple neck cloth. He bared his fangs for the entire palace to see. Her heart rate quickened when the vampire moved forward by his lonesome, not a single soul accompanying him as he approached the royals. Again, she fingered the arrow, debating whether she was mad enough to attack this vampire, or if she should wait for another opportunity.

"Lucian Dragomir," the emperor greeted with a dip of his head. "I assumed we'd be visited by Nicolae instead."

"Nicolae has family matters to attend to," Lucian said. His nose twitched so subtly that she might have missed it if she hadn't already been staring at his fangs. And then his gaze traveled over Kirsa before landing on Chloe, a hardness taking root in his eyes. Chloe shifted as if uncomfortable under his scrutiny, and then her gaze lowered to the floor.

The vampire took another step forward, his nose twitching once more. Although he took his gaze off the princess, he certainly didn't remove his attention from her. "I hope no vampires have been causing mischief in your city, Your Imperial Majesty."

"None," the emperor replied. "Will you be staying in Ironfell, Your Grace? The servants have made up a room for you."

Lucian shook his head and cast a furtive glance toward the princess once more. "No but thank you. My business here won't take long."

"Then come. I'll show you to the prisoners. They're yours for the taking."

A grimace involuntarily found its way onto Kirsa's face as the emperor led Lucian away. She'd heard stories about the emperor rounding up human criminals to give to the vampires in exchange for peace. She couldn't argue with the effectiveness when peace had existed between the two races for centuries now, but the idea was still gruesome.

A very unladylike word escaped Chloe's mouth the moment her parents disappeared from the room, and she spun on her heel toward the door.

"What is it?" she asked, following after. They reached the gardens when the princess finally turned and pointed a finger at her chest.

"Don't you dare follow. I need to warn him."

"Warn who?" When Chloe didn't answer, Kirsa moved closer, glaring at her. "Tell me who." Again, the princess said nothing, and she finally understood. A triumphant, hopeful grin made an appearance as she reached for her arrow and pulled it from the confines of her waistband. "You found a vampire, didn't you?"

"Please," Chloe whispered with wide, doe-like eyes. "Not him."

"As much as I don't want to do this, I have no choice." With ears deaf to Chloe's begging, she retrieved her crossbow and set out to find the vampire. Each second she spent away from Vrork was another second they might lose another of her kind. Every moment counted. There was much more at stake than an innocent vampire's blood.

Luca cursed his own weakness—both in mind and in body.

The fire and the screams disappeared shortly before a raging thirst scathed his parched throat. Begrudgingly, he thought of Zachariah Degore and the rumors surrounding him that he only needed to feed every couple of months, despite being a younger vampire. Younger than him, even.

In comparison, he needed to feed every couple of weeks. He used to admire vampires who had enough self-control to go long periods between feedings, but now he envied them, especially because one of them snagged Laurel right from under him like someone wrenching the rug from beneath his feet.

He sighed heavily and looked up at the boughs of trees above him. The leaves were thick enough to prevent sunlight from slipping through the cracks, and he'd sat in this same spot long enough for the wildlife to move around him once more after a long period of silence. The previously silent birds began to chirp, rabbits ducked in and out of their burrows, and even the river seemed to course faster down the hillside. Not for the first time, he felt frozen, rooted to the same spot as life moved around him.

The question remained—what was next for him?

Before he could entertain the thought, the birds silenced all at once, the shady forest seeming to grow darker before his eyes. He leaped to his feet and spun around, only to find himself face to face with his father.

A heavy dread pressed on his shoulders. He knew why his father was here before he even spoke. He was about to take something else from him. That's all he ever did when he sought him out.

"I made a visit to the emperor's palace," his father said coldly, a silent rage in the very depths of his violet eyes. "Do you know what I found?"

Luca pushed away his dread and leaned casually against the nearest tree to make a show of ineffectiveness, staring his father down, challenging him. "Enlighten me."

"Your scent," his father spat. "On the princess."

His casual defiance turned into genuine shock. "What? *How?*" During the times he'd visited Chloe, he hadn't touched her once. He'd kept his distance, careful not to let his scent linger anywhere but on and near the balcony.

*Oh.* He inhaled sharply as he remembered she had touched him. On the hand. The platonic touch was enough to condemn him.

*Drat it all!*

Standing straighter, his father's eyes flashed dangerously, as if he was the predator and Luca the prey. "I am tired of your romantic pursuits, Luca, and I refuse to stand by and allow the princess to be one of them. What do you think could ever come of it? You would either start a war by deflowering her, or Their Imperial Majesties would kill you and sweep the matter under the rug."

"That's not what's going on—" he started to protest, but his father cut across him.

"A vampire can never be on a human throne. I want you out of Ironfell, and you are not to return."

He stared at his father, a numbness taking hold of his heart and squeezing it until almost nothing remained but a beaten and battered pathetic excuse for a vampire. He felt small in his father's presence, and even smaller as his father glared at him.

"I've done nothing wrong," he finally said weakly.

But it was as if his father hadn't heard him as he dug into Luca's pack and pulled out the centuries-old tome he'd taken from Ichor Knell. Rage thundered across his father's face. "You took an old record that doesn't belong to you. You left home without telling anyone where you were going." He held out his hand as if to materialize them. "Get your fangs back home right now. The Dragomir coven is to make an appearance at the Covaci—"

"I don't want to be a Dragomir!" he cried, surprising himself with the strength of his conviction, and as the words left his mouth, he realized the truth of them. He loathed being associated with the name. It held him to certain expectations he apparently couldn't live up to, nor did he want to. What he wanted was to simply be Luca, but even he didn't know who that vampire was anymore.

Quieter, he repeated, "I don't want to be a Dragomir. I don't want to be your son. Cut me off. Disown me. I don't care. I'm not going back to the city."

His father stared at him as if confused by the words until finally his eyebrows furrowed. The anger, the authority, the hardness fizzled from his expression, replaced by hurt and disbelief. "You don't mean that, Luca. What of your mother? Your sister? Cosette has asked about you several times a day since you left."

The truth was he missed Cosette with every breath, but she wasn't around anymore. Even his friends, Skender and Gavril, weren't enough to keep him in Ichor Knell. He had nothing to go back to. Only in this past week in Ironfell had he started to feel something other than a numb void. If he returned to Ichor Knell, he feared the city might destroy him.

Luca shouldered his pack and turned away from his father, cutting an invisible thread, one far too weak to begin with. Severing the tie pained him, even more so at the thought of leaving his sister behind.

"Tell Cosette I remain firm with my decision. I will leave Ironfell if it appeases you, but after that, you have no jurisdiction over me."

"Be reasonable, Luca. What kind of world is out there for a vampire? The safest place for you is Ichor Knell."

Without turning around, he replied, "Perhaps there lies the problem."

As he walked away, his father didn't stop him, and he didn't dare turn to see the expression on his face. A part of him hoped leaving would hurt his father as much as his absence had hurt Luca. But he knew better than to hope for such things. Hoping only led to disappointment.

*Stay away from Cosette.*

*Stay away from Kirsa.*

*Stay away from Chloe.*

The words rolled around in his mind as he pulled his cloak over his head to conceal his face from the sunlight and followed the path leading to the outskirts of the city. Although he had no qualms about staying away from a vampire killer like Kirsa, it slowly destroyed him to keep distance between himself and the two others he cared for. But what other choice did he have?

He turned the Dragomir ring around and around on his finger, the mere weight of it causing him to drag his feet through the dirt and slow his progress. At one time, he had worn the ring with pride. But now the burden was too much to bear. He couldn't do it anymore.

Allowing habit to take over, he veered off the path and entered a tavern, one with few people littering the tables at the early hour. The tavern keeper looked up from where he washed the bar with a wet rag, and for a moment, the two of them stared at each other. The familiar scent of vampire filled his nostrils, and for a moment, he wondered if any of the patrons knew the male serving them was the very thing that enjoyed feeding on human blood.

"Hello, stranger," the male finally said, adopting an easy smile. "What can I do for you?"

Luca approached slowly, the numbness inside him growing colder as he twisted the Dragomir ring off his finger and set it on the bar between them. "Where can I sell this for a decent price?"

The male picked up the small piece of jewelry and inspected it close to his face. Immediately, his eyes widened, and his gaze darted back to him with disbelief in his expression. "Where did you get this?"

"Where do you think?"

With still-wide eyes, the male turned his attention back to the ring and brushed his thumb over the Dragomir wyvern seal. "So, you're one of them... I've never met one of the Three Graces nor their offspring. I am humbled. Very humbled, indeed."

The awed reaction set him on edge, and it was exactly why he no longer wanted to be associated with the Dragomir line. When others found out he was a Dragomir, they treated him differently, but he'd never done anything in his life to deserve the awe, the admiration. He wanted to walk his own path—not his father's.

"Are you positive you want to sell this?"

Luca nodded.

Closing his fist quickly around the ring, the tavern keeper said, "I will give you a good price for it. Wait here and I'll fetch the coin. I'll even throw in a drink. You thirsty?"

He watched as the male disappeared, only to reappear a minute later with a coin pouch and a tankard of sangrose he'd missed so much. The smell wafted to his nose, and he took a big gulp of the liquid, breathing out a sigh of relief. It wasn't enough to satisfy his thirst, but it was enough to drown the sorrow that spiraled around him like curling black smoke.

A prickling sensation at the back of his neck made him turn his head to look over his shoulder, but he found nothing that stood out in the dimly lit tavern. None of the occupants so much as looked in his direction. Still, he didn't want to stay any longer than necessary, especially not after the encounter with his father.

After the tavern keeper filled his flask with more of the burning red liquid, he pulled his hood farther over his face and stepped out of the establishment, only for the scent of blood to fill his nostrils. His eyes flashed red, his thirst once more burning his throat. It was the smell of a dying human. If his father wanted him out of Ironfell, then fine. He'd feed first and then leave the city and the one friend he'd come to care for behind.

# CHAPTER 6

Kirsa carefully watched the male she assumed to be the vampire from where she crouched in the shadows on a high limb of a tree. She followed his movements with the tip of the bolt protruding from the crossbow in her hands. He'd been easy to spot—one of the few wearing a hood over his head while outdoors despite the favorable weather. She couldn't tell whether he was young and naive or if he just didn't care what happened to him. Either way, she was glad he hooded his face if only so she didn't have to witness his expression when she shot him.

The vampire stalked across a stretch of green grass, weaving in and out of trees the color of emeralds as he followed the scent of human blood she'd left for him—a man who had been already dying, which helped to appease her guilt of using more innocent blood in her quest to save her people.

She breathed in deeply and held her breath. Her body and weapon blended in with her leafy surroundings as she camouflaged, and she dared not make any sudden movements lest the vampire hear her and flee before she had her chance to release the bolt.

*Come on, little vampire*, she thought. *Just a little closer.*

He paused by the river, cautiously glancing back and forth before approaching the freshly dead human. He paused once more as if to listen to his surroundings, and then his fangs sprouted from his mouth so quickly that she might have missed it if she'd blinked. Her finger itched to release the bolt from its confinement, but she continued to hold her breath and watch.

The vampire knelt to the ground and began feeding on the dead man, and still she waited until her lungs burned from the effort to keep herself concealed. He took one large gulp of blood. And then another. Finally, when she could no longer hold her breath, she released the bolt.

From the way he jolted backward, she knew he'd picked up the weapon's release with his overly sensitive ears, but he wasn't fast enough to dodge as it struck him in the shoulder, burying deep into the fibers of his skin. He screeched in both surprise and pain, and when he spun to face her, his hood snagged on a branch and fell back to reveal his face.

Kirsa was dumbstruck.

He was...beautiful. There was no other way to describe him. Rich black hair. Flawless porcelain skin. A square, masculine jaw. Blood dripped from the corner of his mouth, and the moment he retracted his fangs, his deep burgundy eyes turned violet like the irises that grew on a hilltop near Vrork.

She expected him to run, to fight. But he did neither. Rather, he stayed on his knees and stared at her as she did him, the pain of the bolt in his shoulder obviously forgotten.

With slow, deliberate movements, she jumped down from the tree and landed on her feet, an iron dagger in each of her hands. He still didn't flee, though his throat bobbed up and down as if just now realizing the danger. But he didn't move an inch, as if awaiting judgement.

The way he allowed her to approach unsettled her. In all her time of capturing vampires, none of them had let her win without a fight.

Not wanting to get too close to him to risk him biting her, she touched the tip of her dagger beneath his chin and lifted it so he more fully faced her. Again, his beauty startled her, his violet eyes drawing her in, which made her mission much more difficult.

"The bolt in your shoulder," she said, her voice hardly working against the dumbstruck rasp in her throat. "It's made of barbed steel. You can pull it out, but it will cause a lot of damage. That doesn't mention the vial of liquid iron hiding inside. If you or anyone other than a dwarf pulls it out, the iron will seep into your blood and kill you. If you attack, one word from me will release the iron, and it will kill you. If you run away, no matter the distance between us, one word from me, and it will kill you. Understand?"

"Stop!" a female voice shrieked, and Kirsa's head shot up to find Chloe gasping for air, running quickly with her skirts in her hands as she traversed the rough terrain. Her hair looked disheveled, her cheeks bright red as if the exertion from running had taxed her. "Stop, I beg you!"

Chloe pushed Kirsa away and stood protectively in front of the vampire. She hardly seemed capable of handling a simple knife, so she wondered how she planned to keep her from taking the male.

"Move," she ordered. "You know I don't have a choice."

"Not him," Chloe gasped. "Anyone but him. He's my friend."

"And so am I. Move, Chloe. There's more at stake than his life."

Chloe shook her head, sucking in several more breaths before glaring at her. "If you hurt him, Kirsa, consider our friendship over."

She paused as she glanced between Chloe and the vampire, her daggers now poised with uncertainty. Although she'd told herself she would do anything to save her people, could she truly throw away Chloe's friendship?

Lowering her daggers, she murmured, "Four hundred and twenty-two."

"Pardon?"

"Four hundred and twenty-two," she repeated in a stronger voice. "That's how many dwarves remain. One more breakout and we'll all be gone. Can you tell me his life is more important than an entire race?" She pointed one of her daggers in the vampire's direction, startled to find him watching the conversation intently.

A quivering frown formed on Chloe's face. "That's not fair."

Before she could press her point, the vampire spoke up, making both of them jump. "Why do you need me?"

"Luca, don't—" Chloe started, but Kirsa cut across her.

"Your blood," she replied quietly, shamefully looking down at her feet as every vampire's face she'd killed flashed across her memory. "Somewhere in the fibers of your blood, you have the power to heal from any ailment. I need to figure out what gives you that ability."

"Don't listen to her," Chloe quavered. "She's already killed dozens of vampires. I won't allow her to kill you as well."

The vampire—Luca—stood, wincing as if finally acknowledging the pain in his shoulder. He took a step forward, and she tensed by keeping both of her daggers pointed in his direction. Kirsa herself wasn't immortal like a vampire and could be killed, and she could also still be turned into a vampire. Neither were a viable option at the moment, not when she needed to conserve her race rather than become a different race entirely.

"The dwarves..." he said slowly, his violet gaze fixed steadily on her. "They're dying, aren't they?"

She nodded, still taken aback by how calm he acted. For a moment, she debated keeping the secret from him, but she didn't have much else to lose at this point. "It's a disease only dwarves are susceptible to. I've been trying to find a cure for years."

*But with no luck.*

"How much vampire blood do you need?" he asked.

"Luca," Chloe warned, but he didn't heed her.

"Too much," she whispered, horrified by the images flashing through her mind. She looked away from him, not wanting to add his face to the lengthy list. "I try to be careful, but..."

Her voice trailed off. The last thing she wanted was to explain herself to the vampire she planned to experiment on. Chloe's friendship be damned, she didn't have much time left before the remainder of the dwarves died off.

Before she made a move to press him forward with the tip of her dagger, he said, "I'll do it."

She blinked once, and then twice, her daggers falling to her sides. "What?"

"I said I'll do it. I'll do whatever I can to help you."

A strained sob escaped Chloe's throat, and she turned away from them as if to hide the rising emotions evident on her face. Kirsa still couldn't believe her ears as she stared at Luca, and then stared some more. Was this a game? Or did he genuinely want to help her people?

"Why?"

"Where else would I go?" he shrugged. "What else would I live for?"

Chloe spun around and took one of Luca's hands, tears trailing down her face. "You can live for me. Stay here. Perhaps I can convince my father to give you a position at court."

"I can't stay. My father knows I'm in the city. He wants me to leave."

"Your father..." Kirsa muttered, finally piecing everything together. She frowned as she thought of the vampire visitor who had come to collect. He bore a striking resemblance to

Luca. What had Chloe said? The vampire was a millennia old?

Wonderful. Just what she needed.

Worried over the fate of her people, she asked, "Will your father start a war with the dwarves if you come with me?"

"Start a war over me?" he snorted dryly. "Not likely."

As if trying one last time to convince him to stay behind, Chloe latched onto his arm and said, "My father can get you a position outside the city. He's the emperor after all. He has powerful connections. *I* even have powerful connections. There is no reason for you to give your life for this cause."

"I promise to be careful," Kirsa said in a strained voice. She needed Luca to want to come in order to retain her friendship with Chloe and try to help her people at the same time.

"Just like you were careful with the other vampires?" Chloe's glare could frighten even the burliest of men, so it nearly knocked her off her own feet. "Find another way. Vampire blood obviously isn't working."

Chloe's words held truth. If the cure lay within the healing weaved into a vampire's blood, she would have found it by now. Right?

To her relief, Luca still insisted on coming. "I may not have centuries under my belt, but I could keep up with scholars. Or at least one scholar, in particular." His gaze looked far away, a hollow sadness entering his expression, one she felt a sudden unexpected desire to wipe away. "I'll help you, blood or not. Perhaps an outside perspective is exactly what you need. If vampires are immune to this disease, I can get closer to it than you can."

"Why?" Her voice escaped as a husky whisper as she gazed back into his eyes. Out of all the vampires she had captured, none of them had come willingly. None had wanted to help.

He answered just as quietly. "Because I was helpless once. I don't want anyone else to feel the same way."

Emotion washed over her at the vampire's kindness. This wasn't a game to him. He genuinely cared—enough to give himself body and soul to the cause. At this point, she'd accept any help, even if her mother wouldn't. But her mother wouldn't allow just anyone to walk into the Mountain.

"I accept your aid." And for Chloe's benefit, she added, "And I vow I will do everything in my power to find another way."

"Oh, stars above," Chloe muttered. "I hate you both. If you die, Luca, don't come crying to me in the afterlife."

His mouth twitched. "But you would miss me, no?"

She ducked her head and sighed. "You must make me a promise. You will visit after I get married."

"I promise."

The princess threw her arms around Luca's waist and held him tight, and when she released him, she swiped a tear from her cheek.

Luca turned to Kirsa and nodded to the bolt in his shoulder. "Take it out?"

"Not a chance," she said, pushing him forward. Night was almost upon them, and she wanted to cover as much ground as possible before the sunlight posed a threat to both of their existences. "Consider this my safeguard to keeping your fangs out of my neck. You may be willing to help, but that doesn't mean I trust you."

The vampire pressed his lips together, the only indication of his displeasure.

"I bid you farewell, Princess Chloe of Ironfell," he said, saluting to the princess with a hint of a grin at the corners of his mouth while she watched him leave with a worried look in her eyes. Why did he look excited for this? This was anything but exciting. "I'm off on an adventure with a beautiful dwarf half my height."

"I am *not* half your height," Kirsa seethed, now comparing herself next to him as they walked. The top of her head reached his shoulder. He had to be a foot taller than her at *most*. "I will have you know I'm tall for a dwarf."

He held out his hand as if to measure her height for himself, his palm hovering just above her head. "I'm skeptical, but all right."

She rolled her eyes and turned to say goodbye to her friend, but Chloe had already disappeared. Discomfort settled in her stomach as fear over the state of their friendship resurfaced. She needed to do this. There was no other way. And if it came down to it, she would suck every last drop of Luca's blood dry if it meant saving her people.

She hoped more than anything that wouldn't be the case.

# CHAPTER 7

For years, a heavy weight had pressed upon Luca's shoulders, burying him deeper and deeper into the ground until he couldn't see, couldn't breathe. But mere minutes in Kirsa's company, and his head finally broke the surface of the suffocating earth, allowing him to take his first breath in what felt like an eternity.

A shiver of excitement ran through him just at the sight of her—something he hadn't felt in a very long time. She made him feel something, if only this sliver of an emotion. He preferred it to the nothingness that smothered him with its toxic black dirt.

They stopped their journey minutes before the sun peered over the horizon, seeking shelter from its poisonous rays inside a cave that might have harbored a mountain lion at one point, judging by the pile of bones stored in the corner. The scent of animal was old, reassuring him they wouldn't run into a predator.

His gaze roamed over the weapons Kirsa carried, wondering how she'd come to learn how to use all of them. Aside from being the chieftain's daughter, who was Kirsa Frey?

"Are you going to keep staring, or do you plan to help me build a fire?"

A rare smirk pulled his mouth upward as he leaned against the rocky entrance of the cave, folding his arms against his chest. "I fully intend to keep staring." His gaze veered from her weapons to her attire. She'd taken her cloak off, revealing the garb that exposed her shoulders and stomach. She also wore brown leather gloves that stretched from her fingers to her elbows—an interesting choice to compliment her strange attire. "Do all dwarves dress like you?"

"You mean dress normally?"

He glanced down at his own clothing and wondered what she found distasteful enough to inspire a grimace. "Dwarves can't expose themselves to sunlight. So why wear so…little clothing?"

"It gets hot under the Mountain," she explained, trying several times to spark a fire to life without success. "Our forges are plentiful, and they are constantly in use. Or at least they used to be."

Her meaning came across loud and clear. With the dwarves dying at a quick rate, there were less of them to work the forges.

"These blasted gloves," she muttered under her breath as she set her flint and steel down and tugged at her gloves instead. She pulled the right one off easily but struggled with the left. It wasn't until it came off when Luca's heart dipped with shock. From her fingers to the base of her elbow, her skin was stone, though she could still move her fingers, which made him think her arm wasn't entirely solid rock. It looked heavy, her fingers *clacking* together as she picked up the flint and steel and continued her efforts to spark a fire to life.

"Your arm," he managed to choke out. "What happened?"

With eyebrows furrowing tightly together, she seemed to put more of her concentration into her movements. "I need more firewood," she said, completely ignoring his question. "At least make yourself useful."

He watched her silently for a few moments before throwing his cloak over his shoulders to shield himself from the sunlight raging outside. Even with a cloak shielding him, the sunlight could still make him sick, but he'd be careful not to stay out too long.

When the cloak brushed against the small bolt protruding from his shoulder, he winced at the soreness digging deep into his muscle. His vampire healing kept him from bleeding, but when the barbs constantly irritated the tissues in his body... What could he do to convince Kirsa to take it out?

Making sure to traverse the shadows as much as possible, even with his cloak shielding him from the sunlight, he remained close to the cave as he gathered dry branches to use for firewood. On his way through the trees, he spotted red out of the corner of his eye. Raspberries dotted a leafy, green bush, the pink berries plump with a sweet aroma. Although he didn't know much about dwarves, he knew they ate food rather than lived off one thing entirely as vampires did with blood.

The berries felt soft and fragile against his fingers as he picked them one by one and carefully placed them inside his cloak's pockets. By the time he finished stripping the bush bare, both of his pockets bulged to the brim.

Satisfied with his bounty, he returned to the cave only to find the fire flickering, smoke lazily wafting toward the entrance as it escaped into the fresh air of morning. It wasn't a cold day, which made him wonder after her need to build the fire in the first place. Did it remind her of home?

Unpleasant memories probed at his mind. Screams. Blood. Fire. Lots of fire. He shook them away and kept his distance from the flames.

Kirsa raised an eyebrow at him. "It takes you that long to fetch firewood? You do know what wood looks like, don't you?"

He set the branches down in the corner of the cave and slipped his cloak off, handing it to her. She took it warily.

"Do you like berries?" he asked. "I picked some for you. Can't say I share the sentiment."

She finally spotted the berries hiding in the pockets, and her eyes widened in surprise, at least until she grumbled her gratitude and popped them one at a time into her mouth. Even with a frown of seriousness puckering her face, she still looked beautiful.

He found himself staring, not for the first time. The roughness of her attitude and personality contradicted her sweet, innocent face. A heaviness seemed to press down on her hunched shoulders. Worry puckered her mouth. The gold in her eyes seemed to move as rapidly as her thoughts.

When he thought of dwarves, short, ugly creatures came to mind. But although Kirsa was short, she was anything but ugly. Her beauty awed him. He beat his brains as he attempted to remember many of the flirtatious lines he'd used on other vampires in the past, but his mind came up empty.

After finishing half of the berries, Kirsa pulled out a notepad and writing utensil, one that bore no resemblance to a quill. He'd never seen it before, and he wanted to ask about it, but she spoke first.

"How old are you?" she began with her writing utensil poised above the parchment. "I understand your father is at least a millennia old."

The mere mention of his father put a scowl on his face. A part of him delighted in risking his life for the dwarves' sake, if only to displease his father. If his father managed to find him with the dwarves, would he demand he leave their city alone as well?

"Thirty-nine," he answered, still scowling at the barren cave wall. "The youngest offspring of Lucian Dragomir."

Kirsa's hand scribbled across the page, but when he craned his neck to look, he saw nothing but strange symbols. He watched in fascination, wishing he knew how to read it.

"And how old is that in, say, human years?"

He shrugged, sitting beside her and scooting closer to get a better look at the symbols. They made no sense at all, even when he compared them to the Old Language Laurel had insisted he learn back when they'd courted. He'd caught on easy to the ancient vampire language, and he'd learned several more out of sheer enjoyment. But the dwarven language was something else entirely.

"I can't say," he said, but wished he had more of an answer if only to watch her write again. "I came of age a while ago, but I'm still considered young for a vampire. Anything below fifty is considered young."

"Vampire age is confusing," she muttered while etching another symbol into the parchment. "I'm thirty-one myself. We age much slower than humans, though we are not immortal. I once knew a dwarf who lived to be five hundred. It's a shame we can't all look beautiful and young to our very last day."

Her age surprised him, mostly because she looked much younger than thirty-one.

He smirked and leaned closer, elbows resting on his knees. "Are you saying I look beautiful and young? I humbly accept your compliment."

"Humbly, indeed," she said under her breath, but her lips still twitched in amusement.

She continued as if on strict business. "You were born a vampire, to my understanding, not turned. Ancient blood runs through your veins. I've never studied blood quite like yours. Not Dragomir blood."

"Why not study my venom instead?" he asked. "Immortal blood may run through me, but my venom has the power to turn someone immortal."

Immediately, her hand paused on the parchment, and she looked up at him with wide, excited eyes. "I hadn't thought of it before. What if I could extract the part of your venom that created immortality and transfer it to my people? All without turning them into vampires, of course."

"What's wrong with vampires?" he jested, surprised he could jest at all. "I thought we were beautiful and young."

"And I'm trying to *preserve* the dwarven race, not wipe them from extinction by making them vampires." Excitement swirled in her golden eyes. "Tell me, Luca, have you ever turned anyone? Have you ever used your venom?"

His jesting mood fled entirely, and thoughts of Laurel entered his mind. He stood and walked to the entrance of the cave, staring at the green and lush surroundings bathed in sunlight. His hand reacted on instinct as it reached for the flask he always carried with him and unstopped it, taking a short swig despite longing to guzzle the entire thing.

Realizing he still hadn't answered, he continued to stare outside and replied with, "Not on a human, no. And I've never turned anyone. I don't see a point to it."

Kirsa followed him to the foot of the cave and stood only a couple of feet away, also looking out to the morning skies. "Can you expand?" she asked so softly that he turned to meet her gaze. Her expression was warm enough to fight the frigid memory of Laurel, but even that couldn't expel the chill from his bones.

"Expand on which part, exactly?"

"Why is there no point in turning someone?"

He shrugged and fought his growing emotions, though when he was unsuccessful at suppressing them, he took another swig of his drink. "Vampires either turn their human meals on accident, or they turn someone because they fall in love and don't want to live without the other person. Therefore, there has been no point for me to turn anyone."

"But you said you've used your venom before," she pressed. "Just not on a human."

"I don't want to talk about this," he said quietly.

"You said you'd help me. I need to know. I need to understand."

He fingered the flask in his hand, a wallowing sadness filling his heart. The sunshine might have been rain, the cloudless sky filled with swirling black clouds as his memories took him back to Ichor Knell. And the sunshine he used to see on Laurel's face turned bleak and stale. He'd never talked about what happened with Laurel. Even with Gavril and Skender, he'd used only the simplest of explanations.

Kirsa gently touched his elbow, bringing him back to the cave, back to the present.

"Vampires usually use venom on other vampires, on their mates or potential mates," he said slowly. "It creates an aching desire." A shudder ran through him at the memory.

"Then you are mated."

He shook his head. "No, I'm not."

Several beats of silence. And then she spoke. "Will you tell me about it? About her?"

The thought of Laurel made him ache everywhere—his heart, his body, his face. He attempted to rub the ache away from his eyes, but it remained, festering to the point of a pulsing throb.

He shrugged. "What is there to tell?" But as he stared at the trees just outside, branches bending with each tug of the wind, he realized he needed to talk about it, *wanted* to talk about it. Even with someone he only recently met, someone who created warmth inside him despite the chill swarming through his body.

"Laurel and I courted for two years," he finally said, releasing the words he'd stored away. "I was so in love with her, but she insisted we keep our courtship a secret. She hid me away, kept me a secret like something she was ashamed of…" He paused, thinking back on the way she'd treated him during those years. "The courtship seemed to only be fun and games for her, but it wasn't for me. She strung me along to the point where I thought we would become mates. One day, I asked her if we could start telling others about our courtship. She laughed it off and told me she didn't want anyone to know about us." He swallowed. "I didn't want to be a secret. I was done with her games. What I hadn't expected was that it was more serious for her than I realized. When I started courting someone else, she was devastated. I spent years, *years*, trying to fix what I did. She made me feel like I was the villain, and eventually I believed it. She has a mate now."

Kirsa leaned against the opposite side of the cave, her expression much more serious than it had been moments ago. "I don't understand why people waste something good.

If you weren't meant to be together, then end it at the beginning, not wait until there's a pile of broken hearts. There's only so much time in one's life... You never know when it's going to end."

"Have you experienced a broken heart then?"

She shook her head. "There's no time for courting. Not for me at least. I give up my time so others can enjoy theirs. But it's not enough. My people keep dying. Those in stasis are barely hanging on. I'm just so *weary*."

She slid to the ground as if a sudden exhaustion overcame her. Her troubles made his seem miniscule in comparison. He wanted to throw his own out the window and shoulder her burdens with her, but he wasn't entirely sure how.

He cautiously sat beside her, careful to keep his injured shoulder from pressing against the cavern wall.

"Do you want to rest?" he asked, now noticing the exhaustion in her heavy expression, in her slumped shoulders, on her very breath.

As she met his gaze, his breath hitched as he found himself staring into her golden eyes. Even in the firelight, they almost seemed to glow like embers of a deep underground forge.

"You are the first vampire I've met who has even cared," she chuckled humorlessly. "And no. Resting only delays us longer. We should get moving soon."

Shrugging his shoulders sheepishly with a mischievous grin playing at the corners of his mouth, he said, "I don't know... Secondhand sunlight makes me very sick, which might delay us even longer if we travel during the day."

She pulled her knives closer to her, eyeing him cautiously as if he might attack her. He didn't blame her, as she'd likely already been attacked by vampires plenty of times in the past.

"Like I mentioned before," she said in a dangerous undertone, "one word from me will release the liquid iron into your blood. I don't care if you are Chloe's friend. Me staying alive is pertinent to the well-being of my people. Wake me in a couple of hours, and don't you dare touch me."

"I will keep my hands to myself. Mostly." He grinned at her warning glare, but she said nothing more as she leaned back against the wall of the cave and closed her eyes. She must have been wearier than she'd let on because not even a minute passed before her breathing deepened and her face relaxed.

Luca watched her sleeping form, the flickering flames casting shadows across her features. Everything about her was beautiful from her heart-shaped face to her tan skin to her chestnut-brown hair. Only now did he notice the few small braids weaved into her hair, a texture he longed to feel with the tips of his fingers.

The long-evasive warmth filled him once more, dispelling the frigid ice encasing his heart. In time, would the ice melt completely?

He rolled his aching shoulder and pushed the thought away, turning his attention to the pad of parchment she'd left on the ground. Careful to keep the pages intact, he picked it up, his eyebrows furrowing as he studied the runes. An excitement he hadn't felt in ages clicked inside him as he noticed a pattern in the symbols and compared them with what they'd spoken about earlier.

It matched.

His heart thrummed faster and faster as he poured over the notes, his eyes moving rapidly across each page as he matched symbol to symbol, word to word. It *was* similar to the Old Language in essence, but not in form. The sentence structure was almost exactly the same, save for several variances he couldn't quite understand in the little time he had to study them. But the letters...

Enough time passed that the embers from the fire dwindled to a soft, pulsing glow. He reached for the writing utensil Kirsa had used earlier and pressed it to the parchment, but then he froze when she shifted in her sleep and rested her head against his good shoulder, nuzzling her cheek closer to his. The breath fled his lungs as he turned his head ever so slowly, only to find her face inches from his, her eyes closed in a deep slumber. He didn't dare move and risk waking her, especially not when he enjoyed her nearness far too much.

A smirk grew on his face, and he quietly pressed the writing utensil to the parchment and began writing in the dwarven language. He didn't know if any of it would make sense, but when Kirsa found it when she woke, he would know for sure.

# CHAPTER 8

"By the Mountain," Kirsa swore under her breath when she woke to find her head resting against Luca's shoulder, his arm wrapped around her waist while he slept. She pushed herself away from him and leaped to her feet, her heart beating faster than a dwarf's hammer at a forge.

He furrowed his eyebrows, blinking his eyes as if having trouble opening them.

"You were supposed to wake me!" she cried, her gaze darting to the fire that had long since burned out.

"I fell asleep."

"I can see that. I thought I told you to keep your hands to yourself."

"And I said I would. Mostly. Anyway, how is it my fault you were silently asking to be cuddled?"

She shook her head insistently. "I was not. I would never ask for such a ludicrous thing." Her face burned with heat as she carelessly thrust her things into her pack, but when she picked up her parchment and charcoal pen, she stared back at the open page in shock. Did she write this? She had no memory of it.

*Luca is handsome and strong, especially when I'm wrapped in his arms. I want to peck him on the cheek just to find out if his skin is the same temperature as mine. If he held my hand, would it be dwarfed in his?*

No, she absolutely didn't write this.

Her head shot up and she glared while he laughed, his eyes dancing mischievously. His mannerisms were very dwarfish. If he wanted to play pranks, then fine. He'd soon realize a prank war with a dwarf was nothing to treat lightly.

"I take it you understood what I wrote?" He wiped an amused, red-tinted tear from his eye.

"Clearly," she growled. "I had no idea you knew Akretti."

"I don't, but I am very good with new languages. I learned it this afternoon while you slept. I hoped you might teach me how to speak it."

*This afternoon?* She gaped at him, looking from him, to the parchment pad in her hands, and back to him. Even scholars would have a hard time mastering the written language in a year, let alone a few measly hours. She looked at the vampire before her in a new light, a hopeful, dangerous, terrifying idea forming in her mind.

"You truly learned this just now? You've never seen it before?"

He shook his head. "Not until I saw you write it. I hope I wasn't snooping into anything. Languages fascinate me."

Her heart started beating faster, and he raised an eyebrow at her as if he could hear every thump in her chest. To test his knowledge and find out if he really understood it, she penned a short paragraph and handed it to him.

*There are ancient dwarven ruins where the Rotting Blight originated from. It's dangerous and deadly. We are unable to decipher any of their language, but perhaps you could. I will give you anything you desire if you accompany me to these ruins. Anything at all.*

It took him a bit longer than the average dwarf to read through it, but when he finished, he handed the pad back to her. "Old ruins?" he asked, and she nearly melted in relief. He truly did understand the written language.

She nodded. "The ancient dwarves died long ago, before any of the dwarves in my day started contracting the Rot. We believe someone stirred up a disease sitting dormant for centuries, but no matter how many times we've braved the ruins, we cannot glean any information from the glyphs. We've been left to our own devices and knowledge to find a cure for ourselves."

"Did these ancient dwarves die from the Rot?"

"We believe so, yes."

"Then they likely wouldn't have found a cure either."

He had a point there. "No... But we might learn of the origins of the disease, which will bring us one step closer to finding a cure. Your quick understanding of languages gives me hope, Luca. Please tell me you'll accompany me to the ruins."

He started packing his things, a teasing glint in his eye. "So, you'll give me anything I desire?" She noticed he kept his flask on his person rather than in his pack. A part of her suspected something else other than Laurel kept him going back for more drink.

"This is important to me," she insisted. "I will do anything, Luca. Anything."

They exited the cave, and by then, dusk had arrived, the sun disappearing from view. The world stilled around them, crickets chirping lazily in the tall grass and the gurgling of a nearby brook just barely audible to her ears. She followed close behind his heels, waiting anxiously for his answer.

At last, he said, "The things I want, you can't give me."

Her foot missed a step on the uneven pathway, and she would have tumbled to the ground if he hadn't steadied her in time. "You want Laurel?"

"No, I certainly don't want Laurel."

"Then what is it you want?"

He didn't answer, instead looking out over the field to the right of them. To her dismay, he diverted the subject. "I already promised to help, and so I will. If you teach me to speak Akretti, I will be prepared enough to enter the ruins."

"That's all?" she asked, bewildered by his simple request. "You don't want an enchanted sword? A room of treasure? Land of your own?"

"You are fishing for something," he said, his mischievous smile returning to his face. "Are you trying to get me to ask you for a kiss, Kirsa? Now that I think about it, it's not such a bad idea."

She punched him in his good shoulder with her stone hand. Hard. He hissed, shrinking away from her arm's reach. "How's that for a kiss?"

"I didn't realize dwarves were strong like vampires," he grunted.

"They aren't." Her voice quieted as she flexed her fingers, the weight of her stone hand pulling down on her arm. A shudder coursed through her as the memories tried to surface, but she pushed them back down fast and hard, stomping them into the dirt before they had a chance to breathe.

Although she felt his gaze on her, she didn't turn to look.

"Are you all right?" he started to ask, but she quickly cut across him.

"Lesson one of speaking Akretti," she said. "No dwarf will accommodate you in Vrork. Few dwarves will lower their pride enough to speak your tongue. They will treat you with hostility, like a prisoner, despite you coming of your own free will."

He nodded, a spark of excitement in his eyes. "Teach me everything."

And so, she did. Or at least she tried to teach him as much as possible within the hours they walked during the night. She slowed their pace as much as possible to give him more time to learn the language. He learned quickly, much to her surprise, from everyday objects to sentence structure. His memorization was impeccable, his willingness to learn enviable. Although he still had much to learn, her hope flared brighter and brighter in her chest until it nearly blinded her. She'd never met anyone with such an aptitude for languages.

All she needed was to get him inside the ruins and in front of a stone tablet.

"Let's take another break," Kirsa said as she glanced up at the brightening skies. Dawn would soon be upon them, and she didn't want to be anywhere within the sun's reach when it arrived. She clenched her jaw as she vividly recalled the searing burn of the sun's rays.

"Did you just suggest a break?" Luca snorted. "I never thought I'd hear those words from you."

"It's a rare occasion. Besides, I wouldn't want you to get sick from secondhand sunlight exposure."

He slumped down on a log and slipped his shoes off, rubbing his feet as if they ached from walking all those miles. "You don't ever get sick from the sunlight?"

She began piling sticks, one on top of the other, and glanced up at the boughs of trees above them to make sure they had ample coverage from the sunlight. Personally, she'd prefer more, but for now, they should be safe.

"No," she answered. "If I'm covered, I'm fine."

The flint and steel in her hands showered sparks upon the wood, and as it caught fire, she added kindling little by little until the flames flickered to life. When she glanced at him, she found him watching the flames, an uncomfortable fear in his eyes. But it disappeared just as quickly when he looked away and turned his attention to pulling his shoes back on. Had she imagined his fear?

As her mischievous side took hold, she reached inside her pack and casually spread a thick, gooey substance across her palms, all while hiding her actions from the vampire. The substance quickly dried, seeming to leave no trace behind.

Continuing her casual demeanor, she rounded the fire to sit next to him, scooting as close to him as she dared until their knees touched. A grunt of surprise escaped his mouth, and she held in her own surprise when her heart misbehaved from his nearness. It pounded fiercely, turning her blood into a raging river of lava. The feeling startled her enough that she nearly forgot her objective.

She shook the feeling away and cast him a coy smile, touching his forearms with her hands and sliding them down until she grasped his fingers in her own. His skin was cold to the touch, much colder than hers, but she enjoyed the way it threw a bucket of ice water on her searing pulse.

"You're right," she commented while gazing down at their hands. "My hands *are* dwarfed in yours."

He visibly swallowed, his voice raspy. "Not as dwarfed as I imagined them to be."

Once again, her pulse involuntarily quickened as her gaze shot up to meet his. The entire world stilled around them, her head spinning dizzily while she took in his beautiful violet eyes. The color was so unique. She hadn't seen anything like them before.

"I need more firewood," she finally breathed, gasping in air and releasing his hands. The connection between them faded as she distanced herself across the fire and refused to meet his gaze. "Will you gather some?"

"Of course."

The rasp from his voice had faded, and the only indication he'd left in search of kindling was a sharp snap of a twig beneath his foot before all was still. His footsteps were imperceptible, as quiet as the gentle breeze shifting the strands of hair around her face.

She stared at her hands, ignoring the fact that the residue from earlier was now gone as she remembered the tender way Luca had held them. His skin had felt soft, yet cold. His gaze sweet and kind.

"Stop," she whispered to herself as she picked up her knives and ventured into the trees. "There are more important things to focus on. Your family is dying."

The reminder kept her grounded and erased the burning pulse in her blood. Since meeting Luca, she'd found two new leads in their fight for curing the Rotting Blight—deconstructing vampire venom and taking Luca to the ancient dwarven ruins. Until she followed both leads to the end, she could not afford to lose focus.

# CHAPTER 9

$\mathcal{A}$ new and vaguely familiar emotion clawed at Luca. It was shock this time. Shock from feeling. Shock from wanting. Shock from the burning warmth in his heart. It was as if Kirsa had fired up the bellows inside him he'd long since believed were broken. Feeling something frightened him, despite him craving more. He didn't know what to do with the fired bellows, with the burning embers, with the smoke that curled upward in search of fresh air.

And beneath it all, a fear enveloped him. A fear that someone would take away one more person he had come to care about. First came Tavian, forced to a fiery grave. After it was Laurel when Zachariah stole her away. Then it was Cosette, his father giving her away to Oriel without telling him about the union until a week after it had happened. Next it was Chloe, his father ordering him to leave her be.

And now he feared these churning feelings deep within him for Kirsa because he knew—he *knew*—nothing good could come of it. Patterned fate promised to strip her away from him if he allowed himself to get too close.

He habitually reached for the flask in his pocket and took a swig, relishing the burn sliding down his throat. The brief fire helped clear his mind, pushing away all other unwanted thoughts until they focused solely on collecting firewood. He picked up a branch in one hand, and then another branch with his other hand. But when he tried to release them, his brows furrowed when it stuck fast to his skin, clinging on for dear life.

"What the…" he muttered as he stumbled backward and tried to fling the wood from his hands, but it continued to stick.

Using the nearest tree trunk as leverage, he attempted to pry the branches off, but what he hadn't anticipated was his hands sticking to the trunk as well, no amount of prying releasing him from its hold.

Luca swore loud enough to startle the birds from the boughs above him, and moments later, he heard uncontrollable laughter follow. Kirsa stepped out of the trees with a large, mocking smile spread across her face and a couple of dead rabbits slung over her shoulder.

She didn't move to help.

"I see you've found yourself in a situation." She laughed again, her golden eyes sparkling wickedly. "I wish I could help, but my hands are full."

Understanding dawned on him as he remembered her nearness, her touch on his arms, his hands. "What did you do?" he growled, trying but failing to pull his hands away from the tree.

"You clearly don't understand dwarven culture, do you?" She slunk closer until she leaned against the tree he was stuck to, only inches away. "If you start a game of japes, you sure as hell won't finish it." She nodded to his hands. "It's a dwarven innovation. The substance only adheres to wood. It's meant to build a makeshift shelter quickly and sturdily without the use of nails. Do you like it?"

"I would like it better if it wasn't fastened to my hands," he grunted, once again attempting to free himself. He would have been more worried if he wasn't so amused.

Instead of helping, she moved past him and began to build a second fire, one much closer to him in a shadier part of the trees. They'd be safer here than in the previous location.

He raised an eyebrow at her when she started to skin the rabbits bare with one of her knives. "Are you going to help me or am I just going to stand here all day?"

She made a show of thinking about it until she turned her head toward him, a glint of mischief shining brightly at him. "I think I'll let you stand there all day. I wonder how long you'll last until the wolves get you."

"Kirsa," he begged, putting on his best pitiful display. "My feet are sore and tired. At least pull me up a chair."

"I don't give in easily. You'll have to try harder."

A huff escaped him as he continued to stand with his hands embarrassingly stuck to a tree, shifting his weight from one aching foot to the other. She never ceased skinning her rabbits, and when the fire seemed hot enough, she began roasting them over a makeshift spit. The smell wafted past his nose, making him gag as it shrouded him in a cloud of disgusting cooked meat. He'd rather smell horse dung all day.

"What do you want?" he asked, churning his mind for ideas. "I'll fetch you more berries. I'll teach you about my own culture. I'll rub your feet."

"My feet?" she chuckled. "Tempting. But I still hold true to what I said about keeping your hands to yourself. However..." She bit a chunk out of the cooked meat and stared at him thoughtfully. "I do have more questions for you. About immortality."

"Unstick me first and I'll answer them."

At first, he thought she'd ignore his request, but she got to her feet and approached, placing her hands on top of both of his. A glowing warmth returned momentarily at her touch, and when she spoke a word in Akretti, his hands came loose from the tree. He stared at her, shocked at her display of magic.

"I thought dwarves couldn't perform magic," he gasped, feeling his hands to make sure everything was intact.

She returned to the fire and continued her meal. While she sat with her back against the log, facing toward the fire, he lowered himself on the opposite side to face away from it. He didn't want to see the yellow and orange flames clawing and eating at the wood within its reach.

"We can't, to a certain extent," she clarified. "Not like elves, at least. Dwarves can enchant items using the dwarven tongue and ancient elements taken from the ground, such as gems and other aged rocks. Besides, how is it any different from vampire transformations and materialization?"

"You have a point there." To avoid turning and seeing the fire in full blaze, he picked up a sharp rock and a stick and began sharpening it for no reason other than to keep his hands busy. "I would like you to show me how to enchant in time."

His heart nearly stopped when she leaned back enough that their shoulders touched. When she didn't move away, he found his heart beating faster and faster, making him feel, making him smolder. He nearly turned around and reached for her hand, for her face, but he refrained, if only barely.

"I'll consider it," she finally said as if oblivious to the blaze she'd lit inside him. "It takes years of practice, and even then, I'm no expert. But watching a master forger on the other hand…"

"A master forger?" he asked, curiosity piquing his interest. "If not that, then what are you?"

"A leader, mostly, though I specialize in substance compounds such as isolating certain components from vampire blood or creating elixirs to enhance certain attributes." She shook her head, some of her hair tickling the back of his neck. "Another time about those as well. They are complicated to explain, and I'm supposed to be asking the questions, remember?"

He shrugged sheepishly when she turned her head to raise an eyebrow at him. He said nothing more and allowed her to pose her first question.

"Have you ever witnessed anyone transitioning into a vampire? How long does it take?"

"No, I've never witnessed it, but I've heard it happening in Ichor Knell multiple times. In some cases, it lasts a few hours. In other cases, an entire day."

After a nod and a brief scribble on her notepad, she asked her next question. "Does immortality have any adverse effects on a person?"

"Sanity?" he jested, but when he noticed her serious expression, his smile died on his lips. "It can really destroy someone physically if they get an injury. If healers can't fix it, they have to live with it for the rest of their lives."

This time, her scribbling lasted longer.

His sensitive ears picked up a rustling in the leaves littering the floor, and he glanced toward Kirsa to see if she heard it, too. When she gave no indication, a sly grin pulled up on his mouth for a flicker of a second before he hid it again. He patiently waited for the rustling to move closer until he picked up the nearly inaudible sound of a flicking tongue. The head poked out of the leaves, and he made a quick, casual grab until the snake was in his hand. It didn't thrash, it didn't bite, as if it knew the two of them were one of the same in many ways.

With Kirsa's back still to him, he slowly lifted the snake to his own shoulder and allowed it to slither across. It easily found its way to her shoulder, and he could practically hear the eyeroll in her voice.

"Luca," she chided. "What did I say about keeping your hands to yourself?"

"It's not me."

She glanced toward him with furrowed eyebrows before she spotted the snake on her shoulder. A high-pitched scream burst from her mouth as she shot to her feet, jumping and screeching and flinging the snake from her shoulder. He couldn't stop his own hysterical laughter at her reaction.

"I will kill you," she huffed, red-faced as she clambered onto a boulder, staring warily at the ground as if the snake might slither out of the shadows and attack at any moment.

"I may be new to dwarven culture," he said with a grin as he rested his elbows on the log and gazed up at her, "but there are a few things you don't know about *me*. We'll see who will be the one left standing after this game of japes."

Her glare burned with a bright intensity as she stared him down. "You don't know what you just got yourself into, vampire."

He smiled amusedly. "I look forward to finding out, dwarf."

"Why don't you get some rest?" she asked, nodding her head toward the ground, though the glint in her eye hadn't yet disappeared.

Shaking his head, he replied, "Not a chance. You'll do something to me in my sleep."

The eyeroll she gave him could have been the size of a mountain itself. "What's the fun in provoking an unconscious enemy? On my pride, I won't do anything while you sleep."

"Aren't you going to sleep?"

"With the snake still out there? I couldn't sleep even if I tried."

Although he continued to eye her cautiously, he laid on the ground and threw his cloak over himself to shade him from the sunlight if by a miracle, it happened to break through the trees. Sleep came fast but fitfully, and he tossed and turned for what felt like hours as images and noises crept into his mind.

Screams.

Chaos.

Fire.

A haze of smoke filled the air, entering his lungs. Heavy. Suffocating. He coughed and tried to shield his eyes with his elbow. Other vampires jostled him in their escape from the blood hunters and crusaders trying to kill them. They hadn't been prepared. No one had seen this attack coming.

Luca ran away from the disorder with Tavian close at his heels. Panic surged through the burn of his eyes. Cosette! Where was his sister?

*There!*

He spotted a head of black hair, and the moment his gaze met hers, she screamed his name and started to rush toward him.

But then a red, shimmering wall jumped between them, and he slammed into the solid barrier, the impact knocking the air out of his lungs. He blinked in confusion, first at the hundreds of vampires trapped in the box with him, then at the barrier. What was this?

"Luca!" Cosette screamed, pounding on the translucent red wall. Hundreds of vampires also did the same, trying to break it down to save those who were trapped, but to no avail.

His wide eyes stared into hers, fear and understanding passing between them. He wasn't going to survive this. But she still could.

"Leave, Cosette!" he cried desperately. "Run!"

"Not without you," she sobbed.

He didn't get another chance to protest before the slaughter began. He spun around, his eyes widening in horror as blood hunters began beheading vampires with iron swords, as they shoved vials of liquid iron down their throats, as they tied them to stakes and burned them alive. The screams pounded against his skull. Deafening. Heartbreaking.

His body froze, overcome with shock. His feet refused to move. His arms felt heavy, burdened by anvils of fear.

A screech beside him broke through the fog of shock. A blood hunter grabbed Tavian with an arm around his neck. His friend was a young vampire like him, not strong in comparison to centuries-old vampires.

Luca hissed and sprouted his fangs as he jumped on the armored blood hunter, scratching the man across the face with his sharp nails. He sank his fangs into his neck again and again until he finally released Tavian.

But then a metal bracelet made of vodryx clamped over his wrist and depleted his energy. In his daze of distraction, another blood hunter threw him to the ground and pinned him down, his face against gritty dirt.

The other blood hunter dragged Tavian toward a stake.

He knew what came next. He'd watched it play out dozens of different times in his memory, in his dreams, whenever he closed his eyes.

"Don't kill him," he sobbed. "I'll do anything."

But the fire burst to life, surrounding him each way he turned, filling his nostrils with smoke and burning his eyes until they watered. Something touched his shoulder, and he fearfully grabbed his attacker by the wrist. His eyes flashed open, and the fire flickered to life once more, spreading across his vision like a deadly blaze.

He fearfully screeched and leaped to his feet, jumping backward to put as much distance between him and the fire as possible. With his back resting against a tree, he breathed in sharp, rapid breaths as he tried to make sense of his surroundings.

The red barrier disappeared, replaced by a quiet forest. Gentle birdsong took place of the screams. And the fire that had nearly consumed him trickled down into the small campfire hardly capable of doing much damage. When Kirsa approached cautiously with concerned eyes, he suddenly remembered where he was and where he wasn't.

"I'm sorry," he said, his voice shuddering as he pinched the bridge of his nose if only to hide his unrestrained emotions. "I need a minute."

"Luca," she said softly, moving close enough to touch his elbow. Her fingers were gentle against his skin, a soothing warmth compared to the searing heat that haunted his dreams. "I can recognize trauma when I see it. What happened to you?"

He opened his mouth to dismiss her concern, but his chin ended up trembling, and he shut it quickly as he took another several moments to recover from the horrifying images from his dream. It wasn't easy to push everything away when he still saw and heard the horror so clearly.

"I've...I've never spoken about it. To anyone. I don't think...I don't think I'm ready to."

"I understand all too well," she replied quietly, a comforting hand still on his elbow. "Do you know why I build fires during the day?"

He stopped trembling momentarily as he noticed the trace of fear in her own eyes. "I've wondered about it. I assumed it was for cooking."

She shook her head, and he heard her swallow before she lifted her chin to lock her gaze with his. Slowly, she slid her left glove off to reveal her stone arm, her fingers *clacking* together when they moved. His gaze roamed from her fingers to her wrist to the base of her elbow. All stone.

"I am terrified of the sunlight," she said so softly that he almost didn't hear her. "It was my turn to trade dwarven wares with the humans. Of course, we always traveled with partners, but my partner left on an errand, and I was alone to oversee the trading post. Several young human men came by and thought it would be fun to see what happened if they pinned a dwarf down in the sunlight. I was helpless as the sunlight slowly turned me to stone." She shuddered as if she could still feel the pain.

"And then what happened?" he whispered, realizing he'd moved closer to her.

"My partner returned," she explained. "He killed one of the young men and the rest scattered. By then, the harm had already been done. The healers back home could do nothing to reverse the damage, but I count myself lucky. Many sunlight injuries result in the inability to use the limb, or they lose the limb altogether. I can still move everything, though it's slower and heavier than before. Fire helps chase the memories away."

His overactive imagination saw it all—the sunlight, the pain, the helplessness, the cruelty. It reminded him of young boys torturing helpless animals for fun. Their savagery forced Kirsa to live with a stone arm for the rest of her life.

"Do you resent them?" he asked quietly, his fingers brushing against her arm until he took her hand in his. Her skin felt cold to the touch, like a boulder sitting in the shade for too long.

Slowly, she shook her head. "I wish I did, but a stone arm is trivial in comparison to what my people currently face."

He continued to touch her fingers, to puzzle over the chill of her skin. Above her elbow was warm, like a human's, but below was much cooler like vampire skin. He realized this was far from keeping his hands to himself, but he couldn't help it. He craved the comfort she offered from her mere proximity, and he breathed in the warmth of her touch, as if it were air.

After several moments of steeling his emotions, he finally spoke in a small voice. "It was during the Crusader war between vampires and blood hunters. I saw so much death. Death and fire. I lost people I cared about. And…and I feel guilty that I couldn't save them. I feel guilty that they died and not me." He swallowed hard, now thinking of everyone he'd lost over the years, either to death or to other circumstances. "I've lost so many."

"I'm sorry," she whispered, squeezing his hand reassuringly. "Losing those you love is never easy."

For a brief moment, he wondered how many loved ones she'd lost, but he didn't dare ask. Not after she'd revealed so much to him already.

She smiled suddenly and playfully nudged his elbow with her own. "I need fire to survive, and you fear it. What an odd pair we make." They both froze at her choice of wording, and he found his heart beating faster as he watched a crimson blush bloom across her face. She wrenched her hand out of his, and the loss of contact was like a severed limb. "N-n-not that we're a pair. T-t-that's not what I meant."

"It's not?" he teased, his own smile growing as the shadows fled his heart. He hadn't felt this light in many years, and he wanted to take advantage of every moment of it. "Cuddling. Holding hands. Dreaming of kissing me. You *want* us to be a pair."

He certainly deserved it when she walloped him across the good shoulder for the second time with her rock-hard fist. He gasped and doubled over as pain rolled over his shoulder before he felt his body start to heal from the wound. She certainly knew how to throw a punch.

"As a Dragomir, you'd think—"

"I don't want to be associated with that name," he cut across her with the grunt of a breath. Never again.

She nodded. "Then when we reach the Mountain, you will simply be known as Luca. Come. It's cloudy enough to travel, and we'll brave the secondhand sunlight together. We're getting close and should arrive by nightfall."

"So soon?"

Nervousness rumbled through his stomach like thunder on a gray, stormy night. He wasn't sure he was ready yet. He still had a long way to go to learn the language, and besides, he hardly knew what to expect. He could die under the Mountain, and while he'd been prepared for it before, he found he no longer wanted to face the possibility.

Her face became an expressionless mask as she kicked dirt over the fire, as if she, too, wasn't yet prepared to enter her own settlement. "Let's review Akretti pronunciation again," she said as they started on the last leg of their journey. "I'm curious if you remember what I taught you yesterday."

# CHAPTER 10

The change was so sudden from forest to rocky terrain that Luca had to blink twice to make sure he saw it correctly. He stepped backward, and then forward, watching his surroundings transform before his eyes.

Magic rippled around him, making his skin tingle with unfamiliarity. First, he stood on a lush forest floor. Next, his shoes scraped against rocks, scuffing up dirt as he took several steps forward and turned around to find more rocks stretching out before them.

"An illusion?" He reached out and touched the invisible barrier with the tips of his fingers, feeling the tingle threading across his skin like silken cobwebs.

"An enchantment," Kirsa corrected. "It makes Vrork harder to find unless you know where to look. As a people, dwarves prefer isolation from other races."

He raised an eyebrow at her. "Even from vampires?"

"*Especially* from vampires."

She continued with purposeful strides, her focus forward as if she saw something he didn't up ahead. After unclasping her cloak from her shoulders and slinging it over one arm, he copied her actions and followed at her heels, painfully aware of the short bolt protruding from his shoulder.

To keep his anxiety at bay, he continued the conversation with a jest. "What have vampires ever done wrong to you? Have I personally offended you? It must be my kissable lips."

One of her stone fingers pointed at his chest, a menacing glare in her eyes. "I will punch you again. And I'm warning you now that whatever you see or hear within the Mountain's walls, you will take to your grave. You will not tell a single soul. Not your sister. Not Chloe. *No one.* Understand?"

A flicker of worry flashed across his eyes. "What, exactly, will I be subjected to?"

"Just…promise me. Otherwise, I will force you to make a blood pact. It's irreversible. It's deadly if broken. I'd rather not see you die from important information slipping from your tongue."

"I promise?" He still didn't understand her reasoning, but he'd go along with it for now.

She nodded almost imperceptibly before placing her hand in front of her, and it looked as if it rested on something solid. He followed suit and jumped in surprise to find his palm against a second barrier, but this one firm unlike the one before. He'd heard stories of the dwarven kingdom, protected by a supposedly magical force to prevent anyone from entering without special permission.

Dwarven language flowed smoothly from her tongue, and he only wished he understood it better to catch what she said.

His hand melted through the barrier like a candle in a flame, and he jumped again when two dwarves appeared as if from thin air, both standing before an enormous mountain. The enchantment must have unveiled his eyes, allowing him to see the other side of the barrier.

One of the dwarves wearing light, metallic-looking armor and a mask addressed Kirsa in the dwarven tongue. He was proficient enough to recognize the terms "prisoner" and "disease."

Kirsa nodded her head in Luca's direction and replied, also in the dwarven tongue. Everything she said was lost on him, and he frowned in frustration through the entire exchange. He needed to learn this language. He needed to understand it, to speak it, to live it. As Kirsa had mentioned earlier, no one here would subject themselves to speak his own language just to accommodate him.

At last, the two dwarves led them toward the entrance of the Mountain and inside a cavernous room that split into two rooms on either side, each barricaded by a single door rounded at the top to fit the shape of the entrance. Each door was adorned with shimmering gold, glinting off the natural light entering from high above without allowing sunlight in.

The sight alone left him in awe.

And it was just a door. What did the rest of the Mountain look like?

The male dwarf with blond hair and beard pushed him through one door, separating him from Kirsa who entered the opposite door. On one side of the room lay racks and tables full of equipment like masks and weapons, and the other side contained racks and tables full of clothing and shoes.

Once again, the male pushed him forward and roughly ordered something of him in the dwarven tongue. Luca only stared with uncertainty. He certainly was no expert in the language, but did the dwarf just ask him to strip his clothes off?

When he made no move to undress, the dwarf said something else in the language that sounded rather insulting before he produced a knife and grabbed him roughly by the collar. His pulse quickened and he attempted to struggle away, but within moments, the knife tattered his shirt, and it fell right off his torso. The dwarf started for the pants, but Luca yelped and jumped away, hurrying and taking them off himself, leaving him in his undergarments.

The dwarf rolled his eyes and motioned with his knife for him to continue, down to his very shoes. He did so hesitantly, feeling awkward and exposed as he stood completely naked in front of the stranger, who continued to inspect every inch of his body, even beneath his armpits. Without warning, the dwarf grabbed the bolt in his shoulder and pulled. He screeched at the sudden pain, his eyes watering as he took several deep breaths to maintain control as the wound began to reknit.

But he wasn't dead.

Yet.

The liquid iron in the vial hadn't released into his bloodstream.

One last time, the dwarf used his knife to point toward the racks of clothes before he disappeared the way he'd come, leaving him alone in the room. He wanted to breathe a sigh of relief, but he knew what waited for him beyond the next door couldn't be much better than what had already transpired.

He sifted through the clothes and frowned. If he thought Kirsa's clothing was revealing, the choice of male's clothing wasn't any better. He ended up choosing a vest—the largest size—with cording to keep it closed at the front, though it exposed most of his arms and some of his chest. The pants were much more accommodating, surprising him at how comfortable they felt, like silky, breathable cloth that hugged him just right and tucked into his dwarven boots.

Of course, finding a pair of shoes that actually fit was a miracle by itself, and even then, they squished his toes.

At last, he walked through the opposite door, only to find Kirsa waiting for him with her arms crossed, one foot propped against the wall behind her.

"We need to find you a tailor," she said, her eyes roaming him up and down. "Is that the largest size in there? You barely fit."

Ignoring her comment, he said, "When were you going to warn me I'd be stripped at knifepoint?"

She shrugged and inspected her fingernails, though she looked on the verge of laughter. "Standard procedure for those entering the Mountain. It's to make sure the Blight stays out of our settlement. We won't take any risks."

"Kirsa," a female voice barked, which seemed to startle her more than it did him. She quickly pushed away from the wall and placed two fingers over her lips and dipped her head, replying with the dwarven word for "mother."

He realized he faced the dwarven chieftain. She wore a golden circlet across her forehead, large golden earrings that weaved from the top of the ear to the earlobe, and there was a sternness to her expression even Kirsa didn't portray.

His gaze wandered briefly toward Kirsa's ears, and he wondered if she wore similar earrings. Because her hair covered her ears, it blocked his view.

The two of them conversed in Akretti, much to his great frustration. They spoke too quickly for him to understand sentences, but he managed to catch a word here and there, such as "disease" and "blood." When Kirsa mentioned "venom," the chieftain perked up, intrigue in her eyes. It seemed as if none of the dwarves had considered studying vampire venom before. He hoped it might work, because if it didn't, not only would he be in trouble should Kirsa begin to harvest his blood instead, but an entire race could be doomed as well.

The chieftain motioned them forward, and they traversed a long stone hallway, wide enough to comfortably accommodate a group. Again, he found himself marveling at the ornate golden markings lining each end of the hallway, shimmering green, blue, and red stones set into the cavern walls and emitting a soft glow to light their way. He ran his fingers across the smooth, glassy surface of the stones, almost expecting them to pass right through as if it were water.

All too soon, the three of them stopped at the end of the hallway, and he peered over the chieftain's shoulder to find curiosity beckoning him toward the large, waiting cavern. He gaped at the gold and green chandelier dangling from the high-vaulted ceiling, set over even more ornate furniture that reminded him of molten bronze. Nothing in Ichor Knell compared to the beauty in this very room. It drew him in with the crook of a beckoning finger.

One step.

Two steps.

Three steps.

And then he stopped and gawked some more.

"He hasn't seen it yet," Kirsa chuckled behind him, speaking Akretti slowly enough to allow him to understand the sentence.

He turned around to find both Kirsa and her mother watching him amusedly, and he wondered what they were talking about. He opened his mouth to ask, but he froze when a slight movement on the wall caught his attention.

His eyebrows furrowed when he thought he saw his elder brother staring back at him, but when those eyebrows furrowed too, he jumped back in alarm. The other vampire jumped back as well.

"What the..." he muttered, trying to ignore the dwarves guffawing at him.

Slowly, he approached the other figure and reached out, only to touch a smooth, reflective surface. He jumped again, startled at the realization.

This was his reflection. Never in his life had he seen his own reflection.

The dwarves laughed again, but his throat constricted so tightly with emotion that he paid no heed. He touched the mirror again, and then once more, disbelief grasping him with sharp claws. The reflection looked similar to the last portrait painted of him, but different at the same time. He turned his head back and forth, staring into his own violet eyes and taking in his black hair. A small scar on the side of his jaw caught his attention, one he hadn't remembered being there before. He must have received it during the Crusader war, a wound from an iron weapon.

"And here we go again," Kirsa snorted in his tongue, rolling her eyes. "Vampires are in love with their own reflections."

Cautious of the chieftain still watching closely, listening to every word, he attempted to reply in Akretti, "I've never seen it before. How did you do this?"

His effort to speak the language seemed to surprise the chieftain, as her amused demeanor dropped into one of disbelief. But her guard rose so quickly that he couldn't guess her thoughts or read her expression.

After murmuring something to Kirsa, too quickly for him to comprehend, the chieftain took her leave, and he trailed her path with his gaze until she disappeared beyond another door on the opposite side of the spacious cavern.

Kirsa's voice pulled his attention back to her, speaking Akretti and only switching to his tongue during the moments he didn't understand what she said, which was a lot still at this point. "The majority of mirrors are backed with a layer of silver," she explained. "We've found when we back it with other, less pure metals instead, it gives vampires a reflection."

"Incredible," he breathed, glancing at the mirror again and watching his own reflection copy his exact movements. "Why don't you sell this innovation to vampires? I know a lot of my kind who would pay a high price for something like this."

"We have no interest in selling it because we are a greedy and prideful people. Besides, we don't like to share."

"I noticed."

She approached and stood next to him so they faced the mirror side by side, and his throat constricted with unexpected emotion once more. They looked perfect together. Like they belonged at each other's sides. Her golden eyes complimented his violet ones. Her tan face brought out the creamy complexion of his pale skin. And despite their difference in height, they looked good next to one another.

And he didn't know what to make of it.

For a moment, he wondered if she'd thought the same thing because as her cheeks turned crimson, she started leading him toward another door to the right side of the room.

Clearing her throat, she said, "This is the commons. As we are few in number, it isn't likely anyone will spend time here, especially when we no longer receive guests. The living quarters are scattered underground on the south side of the Mountain. We used to have several different entrances and exits, but we barricaded each one, and now there is only one way in and one way out. If you need to..." She glanced back at him and frowned as if worried about saying the wrong thing. "...feed, inform me as soon as possible and I'll have someone take you out."

"Like a dog?" he scoffed. "I'm not exactly fond of the idea."

"Then you'd better get used to it," she retorted. "I'm not about to hunt for you, nor am I going to allow you to put off your hunger until you end up killing several dwarves in your lust for blood. It's happened before. Besides, until you understand the rules here, you aren't about to go anywhere by yourself."

Gone was the Kirsa who he'd traveled with to Vrork, and in her stead was a ruthless leader, one who would do anything to protect her people. It was as if simply stepping into dwarven territory turned her into a different person, and he couldn't help but wonder which Kirsa was the real one.

"Come." She ushered him through a door leading into another hallway, and this time, they weren't alone.

Dwarves, both male and female, traversed the halls and rooms, staring at him as they passed, some out of curiosity and others out of disdain. He towered above all of them, though some of the male dwarves weren't too much shorter than him. But what stood out the most was the jewelry.

Rings, necklaces, earrings, bracelets, and more adorned each dwarf, some made of plain gold while others sparkled with jewels of every size, shape, and color.

His gaze once again roamed to Kirsa, and he studied her with her back turned to him. Although she wore gloves, he remembered her wearing two rings on her right hand, the one not turned to stone. And he still couldn't see her ears. Otherwise, he spotted no other jewelry on her person.

He didn't get enough time to study the dwarves or his surroundings before Kirsa grabbed his arm and pulled him into another room. Compared to the rest of the Mountain, this room was plain, with long, rectangular tables stretching from end to end. Unrecognizable objects lay on top of each table, littering every surface and hardly leaving an inch to spare. He swallowed hard when he noticed needles. Dozens of needles. And vials. Some were filled with liquid ranging in color from clear to blue to red. Others were empty.

"We're getting started?" he squeaked, and he cleared his throat in an attempt to hide the fear layered within. "Already? But we only just arrived."

"I'm not planning on taking any of your blood, Luca." She rolled her eyes while gathering several vials and other objects and ingredients he didn't recognize. "At least not yet. Are you able to produce venom?"

"Yes," he nodded, sitting anxiously in the chair across from her. "Can you leave the room?"

"What for?"

Another wave of anxiety rushed over him at the thought of her watching. Over the past several days, they'd developed something akin to friendship, but they still hadn't known each other for long.

"I feel...vulnerable."

The hardness in her expression vanished, replaced with a soft understanding. The cold leader disappeared in favor of the dwarf he'd gotten to know on the journey to Vrork. That alone helped him relax considerably.

She touched his hand, the bellows within him burning fiercely where their fingers met. "I need to be present to make sure everything goes well. Take your time. I'm willing to wait. If it helps, I'll answer any questions you have about Vrork in the meantime."

His question came easily, waiting on the tip of his tongue. "What's your favorite thing about this place?"

"There are many things I like," she answered, circling him to stand behind him. Her fingers brushed against the spot where the bolt had been earlier, the wound completely healed. "I first must apologize on Gunther's behalf, the guard stationed at the entrance. I usually pull the bolts out, as I do it much gentler than him. He must be having a bad day."

"Clearly." His skin still throbbed, remembering the pain. It hurt worse to get it taken out than to get shot in the first place. "Your favorite thing?" he reminded.

"A meadow near the top of the Mountain." She briefly met his gaze before quickly glancing away. "It's full of purple irises, and when they are in full bloom... It's beautiful." A smile formed on her lips as she turned a vial around in her fingers with her gaze far away. "As a little girl, I'd always dreamt of marrying there. It's a silly dream. It has always been a silly dream."

He shook his head insistently. "It's not silly at all." He opened his mouth to say more but felt the prickle of venom flowing beneath his gums. Quick like a lightning strike, he sprouted his fangs, making Kirsa jump in fright as he snatched a couple of vials off the table and pressed them beneath the sharp-pointed tips. Yellowish liquid dripped free and filled the vials, and with it came an unbearable urge to bite.

He squeezed his eyes shut and backed away from her while focusing on taking long, deep breaths. He desperately wanted to sink his fangs into her neck and sip her blood, to taste it on his tongue.

At last, his flow of venom ceased, and he retracted his fangs and placed the vials down on the table before he might spill them.

"Does it hurt?" she asked, taking a step closer, but she halted when he flinched.

"Stay away for a moment," he warned, still focusing on taking deep breaths. "I told you I'm vulnerable. I really want to bite you right now."

"Oh." Her voice escaped as barely a whisper. "I didn't realize that's what you meant."

Relief flooded through him when she produced an iron dagger and held it between them, but still his desire to bite didn't fade as easily as he'd hoped. It wasn't a desire to feed, nor a desire to turn her into a vampire, but it was a desire for *her*, amplified by venom production.

"Lock me in a room," he begged in a strangled voice. He held his breath, trying not to breathe in her tantalizing scent of earthy gems and wildflowers. Otherwise, he feared what control he had would shatter.

She nodded and led him out of the room by knifepoint, down a corridor, and finally she nudged him into what appeared to be a bedroom, lit by glowing green crystals shaped like sconces that clung to the rocky wall. He wished to admire the beauty and unfamiliarity of it, but his desire pulsed brighter when he turned to look at her.

"This is where you will stay while you're here," she said, still holding the knife between them while remaining in the hallway. "The door is enchanted, and you cannot leave this room until I say otherwise."

The alarmed look in her eyes told him she still hadn't recovered from his confession, and as she closed the door between them, he finally let out the breath he'd been holding.

"By Ylios," he gasped, pressing his forehead against the cool stone wall in an attempt to eradicate the burning desire within him. "What the hell just happened?"

# CHAPTER 11

Kirsa didn't know what to think.

If Luca hadn't told her vampires used venom to bite their mates or potential mates, she would have thought he'd simply needed a vessel to use for his instinct to bite. But what if it had been something more? Had he wanted to bite her out of passion? Would he have felt the same need if another dwarf had been in the room instead of her?

Her distracting thoughts kept her from focusing entirely on the venom in the vials, as she couldn't help but wonder what it might be like for a dwarf and a vampire to marry.

"It's impossible," she muttered, despite knowing her words were a lie. "Besides, I have no time to court. Not that I would want to anyway."

A part of her knew that was a lie as well. She wanted to court. She wanted to marry. To have children. And Luca wasn't exactly atrocious to look at. Quite the opposite, actually.

"Why am I entertaining these thoughts?" she asked herself while carefully dripping several drops of venom into a clear solution, watching as it bubbled for several seconds. "I'm not desperate enough to marry the first man to come around."

Except he wasn't the first man. A lengthy list of suitors had tried to court her, even asked for her hand, but she'd either refused them or they were taken by the Rot. Who knew how much longer she had herself? Days? Months? Years? It was only a matter of time before the Rot claimed her, too. Her priority was her people, not herself. And she didn't need a handsome young vampire distracting her from her ultimate goal.

"I thought I heard you talking to yourself," her mother said as she entered the room.

Kirsa hunched over her work, trying to hide her incriminating thoughts likely evident on her face. She'd eventually need more venom, but she was beginning to reconsider being in the same room while Luca collected a sample for her.

As if realizing she wasn't going to reply to her comment, her mother said, "So the vampire came of his own volition?" She leaned against the table, though gently as if trying not to bump it.

"Yes. He wants to help."

"And does he know how many vampires have died before him?"

Placing her equipment down, she rubbed the fatigue from her eyes, made worse by the reminder of all the blood on her hands. So much blood… "He has a general idea, and he's still willing to help. I think his suggestion of using venom instead of blood might work."

"But?" her mother asked, raising an eyebrow.

Sighing, she pushed away from the table and finally looked her mother in the eye. "I'm sure I can isolate the parts of the venom that create a vampire, but I'm not confident I can isolate the parts that contribute to healing from immortality. If I'm successful, dwarves will become immortal."

She stood and paced across the room, back and forth as the situation weighed heavily on her shoulders. "Dwarves will become extinct if we don't do something, yes. But I want to *preserve* our ways of life, including our long but mortal lifespans. What if we have no other choice?"

"Then we will take it." Her mother's voice held an air of authority, one Kirsa never dared to contradict. "Our people are dying by the mounds. There are only four hundred and two of us left."

Her face paled as she snapped her attention toward her mother. "Twenty more have died?"

"Yes," her mother confirmed with a solemn nod. "While you were gone. Everyone in unit four passed. They were in stasis for too long and the Rot spread."

"Gunther's wife was in unit four," she murmured, remembering Luca's screech of pain when the guard had pulled the arrow from his shoulder. Now she understood

Gunther's awful mood—his wife had passed away. "And Tille? Please tell me my brother is still alive."

"His condition hasn't changed. He's young and more resilient than some of the others. He still has a while yet."

The unspoken words hovered in the air between them, words neither dared to utter. After losing half of their family to the Blight, they were both doing everything in their power to make the death stop, which meant little rest and plenty of attempts to find a cure.

Turning back to her work, she casually brought up what she'd been putting off since arriving. "I'm taking Luca to the ancient ruins. He's very adept at languages."

As she suspected it would, her mother's mouth deepened into a frown. "I don't want you going anywhere near the ruins. They aren't like other settlements. Not with the chasotids running around. I won't allow another incident like what happened to Neeva."

The mention of her sister brought another silent ache, one that had been festering for months. But she would be stubborn about going this time. "You heard Luca speak Akretti. It wasn't perfect, but he learned it in only a few days. Imagine what he can do with Arvitash. No dwarf has ever been able to crack the ancient language, but what if a vampire can?"

"I admit I was taken aback by his ability to speak and understand the language," her mother said, drumming her fingers on top of the table. After a few moments of consideration, she continued. "I will send him into the ruins, but he will be escorted by a guard, not you."

"*Only me*. A guard will die in there. I've already made the trip several times. I know the way like the back of my hand."

"You cannot risk your life going in there!"

"And I cannot risk Luca's!" she shouted back, standing so abruptly that the items on the table rattled. "A guard will die, and Luca will become trapped. He won't make it back out without a guide who knows the way."

Her mother's angry expression melted into one of worry, and she placed her head in her hand as if to try to hide it. "Tille is on his deathbed," she said in a raspy voice. "My son. All of my other children have passed. My husband... But you, Kirsa. You are still alive. You are still healthy. I cannot allow you to go."

Swallowing the emotion in her throat, she touched her mother's hand. "I'm sorry. I won't have another vampire's death on my conscience. Besides, the dwarves need every chance we can get."

At last, her mother nodded, though she continued to frown. "When?"

"Two weeks. Luca needs more time to study Akretti, and I still need to teach him how to wield a weapon."

"You'll be spending an awful lot of time with him," her mother pointed out. "Are you sure that's wise?"

Kirsa's ears burned hot as she started to wonder if her mother had heard her earlier conversation with herself. There was no sense in trying to deny it. "Obviously not. But I've already overseen his studies thus far. I want to continue to keep an eye on them."

"He's a vampire, Kirsa."

They could easily create a serum to take out a vampire's traits in future offspring and leave only dwarven traits. "We both know that doesn't matter." She cringed at the way she quickly defended her choices, and she realized her mother was right. She was getting too close to him already.

*What's the matter with me? A few sparks between us aren't enough to warrant these feelings.*

Except it wasn't simply a few sparks. It was a lightning strike.

"Send someone else to oversee his weapons training," Kirsa said when she at last shook hands with good judgement and rationale. "I should probably keep my distance until we leave for the ruins."

Her mother nodded in approval and gestured to the vials on the table. "The solution needs to sit overnight. Might as well get some sleep while you can."

She simply smiled and walked toward the door, not intending to get any sleep. Not with so much to do still. "Of course."

The hallways and caverns were far too empty for comfort. The Mountain used to be teeming with thousands of dwarves, and now only four hundred and two remained. If death kept up its pace, the rest of the dwarven race wouldn't last the year. The sense of urgency to find a cure was stronger than ever, pulling her toward the library filled with far too many untouched books. With the end of dwarven civilization in sight, the last thing on people's minds was reading.

Using the green crystal sconces to light her way, she located several books regarding writing and speaking Akretti, each more advanced than the last. And when her arms were full to bursting, she made her way back to Luca's room. She stood still for several long moments, her heart racing annoyingly fast. The last time she'd seen him, he'd admitted his desire to bite her. Was she safe yet? Or was visiting a bad idea?

*Definitely a bad idea.*

Still, she knocked anyway and held her breath.

No answer.

She knocked again.

Worry engulfed her, shattering her rationale as she released the enchantment and turned the knob, slowly pushing the door open. The hinge creaked from extensive amounts of disuse, a wince contorting her features as she peered inside. The light from the crystal sconces shone brightly, illuminating the figure lying face down on the bed. Her worry flared like a forge bursting to life, and she abandoned the rest of her good judgement as she rushed toward the vampire who had hardly been in control of his own actions not even an hour before. She touched his back with the tips of her fingers.

And sighed in relief when it rose up and down with each deep, slumbering breath.

"What's wrong with me?" she whispered to herself, rolling her eyes. "He's a vampire. Of course, he's not dead."

For a moment, she'd forgotten Luca couldn't die as easily as dwarves could. But still, memories of deceased vampires filled her mind, guilt and worry forming a massive pit in her stomach.

Her fingers lightly trailed up his back until she touched the tips of his black hair, a beautiful river of molten onyx. No dwarf she'd ever known possessed such a color, but rather ranged from brown to red to blond. But black? She wished to see it more often.

Again, as she looked over his handsome features, she couldn't help but stare. She used a gentle finger to trace his curved eyebrow, his rounded ear, and when she brushed her fingers against his jaw, she froze at the stubble beginning to form. Most male dwarves chose to grow their beards, so the absence of facial hair felt like a breath of fresh air.

He grunted in his sleep, and panic caused her to leap back and hold her breath, blending herself into her surroundings as her heart pounded inside her. She knew any effort to hide from a vampire would be futile. He'd not only be able to pick up her scent but hear her heart as well.

But he simply rolled over and continued to breathe deeply, unaware of her presence. Even then, she didn't dare breathe again until she knew for certain he still slept.

Quickly, she placed the books on the table and hurried out of the room, her strides long and fast until she reached her own quarters and closed the door swiftly behind her.

"What's wrong with me?" she gasped, banging her head against the door to shake the idiocy raging within her. "Luca is a vampire, not a dwarf. Besides, I cannot get distracted by a handsome face. If I lose focus, my people can die."

Despair and hopelessness coursed through her as she slid to the ground, her shoulders trembling as she fought off tears. There was no time for crying either, but she was so afraid. Afraid for her people. Afraid for herself. Afraid for

Luca. And a part of her was afraid to enter those ancient ruins again. Especially after what happened the last time.

Her shoulders quaked even more, and she habitually reached for a familiar piece of parchment she kept hidden in a crag in the wall. When her fingers brushed against a corner of the parchment, she pulled it free and unfolded it until the page stared back at her.

*Things I want to do before I die.*

Out of the ten things on her list, she'd only accomplished three of them.

*Make a human friend.*

*Learn how to throw a knife into a tree.*

*Kiss a man.*

But there were so many things she still wanted to do, and time ate away at her, stealing her future right from beneath her. The seven remaining items stared back at her, taunting her.

*See Ichor Knell in person.*

*Bathe in the star pool under a full moon.*

*Dance in the werewolf soiree during the summer solstice.*

*Taste a honey roll.*

*Get an ardor piercing.*

*Get married in the meadow.*

*Have children.*

"Impossible," she whispered as she longingly trailed her fingers down the page. "There just isn't enough time."

If she could stop time altogether, it would prove to be an efficient solution until she managed to find a cure for the Rotting Blight. But that wasn't possible either. Time would continue to roll forward. Her people would continue to die.

And she would continue to search hopelessly for something she thought might not exist. Were her people doomed for the grave?

"There has to be a way," she said, talking to herself far more than what was healthy. But even as she spoke the words, a deep, gnawing worry clawed at her gut, telling her she'd still be too late.

# CHAPTER 12

"Get up," a gruff voice ordered, and a moment later, something hard landed on top of Luca.

He shot up to a sitting position, bleary eyed with sleep as he took in his surroundings and tried to make sense of where he was. The room was small, made up of a rocky face on each wall with bright sconces above him, blinding him as if daylight entered his room. Above him stood a dwarf, a man, one with long red hair pulled back into a bun, two thick braids trailing down his chin in the form of a coarse beard. Like Kirsa, the man's eyes burned gold, though his contained a scarlet tint and reminded him of a forest fire during twilight.

"I said get up." The man gestured to whatever lay on top of Luca. "Training starts now."

Finally, he glanced down at his lap to find thin armor, a set far too small for him to fit into. For a moment, he wasn't sure what surprised him more—the fact that he'd understood most of what the dwarf said in Akretti, or that he needed training.

"I don't think this is necessary…" he replied slowly in Akretti as he fished for the right words in his mind, but judging by the man's eye roll, he wondered if he'd mangled his sentence.

The man replied too quickly for him to catch what he said, and he frowned in frustration as he finally placed his feet on the cold stone ground. Kirsa had been right—no one would accommodate him in his own language. If he wanted to fit in better here, he needed to speak the tongue. Although he'd made incredible progress over the past several days of doing little more than practicing and studying the language, it still wasn't enough. He needed to do better.

He hardly had time to grab his shoes as the male pushed him in the direction of the door, but not before he caught a whiff of a familiar scent of earthy gems and wildflowers. His eyes widened as he glanced toward the source of the smell, only to spot the brief flicker of a stack of books on the table before the man pushed him into the hallway. He stumbled, only just barely catching himself.

Kirsa…

She'd been in his room last night.

Memories of his desire for her surfaced, and although the carnal part of that desire had faded, he found he couldn't stop thinking about her. Even his dreams had included her. Where was she? What was she doing? When would he see her next?

Warmth spread from his soft smile to his fingertips as he struggled to pull on his shoes while he followed the male dwarf through the winding maze of a mountain. He welcomed the feeling, soaking it into his very core. Part of him was still frozen inside, but little by little, he found himself thawing out. Where numbness used to reside, he now felt a trickle of feeling, a sliver of warmth.

They entered a spacious cavern, the ceiling seeming to stretch for miles. Like the rest of the rooms and halls he'd already seen, this cavern was beautiful. It appeared as if molten gold clung to the rocky surface like vines climbing a wall, pulsing with life. Swords and axes *clanged* together as dwarves fought weapon to weapon, the sound reverberating across the cavern. It reminded him of the training grounds in Ichor Knell.

The tinge of sweat filled the air. Metal sang a familiar tune, one that both comforted and unsettled him. And when he strained his ears, he heard the faint humming of the Mountain itself, as if the dwarves lived in something that also lived and breathed.

Many dwarves stared at Luca with distrust in their eyes as he walked past, their grips on their weapons tightening as if they might find themselves with fangs in their necks at any moment.

How could he wipe the distrust from their expressions?

"My name is Reinhold," the male dwarf finally said. "I will be your instructor."

"My name is—"

"I don't care. Pick a weapon. We will begin with the basics."

Luca grimaced when he only understood half of what the dwarf said, but he gathered the gist of it. Instructor. Fighting. Weapons. It was all he needed to know.

Knowing he wouldn't fit the armor given to him, he tossed it aside. Then, he pulled off his too-tight vest and piled it on top, leaving him bare chested amongst dozens of other dwarves robed in armor. Reinhold raised an eyebrow.

"You want to get hurt?"

The smirk that fought for a place on his lips was almost too hard to hold back as he pulled a sword free from its stand and tested its weight on the tip of his finger. A couple decades ago, the blade might have felt heavy in his hand, but as his strength increased year by year as he aged, it felt lighter now.

"I can only get hurt if you manage to cut me," he replied in choppy Akretti, facing his opponent while holding the sword in a practiced hand.

Reinhold looked doubtful, his eyes scanning him up and down as he stepped forward with his own sword drawn. Without warning, he lunged forward, and Luca easily deflected the attack with his own weapon, surprised at the strength behind it. The dwarf's eyebrows knitted together, obviously taken aback by his skill.

Again and again, Reinhold attacked, and Luca kept up easily by deflecting each blow and delivering attacks of his own. Soon enough, they fell into a bout of parrying, footwork becoming fancier as each of them became braver with each attack.

Perspiration dripped down his forehead, glistening against the skin on his back. He focused on the dwarf's movements, not wanting to make a mistake with his own actions. Fortunately, fighting styles between vampires and dwarves were very similar.

At least until flames spouted from Reinhold's sword.

"What the..." He only barely managed to duck to avoid the dwarf's next attack. He jumped backward.

And froze.

A familiar scent wafted into the cavern, and although he didn't turn to look, he knew who it belonged to. Excitement burst in his chest, and he stood a little straighter, held his weapon with more confidence.

He leaped forward and smashed his sword against Reinhold's, a shower of sparks raining onto the rocky floor. He made sure to maintain a good distance to avoid getting burned. They continued their parrying, but when Kirsa's scent became even stronger, he knew he had to finish this, a desperate need to impress her driving him forward.

With an expert maneuver, he attacked again, this time positioning his weapon in a way that would force his opponent to hold his own weapon awkwardly. Knowing he was stronger than the dwarf, he used it to his advantage. In just a couple of moves, he disarmed the dwarf, the flaming sword flying from his hands and clattering against the ground. The flames extinguished and sizzled as if it had been immersed in a pool of water. Reinhold stared at him, the surprise evident in his features.

"I learned that move from Dracula." Luca rolled his shoulders and stretched to show off his muscles, though he still didn't acknowledge Kirsa's presence.

"Lucky hit," Reinhold argued.

"Huh…" He smirked as he looked down at his hands, his arms. "I don't think you managed to injure me. How about that?"

Reinhold's mouth twitched as he threw a towel at him and said something too fast for him to catch. Something about cleaning up. And then he left, clearly done with their practice.

Luca returned his sword to the stand and used the towel to wipe the perspiration from his forehead, slowly turning around while pretending he still didn't know Kirsa was in the room.

He feigned surprise when he found her sitting with her arms resting on the chair in front of her, watching him thoughtfully.

He opened his mouth to say something, but her beauty struck him as it had the first time he'd seen her. Even beneath the Mountain, her golden eyes swirled with brilliant gold, the color only seeming to become more intense in their dim surroundings compared to outside.

"You know how to handle a weapon," she mused, her expression still thoughtful.

He snorted. "Do I look like a Covaci to you? Of course, I can handle a weapon."

In fact, he'd spent many years training with the sword purely to impress females. He'd never done it for the right reasons, but then again, he'd never had to. At least not until the Crusader war.

The uncomfortable reminder of the war had his hand sliding into his back pocket for his flask, and he took a quick swig before his mind managed to recall the events of that day.

Kirsa likely noticed, as she continued to watch him carefully.

"I thought you'd benefit from learning how to use a weapon, but now... I'm thinking we can make the trip to the ruins a little sooner than expected. Assuming you'd have a good handle on the language by the time we left."

"Speaking of language..." He smirked as he finished drying the perspiration from his face. "Is there any particular reason you visited my room last night?"

She stood abruptly, her expression tensing into defensiveness like a lioness protecting her cubs. "You were awake?"

"No. But I caught your scent this morning. You do realize I'm a vampire, right?"

Now it was her turn to smirk. She leaned closer, only inches from his face. Her scent tantalized him, filled his nostrils with yearning. The desire to close the distance between them intensified until he barely held himself back.

"If you knew I visited last night," she whispered, her breath tickling his skin and drawing him even closer like a beckoning finger, "then you likely knew the moment I entered the cavern today. Were you trying to impress me with your swordsman skills, Luca?"

Her accurate observation took him aback, and her smirk grew wider as if noticing his surprise. However, he quickly recovered, grinning as he stretched to flex his muscles. Her gaze roamed over his arms and then dipped to his chest.

"Did it work? Were you thoroughly impressed?"

Immediately, her smile fell into a scowl, and even his reflexes weren't fast enough to dodge the punch she aimed at his arm. He screeched and jumped away, putting distance between them as he placed a nursing hand over the spot she'd hit. It pulsed with a stabbing ache, a bruise forming the size of her stone hand.

"You smell like sweaty man," she commented, otherwise ignoring his coy attempts. "Let me show you to the bath."

He didn't dare utter the teasing quip resting on the tip of his tongue as he followed her from the training cavern to a short hallway. Each way led to a dead end, a door on either side. They stood in front of the door on the left end of the hallway, steam wafting toward them from the small cracks between the wall and the door.

She gestured to the door. "Go on in. Towels are available inside. Try not to take too long. I can't have you running around without an escort, and unfortunately, that would be me."

"What? You're not joining me?"

When she feigned a punch, he dodged out of the way, laughing as he opened the door.

And paused right in his tracks.

The bath wasn't a bath at all but looked more like an underground hot spring. And he wasn't alone. Male dwarves stared back at him, their conversations ceasing from where they bathed in the water, completely naked. The same distrust he'd seen earlier echoed in each of their eyes, sending shivers of discomfort down his spine.

He turned around in an attempt to flee the uncomfortable situation, but he caught Kirsa watching him from the door leading to the female bathing quarters, her arms crossed as she gave him a warning glare. He wasn't sure what he wanted to brave—the male dwarves and their likely hidden intention to kill him, or Kirsa and her likely hidden intention to kill him.

*The bathhouse it is.*

Slowly, he closed the door, hearing it *click* behind him. He grabbed a towel from a table and made his way to the far side of the bath, trying his best not to shrink under everyone else's gaze—or glares, judging by the hatred in some of their eyes. While facing away from them, he stripped and entered the steaming water, reminding himself he was a vampire and therefore stronger than all of them if it came down to a fight.

Then the whispers started—though he didn't understand all of it when spoken in Akretti—and with strained ears, he heard it all.

"Another vampire in Vrork?"

"It's only going to end in more deaths. Vampire *and* dwarf."

"Did you hear what happened to the last one? Kirsa took too much blood and the vampire begged to die. She killed her in a show of mercy."

"How long do you think this one will last? I'm betting on a month."

"I hate vampires. One of them killed my nephew. I wish I brought my knife. I want to slit his throat."

Luca dunked his head beneath the warm water to block out the cold words. Although he didn't want to be a

Dragomir anymore, he'd never been ashamed to be a vampire.

Until now.

*I'm sorry*, he wanted to say. *I'm sorry for any misery my kind put you through.*

A lonely ache settled in his chest, weighing him down until his lungs burned from staying beneath the water for so long. He didn't belong in Ichor Knell. He didn't belong in Ironfell. He didn't belong in Vrork.

But he wanted to. He wanted to be accepted here among the dwarves. It had been a very long time since he'd felt anything more than anguish, sadness, or emptiness, and he'd felt many things beyond that since leaving the vampire city. Was he simply making a fool of himself by hoping he could belong somewhere? By hoping he could belong *here*?

He clenched his fists as the bellows started again within him, fueled by raw determination. The dwarves might not accept him now, but if he truly put in the effort, maybe things could change.

His head broke the surface of the water, only for him to be met by snickering laughter as a group of dwarves stole his clothes and rushed out the door. He gasped in panic, scrambling after them while other dwarves laughed boisterously around him. He snatched his towel and only barely managed to wrap it loosely around his waist before he burst into the hallway—

—to be met by Kirsa and Kirsa only. The dwarves had disappeared with his clothing, and with it, the flask that had been in his pocket.

So much for fitting in.

"Something wrong?" she asked, a knowing smile on her lips.

"They stole my clothes."

She placed a thoughtful finger to her mouth, her eyes raking him up and down. "I wish I had thought of it. It's ingenious."

He suddenly remembered he was among dwarves. They were notorious for their mischief—Kirsa had shown him that much already. It was as if they were born with an innate ability to find joy in others' suffering.

Other dwarves had joined them outside the bathhouse, all watching their exchange as if waiting for something to happen. Perhaps a reprimanding. But from the amused glint in Kirsa's eye, he didn't expect any such thing to transpire.

"I apologize on behalf of my peers," she said as she came closer, her proximity making his heart race. Her golden gaze ensnared him, nailing his feet to the floor. "From the very bottom of my heart, I am deeply remorseful for what I'm about to do."

He didn't have a chance to stop her before she grabbed his towel and yanked it from his waist. His hands flew downward to cover his male parts, all while a chorus of guffaws erupted around him, echoing off the walls, the floor, his ears.

He attempted to snatch the towel back, but Kirsa tossed it to someone else in the crowd, far out of his reach. The heat of embarrassment crawled up his neck as he backed up against the wall in the opposite direction of the bathhouse. All he could see was Kirsa's smirk emblazoned in his brain as he hastily backed around the corner before sprinting down the maze of hallways, following his own old scent back to his room, all while dwarves laughed at him on all sides as he streaked past.

He entered his room and slammed the door shut, wishing there was a lock on it as if it could shut out all the laughter and embarrassment—which he still heard even within the confines of the four walls.

His humiliation flared brighter, and he ran a hand down his sweltering neck, only pausing when he realized something important. He felt embarrassed. *Extremely* embarrassed. Something he hadn't experienced in a very long time.

"You sly dwarf," he muttered under his breath. "You're trying to help."

A grateful warmth replaced the utter humiliation as he pondered what he'd just learned. Even after years upon years of emotional emptiness, no one had ever tried to help him. Not a single person except Kirsa and Chloe.

How she'd caught onto his need, he didn't know. But he was grateful all the same.

But by all means, he'd get her back for what she'd done to him today.

# CHAPTER 13

Kirsa found Luca in the dining hall after being escorted by another dwarf other than her to supper, and while he didn't eat the dwarven food, he sat alone in the corner, books splayed out on the table around him. She watched him for a moment, wondering if he hated her for the prank she pulled earlier. Her playful side couldn't help itself, especially with an eager audience that needed as much laughter in their lives as Luca did. His scars ran deep like hers, and a part of her felt as if she hadn't even scratched the surface. He'd hinted at family troubles, and she wondered if he would ever feel comfortable enough to share them with her.

If he ever forgave her, of course.

Across the room, she watched as his nose twitched, and then he finally glanced up to meet her gaze. An immediate scowl pulled on his features, indicating he definitely hadn't forgiven her.

She ignored his scowl and continued to the other side of the room, standing in line for the nightly meal. They all played their part in the settlement. Hunters. Cooks. Seamstresses. Smithies. Warriors. Leaders. When everyone did their part and helped take care of each other, the settlement thrived, and with fewer and fewer dwarves under the Mountain, they needed every pair of working hands they could get.

A couple of snickering dwarves caught her attention, and she found them looking in Luca's direction. Kirsa grinned briefly as she remembered the incident. He was fully clothed now, as if it hadn't happened in the first place.

Standing in line made her antsier by the minute, and by the time she obtained a tray with food, she tried her best to walk slowly and casually toward Luca's table instead of sprinting like her body wanted. He'd made room for her by pushing some of the books aside, as if he'd known she'd join him. When she sat, he continued to scowl.

"You are a cruel, wicked female," he said, glaring at her from across the table.

"Does this mean you concede our prank war?" She chewed her food slowly, trying to maintain her casual demeanor.

"On the contrary, dwarf. You'll get what's coming to you. Just wait and see."

She looked forward to it. After all, this war was far too much fun, especially playing it with him.

When his attention returned to the books on the table, she took the opportunity to rake her gaze up and down him, noticing how well his newest clothing fit him. It didn't hug him too tightly like it had before, and the style suited him much better. Although the pants and boots appeared to be similar to the last set he'd worn, the vest from earlier was replaced by a short-sleeved tunic, one the color of a cloudless night sky.

"I see a seamstress made you new clothing," she commented.

His scowl disappeared. "I'm still trying to get used to the style in Vrork. It's much simpler than in Ichor Knell."

"I've never been there. What's it like?"

She regretted asking the moment the words leaked from her mouth, as the mention of the vampire city brought a shadow upon his mood. Surprisingly, he still answered.

"It's big. And cloudy. The castle alone can house hundreds of vampires. I lived in the castle my entire life. Similar to my sister, Cosette. But she's much older than me and only recently moved out."

That hadn't been the first time he mentioned his sister. Was she someone important to him?

Deciding to press her luck, she asked, "How old is Cosette?"

"Two hundred and thirty-two. She mated with Laurel's brother, who hates me." He ran a hand down his face as if the emotional strain of the conversation had taken a wrong turn. "And what can I do about it? Nothing. Oriel is older. Stronger. He's probably one of the most popular vampires in

Ichor Knell. And he doesn't like me to come around, even for Cosette. She was my best friend."

"Was?" she prompted softly, wishing to hear more.

He didn't answer, but rather flipped the page of his book and furrowed his brows as if concentrating hard on the words. For a moment, she wondered how much happiness he'd experienced in his life, because it seemed as if things only went wrong for him and rarely went well.

"I think the pronunciation of Akretti is the most difficult to grasp," he finally said, glancing up to meet her concerned gaze. "Reading it is easy enough, but saying the words correctly is another story altogether. The sounds come from the back of the throat, rather than at the front like I'm used to."

"That's what I find difficult about speaking your tongue."

Without replying, his gaze flicked to her covered ears, curiosity shining brightly in his eyes. She subconsciously lifted her fingers to her hair, making sure her ears were hidden. Other dwarves may not care to show the world their heart or their past, but she wanted to hide it, especially from Luca. A vampire. What would he think if he saw the numerous earrings in her ears? Would he despise her? Fear her? She wanted his friendship, but the last thing she wanted was another hole in her ear.

Except an ardor piercing, of course. She wanted one of those very much.

Remembering the list she'd placed in her pocket earlier, her fingertips brushed the corner, taunting her of goals unfinished, far too many things still not crossed off her list.

She retracted her hand just as quickly, trying to hide the regret in her expression as she continued with her meal. A couple of her goals would be easy enough to accomplish, but they required leaving Vrork, and she just didn't have the time for it. Not when she worked day in and day out trying to isolate the components of Luca's venom.

Speaking of...

"I need another venom sample," she said, a flush creeping into her cheeks the same moment his ears reddened. "If I give you the vials beforehand, can you return them to me the same day?"

"I think I can manage it."

"Good, because—"

Her words were interrupted by the ringing of a loud bell that reverberated throughout the Mountain, deafening her ears. The entire room flew into a panic—screams leaping off the walls, cries of help to locate loved ones, and people frantically running to and fro. Kirsa wasted no time. With raw determination in every movement, she jumped to her feet and ran to a bin that used to be filled with masks, but now only a few remained. She strapped one over her face and hurried into the hallway where other masked dwarves rushed past her in their flight for safety. The crowd jostled her backward, away from the hazard, but she pushed through, ignoring the warning bells grating against her mind.

Footsteps sounded behind her, and she looked back for a brief moment to find Luca following close at her heels, no mask on his face. He didn't need one but worry over him surfaced when she realized she didn't know for certain if that were the case.

The hallways started emptying as dwarves fled to safety, and when she was about to turn right, she skidded to a stop when she spotted a lone figure in the corridor, a little girl crying for her mother.

Except she wore no mask.

To take off her own mask was suicide. She knew that. But it didn't stop her from taking the first initial step toward the little girl. And then another one.

A hand grabbed her from behind, halting her in her tracks.

"Keep going," Luca shouted, his voice hardly discernible over the warning bells. "I can smell the Rot coming from that direction. I'll get the girl. We'll come find you."

She swallowed hard but finally nodded, continuing the way she'd first started. However, she turned around in time to witness him stripping himself of his shirt and wrapping it around the girl's face. He picked her up and buried her face into his chest, and she wasn't able to see anymore before she burst into the infirmary where several other masked dwarves resided, including her mother.

"I need another mask!" Kirsa ordered, her voice muffled by her own. "Hurry!"

Her mother hastily snatched one from a top shelf, just in time for Luca to rush into the room carrying the girl. Kirsa slipped the mask onto the girl's face and tried to take her from him, but she clung tightly, refusing to let go.

At last, the warning bells ceased ringing, though they still echoed inside her head. A deafening silence replaced the bells, and everyone in the room stood still. Quiet. Listening.

And then the screams began.

They were muffled by a barricaded door, closed off from the rest of the Mountain. Luca slid his fingers into hers, and her tears flowed fast as she gripped tightly until her own hand ached.

Little by little, the screams died down until they finally stopped completely. She said a silent prayer to her four gods to spare the dwarves of the pain, to bring them to a better place.

"That's the third outbreak this year," her mother finally said, breaking the tense, mourning silence.

"How many?" Kirsa asked hoarsely, still clutching tightly to Luca's hand. "How many did we just lose?"

"Fifty-two. It was sudden, and we acted quickly. We couldn't inject them in time. Not without putting ourselves at risk. We did the next best thing—we isolated them."

*And left them to die.*

She understood the sacrifice and why it had been necessary. If the isolation hadn't happened, the Rot would have spread to the rest of the inhabitants under the Mountain. Losing fifty-two dwarves was better than losing four hundred and two. Which left them at three hundred and fifty. Their numbers were dwindling. Fast.

Remembering what Luca had said in the hallway, she snapped her head in his direction, her eyes wide, and she almost forgot to speak slowly to give him a better chance at understanding her Akretti words. "You can smell the Rot?"

He paused, his eyebrows furrowed as if he tried to piece together her words. Finally, he nodded. "Yes. It's rather stuffy, like decay."

She shared a look with her mother, and it was as if they'd come to the same conclusion together. Turning back to him, she said, "It takes our ventilation several hours to clear the Rot from the Mountain. And even then, we don't know if it's gone. Will you go out there when we give the go ahead?"

"And sniff it out like a hound dog?" he asked, and although his words were joking, his tone was not. He seemed to be as shaken about what had transpired as she was. "Of course, I'll help."

"Are you hurt? Did it affect you?"

"No. I breathed it in, but it did nothing." He held the child at a distance as if to look her over. She showed no signs of being infected by the Rotting Blight, none except the fear shining in her tear-stained eyes.

Kirsa realized she still held Luca's hand, and she quickly snatched it back, her heartbeat quickening as she crossed the room to where her mother stood, looking down at a familiar face. Tille was still alive. He hadn't been a casualty.

"Who's this?" Luca asked, approaching slowly, cautiously, curiosity in the violet depths of his eyes.

"My brother, Tille," she answered, emotion rising in her chest. "He contracted the Blight a year ago, and he's been in stasis ever since."

She ran her fingers through Tille's thick chestnut brown hair, wondering if a time might come when she'd see him alive and well, rather than dying slowly on a cot.

"I don't understand what stasis is," he admitted.

Her mother answered this time. "After a dwarf contracts the disease, they only have a few minutes to be injected with a serum to keep the Rot from spreading too quickly, and to make it so it's not contagious." She slowed her words as if realizing Luca needed more time to piece them together. "That person will still die quicker than if we put them in stasis, a deep sleep which slows the process of death even more. Those in stasis will eventually die, but it gives them more time to live, a chance for us to find them a cure."

"But what about leaving the Mountain? If dwarves are confined within a space, wouldn't it give them a higher chance to contract the Rot?"

"This is our home, vampire." Her mother frowned, placing a hand on top of Tille's chest, which rose slowly with each inhale of breath. "We will not abandon it. However, we have sent out other dwarves, volunteers, to participate in the breeding program. Several predetermined couples now live out in the open, mating and having children to keep the dwarven race alive should we fail at finding a cure here." She nodded toward her. "Kirsa volunteered for the program when we first proposed the idea. But I wanted her here instead."

Kirsa felt Luca's gaze on her, but she didn't raise her head to look. Rather, she focused on a particular black Blight etching on Tille's face to distract her from his stare. Although her mother was right to keep her here where she could do more good with her particular skill set, the desire to marry and have children was nearly too great to bear. Her primal instincts told her if she didn't start soon, she wouldn't have a chance at all.

But she'd accepted that. Even if the realization made her ache inside.

"You'd mate with a stranger?" he finally asked when her mother moved to the other side of the room to help the nurses with another patient.

"That's not the point," she replied, now braving to meet his gaze. But she almost regretted it when she noticed the frown on his face. "I'll do whatever it takes to save my people. Of course, I'd prefer to be intimate with someone I love, but where is that luxury, Luca? We cannot afford it."

"Then perhaps that's a difference between vampires and dwarves. We are much more selfish when choosing our mates."

She glanced from the little girl now sleeping in his arms to him once more. Immediately, her heart melted into a puddle at the tender display, one that if she wasn't careful, she might slip on and injure herself. But she couldn't help but admire the way he'd saved the girl with hardly a thought for himself. He cared. He truly did. It was more than she could say about any of the other vampires who had stepped foot under the Mountain.

Not able to speak of the subject any longer without wallowing in the ache, she changed the mood between them.

"How is it you always manage to find yourself shirtless in front of me?" She smiled coyly, her heart picking up its pace when he returned her flirtatious smile.

"How is it I always find you looking? And the incident with the towel earlier... What, exactly, were you hoping to see?"

"Self-obsessed vampire," she muttered, though she couldn't wipe the grin from her face as she left his side to speak with her mother. She lowered her voice, glancing toward Luca to make sure he didn't watch the exchange. Instead, he busied himself with finding empty vials and placing them on a near-empty table, all while balancing the sleeping dwarf in one arm. "He's proficient enough. We can't afford to wait any longer."

Her mother lowered her voice as well. "I still don't approve of this, Kirsa. I'll ask one last time. Send a couple of guards in your stead."

"You know as well as I that Luca's best chance at survival is me. Like I said before, I will not risk his life by sending someone else."

"I cannot lose you." Her mother placed a gentle hand on the side of Kirsa's face, a look of motherly affection in her eyes. "I've lost so many already."

"And I cannot lose Luca. The chasotids are dangerous, even for a vampire."

They said nothing for a few long moments, until her mother finally dropped her hand to her side and released a long-suffering sigh. "It's not a good idea for you to travel alone with him. I saw the way you looked at him."

"Shh," she hissed, her frown deepening as she glanced Luca's way while a blush crawled up her neck. "He can probably hear you."

Although he gave no indication of overhearing the conversation, she didn't understand the full extent of vampire hearing. She'd heard stories of some vampires hearing over great distances, and she wondered if the information pertained to older vampires or younger ones as well like Luca.

Her gaze involuntarily flashed to him again, only for alarm to rise within her when he began filling the vials with his venom. She nearly rushed forward to snatch the sleeping dwarf away from him, but she stopped when he hung his head, squeezing his eyes shut while plugging his nose. Each breath he took through his mouth was slow and concentrated, making her rethink jumping in. He appeared to have no interest in biting the girl, but Kirsa on the other hand... She couldn't help but wonder if that same desire to bite her had surfaced as it had the last time he produced venom.

Therefore, she kept her distance.

Instead, she helped her mother and the nurses with caring for the unconscious patients while they waited out the hours until they deemed it safe to open the door and let Luca into the hallway. After giving him permission to enter any room within the Mountain, she sent him off with anxiety churning in her gut.

Her earlier conversation with him brought on a new ache, the desire to *live* before she *died*. Needing the reassurance her list brought her, she reached for it and—

It was gone.

Panic surged through her as she emptied her pockets, checked the floor, searched beneath tables, but the list was nowhere to be found. If anyone found it, if anyone saw it, she'd be mortified.

Absolutely mortified.

# CHAPTER 14

Stealing the parchment from Kirsa's pocket had seemed like a good idea at the time, an amusing practical joke. At least until the bells had started ringing and panic had ensued. Now Luca didn't know how to give it back, though he wasn't sure he wanted to.

As he traversed the dead and empty hallways, searching for traces of the Rot, he unfolded the piece of parchment and scanned the list again while wishing for it to be anything but her items to cross off before her death. Did she really expect to die soon? Did she not have any hope for a cure?

His eyebrows furrowed at the mention of a star pool and an ardor piercing. He hadn't the slightest idea what either one of those things were.

He couldn't help but frown that the "kiss a man" was crossed off the list. A surprising spark of jealousy shot through his body, adding its flame to the bellows churning within him. It wasn't fair for him to be jealous. After all, he'd kissed his fair share of females.

A whiff of musty decay stole him away from his thoughts, and he tucked the list safely within his pocket as he focused on the smell. Although he didn't run into it directly, he followed the trace of it down the hallway until he approached a door tucked in the very corner of the Mountain. He tugged on the door, but to his dismay, it was locked.

However, he was a vampire, and Kirsa had already given him permission to enter every single room in Vrork.

With one carefully placed kick, the door handle broke free and skittered across the ground, the door hanging ajar. He opened it slowly.

And gagged.

The Rot lurked heavily inside the room, the small spores floating dangerously in the small space. Covering his nose with his shirt, he forced himself to take a step inside. And then another. The spores were thick enough to obscure his vision through the haze, but finally he traveled far enough inside to gather it was a supply closet judging by the rusted brooms, dusty masks, and rotted buckets. An old supply closet, one not likely opened often, and one likely the cause of the three breakouts in the past year.

He closed the door firmly once more and explored the rest of the Mountain, and when he didn't find any other traces of the Rot, he returned to the infirmary where Kirsa and her mother waited anxiously on the tips of their toes. Kirsa stopped pacing entirely and dropped her hand from her mouth where she looked to have been biting her nails.

"Well?" she asked.

The moment he stepped inside the room, the little girl—whose name he discovered was Alda—rushed into his arms and held on tightly around his neck. He was glad the Rot didn't cling to clothing, otherwise, his arms would be an unsafe place.

"I found an old supply closet," he said, leaning against the end of a table. "It was locked, but I broke it open. It was so full of the Rot that I could hardly see through it. Your ventilation system might not reach this closet, and it looks to have been collecting for a while."

Kirsa muttered a profanity before turning to her mother, speaking far too quickly for him to keep up. He frowned, wishing to be completely fluent in Akretti. He'd work up to it, but at least he'd made exceptional progress thus far.

At last, the chieftain turned to him. "Is this the only place?"

"Yes. Other than the infirmary, of course. But it's not as strong here, likely because it's in a controlled setting."

The chieftain turned to her daughter and spoke quickly again, but Luca caught several words here and there about taking care of the problem. She left the infirmary moments later with her mask secured to her face.

"Come," Kirsa said, beckoning him through the door. "I'm not about to wait hours until my mother rings the safety bell. We'll return the child to her family and set off for the ruins. I had weapons and your new attire sent to the male entry room. It should fit you." Her gaze traveled from his feet to the top of his head. "I think."

Nervousness pricked at him as he followed her from the room and through the maze of corridors he was only starting to become familiar with. Her words he'd overheard earlier echoed in his mind, and for once, he hoped he hadn't understood her Akretti correctly.

*And I cannot lose Luca. The chasotids are dangerous, even for a vampire.*

What were chasotids? And more importantly, how had Kirsa looked at him that warranted her mother being concerned about them being alone together?

He peeked over at her as she determinedly led the way. Her mask covered half her face, leaving only her eyes visible. Every dwarf he'd seen beneath the Mountain had golden eyes in a variety of shades, but he thought hers were the most beautiful shade of gold. If only she'd allow him to stare into them for longer than five seconds without punching him.

She continued to keep her ears covered with her hair. The longer he went without seeing them, the more he wondered about what they looked like. He caught the scent of faint traces of metal, which meant she had at least a few piercings, and now that he knew she wanted an ardor piercing, he couldn't help but wonder what it was.

When they reached the housing tunnels, Kirsa knocked loudly on a door, and moments later, it opened in a flash. A female stood on the other side with gold-tinted tears streaming down her face. She glanced from Luca, to little Alda in his arms, and then she burst into sobs.

"You've brought my baby to me," she cried through her mask, taking Alda from him. "I thought the Rot got her."

To his complete surprise, she pulled off her mask, took his face in her hands, and kissed one cheek, and then the other, before she smashed her lips against his. When she released him, she wept even harder as she held her daughter close.

"Bless you, vampire. Bless you."

The female closed the door behind her, leaving him staring wide-eyed at the scarred wood, his mouth hanging agape. At least until Kirsa burst into laughter.

"Something wrong?" she asked with a knowing grin.

He turned slowly, surprised—and a bit appalled—that she thought this was a joke. He hoped not, as it was his turn to give her a good embarrassment for a change. "She kissed me!" He gestured to the closed door while lowering her voice. "I hope she didn't get any ideas."

"You still have much to learn about dwarven culture," she snickered, her voice muffled by the mask she wore as she led him toward Vrork's entrance. "It's not uncommon to be kissed from a show of deep gratitude. It's different from a romantic kiss, which is also not uncommon."

"How is it different? In my culture, the only kissing that happens is a show of affection."

They passed through the spacious commons, walked down the hallway, and stood outside the two doors leading to the antechambers, both closed and waiting for them to enter. He wished to spend more time in the commons, if only to admire the ornate handiwork that weaved throughout the rest of the Mountain.

She placed her hands on her hips, her golden eyes sparking with annoyance as she stared back at him. "Now, I'm not saying I let just anybody kiss me, vampire."

He enjoyed fanning her flames, so he leaned closer and rested one hand on the wall just above her head and with the other, he lightly trailed her hair through his fingers. The tendrils felt soft against his skin, reflecting a golden hue within their chestnut depths. It reminded him of the way her eyes shimmered in the candlelight.

He dropped his voice to a whisper, his fingers moving dangerously closer to her ears as his curiosity at what lay beneath her hair continued to prod at him. "I've always wanted to be kissed by a dwarf. Just not *that* dwarf."

As he'd hoped, her cheeks turned crimson, and he braced himself for the punch surely to follow but was surprised when she smacked his hand aside and pushed him away instead.

"Hands to yourself, vampire. Now go on in and change clothing. Gunther will have everything ready for you on the other side of the door. Don't keep me waiting."

When she disappeared behind the female's door, instead of the amusement he expected to feel, his heart pricked with ache as he realized he *wanted* to kiss her. Up until now, it had only been games he played for the sake of her reaction, but now the warmth he previously felt had turned into something resembling affection. Or at least he thought as much. It had been a long time since he'd felt any of these emotions.

Shaking the disappointment of rejection away, he entered the male's entryway to find Gunther waiting, adorned in a mask and weapons just like when Luca had first seen him. But this time, the guard wasn't alone. Another male stood waiting with an armful of weapons while Gunther handed him clothing to change into. As he changed, the two dwarves spoke as if he wasn't in the room.

"You'd better be careful, Elric," Gunther said in Akretti, though Luca caught onto each word this time unlike their first encounter. "Don't get too close or he might drink your blood."

Elric scoffed, rolling his eyes. "Vampires don't drink dwarven blood. Everyone knows that."

They laughed, and Luca couldn't help the amused smirk that came out of hiding. He sprouted his fangs, and both dwarves jumped backward in alarm while staring at his mouth.

He replied in Akretti, "We might if given a good enough reason."

Only when he retracted his fangs did they visibly relax, but he sensed nervousness in their movements, nonetheless. Elric strapped weapons to his person while Gunther gathered rolled parchment, writing utensils, and a bedroll into a bag. After packing, his hands paused, and he glanced toward Luca.

"I'm not sure what else a vampire needs for a two-day journey. You don't need food or water." He still looked shocked that Luca knew how to speak the language. Or at least some of it.

"No, but perhaps a cloak? In case we run into sunlight."

"Oh, right. I forgot dwarves and vampires are similar in that aspect."

Gunther seemed much friendlier to him than during their first encounter, so he dared to ask the question burning in his mind all evening. "Can you tell me about the star pool? What is it?"

The dwarf looked at him suspiciously. "Where did you hear about it?"

"I read about it somewhere," he said with a casual shrug, not wanting to share Kirsa's list.

After what seemed like much contemplation, Gunther finally answered, "It's something dwarves hold sacred to our religion. Our four dwarven gods, Austri, Vestri, Nordri, and Sudri, hold aloft the four corners of the sky. In the very center lies the star pool."

Although Luca couldn't understand some of what he said, he tried to piece it together with the bits he *did* understand. He didn't know much about dwarven religion, but now he was curious to learn more about what the race believed.

"What's the significance of this star pool?"

"It cleanses the spirit. Some dwarves will travel great distances to bathe in the pool during a full moon if only to do it once. Others will bathe in it multiple times during their lives. Since we live so close to the pool, most of us bathe in it at least once a year."

*If it's so close to Vrork, why hasn't Kirsa crossed it off her list already?*

The conundrum worked his mind into a fray. The more he tried to understand her, the less he understood. Not only was she confusing, but she had secrets. Many secrets. Ones she didn't seem to care to share with him. But perhaps he could get her to talk on their trip to the ruins. He wanted to learn more about her, more than he already knew.

"And…and…what's an ardor piercing?"

The dwarves looked at each other before bursting into laughter, and Gunther smacked him amusedly on the shoulder as if he'd just told a hilarious quip. "Planning some risqué behavior? Tell me, vampire, who's the unfortunate dwarf?"

His expression turned blank as he tried to figure it out himself. But try as he might, he couldn't fit the pieces of the puzzle together, not with how little he still knew about dwarven culture.

"Tell us who," Elric smirked with a crinkle of his eyes. "You wouldn't be mentioning the star pool *and* an ardor piercing in the same breath otherwise."

Knowing the dwarves wouldn't explain enough to him, and wanting to save his pride, he went along with the charade and returned the dwarf's smirk with one of his own. "That piece of information is confidential. Now if you'll hand me the pack. I'd best be off."

Gunther smacked him on the shoulder again, sending him out the door while laughter resumed. The night greeted him moments after the door shut behind him, and he welcomed the fresh air with a long intake of breath. He filled his lungs with the clean Mountain air and let the breath out slowly as he stared up at the sky, millions of stars blinking back at him far out of reach. In Ichor Knell, he rarely saw the stars unless he hiked all the way to the lake or left the city altogether, but here on the Mountain…

The sky was beautiful.

He wanted to lay on the ground and gaze up at the sky all night long, examining each mystery shrouded by the dark blanket above. Perhaps if he stared long enough, the mysteries might just begin to make sense.

"See your own reflection up there?" Kirsa asked, startling him out of his thoughts. "I told you to not keep me waiting."

She stood with her arms crossed, a stern expression on her face that hadn't been there minutes earlier. He took in her attire—the same as his own. Long, dark sleeves, long pants stuffed into sturdy shoes. The outfit looked to be infused with some sort of armor he was unfamiliar with, but it felt light, easy to carry.

As if noticing his stare, she explained, "Enchanted armor. It's nearly impenetrable, which is crucial when we face the chasotids. They're harmless as babies, but in their adult form, they're deadly."

Mention of the chasotids made him uneasy, and as he followed her west onto a rocky mountain path, he said, "Tell me more about them. They must be dangerous, otherwise, I wouldn't need this many weapons."

"They are arthropods. Something between a beetle and a centipede, but they're *large*." She held out both of her arms to emphasize her point. "Many even bigger than you. They mainly feed on mushrooms and other cave plants, but they are incredibly territorial. Although they won't eat you, they *will* kill you if you step into their domain."

"So, these weapons are to kill them first."

He noticed her grip tightening on the hilt of her dagger, her expression turning from sour to somber within moments.

When she said nothing, he started to press her for more information, but then she finally spoke.

"This will be my third trip to the ruins," she said softly. "The first time was uneventful, so we thought it was safe to go a second time. I brought my sister along. Neeva. She didn't make it out alive. I had to bring her shredded body back home." When her voice caught, she took a deep breath and continued. "I will never forget my mother's grief. Each child she loses is another piece of her soul that goes with them. It's only me and Tille left. We're doing all we can to keep him alive, and I'm doing all I can to remain healthy and unafflicted."

"I'm sorry to hear about your sister." He creased his forehead in worry. "You'll not just be in danger of the chasotids, but of the Blight as well. Draw me a map. I'll go in by myself."

She smiled teasingly as she glanced over her shoulder at him. "I can hold my own against the chasotids. Besides, it's damned difficult to make your mask slip, and even more difficult to break it. I'll be fine against the Blight. Going in the ruins with you isn't up for discussion."

There were few females in his life more stubborn than Kirsa, and when it should have annoyed him, it instead fueled his desire to hold her in his arms.

He shook off the feeling and continued to follow her on foot. They traveled many miles, only stopping a couple of times for her to replenish herself with food and water. Like humans, dwarves were fragile, susceptible. He couldn't help but wonder what it felt like to have to feed every few hours and consume a steady intake of water. Not to mention healing slowly. As a vampire, his wounds healed quickly, even within minutes at times. Whereas it could take days, weeks, or longer for another race to heal from a wound of the same severity. And as for him, personally, he needed to feed every few weeks rather than daily before suffering the consequences of losing control in his need for blood.

When dawn began its steady approach, they rounded the top of a hill, and Luca gasped as a massive structure rose from the landscape like a large sea creature jumping from the water. Unlike Vrork, which was hidden within a mountain, the ruins stretched tall with surrounding pillars. Judging by the metallic sting wafting through the air on a decaying breeze, he reckoned the structure used to be made of gold, but now only green flakes and crumbling rock remained. It almost seemed as if it would collapse at any moment, the idea becoming more solid when he detected a chilling groan coming from deep within the ruins.

What sounded like pincers clattering together made gooseflesh crawl up his arms and dig into his scalp. He stretched his hearing farther and listened to skittering legs, shrill screeches, and more clattering.

"How big did you say these creatures were?" he asked, now feeling as if the number of weapons he carried on his person weren't enough to combat these monsters.

"You hear them, don't you?" Her inquisitive and curious gaze returned to the ruins. "They're large. If you get cornered by one, I've found it's easiest to kill them with a blade to their underbelly, which is their softest point."

He nodded, still uncomfortable with the idea of entering the ruins at all. "Where will we find a sample of Arvitash?"

Dread filled him when he realized something vital. "Books wouldn't have survived this long, not after a thousand years of decay."

"We discovered several stone tablets," she explained. "They're attached to the wall, unable to come off, which is where the parchment in your pack comes in. That's how we'll make a copy."

"And you don't have any other copies in Vrork?"

Her lips turned downward, and her steps sounded heavier as they continued toward the ruins. "We *did* make a copy," she said in a tone of annoyance. "But the last scholar burned it all in a fit of frustration. We have nothing left."

Despair washed over him as he realized why the dwarf had burned the copies. "It's because the scholar couldn't decipher it, isn't it?"

A sigh escaped her, and finally she turned to face him when they stood beneath a maze of green-flecked pillars. "He studied it for years, Luca. *Years.* We don't have that kind of time. If you can't do this, I don't think anyone can."

The weight of this undertaking crushed his shoulders, trying its best to collapse his legs from beneath him. His words escaped as barely a whisper. "You do realize I'm a young vampire. I may be proficient with languages, but surely there are better candidates for this task."

Kirsa shook her head, and when her fingers brushed against his, his heartbeat picked up at the simple touch. He nearly pulled her in for a kiss then and there. "You misunderstand our predicament. To ask for help in a widespread manner would mean to risk letting other races know we are vulnerable. Unfortunately, our discretion is what keeps what's left of us safe. You are our best and only candidate for the task. I believe you can do this."

He doubted his own ability, but if she had faith in him, he couldn't possibly deny her this request.

Nodding his head, they continued toward the ruins, at least until she stopped with a frown on her face. She placed her hand against the rock, her fingers trailing over the rough surface until she paused at an opening only large enough for a small animal to fit through.

"This didn't used to be collapsed," she said, her frown deepening. "We'll find another way in."

"Why not just send an animal inside?" he asked with an amused shrug of his shoulders, which only earned him a roll of her eyes.

Her tone turned sarcastic. "Why didn't I think of that, Luca? It would work so well."

He realized she had never seen his vampire transformation before, which only served to heighten his amusement. "I'll slip through and find a way to widen the crevice. I'd stand back if I were you, just in case."

With a raise of her eyebrows, she answered, "I don't know if you've noticed, but you're bigger than me, and I can't even fit."

"My dearest Kirsa." He leaned closer to her so his breath ruffled the few strands of hair around her face. To his delightful surprise, she didn't move away, but he heard her heartbeat pick up in an unnaturally quick rhythm. "I think we need to get better acquainted. There is still far too much you don't know about me."

Not giving her time to reply, he released his hold on his transformation and let it wash over him. One moment, he stood in front of her as a vampire, and the next moment, he gazed up at her with the slyest smirk he could manage in his fox form. He swished his tail back and forth, watching as her eyes widened for a moment before she sighed.

"Right. I forgot vampires could transform." A grin spread across her face. "You are rather adorable. And you look so soft. Come here, little foxy. Let me hold you."

When she moved to grab him with a teasing smile on her lips, he leaped out of the way and huffed before he slipped into the crevice in the side of the ruins. How degrading it would be to allow her to hold and pet him like an actual animal! Although he craved her touch, he didn't want it like that.

He easily made it through to the other end and transformed back into a vampire. When he tested the stability of the rock with the weight of his foot, he was surprised when it crumbled beneath his strength. The rock was weak. Weak enough for a vampire to kick the hole larger.

Waiting until he heard Kirsa move out of the way on the other side, he kicked at the rock once, twice, three times, until his foot smashed through, bits and pieces splaying out in all directions.

He cringed and held perfectly still for several long moments as he listened to the ruins within, but no chasotids charged in their direction. None seemed to pay notice to the commotion, as if they were used to parts of the ruins crumbling to a rocky grave.

Kirsa slipped her mask on and breathed in deeply, followed by a brief flicker of fear in her eyes. "Let's get going. I don't want to be here any longer than necessary."

# CHAPTER 15

An icy shudder crawled up Kirsa's arms as she tiptoed down the dank and mildewy hallways, crumbling rocks surrounding all sides of her. The last time she'd visited, her sister had met a gruesome and untimely death. The memory of holding Neeva's limp and bloodied body in her arms spurred her onward with determination to not allow the same thing to happen to Luca.

Darkness filled every inch of the ruins, blinding her to what lay within the crumbling structure. The air felt heavy as they walked through a thicket of spores traveling lazily through the air. The spores appeared innocent, but if her mask slipped, it would mean a swift and painful death.

Her feet sloshed through puddles of water on the ground, and she kept one hand on her weapon at all times as she listened to her surroundings. Chasotid movement echoed all around her, from skittering feet to gnashing pincers. But none of it sounded threatening. At least not yet.

Knowing Luca's eyesight and hearing was much better than hers, she relied on it and stuck close to him as they traversed the hallways making hardly a sound. She slipped her hand in his, noticing his breath hitch before she led him down another hallway, this one much darker than the last. Unfortunately, she had to release her grip on her weapon to feel against the wall, using it to guide her to their next destination.

If only she could light a torch, the journey would be much easier. But not only did the thickness of the soggy atmosphere prevent fires from sparking to life, it also attracted the very creatures lurking within the ruins.

The hallway became dead silent, and her heart pounded harder in her chest as she paused in her tracks, holding absolutely still. Luca did the same, following her lead.

Very suddenly, he shoved her roughly away from him, and she landed on her hands and knees moments before a screeching chasotid tackled him to the ground, ripping into his arms with its talon-like legs. It was the same size as him and likely just as strong.

Kirsa wasted little time as she leaped to her feet and drew her knife, shoving the chasotid off Luca and jumping on top. The creature screeched as she stabbed it through the neck, but she didn't get it in the right spot, as it threw her off and lunged forward with its pincers bared. She rolled out of the way just in time to dodge its next attack. It stood on its back legs to attack again, but before it moved another inch, Luca darted forward and used his sword to stab the creature through the abdomen, in its weakest point of the underbelly.

The creature flailed. It screeched. Until it fell backward and crashed to the floor, unmoving.

Stillness reigned once more.

"Thank the Mountain," she said as she took several steps toward Luca. "Are you all right—"

Her question turned into a yelp of surprise when the floor crumbled beneath their feet. She scrambled for anything to stop her fall, but to no avail. Dust surrounded her like a thick cloud of smoke, and for several long seconds, she found herself suspended in the air moments before she smashed face-first into the ground. She gasped in air but then froze in horror as it far too easily entered her mask.

Now holding her breath, her hands flew to her mask, only to find it broken straight down the middle. Even more horrifying were the spores floating menacingly around her, filling every inch of the room and beyond.

She had breathed in the Rot.

An intense pain not associated with the fall burned inside her lungs, and she hurriedly expelled the ghastly air. But it was too late.

"No," she whispered with wide eyes. She didn't take further precautions to avoid being infected, not when it was already inside her. Pain pulsed from her lungs to her throat, and her fingers scrambled to empty the contents of her bag. In her haste, she scattered several items, and then her fingers curled around a syringe she had never thought she'd need to use.

Stabbing the needle of the syringe into her arm, she squeezed the liquid straight into her bloodstream. An immediate cooling sensation filled her body, encasing her lungs as the serum halted the Blight in its tracks.

Only one thought filled her mind, in perfect sync to the rhythm of horror banging its drum within her chest.

*I'm infected. I'm infected. I'm infected.*

Her second thought was she didn't want Luca to find out.

She gathered her scarf from the ground and wrapped it tightly around her face, making sure to hide the evidence of her broken mask.

But when she raised her gaze, horror engulfed her once more when she didn't see him. Debris covered the ground, dust still raining down from the floor they'd fallen through, but he was nowhere in sight.

"Luca," she gasped as her gaze darted in every direction, but she didn't spot a head of black hair anywhere in the chaotic mess of fallen rock. "Luca!"

She stumbled to her feet. Fear caused her hands to tremble, but she forced the emotion aside in her desperation to find the vampire. A thousand possibilities of his demise sprinted through her mind, which only worsened her distress.

A grunt followed by sifting rocks sounded around the corner, and she sighed in relief, at least until Luca stumbled into view on what seemed to be dizzy feet. He held his hand to the wall as if to steady himself.

Dread shook her to the core as she noticed the gash in the side of his head, blood trailing over his ear and down his chin. Much of it was already dry, as if the wound had been far worse and this was what it looked like partially healed.

"Luca," she choked, stumbling toward him.

She caught onto his arms and gently turned his head, watching him wince as if the small movement pained him. The gash looked deep, and she knew if it had been her, she would have died from such a wound. A vampire was immortal, and the injury closed as the seconds passed. He wouldn't die from it, but if they didn't leave soon, there was a possibility they would both get mauled by another chasotid.

A part of her wondered if it even mattered at this point. The Blight had already claimed her. She would die with or without being mauled to death.

"Can you continue?" she asked, her voice trembling despite her best efforts to appear brave. "We're not far."

"Yes," he nodded, and once again, he winced as if simply speaking pained him. She wished to hold him close, to seek comfort in his embrace, but instead, she slipped the blank parchment from the pack he carried on his back.

She wanted to cry, emotion bubbling up inside her like a witch's cauldron ready to burst free of its spell. But they were still inside the ruins, very close to danger. There was no time to dwell on unhappy circumstances.

Once more, she grasped onto his hand, not just to keep him steady and lead him along, but to seek the comfort of his touch.

They continued forward, luckily avoiding other chasotids as they followed a corridor and then entered the room with stone tablets. The tablets clung tightly to the wall, as if they had been carved from the rocky surface rather than mounted there. She pressed one of the parchments to the wall and drew over it with her charcoal pen to copy the sample of Arvitash. As she did this with all the available parchment, Luca located a puddle of water on the ground and hissed quietly as he cleaned the blood from his face. The gash was smaller now, no longer gushing blood, but she reckoned it would take a while yet to heal completely.

"So, this is Arvitash," he said quietly as he approached with water dripping down his chin and watched her take the last sample of the language. He touched the symbols etched into the tablet and frowned, his gaze scanning the contents. "This is complete gibberish."

"I know," she sighed, making sure to keep her voice low to avoid attracting more of the foul creatures plaguing the ruins. "Dwarves have been trying to decode it for many years. Without success, I might add. I'm hoping a fresh set of eyes might help."

He continued to frown but said nothing as she rolled up the pieces of parchment and slipped them back into his pack. She didn't like the look of his frown. It made her think he didn't believe it was possible to decipher the language.

In a startling movement, he swore under his breath and grabbed her hand, pulling her toward a staircase moments before another chasotid burst through the wall, exploding dirt and debris over their heads, and charged toward them. She gasped in shock, struggling to keep up with his long strides as he tugged her along. They scrambled up the staircase with the creature nipping at their heels. They trudged through ankle-deep water as they darted down the hallway. And finally, when a sliver of light came into view at the end of the hallway, they hurried their steps even faster.

Fear escalated within her when the chasotid lunged forward and managed to nick her calf, but she pumped her legs faster and harder until they burst outside into the fresh air. The creature fell back as if it didn't want to leave its rocky confines.

They both breathed heavily, her hands on her knees in the cloudy atmosphere absent of sunlight as she listened to the chasotid retreating into the ruins. She pulled her broken mask from her face, her gaze flicked up to meet Luca's, and it was as if the dangerous experience loosened the knot of passion within her.

Heat burst upward from her feet like a billowing fire, consuming her with her every breath. In one moment, her gaze lowered to his lips, and in the next moment, she found she couldn't stop herself from reaching out for him. He met her halfway, pulling her toward him until their lips crashed together in an all-consuming forest blaze.

She gasped for air each time their lips parted, but the flames within her needed more of him, the heat searing everything in its path.

Her hands roamed over him, feeling every knot of muscle, touching the lush softness of his black hair. He returned the kiss with equal fervor, as if he was as hungry for her as she was for him. All rational thought dispersed from her mind, replaced by the need for more, more, more.

A hot exhale left her mouth when he backed her against the nearest tree, taking the kiss deeper. Their lips melded perfectly together. Every soft curve of her body fit against each hard muscle of his. Their fingers fit like two tailored gloves.

When she could no longer fight her desire, her hands dipped lower to his waistband. She only managed to unbuckle his belt before he breathed in sharply, his hands darting to hers and firmly grasping them to prevent her from going any further.

Luca broke the kiss, and she still breathed heavily as she stared back at the shock evident in his eyes. The heat of embarrassment flamed in her cheeks as he shook his head, gently pushing her hands away until she held them at her sides.

"I can't, Kirsa," he whispered, which only made the heat in her face burn hotter. "I'm a vampire. I only get to do it once before it dictates the rest of my life."

Or in other words, he didn't want her as a mate. What else could he mean by it?

Before she allowed him to see the hurt in her eyes, she spun around and forced herself to take a deep breath of cool air, which helped disperse the billowing flames from her lungs until nothing remained in the hearth but dwindling embers.

She wanted to cry, not because he had rejected her, but because she was going to die. Death had sprouted so quickly from the earth and snatched her up, and she hadn't been able to dodge it in time before it ensnared her in its black, unforgiving talons. The Rot had found her, despite how careful she'd been. What she wanted was comfort, and she had sought it in Luca's embrace.

What a fool she was.

"I think I need a few minutes alone," she whispered.

He said nothing for several very long, very torturous moments. And then she heard him walk away, his feet scuffling the dirt with his movements.

"I need to feed," he said. "Find somewhere to make camp. I'll track you when I return. I shouldn't be gone long."

For a while, she stood still, numb as she stared into the forest beyond, even long after Luca left her side. It wasn't until she heard the scratching claws of a chasotid when she urged her feet forward, sprinting past a blur of trees, over a sea of rocks, and only when she reached a clearing far from the ruins did she allow herself to collapse onto her hands and knees and weep.

Rocks dug into her knees as tears cascaded from her eyes. Her lungs could barely draw a single breath before the next bout of sobbing ensued. Tears wet her face, clinging to her bruised cheek and soaking into her shirt. Years of grief and heartache escaped through each droplet, memories of her family weaved into the watery essence. Her father. Her two brothers. Neeva. And now her. The ruins…the Rot…they had taken everything from her. *Everything.*

A sharp pain pulsed through her arm, enough to stop the next bout of weeping in its tracks. Through her blurry, tear-filled vision, she tugged her sleeve up to her elbow, only to find the dark etchings of the Rot creating a webbing beneath her skin like a crudely drawn tattoo. From watching the disease spread in Tille, she knew the webbing would grow up her arm, across her chest, down to the rest of her body, and then it would make its final destination to her heart and lungs. Only then would it kill her. But there was one thing she knew for sure.

It *would* kill her.

There was no escaping the disease, not unless the dwarves found a cure.

"If finding one is even possible," she whispered to herself. "It now seems likely that I will die before then."

Not wanting to see the ghastly disease staring mockingly back at her, she tugged her sleeve back down, dried her tears, and set out for firewood. The vitality she had felt in the ruins long since disappeared, her strength depleted now that the Rot had found a home within her body. Still, she pushed past the fatigue in search of wood.

The forest floor composed of dried, brown pine needles caved beneath each of her footfalls, a gentle wind whispering through the trees with the approach of dusk. She forced her thoughts to retreat behind her mental wall of solid willpower, and instead focused on the task at hand.

When she gathered enough firewood, she stacked each branch and twig before setting the kindling ablaze with her flint and steel. When fire used to dispel the chill set deep in her bones, it had no effect this time.

This time, she felt cold, empty, hopeless.

With or without the Arvitash copy, she felt sure the dwarves would die. Every last one of them, including herself.

She pushed aside her hair to trail her finger over the earrings in each of her ears. Fourteen piercings. Eight on the top of the helix of the right ear, six on the top of the helix of the left ear. So much blood on her hands. All for nothing.

"I've always wondered what secrets hid beneath your hair," a voice said at the edge of the clearing, making her jump.

Her gaze darted in Luca's direction, startled by him so easily sneaking up on her. Another embarrassed flush crept up her neck when her thoughts turned to their earlier encounter, but she forced it away and maintained a neutral expression.

"I prefer to keep my past private." She prodded at the fire with a branch lying at her feet, watching as sparks shot upward into the darkening sky.

He warily eyed the flames before he sat across the fire from her and set a sack down beside him. For a moment, she thought the sack might contain alcohol, but she decided it wasn't the right shape for a bottle.

"I've heard rumors," he said hesitantly, still staring at the earrings she hadn't bothered to hide again. "Is it true you killed all those vampires?"

Unable to hold his gaze for long, she stared into the fire once more and debated for a moment if she should tell him anything. In the end, she brushed each earring with the tip of her finger, remembering each face with the clinking jewelry.

"Yes," she whispered. "One earring per vampire death on my hands. Fourteen vampires in total. I wish it hadn't come to death, but I couldn't stand idle and watch my people die without doing something about it. I give each a piercing to remember what I did, to never allow myself to forget the cost."

"What about humans?" he asked. He didn't move closer, but he leaned forward as if to get a better look at the jewelry in her ears.

"I've never killed a human."

"No? Then what about the one you used to ensnare me?"

Kirsa shook her head as she remembered the human Luca had feasted on moments before she shot him with a dwarven bolt. "I didn't kill him. He was already dying—got beaten too hard in the palace prison."

As she draped her hair back over her ears, she watched as he touched his own ears, both bare and void of decoration.

"If each earring means a death on your hands, I'd probably not have any room left on my ears. I've killed far too many humans to count."

"You don't sound remorseful."

"I'm not," he shrugged. "It's the way of things, and I need to feed somehow. I almost killed Chloe before I met you. That would have been incredibly unfortunate."

A frown pulled his lips downward, and a pit of guilt entered her stomach as she thought of their shared friend back in Ironfell. Chloe was to be married soon, and Kirsa had nearly stripped her of the chance by sending her out into the forest to face a vampire alone.

Her thoughts of Chloe and Ironfell pulled her deeper and deeper into her own mind, and it startled her when Luca spoke.

"Are we going to talk about what happened?"

Her gaze darted across the fire to meet his discomforting serious expression. With the yellow and orange flames flickering between them, the color of his eyes appeared to reflect a lighter tone. Gone was the light violet, replaced by a fierce rhythm of dancing firelight. Still, she held his gaze unflinchingly, even as the warmth from the fire seemed to burn hotter by the second.

"Of course," she replied casually as she picked up the stick beside her to once more stir the fire. "We entered the ruins, suffered a few scrapes, but we got out alive."

"That's not what I was referring to, and you know it."

Again, she prodded the fire while trying to ignore the flames shooting up through her body as she recalled the desperate need to taste his lips, to touch him, to breathe his air. And then his stinging rejection. Deep within her, she knew it was unfair to become his mate when she was dying, but she had wanted it so badly…

"It was simply an impulse of fear. Nothing more."

He grew quiet, and this time, she didn't dare raise her gaze to look him in the eye, and instead settled her attention on the dancing flames. Her mother had been right. It was dangerous to be alone with the vampire, especially when her feelings continued to grow despite how hard she tried to stamp them out.

Finally, he shifted his position to reach around the fire, and for one terrifying, exhilarating moment, her heart hammered in her chest when she thought he might try to kiss her again. But it slowed in disappointment. He didn't touch her, but rather placed the sack he'd brought earlier into her hands.

"I was out hunting," he explained as he motioned his head toward the sack, "and I passed by a vendor selling baked goods. I thought you might like something. I can't say for sure if it will taste good, as it smells awful to me."

Curiosity won her over as she reached into the sack and pulled out a lump of something sticky. Immediately, her throat constricted, and tears threatened to overwhelm her as she found herself staring back at a honey roll. The roll glistened as the light of the fire reflected off the sweet glaze. She'd never had time to track one down, not even to cross it off the list she'd lost. But here it was now, right in front of her, a gift from Luca. Could he possibly understand just how much it meant to her?

Not able to wait any longer, she took a bite of the honey roll and sighed through her nose as the sweet, honey flavor hit her tongue. Years of dreaming what it might taste like came to a beautifully delicious end. It tasted better than she'd ever imagined, bringing her to a meadow of gold, birds singing cheerfully in the trees, and the sweet scent of honey surrounding her at every turn.

And then the image shattered the moment Luca opened his mouth. "You know... You're the only female I've ever kissed."

Her head jerked upward in time to see the playful, flirtatious grin he gave her every so often, one that made her want to punch him and smother him in more kisses at the same time.

"I don't believe it for a single second," she scoffed before taking another bite of the roll, almost losing herself on a golden cloud of sweet nectar in the middle of an amber meadow.

"No?" he said with a coy curve of his mouth. "And why do you say that?"

*Because it was the best kiss I've ever experienced.*

No one who kissed as skillfully as he did didn't already have a lot of practice beforehand.

But she didn't say as much. Instead, she finished her treat in silence before curling up in her bedroll, facing away from him. With each beat of her heart, she was painfully aware of his proximity and what, exactly, she still wanted to do with him. The burning desire had faded, yet a warm pulse still taunted her.

However, she was glad he had refused her. It wouldn't be fair to him, not when she was dying.

She shuddered as she tried to ignore the ache pulsing through her elbow. No, it wouldn't be fair at all.

The journey home was quick, as Kirsa had no time to waste, and she didn't want to be around Luca any longer than necessary. When Adrietta ushered her into the female entry room, she slumped defeatedly into a chair and held up a hand to keep the other dwarf from searching her.

"Keep your mask on," she said quietly, her voice sounding weary to her own ears. "I'm infected. Fetch my mother, please. And don't tell a soul what I just told you now."

Adrietta didn't move from her position, and she glanced up to find her staring with wide eyes. "Infected? How?"

"Fetch my mother. Please. I injected myself with the serum, so I'm not contagious."

Finally, Adrietta nodded and returned only minutes later with her mother in tow. By the alarmed look in her mother's eyes, she knew Adrietta had told her.

"Leave us," her mother ordered, and Adrietta obliged. Even when the dwarf left, her mother still didn't place a mask over her face, almost as if she'd rather risk catching the Blight than putting a barrier between herself and what used to be her last healthy offspring.

"I'm sorry," Kirsa whispered as she tugged up her sleeve to reveal the Blight latched to her elbow. "I swear I was careful, but the ground crumbled beneath my feet and then I fell, and I smashed my face against a rock. The mask took the brunt of the fall, but it broke."

Her mother gently touched the bruise on her cheek, a testament to her unfortunate tale. Although her mother didn't cry, she wore a look of devastation in her eyes that made *her* want to cry.

Instead of saying anything immediately, her mother produced a vial of serum and injected it into Kirsa's arm, closest to the Blight. A cool sting shot up her arm, engulfing her entire elbow as if warding off the deadly disease. At least for a time.

"We can put you in stasis—"

"No," Kirsa objected. "Our people are important to me. I won't abandon them."

Silence entered the room like a sinister fog, latching onto every surface and clogging up her throat until she struggled to speak. But she didn't need to, as her mother's concerned expression turned furious in the blink of an eye.

"I hope that boy was worth it. He may have lived, but at what cost?"

And then she stormed away, leaving Kirsa alone in the too-quiet room.

A shudder started from her toes and traveled up her body until it took hold of her trembling fingers. Finally, her shoulders shook as she began sobbing. The ruins had taken everything from her.

Absolutely everything.

# CHAPTER 16

irsa was avoiding him.

Weeks had passed, and Luca could count on one hand how many times he'd seen her, and only in the briefest of settings. Instead of collecting venom samples herself, she sent someone else to do it, and he noticed she avoided spending time in the dining hall, and the commons, and he never saw her in the library either, where he often worked his hardest trying to decipher Arvitash.

He could think of only one thing that might have pushed her away—the kiss.

The kiss had been everything he'd ever hoped for and more. It had awakened a sleeping beast, ravenous for its first taste of food and warmth after a long stretch of winter. He felt more alive than he had in many years, his heart open to so many more emotions than he'd remembered feeling.

He tapped an open book with the tips of his fingers as his mind drifted off.

The kiss had also taken him by surprise. When she'd wanted to go further, he hadn't had enough time to ponder what he wanted should they jump into a relationship. It had happened so suddenly that the only smart response was to say no.

Then why did he regret it? She could have become his mate, and she likely wouldn't be avoiding him now. If he could just explain his reasoning…

But her earlier words filled him with doubt. She only kissed him because of the tense situation, fear being her guide. If they mated, as a dwarf, she'd be free to court and even marry another. As for him, he'd be connected to her body and soul, and part of him feared she would regret having a vampire so completely infatuated and attached to her.

He sighed and ran a hand down his face as he pushed his work aside, no closer to deciphering the gibberish in front of him. He needed to see Kirsa. Now. If she wanted to hide, then fine, but she'd soon learn she couldn't hide from a vampire's keen sense of smell.

Wandering the halls for a few minutes, he tracked down her freshest scent and followed it, and to his surprise, the scent led him almost all the way around the entire settlement.

Finally, he found himself back at the library, the door slightly ajar. He opened it slowly, only to find Kirsa staring at the progress—or lack of—he'd made. He watched her for a moment, his heart quickening when she placed a thoughtful finger to her lips while peering at the Arvitash scrolls laid out on the desk. He acutely remembered the taste of those lips, full of spring and rosebuds and birdsong.

Not wanting her to catch him staring, he cleared his throat and entered the room, which still managed to make her jump. She turned to him, biting her lip sheepishly, though he didn't know why.

For a moment, his hope surged. Had she wanted to see him as much as he'd wanted to see her?

"Just the dwarf I was looking for," he said before she spoke. "I have an important errand I need to run for..." he coughed, "...research. I hoped you might accompany me to the werewolf settlement."

"The werewolf settlement?" she asked with wide, disbelieving eyes.

Luca tried his hardest to keep a straight face, to hide his true intentions beneath his easy mask. "Exactly. It's rather urgent, so we need to leave straight away."

She still raised an eyebrow at him, looking as if she didn't believe a word he said. "And what is so urgent that it can't wait until tomorrow?"

He'd been prepared for this answer, knowing she'd ask that very question. Pushing aside the Arvitash scrolls, he looked at her with the best innocent eyes he could muster. "One—I'm not used to being cooped up inside for so long and I need to get out. And two—I need a sample of the werewolf language to compare side by side with the scrolls to see if I can find any parallels."

It was a lie, one he knew very well wouldn't be helpful. He once tried to woo a werewolf, if only to anger his father, and to accomplish the feat, he learned the language.

The wooing had worked. The angering had especially worked.

But the relationship hadn't. There was a reason vampires and werewolves didn't get along, and those reasons quickly became transparent, resulting in snapping the relationship in half like a stick used for kindling.

A rare uncertainty crept into her expression, and she bit her lip as she glanced toward the door as if hoping for someone to enter.

"It's the summer solstice today." She drummed her fingers against her arm as she finally glanced back at him. He only wished to smooth her uncertainty away with a brush of his thumb.

"Hence the urgency," he insisted. He leaned against the table, and it took every ounce of willpower not to reach out and touch her. "In Ichor Knell, vampires celebrate the winter solstice, and there's not a single vampire who doesn't enjoy at least one cup of sangrose. The werewolves will be too busy enjoying themselves to notice a vampire and a dwarf sneaking onto their borders."

"But it's dangerous for you."

"I know." He tried to hold back a frown but was unsuccessful. For a moment, he was glad she didn't have keen senses, otherwise, he wondered if she might smell the fear seeping from his skin.

To distract himself from his own distress, he glanced down at the Arvitash scrolls laid out on the desk and ran a finger over the coarse, yellowed parchment. The words on the page taunted him. It was no wonder why the last dwarven scholar had burned his Arvitash copies in a fit of frustration. The language was impossible to decipher.

"Then why?"

He chose his words carefully in his mind before lifting his head to meet her gaze. "Right now, the dwarves are my priority." *Including you.* "And I want to do whatever I can to help." *Especially you.*

*The kiss was a mistake. It was an impulse of fear. Nothing more.*

Not for the first time, her words rattled his brain, and a throbbing ache filled his chest. It had been a long time since he'd felt this kind of heartache—the heartbreak kind—but he supposed he should be grateful to feel it at all rather than the mind-numbing silence of nothingness from before.

"Fine," she relented at last. "We'll get in and out quickly to protect you from being spotted. I don't know what they'd do to a vampire on the summer solstice."

*I do, and it's not pleasant.*

Images of being impaled by iron weapons and strung up at a stake half-alive filled his mind. Fortunately, there would be plenty of werewolves surrounding him, which would effectively hide his scent if he mingled with them enough.

"Perfect," he said while forcing a smile to his face. "If we don't leave immediately, we'll be late."

Her mischievous smirk returned, a smirk he'd missed all too much during their far-too-long separation from each other. "I have something to get us in and out quickly. I can only use it for a round trip before the enchantment fades, but it should be enough. Are you ready for a little taste of what dwarves are capable of?"

"You mean to say I haven't tasted enough already?"

His suggestive grin implied their kiss earlier, though her smirk quickly faded, and his comment earned him a smack to the shoulder. He rubbed the throbbing bruise as if it could make the pain fade quicker, but he had no regrets. Not the kiss nor the comment. Rather, he wished to kiss her again if she'd ever allow such a thing.

"We won't be long," she said in a gruff tone. "Grab a cloak and meet me in the commons. I need to track down a crystal and I'll be there shortly."

Before he could ask what the crystal was, she disappeared from the room. He took a moment to steady himself for his next obstacle.

Werewolves. And a lot of them. On the summer solstice of all nights.

"I think I might be insane," he whispered to himself as he gathered a cloak and a couple of weapons and made his way to the commons, which was once again empty as it had been when he'd first arrived in Vrork. He sat on a golden-embroidered sofa but couldn't stay still for more than a few moments before he stood and walked the length of the room. He touched the lightly glowing sconces. He admired the intricately embroidered tapestries. And somehow, he found himself standing in front of the mirror, once again shocked to find himself staring back.

However, the vampire gazing back at him wasn't the same one he'd seen upon his first arrival. Instead of dark, sunken eyes, he discovered bright, lively ones. Instead of a permanent frown, he found his mouth curving upward in an almost smile. Gone was the sunken, gray, deflated vampire. Something about Vrork had changed him.

Or perhaps *someone*.

"Admiring yourself again, vampire?"

He spun around to find Kirsa snickering at him while she held a clear crystal in her hands. Though, as he focused his eyes, he noticed a tinge of purple giving off a lavender hue. His curiosity got the best of him as he approached, wondering how a simple rock could hold an enchantment in the first place. If he ever cracked Arvitash, he wanted to learn how to enchant items next.

If Kirsa allowed him to stay in Vrork, of course, and if they managed to live long enough.

"I was," he chuckled with a teasing glint in his eye, "but now I'm admiring you."

"Please," she snorted with a roll of her eyes. "Save your wooing for someone who believes it."

She pushed past him and walked quickly down the long hallway leading to the entry rooms. For a moment, he was too dumbstruck to follow. He'd been blatantly flirting with her over the past several weeks, and she didn't believe him to be serious?

He didn't care that she was a dwarf and he was a vampire. He pushed aside each of her rejections and focused on the fact that she'd kissed him first, despite her insisting it had been an impulse of fear. Instead, he turned his attention to the burning bellows within him, churning in sync with his emboldening emotions. His heart worked again, and it was Kirsa's doing.

Before he could stop himself, he took several long strides toward her and grabbed onto her hand, tugging her toward him. She gasped in surprise, but he stifled it by capturing her lips with his own. Unlike their first passionate kiss, this one was soft, sweet, gentle, and it made his heart flare alive in full force as the bellows turned into a forge, ready to be worked and molded if she picked up the hammer to his anvil.

But she didn't.

One of her hands touched his chest, not tenderly, but to push him away. "Luca," she whispered as she broke the kiss. "I—"

He kissed one corner of her mouth and noticed her will deflating when her hand slackened against his chest, and then he kissed the other corner. A tickle of breath caressed his cheek, tantalizing as her scent rushed into his nostrils. His control nearly fled him, but he forced it back and kissed her fully on the lips once more.

Again, she didn't return his kiss, but pushed him away with both hands this time as she said in a breathy whisper, emotion catching on her quivering voice, "I can't do this, Luca."

She spun around, but he caught onto her hand before she managed to escape behind the female's entry room door.

"And why not?"

Her shoulders began shaking, and rather than turning to face him, she wrenched her hand out of his grip and slipped behind the door, leaving him standing alone in the hallway.

Confusion hit his heart like a hammer to a nail, pounding again and again until only an aching throb remained. It had been a very long time since he'd put his heart on the line, and to have it so soundly rejected?

The throbbing ache continued as he finally gathered enough courage to step through the male's door. It might be best for everyone to simply act like the kiss hadn't even happened.

# CHAPTER 17

*'m dying.*

*I'm dying.*

*I'm dying.*

Those words echoed in Kirsa's mind again and again as she leaned her head back against the wall and allowed her tears to run freely down her face. Adrietta turned a blind eye to give her a moment of privacy, but even if the other woman stared, Kirsa wouldn't have been able to cease the flow of tears. Luca had turned into something more than just a handsome face. She cared for him. Too much. And to give in to his wooing, to allow herself to return his affection, it could only break both of their hearts.

She lifted her sleeve to view the ominous black etching on her skin that indicated the Rot was spreading. If she went into stasis, it would give her more time. Maybe a year. But to give up her consciousness meant to give up her help. Luca needed her help. She knew that. Her people needed it, too.

And despite her deep desire to surrender to Luca's wooing, it wasn't fair to him. She was dying, and if patterns proved correct, she only had months before the Rot would kill her without the aid of stasis.

Until now, she'd never feared death. But with Luca in her life… It changed things.

Dragging a hand across her eyes to collect the watery tears, she proceeded to hold her head high and throw a cloak over herself. She checked to make sure her daggers were tucked safely in her belt and forgoed the pack full of food Adrietta offered. As much as she longed to dance tonight to cross another item off her list, she knew staying longer than necessary would put Luca's life in danger. She wanted to get in and out as quickly as possible.

She took a deep breath and let it out slowly before exiting the Mountain. She held her breath as a subconscious defense tactic when she found Luca waiting with his back turned, staring out over the valley. None of her muscles moved an inch, her entire body blending in with her surroundings in her stillness.

The setting sun spread an array of yellow, orange, and pink across the sky and bathed the valley in color. She wanted to stop to admire the view as well, but she stared at his back instead as if he was a predator ready to strike.

He peeked over his shoulder at her, and to her surprise, he smiled.

"I still can't get used to that," he chuckled before adjusting his hood as if to continue to keep the last remaining rays of sunlight from burning him. "I can smell you, but I can't see you. It's what caught me in your trap in the first place."

Slowly, she released her breath, and with it, her body emerged from its surroundings, as hesitant as her emotions. He didn't act strange nor address what had happened only minutes before, and neither should she.

"What would it take to keep you from noticing my presence altogether?"

She cringed as she asked it. It was the type of question that invited a flirty jest. However, he seemed to push aside the opportunity to flirt, and she wasn't sure why a surge of disappointment rose within her.

"It's not easy," he answered, still not closing the distance between them as a part of her desperately wished he would. "You have to hide yourself from my sense of smell and my keen ears. The trick is to become something else entirely. Make yourself smell like your surroundings. Cover yourself in mud or sap. Don't make a sound your surroundings wouldn't."

The information might prove useful in the instance they needed to hide from the werewolves, so she tucked it within her mind just in case.

Still, one more question pressed heavily on her mind, driven by worry for him. "How will you hide *your* scent from *their* keen senses?"

"By touching as many werewolves as I can." He smirked, and she sighed in relief at his familiar playfulness. "Don't get jealous, love. If it looks like I'm enjoying myself, it's because I am."

She rolled her eyes and held out the crystal as she approached him. "Let's just get this over with. Place your hand on the crystal. I've never materialized before like older vampires can, but I assume this will feel like something similar."

Their fingers brushed, the touch spreading an agonizing heat through her body like a rose in bloom and reminding her of when he'd grasped her hand moments before pulling her into a kiss. It had taken every ounce of her self-control to keep from returning the kiss. But if she distanced them as much as possible before the Rot took her, it would be for the best. Especially because even she wasn't that selfish. Vampires could only mate once. If she gave into her fight against the aching desire for intimacy with him, it would be just as cruel as killing him with her own two hands.

Akretti words flowed from her tongue and ignited the crystal's enchantment. The crystal glowed a brilliant purple, forcing her to squint against the blinding light. And then in a flash, their surroundings were swallowed up into darkness, a void of swirling black masses tickling her skin. Moments later, the void spit them back out onto a lush green field surrounded by tents, tables, and lots and lots of werewolves—all in their human forms, as it was not yet a full moon. Beating drums filled the sky, each strike more appealing than the last as it dared her to join the throng of dancing.

There were few things she wanted more.

"That does *not* resemble materializing at all," Luca choked, gasping in air as if struggling to draw breath into his lungs.

"Then what is it supposed to feel like?" she asked quietly to not draw any unwanted attention from the werewolves. None of them glanced their way, either too busy dancing, laughing, or participating in the celebration of the summer solstice. A bonfire blazed in the middle of the dance floor, growing higher and higher as the reverberating drums once again enticed her to follow.

"It feels like...flying. As if I'm a snowflake drifting on the breeze. And why didn't we use one of those when we went to the ruins?"

"I brought one just in case," she huffed. "But we need to conserve our resources as much as possible, which is why I didn't use it."

At last, she spared a glance for him, watching as he struggled to his feet after the teleportation enchantment. She might have laughed at the ludicrosity of it if she wasn't so concerned about getting caught.

She got straight to the point. "Find what you need. I want to leave as soon as possible."

A grin spread across his face when he finally seemed to recover from teleporting. "I don't think I want to start looking yet. If there's fun to be had, I think it's best to let loose. Catch me if you can."

"Luca!" she hissed and dove for him as he spun toward the crowd of werewolves, but her fingers only barely managed to graze his cloak before he slipped from her grasp.

Terror gripped her as she watched him slip easily into the crowd like water flowing nimbly around rocks in a stream. He wrapped his arm around a female's waist and spun her around once before moving to the next female. This one laughed and wrapped her arms around his neck, clearly intoxicated as she stumbled along with the movements. He pulled her even closer so their bodies touched, not even an inch between them.

Kirsa's terror slowly turned into annoyance, which veered sharply into jealousy. The female was placing her hands *all over him*! It was as if she expected to mate with him right there on the dance floor. And judging by the blatantly coy looks she gave him, she had no doubt what was on the female's mind.

She balled her hands into fists and marched toward him, but she didn't make it far before someone pulled her in the opposite direction and forced her into a chair. For a moment, she thought she'd been caught. At least until the werewolves grinned.

"You look like you need a drink, lil' lady," a man said. His large eyes were black like a bottomless ravine, one cold enough to send shivers down her spine. His cheekbones stood out prominently when he smiled and handed her a tankard filled with what she assumed was alcohol.

"Lil' lady is right," another werewolf laughed, this one female. Her red hair was pulled back at the nape of her neck, her similar black eyes small and beady as she looked Kirsa up and down with suspicion in their depths. "You're so small, I could mistake you for a dwarf."

Her heart quickened as she realized they might catch onto her dwarven scent if she didn't hide it soon. Luca had been smart to hide his vampire scent first thing, even if she didn't like his methods.

"Give me that," she muttered as she snatched the tankard from the man and downed its contents as the group of werewolves cheered her on. Her throat burned from the strong liquor, and when the tankard was empty, she coughed up what felt like fire escaping from her lips. She'd never had alcohol this strong. What was it?

"Have another." Pointed teeth hiding behind his lips caught her attention as he pushed a second tankard in her direction. "I'm sure you're parched."

"Drink it yourself," she snapped, and when she attempted to stand, her head swayed dizzily until she found herself careening forward, straight into him. He caught her with his gigantic hands on her shoulders, a malicious smile on his face.

The dizziness faded, but a lightheaded elation immediately replaced it. "What did you give me?" she laughed. She quickly clamped her hands over her mouth, but even they weren't enough to keep her smile hidden.

"Another newbie," the woman said with a chuckle. "We have a few of them this year."

That didn't explain what she'd just consumed, and she didn't get another chance to ask before the male pushed her back out onto the dance floor. A blazing fire spun past her line of sight, followed by body after body until someone caught her and spun her around once, twice, and when they stopped, she barely managed to make out black hair and pale skin through her dizziness.

"I know you," she laughed, trying but failing to fight against the elation rising within her. It was the blasted drink! She couldn't think past its quick and unwanted effects.

"I should hope so," Luca answered close to her ear, and a moment later, he breathed in deeply, and she couldn't help but close her eyes and enjoy the way his lips almost grazed her skin. "I don't even want to ask why you smell like male werewolf."

Another laugh escaped her as they twirled, and more than once, he stepped on her toes. "You need to try that drink. Also, you're a horrid dancer."

He joined in her laughter and pulled her closer, once again leaning near enough for her to feel his breath caress her ear. "Last I checked, I'm no Covaci. I may not be a graceful dancer, but at least I know how to let loose."

"I witnessed as much," she replied dryly as she glanced around for the female he'd been dancing with earlier, only to find her pouting with a large lower lip as she danced with another male and stared in Luca's direction. "I should hope she doesn't get her way tonight."

When he smirked, she couldn't even be bothered by it. "Are you jealous, love?"

The alcohol continued to swirl in her mind, churning her thoughts until she couldn't stop the words from escaping her mouth. "I'm raging with jealousy."

She released a carefree laugh when he spun her again, and she wasn't sure how much time passed in his arms, nor did she care. The moon rose higher and higher, a silver gleam shining brightly against the bonfire.

*Why did we come again?*

The answer pricked and prodded at her, but her mind wouldn't open up to swallow it. However, it did swallow plenty of something else. Something that continued to take her higher and higher, and she didn't want it to stop.

"I need another drink!" she shouted over the beating drums. "You need some too, Luca."

They stopped dancing, and he glanced toward a human impaled with a stake at the edge of the field. A part of her mind sounded an alarm, but try as she might, she couldn't bring herself to care like she knew she should.

"I have to mix something up myself, so my body won't reject it," he said slowly while guiding her to a bench. "Wait here. And don't drape yourself over any other males unless they're me. Believe me, I'll know."

He slipped away as she laughed. It felt good to laugh carefreely again. It seemed like such a long time had passed since she'd allowed herself this much freedom, what with her emotional burdens too great to bear. But this drink, whatever it was, and Luca's presence…they helped lift those burdens, if only for one night.

Leaning back on the bench, she allowed her gaze to drift over the celebration. Werewolf culture was strange but interesting. They often traveled in large packs. They transformed beneath a full moon. And unlike vampires who mated only once in their entire lives, werewolves took multiple mates.

She craned her neck to peer inside the tents stationed around the camp. Some tent flaps were closed and prevented her from seeing inside. Others were wide open, revealing shops selling trinkets and wares, games played by exuberant werewolves, and one shop, in particular, caught her eye—a tattoo lounge. Never in her life had she gotten a tattoo. The idea appealed to her now, though she wasn't sure if it was because of her impending doom or the drink nudging her thoughts.

A moment later, Luca slid onto the bench beside her, holding two tankards. He handed her one and clinked his tankard against hers. She eagerly lifted it to her lips, and an exhilarating rush followed, filling her mind with complete ecstasy. An uncharacteristic giggle escaped her when Luca coughed as she had done at first. He squinted his eyes shut and opened them as if to refocus.

"This is strong," he coughed again. "What is it made of?"

"He didn't tell me when I asked," she said, another giggle escaping. "Can't handle the heat, Luca?"

"Oh, I can handle it just fine. It's you I'm worried about."

The music rushed over her, and she closed her eyes and allowed her body to sway with the beat. Dancing with werewolves had been better than she'd ever imagined. She never thought she'd get the opportunity.

She opened her eyes to find Luca draped across the bench with his face upturned toward the sky. With nothing holding her back any longer, she said, "I've been wanting to ask about your sister. Why don't you ever talk about her? About your family?"

He took another long swig from his tankard and said with a laugh, "I hate my father. We can never see eye to eye, no matter how hard I've tried."

"And Cosette?"

"Now *she* is the best vampire who has ever lived." He chuckled again as if he couldn't stop it against the influence of the drink. "I wish I could write to her, to tell her how much I miss her, but I just can't find the words."

"Does your family know where you are?"

This time, he laughed loudly and downed the rest of his blood-tinted alcohol. "I already told you, I'm not one of them anymore. And whether you're referring to me being *here* or my recent living situation with the dwarves, I think I'd be skewered alive either way."

Enough of her inhibition had liquified like the alcohol running through her veins, and she reached out to run her fingers through his hair. Black as night. Silky smooth like a raven's feathers.

"Have I ever told you I love your hair?"

"No," he grinned. "What do you love about it?"

How he could still appear so relaxed when she floated on a cloud herself in mind, body, and soul, she would never understand.

She gazed into his eyes and continued to lightly stroke his hair. "I love how it's different. It's shiny and soft, and no other dwarves have this coloring. I think I want children with black hair."

The words slipped from her mouth much faster than she could stop them, but she couldn't bring herself to care, not even when Luca became still against her fingers exploring his ebony locks. They wandered from his hair to his ears, until she trailed a single finger down his neck. Temptation curled around her hand, enticing her to explore more of him. She only reached his chest when a single rational thought entered her mind, one reminding her that it wasn't fair of her to go any further, despite how much she wanted to.

A physical ache gripped her heart as she dropped her hand and leaned away from him, turning her attention back to the dancing werewolves. The dancing distracted her enough from her desire for Luca.

"I think I'll get you another drink," he said teasingly, lightly touching her knee as he stood. "Loose lips make for good confessions, don't you think?"

"There's not a chance I'm drinking another one of those," she said with a firm shake of her head.

"Well, I won't say no to another."

He moved to walk away, but before he took more than two steps, the werewolf male with black eyes took his elbow and steered him toward a large tent, and the female with red hair did the same for Kirsa. She attempted to struggle against her strong grip, but she only managed to stumble over her own foot in the process.

They were escorted inside the tent, only to find themselves face to face with several werewolf guards flanking a female with eyes as equally white as her short hair. She stood tall and proud, her shoulders back as she looked just beyond them, as if she couldn't see where, exactly, they were.

She was blind.

"Hello," the female said with a calm smile, one that revealed sharp teeth beneath her lips. "I don't believe we've met. I am Aoni, werewolf chieftain. And I believe you two are trespassing on werewolf territory."

Kirsa swallowed the fear lodged within her throat. She glanced toward Luca, only to find his expression unreadable. Her fingers inched toward the transportation crystal tucked in her pocket, but the female holding her arm tightened her grip, preventing any further movement.

"We meant no harm," Luca insisted calmly, and she was suddenly glad one of them had a level head at the moment. It certainly wasn't her.

"Ah," Aoni said, her white eyes sparkling with amusement. "This is the vampire I thought I caught a whiff of. You can hide your outward scent by mingling with werewolves, but you can't hide the very blood coursing through your veins." Her nostrils flared. "I knew I recognized your scent. A Dragomir. But not just any Dragomir. The youngest son of Lucian."

"I am no Dragomir," he replied hoarsely. "I gave up my birthright."

Kirsa's heart skipped in surprise as she stared at him, trying to unveil the truth. Although he'd mentioned not wanting to be associated with his family, he'd never said anything about a birthright. Did he truly detest his father so much as to sever all ties?

"Very interesting," the chieftain continued, her senses seeming to look him over in a new light. "And in very peculiar company, it seems. I have not come in contact with the scent for a very long time, long before I lost my sight. But I never forget a smell. You are a dwarf. A Frey. News of your siblings' demises have already reached me, but no news of yours, Kirsa Frey. Daughter of the dwarven chieftain."

A shuddering chill raced across her skin, the tent suddenly feeling much colder even beneath the summer night. The werewolf before her had no sight, yet the woman saw more than anyone else she'd ever known.

Aoni's smile returned, showing each pointed tooth. "Tonight is a night for celebration, not hunting. I will allow you two to stay."

Finally, the female holding Kirsa's arm let go, and she immediately rushed to Luca's side in case they needed to escape with the crystal. But no one made a move to capture them again. She held tightly onto him as they turned toward the exit, but Aoni's last chilling words froze her in her tracks.

"I am curious about how he will react when you tell him the truth, Miss Frey."

The heat of guilt thawed her feet, allowing her to move again as she hurried through the tent flap with Luca at her side. They didn't get very far before he turned to her with a question in his eyes.

"What was she talking about?" he asked, but she feigned ignorance with a raise of her shoulder.

"I don't know, but I want to leave. Now."

"I was having fun."

"You can have fun somewhere else." She swayed on her feet and reached out to a table full of werewolves playing a card game to regain her balance. "We've put ourselves in enough danger."

"Fine," he relented. "We'll leave after one more drink."

# CHAPTER 18

Luca struggled to maintain control.

One more drink came and went, and since then, he wasn't sure how many more he'd consumed. Two? Three? From the buzzing in his mind to his swaying surroundings, he guessed it was the latter.

His mind drifted past him, and he only managed to grab a hold of it and tug it back toward him before it floated out to sea once more. He'd had too much to drink, and by the looks of it, Kirsa had, too. Her laughter rang out as she gambled with werewolves, no longer paying heed to the danger they used to be in. At least after the chieftain had pardoned them for the night.

But he was taking a chance on Chieftain Aoni's word, which was the only reason they stayed. That and watching Kirsa enjoy herself entertained him far too much.

"Ha!" Kirsa shouted, slapping her cards down on the table. "I won this round. Hand it over."

A werewolf appeared to begrudgingly hand over a couple of wooden chips, which Kirsa snatched up eagerly. She saluted to her opponents and before his mind could grasp what was happening, she grabbed his hand and pulled him in the direction of a tent. His feet struggled to follow, as heavy as they felt.

"Where are we going?" he asked, though he'd go anywhere with her. Anywhere at all.

"You don't think I was gambling just for fun, do you?" She stopped, and he didn't react fast enough before he ran into her, their bodies melding together. However, neither of them moved away, despite him knowing he should. She smelled nice, her alluring scent spilling from the very fibers of her hair.

Once again, he struggled to maintain control of his actions. It was hard enough to remind himself she hadn't wanted to kiss him the last time. Nothing had changed since then. Absolutely nothing.

Then why did she sift her fingers through the ends of his hair?

He sighed and leaned into her touch. His control momentarily lapsed as he placed his hands on her hips. Although she was smaller than him, they still fit together perfectly from her height to each curve of her body. His fingers grazed her skin beneath her shirt, and he pulled her even closer and caressed the nape of her neck with his nose. Her scent once again filled his nostrils with sweet rapture, ensnaring him within the very desire to take her as his mate.

Not once in his life had he ever felt this level of intensity to settle down with a mate, not even with Laurel. Kirsa was the one he wanted to choose. If she'd only choose him back.

"You're in trouble, dwarf," a voice behind them said, startling them both apart. Luca spun around to find the male from before as well as his red-headed companion, the ones who had brought them to the chieftain.

"But the chieftain said we could stay," Kirsa argued with her hands on her hips, right where his hands had been only moments earlier.

The male laughed and nodded his head toward Luca. "I wasn't referring to that. I meant it about him." He wiggled his eyebrows suggestively. "Do you know what it means when a vampire roots out your scent? He wants to mate with you. I know of a currently empty tent you can borrow for the night."

As the two werewolves laughed, Luca's face lit up with fire. For them to have so blatantly told her his deepest wishes... He was mortified. He couldn't even look at her to gauge her reaction, such was his embarrassment. If she hadn't wanted to kiss him earlier, she certainly wouldn't want to become his mate.

"I think I know where you can shove it," she spat, and he dared to peek over at her to find her nodding toward the male's lower regions.

Once again, the werewolves laughed, and she grabbed onto his hand, pulling him toward the same tent they were headed to earlier. Upon entering, a darkness swallowed them, only lit by several lanterns throughout the space. He was grateful for the dimness, as it effectively hid the flush that continued to creep up his neck.

Kirsa tossed the two wooden chips on the table before several werewolves and said, "We're both getting tattoos."

His surprise had to push through layers and layers of mud to reach the surface of his mind. Before he churned the idea around, someone pushed him into a chair and placed his right arm on the table, his wrist facing upward.

"I'm getting a tattoo?" he laughed before drinking another tankard of sangrose. The high helped dispel his previous mortification and managed to muddle his mind even more until the entire room spun with each passing breath.

"Not just any tattoo," she said, returning his laugh with one of her own. She drew a design on a piece of parchment and slid it to the artist, and moments later, he felt a pricking sensation on his wrist. His head spun far too much for him to make sense of the design, nor did he feel the pain of the chisel as much as he thought he should.

In Ichor Knell, very few vampires had tattoos. They were considered barbaric traditions of werewolves, taboo in society. A part of him thrilled at each prick on his skin— another way to rebel against the culture he'd grown up in.

His surroundings swayed again, as did everyone's voices, and it wasn't until Kirsa pulled him back out of the tent when he realized the tattoo was finished. He attempted to get a better look at it, but his hand split into two, as did Kirsa when he raised his gaze. Even doubled, his desire for her amplified, and he finally lost control after the last round of sangrose.

"You are the most..." He stopped to swallow the hiccup rising in his throat before continuing. "...the most beautiful creature I have ever laid eyes upon. You must..." Again, a hiccup threatened to escape but he pushed it down as he swayed on dizzy feet. "You must become my mate."

Kirsa wasn't much steadier on her feet. She leaned toward him with a lopsided smile, pointing a finger at his chest. "I knew you were trying to get me alone, vampire. I've been waiting for you to..." She tipped precariously to the side, and he reached out to steady her by clasping her shoulders, but the world tipped to the opposite side, and he wondered how he managed to stay standing on his own two feet.

"To what?" he asked, this time not able to stop his hiccup from escaping.

She smiled again with a wicked glint in her eye as she grabbed his hand and pulled him toward another tent. He followed while hardly managing to keep one foot in front of the other, and when he ran into a table and knocked a tankard to the ground, she started giggling uncontrollably as she looked over her shoulder.

"Shh!" she hissed, though her voice was far from quiet. "We don't want anyone to know we're here."

The tent was empty, but at this point, he couldn't find himself to care whether they did this behind closed doors or in front of an audience.

His head continued to spin dizzily as he reached out for her and pulled her to him. He only managed to graze his lips against her throat before they both stumbled and fell to the ground. Laughter broke out between them as they tried to untangle their bodies, but he gave up when he couldn't lift his hand without it splitting into two.

"I just need to close my eyes for a moment," he said, resting his head back against the lush grass.

With a giggling laugh, she replied, "You are a fun one, Luca. I like you."

A smile tugged at his mouth, but try as he might, he couldn't lift his eyelids as darkness pulled him downward like a heavy blanket trapping him beneath the water. "That's a coincidence. You're my most favorite person I know."

And then the darkness finally pulled him under, and he fell into a deep slumber.

"Blistering blood," Luca muttered under his breath as he opened his eyes against a bright light, his head pounding fiercely as if the drums from the previous night remained beating against his skull.

He blinked once, twice, until his eyes finally adjusted to the offense that was morning. Where was he? This wasn't Vrork. It was a tent.

For a moment, his heart ceased to beat as he glanced over to find his hand resting against Kirsa's sleeping shoulder—her *clothed* shoulder. They were both clothed, and he wasn't sure whether to be relieved or disappointed.

Relieved, he decided. If he was to take a mate, he didn't want it to be under the influence of liquor. Rather, he wanted a level head. Besides, he feared if he gave his heart to her, if he gave all of himself to her, fate would find a way to snatch her from him. Fate was cruel, and they certainly weren't friends. It took everything away from him he held dear.

"Wake up," he said in a groggy voice while shaking her shoulder. She groaned and slapped his hand away, nuzzling into his chest.

"Kirsa," he tried again, though he wished to spend another moment enjoying her nearness. "We're in werewolf territory. I think it's best we leave before someone catches us."

At the mention of "werewolf," she bolted upright, only to squeeze her eyes shut as she, too, met with the unforgiving light of morning.

She swore under her breath at seeing their position, their legs still tangled from their drunkenly unsuccessful attempt to mate. He remembered that part clearly despite everything else being a blur, cringing at the memory of his embarrassing efforts to woo her. It had worked, it seemed. If they'd only been slightly more lucid, he may have woken with an intense bloodbond churning within him for his new mate.

"Did we..." She didn't finish her sentence. She didn't need to.

"No, but I think it's safe to say if we ever get drunk again, we should not be near each other."

"Agreed. You are far too tempting for your own good."

They both froze at her words, and she lifted her gaze to his, her eyes wide as if shocked the confession had escaped her mouth. His lips parted, and he wasn't sure whether in his sleepy stupor he was about to kiss her or reply, but in the end, he continued to stay still.

"We should leave," she said with a grimace, nodding her head toward the tent flap.

"Right. Of course."

He put his focus into untangling himself from her, groaning at the strain it put on his aching, protesting muscles. It took a few moments too long to untangle themselves, but finally they managed the feat, both of them red-faced and flustered by the time they reached the tent's exit.

The sun had yet to break free from the confines of the nearest mountain, which gave them ample cover to sidle across dew-tipped grass and past sleeping werewolves. Neither of them knew where their own cloaks had ended up the night before, so they stole a couple hanging over the side of a tree branch. Kirsa's cloak drowned her, and she kept cursing as she tripped on the hem multiple times.

A few werewolves had yet to retire to bed, and as the two of them attempted to sneak past, one of them whistled suggestively before the group of them burst into laughter.

Heat crawled up Luca's neck, and he pulled the hood of the cloak over his head to hide his evident flush. It wasn't until they were far from the camp before his posture relaxed. He lifted his hand to pull the hood from his head but froze when he found symbols etched onto his wrist. Dwarven symbols.

However, he didn't recognize what it said.

"Umm...Kirsa?"

"Yes?"

He tentatively held his wrist out to show her the tattoo that hadn't been there a day earlier. "What does this say?"

Not for the first time that morning, she cursed, hastily pulling off her glove to find themselves staring back at the same exact symbols on her own wrist, though hers was red and inflamed while his had already healed. They matched.

"Why did we think it was a good idea to drink?" she groaned while pulling her glove back on. "Never again."

"But what does it mean?"

His heart pounded when she avoided looking at him. When it was evident she wouldn't answer, he grabbed onto her hand and spun her to face him until they were only inches away from one another. For a moment, he forgot his question as he gazed into her eyes. This female had almost become his mate, and although he didn't think he deserved her, he found she had taken up every inch of his heart, nonetheless.

His chest squeezed so painfully tight with emotion that he couldn't breathe.

At last, she answered, "Dwarves are better known for piercings rather than tattoos, as werewolves are. There is a certain..." She took a deep breath and let it out slowly as her gaze slid from his eyes to his feet. "...a certain piercing we get when we find someone we want to spend the rest of our lives with. This tattoo is the equivalent of an ardor piercing."

*Ardor piercing.*

He'd been wondering for far too long what it was after he'd seen it mentioned on Kirsa's list—a list he had yet to return.

Once again, his heart pounded so loud that it pulsed in his ears, deafening all other sounds. His emotions flared alive, no longer bound by the cage trapping them deep inside him. More than anything, he wanted to hold Kirsa's hand, he wanted to kiss her lips. But he refrained, even if it was one of the most difficult things he had to do.

"You know what almost happened last night," he said slowly as he tried to hear his own words over his raging pulse. "You would have become my mate, and I would have been tied to you forever. What would you have done in such an instance?"

"The right thing," she answered quietly, still refusing to meet his gaze.

"Which is what?"

He needed to hear her answer, though he both hoped for it and dreaded it at the same time. If he allowed himself to care for her too much, she'd be taken away from him. Fate would see to it.

However, he quickly realized he already cared too much. Far too much. But he dared not put a name to the feeling burning brightly in his chest.

"I would have married you. If I'm bold enough to be intimate with a vampire, then I'd better be ready to face everything that comes with it."

It was noble, indeed. He'd heard stories of vampires giving themselves to other races, only for them to be brokenhearted and abandoned, not able to take another mate for the rest of their immortal lives.

He decided to let the matter drop. To prod for more information meant to unravel his own feelings for the dwarf, and he wasn't sure he was ready to face them. He wasn't sure if he'd *ever* be ready to face them.

They continued forward in silence, and despite him dropping the subject, he found himself thinking about it far too long. Would she have wanted to marry him should they have mated? Or would she have detested the idea?

Not able to push the matter away completely, he asked, "Where on the body does one get an ardor piercing?"

To his complete surprise, she pushed her hair aside to reveal one of her piercing-covered ears, and his eyes couldn't help but roam over every piercing, a desire to learn the story behind each one tugging at him hard.

"Right here." She pointed to an empty spot on the crus of helix, void of all piercings. "Dwarves consider it the heart of the ear. It's a tradition to receive an ardor piercing on one's wedding day, right after reciting vows."

"And do males receive them, too?" He couldn't help but express an interest in the culture. Although he'd grown up as a vampire, he felt like he belonged with the dwarves. Vrork felt more like a home to him than Ichor Knell ever had.

Kirsa smirked knowingly and covered her ears once more with her hair. "Men have plenty of piercings, too, and that includes ardor piercings."

"Only on the wedding day? What if someone received one before then?"

"My, my. You have plenty of questions, vampire. And honestly, it doesn't matter when you get the piercing. You don't have to be married. It's only a wedding tradition."

When she turned her back, he studied the symbols on his wrist with a newfound curiosity. He only remembered so much of last night, and he couldn't recall whether the tattoo had been his idea or Kirsa's.

"Did you get what you came here for?" she asked suddenly, and he dropped his hand to his side lest she catch him studying the tattoo too closely.

For a moment, he had no idea what she was talking about, especially amidst the post-drunken fog spiraling in his mind. At least until he faintly recalled using the "errand" as an excuse to cross an item off her list. Now only five things remained unless one counted the ardor tattoo as an ardor piercing. It was close enough.

Unfortunately, he could only help her cross off one more thing. After that, he was useless. He refused to return to Ichor Knell, and therefore wouldn't take her there. He doubted their relationship would blossom into marriage, and even if it did, he could never give her children in time before the dwarves died off from the Rotting Blight. It could take decades for a vampire male to produce a child due to their low fertility.

Not that he was ready to sire children anyway.

Still, a triumphant warmth rose within him at what he'd accomplished for her—dancing in the werewolf soiree during the summer solstice.

"I certainly did," he replied with a sly smile. "I certainly did."

"Good, now let's get home."

*Home...*

She slipped the transportation crystal from her pocket, and once they both placed their hands on it, it transported them in a dizzying array of darkness until they stood at the foot of Vrork's door. They crossed the barrier in silence, and when they reached the entryway, he turned to her to express his gratitude for her company, but she had already disappeared.

Instead of dwelling on her quick departure, he followed Gunther into the male entryway and followed protocol by stripping down to nothing. At this point, it no longer fazed him.

Gunther snorted at Luca's tattooed wrist. "Ah, I finally understand who the unfortunate dwarf is. It seems you are rather unfortunate as well. Bad timing."

"Bad timing?" He scrunched his eyebrows together as he dressed once more, turning the dwarf's words around in his mind. "What do you mean?"

"She still hasn't told you?" Gunther pressed his lips tight together as if realizing he made a mistake by saying anything at all. "I think you need to hear it from her mouth, not mine."

As he followed the maze of hallways back to the library to continue his studies, he stared down at his wrist, brushing his fingers over the dwarven symbols etched onto his skin. Something was wrong, and now he vaguely understood Chieftain Aoni's words.

Kirsa was harboring a secret, and he couldn't even begin to guess what it was.

# CHAPTER 19

"Blasted thing won't come off," Kirsa muttered to herself.

She'd used every possible trick imaginable to scrub the ardor tattoo from her wrist until the skin around it became raw and tender, an inflamed red patch with a glaring black design stark in the middle. But short of cutting her very skin off with a knife, she was stuck with the tattoo.

Forever.

Or at least until the Blight took her in several measly months.

The excursion to the werewolf territory had taxed her body greatly, and usually when she'd still have plenty of energy to spare, she felt her vitality draining. Yet, a smile crept across her face as she thought of her shortened list of things she wanted to do before she died. What a fortunate coincidence Luca needed werewolf text to use as a reference for his project. Going at all had put his life in danger, but they'd gotten out unscathed.

Well, mostly unscathed.

Her mind hazily recalled his hands on her waist as they had danced carefreely surrounded by large, flickering fires. She remembered the intensity of her desire for him, enough for her to suggest the ludicrous idea of getting these matching tattoos. However, the tattoo only reminded her of her fast-approaching death, and it was more than selfish to involve him in her carnal desires when such a short time remained of her life.

"By the Mountain." She rolled her eyes and finally reached for a knife and wasn't able to press it against her wrist before the door to the lab opened. The knife clattered to the table in her haste to hide her wrist behind her back. Her mother entered and stopped short.

"I saw that."

Heat claimed her face as she pushed the knife away and continued to work on her latest venom sample, her head hanging over her work. She wasn't finding much success in her attempts to isolate the healing aspects woven within the venom from the immortality.

Her mother pulled up a chair beside her, and although Kirsa felt her stare, she refused to acknowledge it. At least until her mother spoke first.

"You can't stay away from him, can you?"

"I had a bit too much to drink is all."

Slowly, her mother's eyebrow rose with every inch of it covered in skepticism. "I doubt that was all." But then a reminiscent smile replaced her skeptical expression. "I remember when I met your father. His title as chieftain did nothing to sway my interest in him. I had come from another settlement at the time, and the last thing I wanted was to be married off so quickly to a dwarf with an ego the size of a mountain." She slid a glass plate toward her as if noticing she needed one for the next step in the process. "He grew on me, though, and we started sneaking off to be alone far too often. I can recognize a dwarf in love when I see one."

Kirsa made a show of glancing around the room, but it was currently empty save for the two of them. "Where? I don't see anyone myself."

"You are such an imp," her mother laughed, and the sound alone caused her own smile to sprout from darkened soil. It had been far too long since she'd heard her laugh. "I don't exactly care for you to be with a vampire, let alone one I believe put you in danger at the ruins, but consider living your life before you can't anymore."

"No." She rubbed the persistent ache in her shoulder where the Rot was spreading farther up her arm by the day. "Why do you think I keep my distance? He's a vampire. *Immortal.* I am terrified of hurting him."

"Then he doesn't know, does he?"

She shook her head. "I know he'll find out sooner or later... But I know he cares for me like I do him. If the situation was reversed, I'd be heartbroken and angry. I don't think I can handle witnessing his expression if I tell him."

"If you want my sage advice—"

"—I don't."

Her mother continued anyway. "It's better for him to hear it from you than to learn of it from someone else. Let him decide for himself after that."

Kirsa shoved her equipment away and stood abruptly before walking toward the door.

"Where are you going?" her mother called after her.

"To get it over with. That way certain chieftains can stop bothering me about it and leave me alone in peace."

She ignored her mother's laughter as she escaped the confines of the room. Each step she took toward the housing district made her heart pound harder and harder, and when she finally stood in front of Luca's room, she didn't bother to knock before she stepped inside. She opened her mouth to say the words that would condemn her…

Only to find the room empty.

"Where are you, vampire?" she muttered to herself while closing the door. For once in her life, she wished she possessed a vampire's ability to follow a scent, because when she checked outside the bathhouse and in the commons, they were both empty as well. The last place she thought to check was the library. When she entered the room, her throat constricted at the disarray of it. Luca didn't notice as she entered, such was his concentration as he pinned diagrams to the wall, threads connecting bits and pieces of Akretti to Arvitash. Dozens of open books littered the tables, along with scrolls and parchment, his handwriting occupying every inch of free space.

He truly was trying his absolute hardest to crack the Arvitash language, and from the looks of it, he was getting farther than any of the dwarven scholars who'd tried.

Luca picked up the quill resting behind his ear and dipped it in ink before scribbling down another note, and his look of concentration as he turned toward his diagram endeared her to him even more. His eyebrows furrowed as he turned his head.

And he jumped so high she might have laughed if her heart didn't beat with sickening nervousness as it was.

"Kirsa!" he gasped while placing his quill down. "You startled me. How long were you standing there?"

"I only just arrived," she replied with a half-hearted shrug. The words she wanted to say to him died on the tip of her tongue, the sinking feeling in her chest becoming nearly unbearable. "I thought you could use some fresh air. Take a walk with me?"

"Absolutely," he said eagerly, and she couldn't help but smile when he cleared his throat sheepishly.

No words came to her mouth as she took the lead, and when they were outside in the fresh mountain air, words still didn't come. Dusk greeted them, making cloaks unnecessary as they traversed the mountainside in silence.

What was on his mind? Was it anything as heavy as what pricked at her own conscience? Or was he still so focused on his work that it had followed him outside?

Her contemplation quickly turned into a scowl as she noticed his bare wrist, the ardor tattoo emblazoned on his skin for all to see. "You're not covering it? At least have some decency to wear gloves."

"Cover it?" He turned to give her one of his most irksome grins. "Why cover something I'm not ashamed of?"

They reached the nearby glassy lake, beautiful beneath the twilight skies. The surface of the water reflected hues of orange and purple, signaling the waning day waxing into night. It perfectly mirrored the tumult raging inside her own heart and the darkness that would surely follow once she told Luca the very thing she'd been hiding from him.

"You're not the least bit worried about what others might think about us having matching tattoos we drunkenly received at a werewolf soiree?"

"Why does it matter what others think?" He stooped to pick up a flat rock. She watched as he took aim and skipped it across the lake, and it took every effort to keep her mouth from dropping at the strength behind the throw. The rock skipped several times and made it over halfway across the water before sinking beneath the surface. But she quickly hid her astonishment when he turned back to face her.

"It matters when I'm the chieftain's daughter."

He shrugged and picked up yet another rock, but he didn't throw it yet and instead tossed it into the air and caught it multiple times. "I used to be held back by the person others expected me to be. I feel much more at peace now that I've let it go. Besides, aren't people supposed to be more truthful when they're intoxicated?" He laughed and tossed the rock up again. "I think I remember you saying something about wanting children with black hair."

Her face heated as she stared back at him, completely mortified. "I never said that." Or at least she didn't remember it.

"You did. And I especially remember when you told me you were raging with jealousy when I danced with another female."

All right, she did remember saying *that*, but it wasn't quite as horrifying as the first confession. "And your point is?"

"Stop skirting around the truth. Admit you have feelings for me."

Icy fear spread from her fingers to her toes as she stared back at him with a blank expression. She hadn't sought him out to bleed her heart dry. She'd sought him out to tell him something far more sinister.

"I...I can't."

He stepped forward and placed his hands on her shoulders, and she hid the wince of pain when he brushed the part of her shoulder covered in the Rot, hidden just beneath her sleeve.

"Then I'll go first," he said softly. "I haven't felt anything in years. *Years*. Until I met you. You make me feel alive. You've managed to spark life back inside me when I thought all hope was lost. I love you, Kirsa."

And then the ice frosted over completely, covering her entire body and weaving its way into her heart until it beat slower...slower...slower. Until her heart squeezed with enough pain to cause one lone tear to escape the corner of her eye. This was not how she'd wanted to tell him. But now she had no choice.

"Luca, I'm dying."

Luca's smile melted slowly as he gazed back at Kirsa for what felt like an eternity. As if on their own accord, his hands dropped from her shoulders, and he stared at her as he searched for the lie in her eyes.

It wasn't there.

"What?" he rasped.

He refused to believe it.

Another tear escaped her eye, and he willed his finger to wipe it away, but his hand wouldn't budge from his side. It stayed still as if it had turned to stone, the rest of his body following suit. But instead of the emptiness he expected to feel, an agonizing ache filled every pore in his body. Still, he waited with bated breath.

"I should have told you when it happened," she replied hoarsely. "That's why I've been avoiding you. I didn't know how to tell you. When we went to the ruins, the fall we experienced..." She blinked several times as if to hold in her tears. "It broke my mask. I breathed in the Rot. I injected myself with serum in time, but it will still spread. I give myself a few more months until it takes me, too."

In a single instant, his world shattered into a thousand pieces. Every laugh he'd experienced, every smile, every kiss. Shattered. Broken. Shards of his fragile heart scattered in the wind. The pulsing ache urged his nose to seek it out, to see it for himself. He moved closer to her and breathed in her scent, searching. He found what he was looking for on her right arm.

She didn't stop him as he slipped her glove off, but his roaming gaze didn't pause at the ardor tattoo on her wrist. He lifted her sleeve higher until he found the evidence in the form of black vein-like etchings.

There it was. Plain to see. Evidence. Truth.

"No," he whispered, stumbling backward as his face contorted with pain. "Not you."

Ache flared in his heart, nearly crumpling him where he stood. He spun around and approached the edge of the lake with a hand clutched over his bleeding heart. But no matter how hard he tried to keep the pain in, it overflowed from his fingers like water in a gushing river.

*Cosette. Tavian. Chloe. Kirsa.*

Fate took from him everyone he ever cared about. He knew—he *knew*—if he got closer to Kirsa, fate would take her away, too. For the first time in years, he'd learned how to love again. How to live. How to care. And now the very dwarf he'd given his entire heart to, she'd be taken from him as well.

Grieving anger coursed through him in a sudden wave, and out of habit, he reached for his flask and opened it, but he didn't drink. He couldn't. He didn't want to ease the pain. He wanted to feel it. He wanted it to consume him.

A loud, anguished cry erupted from his mouth as he threw the flask with all his might, watching as it soared through the air and splashed into the lake, disappearing beneath the surface. Tears came unbidden to his eyes, and they overflowed onto his cheeks, down his chin, and dripped onto his hand that attempted to wipe them away. A strangled sob caught in his throat as his anguish nearly devoured him.

His chest felt as if someone had taken an iron knife and cut him deep, far too deep for him to even begin healing from it. This wonderful, beautiful, extraordinary female he wanted as his mate…

Fate was slowly taking her away.

He wept silently into his hand, and when it became clear the pain wouldn't lessen, he turned back to Kirsa, only to find her hands pressed to her heart, her tears flowing as unceasingly as his. Unlike his red tears, hers contained a golden sheen. And seeing them brought a whole new ache to his heart. A determined, unselfish ache.

He'd cross off every item on her list. Every last one. No matter what it took. And if she decided she didn't want to marry him, then he'd find someone she *did* want to marry. But damn it all! He would help her finish her list no matter what it cost him.

In several strides, he closed the distance between them and pulled her into a tight embrace. She immediately broke down sobbing into his chest, and with each aching moment that passed, he held her close, tenderly, allowing his love to pour out from himself and into her.

One thing he was sure of—he wouldn't rest until he cracked the Arvitash language. Aside from her list, it was his number one priority.

# CHAPTER 20

$\mathscr{A}$nother week passed and they still made little progress toward finding a cure for the Rotting Blight. Luca worked day and night on cracking the uncrackable dwarven language. At times, he wanted to pull his hair out in frustration. At other times, temptation nearly lured him back to Ichor Knell where he might receive some help figuring it out. He'd seek out Nicolae Covaci, and dare he think it, even Laurel. He'd lower his pride enough to grovel at the feet of a couple of the greatest scholars in the vampire city. But in order for them to help, they needed to also learn Akretti, and the dwarves didn't have that kind of time. *Kirsa* didn't have that kind of time.

Which resulted in more frustrated groaning and hair pulling.

He blew out a long breath as he once again compared what he thought the Arvitash scroll might say to what he'd written in Akretti. It didn't match, nor did it make any sense. He was missing something here, and he knew it was right in front of his eyes. All he needed was a key, but what was the key?

"What about this passage?" Elric asked as he handed Luca a book on ancient dwarven history. "It's copied from a stone tablet. Deaths and dates of dwarves, it looks like."

Elric and Gunther had both been helping him in their spare time, and although they hadn't had the best of starts, he was beginning to form a tight friendship with the two of them. And the more he studied and practiced Akretti, the more he understood what they said.

"Yes, this is good," he said with renewed enthusiasm as he cross-referenced the passage with another book of death names and dates from Vrork. However, the names looked to be remarkably different in appearance, and he couldn't make sense of a single symbol in the ancient language.

"It's good for a different perspective," he amended. "Is there anyone in Vrork who knows any ancient dwarven names?"

Gunther leaned back in his chair and stroked his short blond beard. "We're talking about names thousands of years old. Your father is a thousand years old, yes? He may be a good resource."

Luca shook his head and scowled at the passage as if it had personally offended him. "He's the last person I'd use as a resource. We are not on speaking terms right now, and I doubt we'll ever be."

Guilt consumed him at the notion of his pride hindering Kirsa's recovery. His father might not even know anything about the dwarves of ancient times, but could Luca really not lower his pride enough in the chance that any of the information his father provided proved useful?

He shook the guilt away and focused harder on the information in front of him. It was not a decision he'd make right now.

The door opened, and he knew exactly who it was before she stepped foot in the room. Her scent wafted through the air, caressing his nostrils, filling him with excitement.

"Glad you could join us, Kirsa," he said with a grin moments before he turned around to find her carrying a plate of dwarven sweets.

"How does he do that?" Gunther asked.

"I wondered the exact same thing," Elric replied. "It's rather eerie."

Kirsa gave him a sweet smile, one he locked away within his memory to cherish at another time. She hadn't said anything to him to indicate she might return his feelings, but he no longer brooded over it. Her survival and happiness were more important than requited love, and if he had a say in it, he'd see to both.

"I stole some fairy cakes from the mess hall," she said, coming more fully into the room. "I thought you boys might enjoy them."

"Don't mind if I do," Luca said as he reached out for one, but she quickly smacked his hand away.

"You don't eat real food and you know it." She laughed before handing the plate to the other two dwarves, who devoured the cakes ravenously. "Besides, it would be a waste for a vampire to try it. Remember several days ago?"

"Those strudels were disgustingly bitter."

She playfully kicked his leg. "They were not. Your sense of taste is far from normal."

He sighed dramatically as he rested his head against his hand and gazed at her with longing in his eyes, though he tried to pass it off as longing for the food. "I wish I could taste things the way you do. Though, if you tasted blood the way it tastes to me, I'm sure you'd be ravenous for it more than your little fairy cakes."

"You just transitioned from eerie to disturbing," Elric grimaced. "I can't believe you actually drink blood and enjoy it."

His fangs sprouted from his mouth, and he grinned wickedly. "Very much."

Gunther chuckled and pulled Elric toward the door. "I think that's our cue to leave. Don't want fangs in our necks."

"You mean you don't want to witness these two sickening lovers?" Elric laughed right behind him.

Kirsa raised her hand as if to stop them, but before she uttered a word, they disappeared, leaving them alone in the library. His playful demeanor immediately melted into concern as he looked her over. Long sleeves covered every inch of her arms and shoulders, and today, she wore a top to conceal most of her neck. The Rot must be spreading.

"How are you feeling?" he asked before he retracted his fangs.

"They know we're not lovers, don't they?" Her attention turned distractedly toward the door as if she itched to escape the confines of the room.

"You're ignoring my question."

"On purpose, too. I don't want to talk about it."

The legs of his chair scraped against the ground as he stood, and she continued to stare defiantly at the door rather than meet his gaze. A hundred different words and feelings and questions churned in his mind, but he forced them to the side despite how much it pained him.

Instead of addressing any one of those thoughts, he said, "I'm tired of spending time with Gunther and Elric. I wanted to do something else tonight, and I hoped you might accompany me."

She still didn't look at him as she answered. "It's not a good idea, considering what you know about me now."

The Blight? Of course, he knew about it, much to his over-worried heart. But what did it have to do with not being a good idea? Was she hurting? Did she not have enough energy?

"It's a bit of a hike," he continued, rubbing the back of his neck. "I will carry you the entire way. You don't have to lift a finger."

Although he didn't see it, he heard her swallow moments before her shoulders drooped. "How did it come to this? I can't go on a measly hike without needing to be carried. I'm far too weak for comfort."

*It must be her pride holding her back. I forgot dwarves are prideful creatures.*

"Or you can carry me," he jested in an attempt to distract her from her own shortcomings. "I've become accustomed to sitting at this desk all day, and I'd rather not get my feet dirty."

"Vain vampires," she muttered under her breath. Louder, she said, "I'm surprised vampires can be so vain in the first place, never seeing their own reflections their whole lives and all."

He leaned back against the table and gave her a casual grin. "Those who can afford it hire a portrait artist to paint their profile for each year of their lives until they stop aging. After, we judge our looks on how others perceive us."

She raised an eyebrow. "Such as?"

"Flirt attempts from the opposite sex, attention we receive from others, how many handkerchiefs we are gifted from interested suitors, how a female responds when I kiss her..."

"You must be down in the pits then. Considering I'm the *only* female you've ever kissed, and I haven't responded well." Her teasing tone brought out his mischievous side, and he couldn't help but flirt.

"Well, you know, you aren't the *first* female I've kissed. There may have been a few before you."

"What?" Kirsa gasped sarcastically. "You're jesting."

"I know, I know. It's hard to believe."

The teasing glint in her eye disappeared so suddenly it took him by complete surprise. "How many females *have* you courted?"

However, he wouldn't allow her seriousness to ruin their playful encounter, so he gathered several of the books from the table and cradled them in his arms. When he reached the doorway, he turned back to her. "Where's the fun in telling you? Besides, the only female I want to court is you. Meet me outside an hour before midnight if you decide to take me up on my offer. I promise you'll love it."

He left her gaping after him, and he thanked the heavens she couldn't hear his pounding heartbeat during his departure. She already knew of his feelings for her. If she decided to meet him before midnight, then he'd know for sure she returned at least a fraction of those feelings.

He'd never wished for anything as much as he did for her to turn up tonight.

Waiting until midnight was agonizingly painful, and when the time finally arrived, it took all his self-control not to race through the hallways and burst out into the open air. Instead, he forced himself to take slow, deliberate steps until he stood on the edge of a cliff and looked up at the skies above. The luminous light from the full moon cast shadows across the mountainous terrain, and he found his mind wandering back to Ichor Knell, back to Cosette. What was his sister doing right now? Was she looking out the window of her new home and staring at the same moon? Or was she fast asleep, her little Leif tucked into bed in the nursery?

A somber smile forged its way to his mouth as he thought of the two of them. He'd been a good uncle to Leif, and he longed to see both him and Cosette again, but to return to Ichor Knell to do it?

"I suppose I have to go back anyway," he said to himself as he thought of Kirsa and her list. He'd vowed to himself to cross every item off her list, and if visiting Ichor Knell in person was on there, he'd personally see to the task. No matter how hard it was to return.

"Go back where?" a voice asked behind him.

He turned around slowly to face Kirsa, his eyes widening in surprise while his throat simultaneously closed up with emotion. "You came."

"Of course, I did. Why would I pass up the opportunity to carry you across the mountainside?"

When she smiled at her own jest, he allowed himself to chuckle. Relief flooded through him to the point where it became overwhelming. She cared for him, too. Otherwise, she wouldn't be here.

Reaching for her hand, he grabbed onto her fingers and held on tight. She returned the gesture with a gentle squeeze. His hand dwarfed hers, and when it had once been a strange sensation, it had become all too familiar and welcome. He loved this female, and although he hadn't wanted to put a name to these feelings churning for her, he hadn't been able to help it. He loved her. He wanted her as his mate. No matter how short their union might be.

But he didn't have much time left to ask her. If she responded well to tonight, he'd consider asking soon.

*Every single item on the list*, he vowed yet again. *No matter what it costs me.*

"Where are you taking me?" she asked once he started leading her down a well-worn path, one he'd studied from a map in the library until each curve in the trail was seared into his memory.

"You'll see."

She endured about a half mile down the path until her lungs finally gave out, and she made the excuse of fixing her shoe to sit down to rest. He saw straight through the lie, and making an excuse of his own that he was cold and needed to share body heat, he picked her up into his arms and cradled her close as he continued forward. Surprisingly, she didn't protest, nor did she fight him. Rather, she wrapped her arms around his neck and leaned against him as they continued their journey.

The placement of her head positioned her hair far too close to his nose, and temptation lured him closer until he leaned in to breathe in her scent. Alluring. Tantalizing. And it vexed him enough to steal every coherent thought from his mind.

A soft vampire whine trickled from his throat, one that caused his arms to become rigid around her. He hadn't meant for it to escape, to weave tales of his conspicuous desire. Kirsa lifted her head and looked into his eyes, their golden hue shining beneath the light of the moon.

Suddenly, those eyes widened, and she pushed away from him until she landed on her feet. It wasn't until then he realized they had reached their destination.

The star pool stole the very breath from his lungs. Under the full moon, it glistened beautifully, each small ripple moving like liquid silver. The atmosphere held a reverent stillness to it he feared even the faintest of whispers might break. The pool was as large as a small lake. While several dwarves bathed on the opposite side of the pool, they didn't look their way upon their arrival.

His wonder broke as a fist came flying at him, and he didn't have time to dodge before it smashed into his shoulder.

"You stole my list!" Kirsa cried.

He grunted in pain, but the pain quickly turned into shock when she grabbed a fistful of his shirt and pulled him down until their lips met in the sweetest, gentlest of kisses. The flare in his shoulder ebbed into a warm throb as he melted into the kiss, only wishing to take it further when she pulled away with a joyful smile reaching her eyes.

He rubbed the back of his neck sheepishly. "Was that a kiss of gratitude or affection?"

"Both," she answered. "I feel like a halfwit right now. First the honey roll. Then the werewolf soiree. You didn't need a sample of their language, did you?"

"No," he admitted. "But we both survived it, and for the parts I *do* remember, I enjoyed myself quite a bit."

"So did I."

The way she looked at him leaked gratitude, at least until her expression fell into uncertainty as she looked out over the water. "It's so close to home," she whispered, and he watched as her gaze drifted from one end of the pool to the other. "I'm here. It's a full moon. Yet, I don't think I can bring myself to wade in. I don't deserve it. Not after everything I've done. Not after all the blood on my hands."

Now it finally made sense—why she hadn't visited the star pool already. Her guilt over killing vampire after vampire held her back. He didn't know if he could ease her guilt, but perhaps he could try.

"You may have killed vampires, but you did it to save your people."

"But they all died in vain. I'm hardly closer to finding a cure than I had been in the past."

"Then perhaps you need to hear it from a vampire." He stepped closer and took both of her hands in his, a sincerity in his eyes as he gazed down at her. "I forgive you, Kirsa. For each vampire you've killed, for all the blood on your hands. I forgive you. *We* forgive you."

Tears streamed down her cheeks, and she closed her eyes as they dripped one by one from her chin. "I regret it so much. I wish I never had to do it."

"I know, love. I know." When she didn't move from where she stood, he said, "If you don't want to go in, I will just sit here with you, and we can enjoy the peace. Or we can return home right now if you'd prefer."

*Home.*

Vrork was his home now. Finally, he'd found somewhere he belonged. Although he may be a vampire, he'd found his place among dwarves, especially now that they were beginning to accept him. Here by Kirsa's side was where he wanted to be. Always.

After a moment, she opened her eyes. "I'll go in."

She stepped away from him and faced toward the water. He knew he should have looked away when she started stripping, but his gaze remained fixed on her until she was in her undergarments. His gaze traveled over every curve of her body from her bare legs to her bare lower back, but then it froze at the sight of the winding black etchings that started from the fingers of her right hand and stretched all the way to the base of her neck and across one shoulder. His stare continued along those etchings until she submerged herself beneath the water, hiding them from view.

What he wouldn't give to take her pain away, to give her more life than she currently had. But he knew her position on becoming a vampire, and therefore, he would never ask to bite her, even if it would give her forever rather than a short few months. He hoped to find a cure before then. Long before then. If he could only make sense of a single symbol of the Arvitash language…

"Why are you still standing there?" Kirsa asked, breaking him away from his thoughts.

He raised his eyebrows at the obvious issue and gestured to the whole of him. "I'm a vampire. I don't belong in the sacred dwarven pool."

Her response was quiet, yet he still detected it with his keen hearing. "You're more of a dwarf than anyone I've ever met. For everything you've been doing for us, you most certainly belong here."

Still, he hesitated. Dwarves revered this pool. They held it sacred above most other things, and he certainly didn't want to taint it with his vampire origins.

"You won't taint it," she said, and for a moment her comment took him aback, at least until he realized he had voiced his concerns out loud. "Please join me?"

"All right," he said slowly. He pulled his boots off his feet, and undoing a button at a time, his tunic fell off his shoulders and lay at his feet. He caught her staring, and he grinned as he held her gaze while undressing the rest of him until he waded forward in only his undergarments. The water's chill caught him off guard, but within moments, it felt refreshing against his skin, exactly how he'd imagined spiritually cleansing water might feel.

The atmosphere continued to hold a sacredness within its soft, fluid hands, and he made sure to respect it with slow movements and a hush to his voice as he would in the cathedral back in Ichor Knell.

When he reached Kirsa, he held one of her hands and led her farther into the lake. She quickly couldn't reach the bottom, and flipped onto her back, allowing him to guide her closer to the center of the body of water where the moon reflected the brightest.

Kirsa closed her eyes, and with one hand helping to keep her afloat at the small of her back, he turned his attention to the sky above. The moon was large and round and bright, the second most beautiful thing he'd seen in the past five minutes.

She repositioned herself and nearly dunked her head beneath the water as if trying to stand on her own two feet. He grabbed a hold of her to keep her steady, pulling her closer until they were only inches apart.

"Why?" she whispered, searching his eyes. She didn't need to explain for him to catch her meaning.

"It was supposed to be a practical joke at first, stealing your list. But your list was serious, as are my feelings for you." He gently tucked her hair behind her ear and allowed his gaze to roam over each of her piercings. His fingers grazed each one of the earrings, stories he longed to hear one day from her own mouth. "I don't know if we'll ever find a cure for the Blight, but I swear to you, Kirsa, I'll find a way to cross every item off your list. One way or another, I promise to make it happen."

The tip of his finger moved from her earrings to the bare spot on the crus of helix saved for an ardor piercing. He leaned forward and grazed his lips over it in the barest of kisses. The action felt intimate, full of meaning and intent. When the time was right, he'd ask for her hand, even if he knew the answer might be "no." But not just yet.

"Luca," she whispered, and she pulled away enough to reveal the anxiety evident in her eyes.

"I know," he sighed, expecting another rejection. "Keep my hands to myself. Put some distance between us. You're not interested in me that way."

She shook her head, and he heard her swallow as she continued to hold his gaze with the same nervousness growing in her expression. "No. Quite the opposite, in fact. I only have a little time left as far as I'm concerned. I hoped you might marry me."

His body iced over in shock as he stared at her...and stared...and stared. But no matter how hard he tried to pick apart her words, he couldn't bring himself to believe them to be real. Finally, his body thawed just enough for his tongue to work, though his heart still beat slowly as it trudged through a thick layer of disbelief.

"Is this a practical joke? Because it's not funny."

"No. Of course not." Water dripped from her hands as she lifted them from the water and placed them on either side of his face. Her skin felt cold against his cheeks, her stone hand even colder, but heat managed to seep through and thaw him just a bit more. "This list is one of the most significant things in my life. Crossing marriage off is important to me. I want to experience the engagement, the ceremony, the joyful elation of simply being married. I'd rather not be intimate with you, as I'd feel awful if I made you do it when you can only choose one mate for the rest of your life. And after the Rot takes me, you'll be a free male again."

He wasn't sure what bothered him the most about her rush of words—her unwillingness to become his mate, the fact that she thought she needed to beg for this favor, or that she didn't seem to believe they'd find a cure.

At last, his entire body thawed, warmth replacing the ice despite the frigid water.

"I will marry you under three conditions," he replied as he took her hands from his face and held them tightly in his.

"Anything," she breathed.

The word sent a rush of elation through him. This was what he'd wanted for a while now. It felt surreal to be so close.

"First, I want to take your name rather than you taking mine." He didn't want to be associated with being a Dragomir, and this would effectively separate him from his family, despite the notion being untraditional.

"Done."

"Second, I want you to tell me how you feel about me. Nothing held back."

Kirsa nodded and slowly snaked her arms around his neck and pulled him in for a sweet, tender kiss. He released a breath so hot it felt like fire as he wrapped his arms around her waist and pulled her closer to him through the water. Her lips were soft, tempting him to explore. But he couldn't lose his mind before his third request. Not yet at least.

"I love you, Luca," she whispered when she finally pulled away. "I may have helped you feel again, but you have helped me live again. I am ever grateful to you."

He kissed her palm and then her wrist where the ardor tattoo stood out against her skin. He could hardly believe she returned his feelings. That alone brought him more happiness than he could have imagined.

"And my final condition… You will allow me to take you as my mate."

She snatched her hand back so quickly he almost didn't catch the movement, save for the small splash it made when it dove beneath the water. His heart panged with an ache, one he stuffed back inside himself before he gave her a chance to see it.

"I-I-I can't. It's not fair to you."

"I've already made my choice. If I must live out the rest of my days without you, then so be it. But I stand firm with this. If you can't become my mate, then I can't become your husband."

"Luca, you can't ask that of me."

"I just did. Vampires are careful when selecting their mates. I have wanted you for a mate for a while now."

Once again, she shook her head and refused to look him in the eye, though she still held onto his arm to keep herself afloat in the water. "I don't understand the complexities of vampires and finding mates, but what I do know is my death will destroy you more after mating than it would before. I can't do that to you."

He swallowed the lump in his throat. For a moment, she had felt so close, but now his future with her, however short, was slipping right through his fingers. But for this, he refused to budge.

"As I said earlier," he replied with a bubble of dread in his chest, "I will do whatever it takes to help you finish your list. If you want to experience marriage, I will find someone who will make you happy."

"No." Golden, shimmering tears fell from the corners of her eyes. He caught them with his thumbs and slowly pulled her toward a place where she could stand on her own without his help. "I want to marry someone I love. I want to marry you."

Closing his eyes, he repeated her words again and again in his mind, memorizing the sound of them, the feel of them. For years, he had felt as if his existence didn't matter, as if no one would love him for the person he was. But here was a dwarf of all people who loved him unconditionally, a dwarf he felt he didn't deserve.

"You are too selfless for your own good," he finally said, opening his eyes to gaze back at her golden, teary irises. "And mine. Vrork is the only place I've ever felt like I belonged, and I would give my very last breath dedicating myself to the survival of your people, whether or not you live to see it. This is what I want. *You* are what I want. And so, it remains my final condition for your proposal."

If the situation wasn't so serious, he might have chuckled over her proposing to him rather than the other way around.

"It's a hard one to accept." She wiped her tears from her cheeks before placing her wet palms against his face. "Then allow me to make one final adjustment. I will agree to your condition as long as you know you can back out at any time. Of any of it."

"I won't back out." He took her hands again and kissed her stone fingers before kissing the ones of flesh, and then he drew her in for a long, affectionate kiss. He threaded his fingers through her wet hair, caressed each earring in her ear with a finger, and breathed in every breath she let out, wallowing in her delightful scent exuding from every pore. But the kiss ended far too soon when she pulled away first.

She twisted the ends of his hair around her fingers, and he sighed at her gentle touch. "I want to do this right, and to give you a little more time to make sure you're absolutely certain." He found himself nodding before she even continued with the rest. "No intimacy until after our vows."

"I can manage that." He knew humans, dwarves, and elves harbored similar views on chastity, and aside from unsuccessful drunken attempts to mate, he'd been expecting it. "What I'm concerned about is your mother. Who will tell her about our engagement? You or I?"

Soft laughter escaped her mouth, and he couldn't help but smile at the beautiful sound, a melody against the silver, moonlit stars. "Good luck, vampire. This will be your true test."

He nuzzled his nose against hers and lifted her from the water. "I look forward to it, dwarf. Every second of it."

# CHAPTER 21

Kirsa was a jumble of nerves.

The wedding was hastened to only a week after the engagement, and the entire whirlwind was still difficult to believe even as she stood in front of a full-length mirror, staring back into her overly wide, eager eyes. She wore the finest clothing she owned, or at the very least, the finest outfit she owned that still covered nearly every inch of her diseased skin. The fabric was a deep burgundy—a reflection of the male she was choosing to marry this evening at dusk. A vampire.

When was the last time a vampire and a dwarf had married? She couldn't recall a single instance, at least not in Vrork, and certainly not within her lifetime.

"You know…" her mother said as she walked into the room and draped a sheer matching ceremonial wrap over

Kirsa's right shoulder, "when I said to live your life before you can't anymore, I didn't mean marrying a vampire."

"You like him despite the fangs. Admit it."

Her mother placed a hand on either of her shoulders and smiled at her through the mirror. It was the same smile she used to see on Tille's face before he entered stasis. "I will admit he has grown on me. If the dwarves weren't in such a dire situation, I'm not sure I would allow this union to happen at all."

"You know I won't last long enough to produce any offspring."

"You don't know that." Deep sadness entered her mother's eyes as she trailed her fingers through Kirsa's hair. "Besides, I'm looking forward to seeing his face when we give him the vial."

Kirsa chuckled and pulled her hair over the right shoulder, exposing her entire left ear, earrings and all. After Luca had accepted her and her bloody past, she wasn't quite as afraid to lay it bare for others to see.

"He's the one who insisted on this," she said as she tied her hair in place with a good tug of a ribbon. "I just don't think he understands what it entails in a dwarven ceremony."

"I'm not sure he *can* understand. The idea would be completely foreign in his culture."

Someone knocked at the open door, and Kirsa turned in time to find Luca poking his head around the corner, but not enough to actually enter the room. Her entire expression lit up upon seeing him, and she gave him permission to enter by waving him inside. He looked striking in his own ceremonial garb, wearing a dark golden outfit with a matching sheer wrap draped over his right shoulder in a similar fashion to hers. He was handsomer than usual in the nice clothing, his dark hair and violet eyes a beautiful pairing with the gold. His eyes were full of life and excitement. It was a stark contrast to the shell of a vampire she had first met in Ironfell.

"I felt my ears burning," he said with a teasing grin. "I simply followed the burn, and lo and behold, I hear something about a strange vial."

She stood with her hands on her hips and stared him down. "Isn't it considered rude to eavesdrop in your culture?"

"Yes, and I try not to do it. But I've been keeping my ears peeled in case someone wants to assassinate me for being a vampire taking a dwarf for a mate."

Although his eyes danced mischievously, she spotted uncertainty within their depths, as if he actually believed a dwarf might be daft enough to try and take his life before the marriage happened. After all his efforts to save her race, she didn't suspect any of her kind were cruel enough to do such a thing.

"Ah," her mother said, her previous smile replaced by a hardened expression as she reached for a long dagger on her belt. It took every effort for Kirsa not to roll her eyes. "Since we're on the topic, Luca. I don't believe you're familiar enough with our marriage ceremony traditions. In our culture, on the wedding day, a champion will step forward to duel you to the death. If you win the duel, only then can you marry the female. As it so happens, it will be me you fight to the death."

All the blood drained from Luca's face, making his pale skin appear even paler. He reached out to the wall as if to steady himself as he stared incredulously at her mother.

"What?" he rasped.

"I will give you ten minutes to pick your weapon and meet me in the arena."

He stared blankly at her before he turned his pale face to Kirsa. He opened his mouth, but no words came out. The poor vampire looked either close to passing out or running for the hills.

"She's jesting, Luca," Kirsa said at the same time her mother burst into laughter and sheathed her dagger. "Though, I'm glad to know you're hesitant about killing my mother for my hand. I'd prefer such a thing not to happen."

He released an audible breath and ran his fingers through his hair, and finally, his mouth started working again. "I'm relieved to hear it. Are there any other surprises I need to know about?"

"Just one." She bit her lip before handing him a vial filled with clear liquid, one she had created herself for this very day, adapted to her and Luca's unique union. "I'd like you to drink every drop of this. It's a wedding tradition."

His eyebrow rose with skepticism. "Just like how dueling to the death is a wedding tradition?"

Her mother cut in right then, and Kirsa had never been more grateful, especially as the heat of fluster began rising up her neck. "This is actually a tradition. At least it has been in the past several centuries as the dwarven race rests on the brink of extinction. How familiar are you with our wedding customs?"

He shrugged. "I admit I haven't had much time to study up on it, as I've been far too occupied with Arvitash."

Kirsa admired his dedication to finding a cure for her people. He'd been working endlessly both day and night, so much that they'd hardly been able to see each other much this past week.

Continuing, her mother said, "A wedding is held on the peak of the female's fertility that month, and in turn, the male drinks a specially made elixir to heighten his own fertility. It increases the chance of producing offspring."

Luca frowned as he turned the glass vial between his fingers. "Kirsa, if you want children, you shouldn't marry a vampire. Do you know how long it took my brother Cristian and his mate to have a child? Twenty-six years. It can often take longer."

She didn't know how to explain to him how the elixir worked. Of course, it was a gamble with a vampire, but the mechanics of the elixir should theoretically work the same as it would for a dwarf.

To try to put him at ease, she placed a hand on his arm and smiled reassuringly. "It's only a tradition, Luca. Whether or not it works doesn't matter. I likely don't have enough time to carry a child to term."

"I hate the reminder."

The atmosphere had suddenly darkened, heavy on her shoulders as she watched the worry crawl through in his eyes. She wanted the darkness to evaporate, so she said the first thing to come to mind. "I wish we could have invited Chloe to the wedding. I think she would appreciate the fact that I didn't kill you, but rather I am marrying you."

As she had hoped, the atmosphere lightened considerably, allowing her chest to draw air into her lungs once more.

"I think she would be in for quite a surprise," he chuckled.

They had agreed not to invite Chloe, as a week wasn't quite enough notice for their friend, and Luca hadn't wanted to invite any of his family members either. She didn't question his decision to keep them in the dark, despite her growing curiosity about who his family was and why he continued to keep his distance from them. Only dwarves would be in attendance, and plenty of them judging by the stir their marriage had caused in Vrork. She was pleasantly surprised at how quickly her people took to Luca, despite him being a vampire. They recognized his efforts to help them. How could they dislike him for that?

"Now go drink it and meet me outside." She smirked and slapped his arse when her mother wasn't looking. He grinned at her coyly as he started to walk away, but before he disappeared, she grabbed onto his hand. "Wait. I've been meaning to ask." She bit her lip, knowing her request likely wouldn't be met with any sort of enthusiasm. "Can we go on a honeymoon to Ichor Knell?"

He grimaced and stared at their clasped hands rather than looking her in the eye. "I don't know, Kirsa. I burned a lot of bridges when I left."

"We don't have to talk to anyone. No one needs to know we're there."

Finally, he lifted his gaze, but his grimace remained. "Trust me, my father will know." For several moments, he played with her fingers. "But I'll think about it. Is that all right?"

"Yes," she breathed. And when she placed a kiss on his cheek, his expression lightened, followed by a bright smile. She watched him disappear around the corner.

A flutter of nervous butterflies filled her stomach as the realization dawned on her for what felt like the hundredth time that week. She was getting married. The one thing she had dreamed of her entire life was finally happening, and to the most unexpected candidate. But she loved Luca. Despite how short their marriage might be, she knew she would cherish every moment with him.

When her mother left the room, she sat down and penned a letter to Chloe, though it took a few moments to remember to switch from her own language to the princess's.

*Dearest Chloe,*

*Your marriage has likely already happened, and I would like to congratulate you on the nuptials. I know how nervous you were for the event, and I hope you have not only found happiness, but you're enjoying your new companion. Perhaps someday I might be able to meet him, if you ever forgive me for taking Luca back to my home.*

*I have some news, which might come as a bit of a shock to you. I'm still in a bit of a shock myself. No, Luca is not dead. In fact, I haven't taken a single drop of his blood. Rather, the two of us are getting married today. It is you I must thank. Without you, we never would have met. I am a nervous mess, and I wish I could talk to you in person, but time is short in Vrork. Thus, the engagement must be quick, and the marriage quicker.*

*I hope this letter receives you well, and I hope to receive a reply. You cannot remain angry with me forever, right?*

*Your friend, Kirsa Frey*

Not wanting to keep Luca waiting any longer than necessary, she sealed the letter and addressed it before placing it in the post. She took a deep breath, wiped her sweaty palms on her clothing, and exited the Mountain.

Dusk had fallen over Vrork, and along with it, a serene stillness as the sun hid from view behind the peaks, casting yellows, oranges, and pinks across the sky. The sweet smell of blooms filled the air, and she breathed it in, reveling in the momentary peace in the land. In her soul.

And then as she glanced around. The teeming number of dwarves waiting in the procession took her off guard, each one holding wildflowers, joking and laughing with Luca of all people. She watched for a moment with a smile on her face as they traded jests, and she nearly melted where she stood when he laughed loudly, the sound setting the kindling on fire within her heart.

He noticed her only moments later and grinned back at her. The sight alone stole her breath away, and she could scarcely breathe when he took her hand and kissed her fingers. His violet gaze ensnared her, trapping her within the walls of a lovely cocoon. Being engaged felt far more wonderful than she'd ever imagined, and she just knew being married would be even better.

Her mother approached, which forced her to tear her gaze away from Luca. She draped a garland of flowers over the top of her head and kissed her brow, and then she stood on her tiptoes and did the same for Luca, except his was a garland of vines.

"To the happy couple," her mother said. "May the rest of your days together be wonderful."

Kirsa didn't want to think about how many days, exactly, they still had together, so she smiled and squeezed Luca's hand before they both started forward.

Dwarves formed a path for them on each side, creating a long trail leading to the meadow of irises she loved so dearly. Each dwarf she passed handed her a wildflower to add to her growing bouquet, and when they finally reached the meadow, her hands were full to bursting with beautiful flowers. Tears shimmered in her eyes when she glanced at the irises in full bloom. She had been right. They were the same color as Luca's eyes.

While they took their places to stand beneath a wedding arch with wildflowers weaved into it and strands of gold and silver dripping down like trickling water, the rest of the dwarves filed into the meadow until they were surrounded. She didn't know many of the dwarves well, but she did know their names. The fact that they were here to witness the marriage spread warmth through her.

Luca may be a vampire, but he was one of them.

The priest had died long ago from the Blight without a replacement, so her mother took her place at the front to lead the ceremony. Only when the meadow fell into a hush did her mother begin.

"Today we are to witness an atypical wedding between a dwarf and a vampire, and it brings me great joy to see the smiles on your faces. From the moment you arrived in Vrork, Luca, there was no doubt in my mind about how my daughter felt about you. And now, we get to celebrate by joining the two of you in matrimony."

She continued with the ceremony, and when it came time to exchange rings, Kirsa's hands nearly shook from nervous excitement. She slipped a gold and silver band onto his finger, and he slid a beautifully crafted ring onto hers, made of strands of woven gold with a single amethyst gemstone as if to serve as a constant reminder of him.

"Elric helped me craft it," he explained with a mischievous smirk. "And we even enchanted it. The wearer will fall madly in love with me."

Kirsa laughed and rolled her eyes as she playfully shoved his shoulder. "I can recognize an enchanted item when I see it, and this isn't one. But I don't think it will be too hard to fall madly in love with you."

He gave her a look of pure adoration, and when he started to pull her toward him for a kiss, her mother stopped him with a hand to his elbow.

"Not yet," she said, followed by a rumble of laughter from the audience. "Kirsa has opted into receiving an ardor piercing. Luca, will you receive one today as well?"

"Absolutely," he breathed, and her heart burst alive with joy. "Will this hurt?"

"The first time is always the worst," Kirsa said as they knelt side by side in the grass as the piercer came forward with her equipment. "After the tenth piercing, it isn't so bad."

Luca leaned closer to her, his lips hardly a breath away. "How many piercings *do* you have, love? Any I should know about not on your ears?"

A teasing grin pulled up on her lips as she gave him a coy look. Making sure to keep her voice low to avoid someone overhearing, she said, "I suppose you'll just have to keep your curiosity in check until later tonight."

They shared a roguish look before she forced her attention to the piercer. Like every piercing she'd ever received, she balled her hands into fists and held her breath as the piercer carefully positioned the needle. Though, she made sure not to turn invisible this time, as she had done it only a few piercings ago and almost made a mess of things. A short burst of pain shot through her left ear, and she finally released her breath as it pulsed with aching satisfaction. It was symbolic of her love for Luca, a love that would never fade no matter how little time they had together.

As the piercer moved onto Luca, he yelped as he received his own piercing, which inspired another rumble of laughter through the audience. His hand darted to his ear, fondling the rod-like earring now pierced through the crus of helix, through the heart of the ear.

"Careful not to touch it too much," she warned. "It could…"

Her words trailed off when she noticed his ear had already healed from the piercing, much to her astonishment. She knew vampires healed quickly, but it took her off guard every time she witnessed it.

Without waiting for permission this time, he reached for her and pulled her into a kiss, one that burned as hot as sunlight but as cool as a gushing waterfall. Through the haze of pure warmth and love, she hardly registered her mother saying, "Join me in congratulating the newly married couple, Kirsa Frey and Luca Frey."

Elation filled her entire being, both body and soul, when they broke apart, their smiles mirroring the other's. She couldn't believe it. She was married. To Luca, a vampire, the most incredible male she had ever met. Although only two things on her list now remained—seeing the vampire city of Ichor Knell and having children—she knew she could pass from this world in complete contentment if neither were to happen.

Their audience cheered, and she laughed joyously as they ushered the two of them from the meadow and into a small field where enchanted crystals had previously been placed for the occasion. Shimmering hues of blue, green, purple, and pink glowed brightly to ward off the darkness as a troupe of musicians struck up a lively tune. Luca wasted no time before pulling her into a dance, and she laughed as he spun her around and around, reminding her that although he was a horrible dancer, there was no one else she'd rather dance with. She easily lost herself in the music, in the energetic celebration happening around them, in the arms of her vampire husband.

They feasted—well, at least she did—they laughed, they danced well into the night, until she noticed a sheen of perspiration begin to gather on Luca's forehead. He wiped it away with his forearm, but his discomfort showed clearly in his expression.

The elixir was working.

"I didn't eat anything, did I?" he asked when they stopped dancing due to her fatigue from the Blight. "I have an awful stomachache."

She knew it wasn't a stomachache, but rather something a smidge below the stomach. But again, to explain how the elixir worked wasn't worth the effort, not when he wouldn't understand because he was too accustomed to vampire culture and the restrictions that went with it.

"It's the elixir," she said, but didn't go into detail. Rather, she gave him a coy smile and pulled him close enough to whisper in his ear. "You'll feel better soon. I promise. Now, I don't know about you, but I'm ready to claim a little peace and quiet to ourselves."

"Yes," he replied immediately, and she couldn't help but laugh at the enthusiasm leaking from his voice. "Absolutely yes."

They bid farewell to their guests, who showered lavender buds over their heads in their departure. The walk to their destination wasn't far, but Luca held her the entire way up the path before carrying her over the threshold of a vacant family cabin—only after giving him permission to enter, of course.

Although she'd had little to drink, she still laughed blissfully when he set her down and wiped his perspiring forehead once more before closing the door behind them.

"I have been waiting all week for this, Mrs. Frey," he said, kissing her between breaths as they became tangled together on their way to the bedroom.

"I've heard it's a big moment for a vampire, Mr. Frey," she teased right back, hungrily drinking in each of his kisses.

"I can't lie." He stopped kissing her for a moment to take the tie out of her hair until chestnut brown locks cascaded down her back. "I love my new name."

"As do I."

He ran his fingers through her hair and then placed a gentle kiss against her neck. She shuddered at the pleasant way he scraped his teeth along her skin but didn't sprout his fangs. And when he inhaled her scent, she grasped onto his tunic to keep herself steady against him.

"I don't think you'll be needing this," he said with a playful grin as he pulled the burgundy drape off her shoulder and tossed it aside.

Her heart hammered in her chest, but despite her nervousness, she played along by unbuckling his belt and slowly sliding it from its casing. "You won't be needing this."

Their kisses continued in earnest, both hardly coming up for air as the heat of passion filled the room until they fell backward onto the bed. She unbuttoned his shirt and ran her hands over the defined muscles of his chest. She'd always admired him from afar, but now she got to touch him. She wanted to take the time to memorize him, but it would have to wait for another day.

A shuddering breath left his mouth as she grazed her lips across the ardor piercing in his ear, followed by her whisper. "You won't be needing this either."

She tossed his shirt aside, freely allowing her gaze to roam up and down his bare torso. Years of practicing swordplay had toned him nicely, and she wanted to linger longer, but he seemed far too eager to claim her as his own. His lips captured hers, and she breathed out what felt like a hot exhale of dragon fire. She was immensely glad she had met him, for without him, life would have been much emptier.

254

# CHAPTER 22

*K irsa. Kirsa. Kirsa.*

Every one of Luca's heartbeats pulsed with the name of his mate.

He quietly slipped out from beneath her arm where he'd cuddled her in his fox form and transformed back into a vampire. The darkness of early morning created a silhouette of Kirsa lying in bed sleeping. As he pulled on his trousers and shoes, he fought his fangs when they wanted to sprout. They resisted his efforts.

He ran his fingers through his hair, battling with the carnal desire to sprout his fangs and sink them into her flesh to share the passion of his most basal instincts. He blinked several times to ward off the prickling sensation crawling across his eyes as they transitioned from violet to red and back to violet. Yet, he knew a bite would hurt her. With or without venom. It wouldn't be enjoyable like another vampire would find it. He refused to hurt his mate in any way.

"I am in so much trouble," he murmured, now realizing just how difficult it would be to have a non-vampire as his mate. To never bite her? It would be difficult to fight his own vampiristic instincts, but he would do it for her. He would practice self-control and keep that part of himself locked away in the deepest recesses of his soul.

But until he had himself under better control, he needed to feed.

Often.

He pulled his shirt over his head and then rested his hands on each side of Kirsa. The scent of earthy gems and wildflowers teased his nostrils with each slumbering breath she took.

"I absolutely adore you," he whispered as he kissed her jaw, then her throat, and finally her bare shoulder.

A flicker of a smile rested on her lips, and her eyes squinted open the slightest bit. "It's still dark. Why are you dressed?"

"I need to feed." He trailed a finger over her collarbones, gently grazing the black etchings of the Blight growing across her skin. It only served as a reminder of how little time remained before the disease took her. He didn't want to waste a single moment.

"I'll come with you."

Hesitation froze his fingers on her skin until he dropped his hand and sat next to her. "I don't want you to see me like that."

"But I want to." Fatigue rested on her brow as she moved to sit, clutching the blanket to cover herself. "I want to know every part of you."

"Kirsa." He quirked his mouth to the side, debating all the reasons in his mind why it was a terrible idea. "I'm…scary…when I hunt. You'll be frightened of me."

"I won't. I saw you fight the chasotid in the ruins. I wasn't afraid of you then." She moved closer until she wrapped her arms around his neck and kissed his ear, sending a pleasant shiver down his spine. "I don't want to be apart from you."

And when she kissed his throat, he quickly lost the battle. He would do anything for this female. *Anything.* His mate.

"Fine." He playfully nipped at her lip before finding her clothes scattered about the room and tossing them onto the bed beside her. "But I'm warning you now. You will have to carry me down the hill."

Laughter escaped her mouth as she dressed and then met him outside in the darkness of early morning. A hush still lingered as the world slept around them. No singing birds. No scurrying animals. And the air remained still, not even a trickle of a breeze running through his hair.

Kirsa didn't protest when he scooped her into his arms, and to keep his hands free, he moved her onto his back where she held on tight around his neck, cheek resting against cheek.

"Show me how you hunt."

A prickle crawled across his face as his eyes transitioned from violet to red. He took several deep breaths to maintain control. Although the scent of dwarven blood didn't interest him in the slightest, he wanted to make sure his instinct to hunt wouldn't lead him toward the Mountain and the dwarves living within it. Instead, he breathed in through his nose and caught the faintest sliver of human scents.

He didn't want to scare her completely by hunting a human in front of her, so he picked apart the scents until he found one with a trace of decay. Today, he would scavenge.

"This excursion will be rather unexciting," he said as he started down the hill, following the faint scent. "But it will get the job done."

Many minutes passed as he followed the scent, moving as fast as he dared to not jostle Kirsa off his back. Not too long passed before her arms started shaking with the effort of holding on. Although he hated not having his hands free during a hunt, he reached behind him to better support her so she didn't have to hold on so tight herself.

They traveled into the forest, trees becoming thicker and a trickle of water greeting his ears. He veered more to the right when the scent became stronger. It led him to a worn-down cottage with the windows in disrepair and the door hanging off its hinges. Stiff clothes hung over a line as if they'd been dried, rained on, and dried again.

No one seemed to live here, yet the decay from within grew stronger as he approached the door.

He frowned at the shimmering barrier over the door, one that prevented him from entering.

"What is it?" Kirsa asked.

"I can't enter. Someone passed away inside, but the house might not belong to them, as the barrier would drop if that was the case."

"Then it's a good thing you have a dwarf for a mate. Wait here."

She slid off his back, and the door creaked as she opened it. After several minutes, she breathed heavily as she dragged the dead human out of the cottage and outside into the open air. The man looked to be a few days dead.

"How about that?" he murmured, arms crossed. "Maybe you should come hunting with me more often. We make a good team."

Her expression softened. "We do, don't we?" The exertion must have cost her because she slumped onto the porch step and struggled for air. She leaned against the wooden railing and closed her eyes in her exhaustion.

Concern stirred within him, but when he moved toward her, she waved him away without opening her eyes. "Just give me a minute."

His eyes misted over to see her so...defeated. The Blight was thoroughly killing her, and just the thought of losing his mate gutted him. But he refused to beat down what pride she had and say anything about it. Not now, at least.

"You never got to see my scary side," he commented, and to his delight, she chuckled and peeked her eyes open.

"Oh, I'm sure I will have plenty of opportunities." Her eyes opened wider. "Unless you plan to scavenge each time you take me on a hunt. I'm not so fragile as that."

"You think I assume you to be weak?" The thought bothered him as he sat cross-legged on the ground beside the dead man and picked up his wrist. It smelled of decay, and the blood would be disappointingly sour. But it would satiate his need to feed for a while. "Remember when I said I felt vulnerable with you watching me collect my venom?" When she nodded, he continued. "I feel just as vulnerable being seen as a predator. I suppose..." He trailed off, trying to find the words. "I suppose I'm afraid you will change your mind about me."

Despite the fatigue visible in every inch of her body, she stood and crossed the space between them until she sat on his lap, her arms wrapped around his waist and her head resting on his shoulder.

"I will never change my mind about you," she murmured into his shirt. "I'm not asking you to be a human or an elf or a dwarf. You are my vampire. And I love you for it."

Emotion clogged his throat, and he attempted to swallow it. All his life, he'd *never* had someone love him unconditionally. It was beautiful. Incredible. Overwhelming.

Instead of answering, he sprouted his fangs, lifted the dead man's wrist to his mouth, and drank.

# CHAPTER 23

Kirsa insisted on walking back to the Mountain on her own. Her body felt weak and exhausted, but she refused to give up her autonomy for as long as possible. Their journey back started at a good pace. However, it slowed as the minutes wore on.

She blinked back tears of frustration. Most of the items on her list were crossed out. She was married to someone she loved dearly, but it wasn't enough. She wanted more. More energy, more happiness, more time. Never in her life had she been so terrified of losing someone.

Luca's grip tightened on her hand as they traversed over slippery rocks of a stream. "This is nice," he murmured. "I know there is so much to do and so little time, but I love spending time with you. Just you and me. Like this."

Surprise lifted her eyebrows. But when she turned her attention to him, her foot slipped on a rock. He darted for her but slipped as well. She yelped as she crashed into the frigid water with a splash. He followed after.

Droplets of water dripped from her hair and into her face, her attire completely soaked through. She glanced at Luca, whose black hair was plastered to his forehead. The violet of his eyes sparked with humor, and at the same time, they burst into laughter. His hand swiped through the water and splashed her, and she splashed him back until every inch of her was drenched. The laughter soothed much of the ache growing in her soul.

Soon, she found him hovering over her, their lips only inches apart. She twisted the wedding ring on her finger, glancing back and forth between his eyes.

"What is it like?" she asked, threading her fingers through the ebony locks of his hair. "The bloodbond vampires feel?"

He grabbed onto her hand and lifted her from the water until they stood on the bank. "It's terror and happiness and gut-wrenching anxiety. Kirsa, I—" His voice broke, and he clamped his mouth shut.

"I'm still here, Luca." She blinked back the overwhelming emotion burning through her veins. "But what will happen to you after I'm gone? Maybe we shouldn't have—"

"Don't say it," he growled. "I don't regret the bond. I never will."

She breathed in deeply and let it out slowly. "I am a selfish dwarf."

"Uh huh." He cast her a teasing grin. "Prideful and selfish."

She scowled and lifted her stone hand to smack him, but he laughed and darted away. When she opened her mouth to reply to his comment, a scream in the distance halted her words, followed by a deafening roar.

Dozens of birds fluttered out of the boughs above them, fleeing from the forest. And suddenly, all became far too quiet. That sound...

Kirsa's stomach dropped to her toes.

*A manticore.*

She tugged on Luca's arm, but he stared in the direction of the sound as if he heard something she didn't. "We have to go—"

"That's your mother," he gasped. "Stay here."

For a moment, she stood frozen, watching Luca disappear into the thicket of trees. But then another distressed cry urged her feet to move. Faster. Faster. Faster. She'd brought no weapons to the cabin with her after the wedding. But now she felt like a fool. The idiotic part of her hadn't thought it necessary when she had a weapon for a husband at her side.

She burst into a small clearing, breathing heavily while her eyes grew wide. One manticore lay dead. A lion head and body, sharp claws, and the tail of a scorpion. Two more cornered a patrol dwarf and her mother.

Horror flared inside her chest. Deep gashes raked across her mother's body, bleeding profusely. She swayed on unsteady feet, the sword in her hand a barrier between her and the two creatures.

"Go!" her mother barked to the patrol dwarf. "Get help."

The woman ran off, and one of the manticores lunged. Luca screeched and tackled the creature to the ground. Kirsa watched with a tight chest as he seemed to transform before her eyes. Fangs bared. Expression contorted with menacing anger. Eyes flashing red. He growled moments before repeatedly biting the manticore in the neck and raking his sharp fingernails across its head and drawing blood.

The manticore roared, its tail lifting in the air with the stinger poised to strike.

"Watch out!" she screamed, and he rolled out of the way just in time to avoid the attack. The creature pierced itself through the neck, and it twitched several times before lying still. Between what she assumed to be Luca's venom and the creature's stinger, the life quickly drained from it.

On the opposite side of the clearing, her mother swayed back and forth as if dizzy from blood loss. She dropped her sword and collapsed to her knees, and then to her side, unconscious.

Kirsa sprinted toward her mother, which drew the remaining manticore's attention. She reached her mother's side, but before she managed to grab a hold of the blade, the creature swiped its claws at her. She dove to the ground, barely dodging the attack.

When she rolled back onto her feet, the manticore rounded on her once more, and her first reflex was to hold her breath to blend in with her surroundings. Her eyes widened when its tail whipped forward, aimed straight for her heart. It was as if time slowed as the sharp point flashed beneath the faintest trace of light and then shot toward her with impeccable speed.

Something slammed into her, knocking her to the ground, followed by a *thunk*.

Kirsa's heart raced as she ran her hands down her body, but she found no wound. And then...

"Luca!" she screamed.

The manticore's sharp tail pinned Luca to the tree through the stomach. Red gushed from the wound, and he choked on his own blood as it dripped from his mouth. His feet dangled off the ground. Strangled hisses escaped his lips as he held onto the tail with one arm as if to keep his own weight from hurting him further, and with the other, he swiped at the creature's face.

Lightning fast, the creature raked its claws over Luca's chest, and he released a pained cry that managed to skewer *her* through the heart.

Fury raced through her blood, giving her the strength to climb to her feet. She grabbed her mother's sword and rushed forward with a battle cry. The manticore turned its head just as she swung the weapon, severing its tail from its body.

Another screech filled the skies as the manticore reared up on its hind legs. She took the opportunity to stab the sword into its heart.

When the creature's front legs hit the ground, it collapsed.

And lay still.

"Luca," she rasped, stumbling toward him. "Luca, Luca, Luca."

The tail still skewered him to the tree despite it being no longer attached to the creature. Blood soaked his clothes, shiny and wet and tinged with a metallic smell. He struggled against the tail, but his effort only resulted in a pained cry. However, when she took a hold of the blasted thing and pulled with all her might, it remained stuck.

"Hold on," she sobbed. "Just hold on."

Blood spattered her chin when he shook his head. He swallowed. Once. Twice. Before the faintest words escaped him. "I'll live. Get your mother…to safety."

She pressed a fist to her mouth. "I can't leave you like this."

"You don't…" He swallowed, and another garbled grunt of pain lingered in his throat. "…don't have a choice."

Tears trailed down her cheeks as she kissed his hand. "I'll be back. I swear." And then she darted toward her mother, who lay still on the ground, her breaths raspy. Gouges from the manticore's sharp claws oozed blood. Too much blood.

Memories of Neeva getting mauled by chasotids flashed across her mind, and for a moment, instead of her mother, she saw her sister. And when she returned to the present, the same devastation crushed her.

Her mother would not survive this.

A teleportation crystal spit Gunther out of the void beside her. The man's expression hardened upon surveying the blood and destruction around them, but he wasted no time as he helped heave her mother up so she rested limp between them. And after one last glance at the agony in Luca's eyes, the crystal teleported the three of them back to the settlement.

They didn't follow protocol as they rushed her mother through the entry room. There was no time, but it was highly unlikely any of them would have brought the contagious Blight into the settlement.

Her heart pounded with each step, and when other dwarves noticed them, they also helped transport her mother. Many others followed behind until they reached the infirmary. A groan escaped her mother when they laid her on a cot, and immediately, a flurry of nurses surrounded them, tending to the horrid injuries.

Sticky blood coated Kirsa's hand as she grasped her mother's fingers, but as her eyes took in the deep gashes in her mother's torso, even she knew nothing could be done.

*No!* she screamed in her mind when her mother's eyelids fluttered open, and she became more lucid. This was the end.

*I'm not ready. I'm not ready. I'm not ready.*

"The manticore," her mother whispered as if it was all she could manage before she grimaced and cried out in pain once more. "We were doing a perimeter check. If I had only brought more weapons," she grunted in pain, "I might have stood a chance."

Now Kirsa's tears streamed so heavily she could hardly see her mother's face through her blurry vision. The blood coating her fingers seemed to become colder and colder by the second.

Her mother reached out a hand to Kirsa and dropped two metal rings into her palm, and although they were covered in blood, she knew exactly what they were, which only inspired more tears.

"For you and your vampire sweetheart..." her mother wheezed. "I pass my mantle to you. This is mine and your father's. Lead these people, Kirsa. *Lead them*! Whether it be through the chaos to the end or to the next generation."

"Please, Mother," she sobbed as her hand tightened around her fingers. "Don't go. I beg you."

This had been far too sudden and terrible timing, too. Kirsa couldn't lead her people. She needed her mother. She couldn't leave. Not like this!

But her mother's body began convulsing, and moments later, she lay still, her eyes wide open in death. The dam broke inside of her, and her sobs became more violent as she leaned over her mother's body and wept.

Another family member, gone. Like Neeva, her mother had suffered a violent death. But now Kirsa was next in line. She was the new chieftain. A *dying* chieftain married to a *vampire*.

Her eyes flew open. *Luca*!

She set her grieving aside as she threw the infirmary door open and raced down the halls of the settlement. When she reached her bedchambers, she sifted through the crystals, vials, and enchanted weapons littering her table and drawers. In her haste, she knocked several items to the floor. Glass shattered. A crystal broke. But finally, her fingers closed around an enchanted jade rod and a transportation crystal.

She spoke a few words in Akretti, and the crystal heated in her hands. The teleportation enchantment sucked her into a void of black, and for a moment, she found herself weightless. Suspended in the air. At least until it spit her back out where she'd left Luca.

Terror struck her like a bolt of lightning in an unforgiving storm. The stinger still pinned him to the tree.

But instead of fighting against it as he had earlier, his body hung limp, his face pale from blood loss.

"Luca!" she screeched, panic shaking her raw as she stumbled toward him.

*No, no, no! I can't lose someone else I love. I can't!*

She swung the jade rod and smashed it against the manticore tail. Starting from the severed end, it disintegrated into ash until finally, the stinger crumbled, and Luca dropped to the ground in a heap.

Careful of his injuries, she turned him onto his back. Dread climbed her spine at the sight of the gashes across his chest and the gigantic puncture wound in his abdomen.

He was pale. So, so pale.

Blood spurted from his mouth when he coughed. A brief flicker of hope passed through her as he slowly regained consciousness. Still, her hands trembled as she tenderly held either side of his bloodied face.

"Tell me how to help. Please." Her voice cracked, and she barely held back her desire to weep.

The skin around his eyes crinkled at the agony he must have felt. A sob of pain escaped him. But he was conscious again. Barely.

Her fingers continued to tremble when she carefully placed his head in her lap. "Take deep breaths," she said calmly despite panic, grief, and heartache rolling through her chest.

He clutched onto her hand. Weakly at first, but slowly, his grip strengthened. Many long, torturous minutes passed, but his wounds began to heal.

A sliver of heartache slipped through her steel doors. She sniffed back the tears burning her eyes. "I thought you should know," she said, her voice trembling, "you were incredibly scary."

He chuckled humorlessly, but then sobbed again. Tears of pain rolled down his face. She held tighter to his hand and leaned down to kiss his temple. "Just breathe," she whispered. "I'm here. I'm not going anywhere. You will be just fine."

Time passed far too slowly as she watched his wounds close one by one. But at last, the agony in his expression melted into relief. He kept his eyes closed as he murmured in a strained voice, "Are you hurt?"

"No." Another sniff. "How did you know I was there? I was invisible."

"Your scent." A deep breath. "How is your mother?"

Her chin wobbled. She didn't answer.

Through the tears blurring her vision, she saw him open his eyes. She didn't say anything, but she didn't have to. He reached for her and cupped a hand around her neck, pulling her to him until her forehead rested against his shoulder.

And finally, she sobbed. "I was supposed to die first!" she wept, her voice muffled. "I would have understood dying from a chasotid or the Blight. But a manticore? This wasn't supposed to happen."

He continued to hold her until her ugly weeping turned into sniffs which turned into shuddering breaths.

"I'm sorry, Kirsa. I'm so, so sorry."

She sat up and wiped the tears from her face. By now, the sun started to rise over the mountains. She helped Luca sit against the tree he'd been pinned to, safe in the shadows where sunlight couldn't harm either of them. As much as she wanted to weep all day, she had a duty to her people. As the new chieftain, she needed to take charge and move forward, starting with a funeral she knew everyone in Vrork would not only attend, but they would mourn the loss of their beloved leader.

A determined but hollow ache followed her movements as she cleaned the blood from her mother's rings on the grass.

"Kirsa," Luca said, but she didn't answer.

"Kirsa," he said again, but still she didn't turn.

Finally, he placed a hand on top of hers, and with his other hand, he turned her head to face him. A deep sadness stared back at her, mirroring the devastation inside herself, and before she could stop them, several more tears fell from her eyes.

"I'm so sorry, love," he whispered. He kissed each of her damp eyelids, her cheeks, and then he rested his forehead against hers while she clung tightly, desperately to his bloodied shirt. His external wounds seem to have healed, but he was still pale.

Her chin quivered, her hands shaking despite the confident facade she had attempted in the infirmary. Her mother was dead. After the happiest day of her life, fate was cruel enough to take her mother away. And now she and Luca were the new dwarven chieftains. Is that what he even wanted?

He held her until her shaking ceased, until her tears dried. And then she turned to him and opened her palm to reveal the rings.

"Every dwarven settlement has a chieftain," she explained in a hoarse whisper. "Though, there are two if the chieftain is married. I thought my mother would outlive me, Luca. She didn't. I am the new chieftain. *We* are Vrork's new leaders. Tell me you don't want this, and I will step down."

His eyes widened as if he finally understood the mantle thrust so suddenly upon their shoulders.

"But...I am a vampire." He grimaced and clutched his stomach, taking several deep breaths as he continued to heal internally. She only wished to take his pain away.

"And these are dire times. We do what we must to survive as a race."

"They won't accept me."

She shook her head in disagreement. "Don't be so sure of that."

His eyes filled with uncertainty as he looked from her to the Mountain towering over them. As his wife, as his *mate*, she would comply with whatever he felt most comfortable with, even if it meant finding someone else to lead the dwarves. But she would stay with him no matter what he decided. "If we don't find a cure, what will happen then? What if you die? Where does it leave me?"

"You will be free to either choose a different chieftain in your stead, or you can continue to lead *our* people without me."

"Our people," he repeated in an incredulous whisper. "It feels nice to be grouped in with the people I feel like I belong to." He looked back into her eyes and took each of her hands, the two rings resting between their palms. "I'll stay by your side, Kirsa. I will help you lead. And I swear to you, I will find a cure. I won't let you die."

Another tear escaped her eye, this time not for her mother, but for herself. Her hope of finding a cure had died along with her mother.

He caressed her hair, her temple, and finally rested his hand against her cheek as he gazed into her eyes, the violet color filled with unfettered determination despite the paleness and pain on his face. "Just tell me what I need to do."

There had only ever been one day Luca had seen so full of mourning and sadness as this one, and it had been after the Crusader war in Ichor Knell. Many vampires had lost loved ones to the blood hunters, and the funeral accompanying the deaths was one to shatter hearts, including his own.

But as he stood at the front of a crowd of four hundred dwarves wearing cloaks to protect themselves from the afternoon sunlight, he felt the deep ache as if it were his own. He hadn't known Kirsa's mother well, but Kirsa's loss was his loss, so strong was the mating bond between them.

The sun finally rose high enough for the sunlight to rain directly from above, and he watched as Kirsa pulled away the drapery covering her mother's body. The moment the body was exposed to sunlight, the skin slowly turned to stone until she looked like a gray statue standing upright with her arms held outward as if in welcome, perfectly preserved in death.

He and Kirsa approached, the first to lay flowers at the previous chieftain's feet. From her hair to her skin to her clothing, everything was stone, including each earring in her ear.

He gazed sadly at her stone face, much more peaceful in death than in her last moments of life. A pit of guilt rose within him. If only he'd been faster after hearing her cry. If only he'd offered to bite her, even with the danger the manticores had posed. She might not have lived through the vampire transition, not with her severe injuries, but he should have offered nonetheless, even if she had rejected it.

Dwarven culture and customs for the dead were still foreign to him, so he sent her off in the only way he knew how.

"Odihneasca-se in pace," he whispered.

Haunting memories filled his mind as he pricked his finger with a fang and dripped a drop of his blood onto the previous chieftain's stone hand. He had done this very thing with Tavian as well, except by the time everyone had paid their respects, Tavian's cold, lifeless hands had been covered in various drops of blood, as loved as he had been.

He lifted his head and found Kirsa watching him curiously, clearly not having been to a vampire funeral before. He simply nodded and moved to stand at her side as one by one, each dwarf laid a flower at Mathilde's feet.

A reverent silence filled the atmosphere, a stillness even in the boughs of trees as if the wildlife on the Mountain, too, were paying their respects.

Mathilde's body was placed beside the stone bodies of her other deceased family members, and the still silence continued as dwarves draped a strand of rubies over her stone neck.

At last, Kirsa stepped forward, and everyone turned their undivided attention to her as if looking for guidance in a dark and unforgiving world.

She said nothing for several long seconds as if trying to gather her emotions before speaking to the crowd.

"I appreciate all of you for coming today," she finally said, though her voice still sounded thick with emotion. "My mother is with the gods, and she has been reunited with loved ones. She dedicated her life to our people, even during her final breath." Again, she paused, and Luca only wished he could pull her in for an embrace, but it wasn't the right time. "As many of you know, or have heard rumors about, I can confirm that I have been infected by the Rotting Blight. My life will be short unless we discover a cure, which we are working our hardest to find. In addition, I am married to a vampire. We want to lead you, but I know our circumstances are untraditional and far from ideal. If the majority of you want us to step down from leadership positions, we will."

She then asked them to vote by raising their hands. He froze at the unanimous vote to keep them both as the chieftains. A vampire… He was a vampire, but these people, these *dwarves,* wanted him to lead them at Kirsa's side.

He blinked back emotion as it threatened to overwhelm him. These dwarves wanted him. The acceptance nearly undid him.

However, he simply nodded his gratitude and looked out over each of the dwarves' faces. Unlike his first day in Vrork, they didn't look down on him, nor did they treat him with hostility. They looked to him with curiosity, and someday, he hoped they might look at him with respect.

Kirsa surprised him by taking his hand and lifting it for all to see. She slid the chieftain ring onto his pinky finger, and then motioned for him to do the same for her. The ring once covered in blood was beautiful, a golden band with small rubies on all sides. His was wider than hers, though the delicacy of the symbolic ring belied the ferociousness inside her.

After he slid the ring onto her finger, they held hands as they turned back to the crowd. Each dwarf held two fingers to their lips and bowed their heads in acknowledgement of their new chieftains.

Once again, he found his throat closing up with emotion. These were his people now. And he swore to do everything in his power to save them.

# CHAPTER 24

Luca rubbed his overtired eyes as frustration took a hold of him. Three weeks had passed since the funeral, and he was still at a loss over cracking Arvitash. He'd looked at it from different angles, he'd snuck into the library in Ironfell—though Chloe hadn't been home during his visit, much to his dismay—and he even considered different cures other than what might lie within the knowledge of the ancient dwarves.

Nothing worked.

Arvitash was impossible to decipher.

In those few short weeks, they lost thirty more dwarves in stasis. Time was running short.

As he reorganized his materials and opened another book he'd read at least three times, front to back, his thumb brushed against the chieftain ring on his pinky, right where his Dragomir ring used to reside. The fire from the hearth glinted off the rubies, creating a deep, pulsing crimson that almost seemed alive with each beat of his heart. Some days, he swore the piece of jewelry was living, giving him strength during the times he thought he had nothing left. It drove him forward, kept him going, reminded him of why he strove for a cure in the first place.

"Kirsa," he whispered as he turned the ring around and around on his finger and stared at it until a deep ache filled him. He couldn't stop himself from imagining her in her mother's place, turned to stone beneath the afternoon sun should the Blight take her from him. Losing her might kill him. His mate. The female he loved down to the very bottom of his heart.

He wouldn't allow it to happen.

A desperate need to see her drove him from the room and down the hallway as his feet found the familiar path to the lab where she worked tirelessly, despite her weakening body. He opened the door and sighed in relief to find her sitting at her desk, alive and unharmed.

She turned and smiled at him, each corner of her mouth begging to be kissed, and kiss them he would.

He took a single step forward—

—and stopped.

Immediately, his smile fell, and his eyes widened as shock overtook him from his toes before it shot up to his chest as if ice water burst through his entire body. He spun around so quickly that he couldn't comprehend his own movements until he crashed into another table and knocked several items to the ground. This time, the shock took root and nailed his feet to the floor. He couldn't move. He couldn't escape. He couldn't *think.*

Kirsa gasped behind him, and he heard her jump to her feet moments before her warm hand took hold of his frigid fingers. "What happened? Is everything all right?"

His body still refused to move, at least until his free hand thawed enough for him to cover his eyes with his fingers. He was surprised to find tears there—shocked, surprised tears. Disbelief filled him, and he strained his ears to hear it again.

There it was, as clear as the water in the star pool during a full moon. There was no mistaking it.

Slowly, he turned around and met Kirsa's fearful, concerned gaze. Her distress only seemed to grow upon seeing his tears, but no matter how hard he tried, he couldn't stop them. He was shocked, and happy, and *terrified.*

"What happened?" she asked again. "Is it Tille?"

"No," he replied through a tumultuous wave of emotion. "Your brother is still in stasis. It's…it's you."

He wiped his tears with the back of his arm and didn't give her a chance to respond before he gently picked her up and set her on the table. She looked at him with confusion leaking from her every pore, so great he could almost smell it.

"I hear your heartbeat," he said as he touched the skin over her heart. And then he trailed his finger down her torso until he touched the space below her belly. "I hear this heartbeat as well." Her eyes widened as she caught his meaning, but he wasn't finished as he touched a place not even an inch from the other. "And this one, too." Finally, he raised his gaze to find tears streaming down her face, mimicking his emotions from only moments earlier. "You've missed your monthly bleeding, haven't you?"

He didn't need her confirmation to know the truth for himself.

She nodded her head and squeezed his hand. "I wasn't planning on telling you until I knew anything for certain."

"You can't fool a vampire," he said, but his voice choked with emotion once more as he listened to the two small hearts beating in unison. They sounded healthy. Strong. Which brought him to the question, "How? Vampire males have such low fertility that the last time something like this happened so quickly was with Dracula and Elisabeta over a thousand years ago."

"It's the elixir I gave you before our wedding," she explained. Her eyes lit up as she placed her hands over her belly, and he couldn't help but treasure the memory, tucking it in the back of his mind for safekeeping. "It helps you create healthy seed, and a lot of it."

The elation he felt inside came crashing down the moment he laid eyes upon the black etchings on her skin created by the Blight. It was spreading far too quickly for comfort.

"You're not going to make it," he whispered. "Our children won't be born. Unless..." He took both of her hands, a desperation in his eyes. "We need to put you in stasis. I swore I'd find a cure for you, and I will."

However, she shook her head sadly. "Putting me in stasis might preserve my own life, but it will kill these babies. I'm not willing to go through with it."

He slumped into a chair and rested his head against her knee as another wave of emotion crashed over him. He was in danger of not only losing his mate, but his children as well if he failed. Fate would take three from him and not just one.

But this time, he refused to allow fate to win.

"What if they were born?" he asked, his voice muffled. "What if the Blight didn't exist, and they were brought into this life? Vampire or dwarf?"

"Dwarf," she whispered as she trailed her fingers through his hair. Her touch was comforting, making him want to lean into the caress like a feline basking in the sun. "I hope you will forgive me for not saying anything. The elixir you drank... I altered it so none of your vampire traits would come through should we produce offspring. They won't be immortal. They won't have fangs, nor will they drink blood. But I certainly hope they have black hair."

"You can do that?" At this point, he wasn't sure why it surprised him. Dwarves seemed to be capable of anything. Well, at least until it came to preserving their own race.

"Yes. Are you angry with me?"

"Not at all. All I care about is being able to hold their healthy, Blight-less little selves." He turned his head slightly to look her in the eye. "I'm terrified, Kirsa. We have so much to lose."

"I know, Luca. I know."

He took her hand and gave her fingers a squeeze, and they stayed in that position for a while as they both silently worried and fretted, seeking one another's comforting presence. One way or another, he wouldn't allow fate to have its way.

# CHAPTER 25

He really wasn't coming home...

Lucian Dragomir ran a hand down his stubbled face as he stared at the river coursing by, watching as a golden leaf twirled carelessly downstream. He'd given Luca plenty of space in hopes he'd come back home soon. But months had passed already. His son had yet to make an appearance.

Late spring had turned into summer. Summer had turned into autumn. And his son was still gone.

A feeling of foreboding encompassed him in a cocoon of dread. What if something awful had happened to Luca?

Her quiet footsteps on the fallen leaves alerted him to her presence before he felt two comforting arms wrap around his middle from behind. He breathed in his mate's scent, an ever-present gratitude filling him that she was still alive. Both Dracula and Nicolae had lost their mates, but he still had his.

"Bridgette," he whispered, still watching golden leaves spiral into the water from the tree above. "It's my fault. I know it is. I have thought long and hard about why he hates me so. After the Crusader war, he had come to me, bearing his heart and soul. And I pushed him aside to help other mourners. My own son."

She said nothing, seeming to know he needed his mind to churn through the problem on its own.

He continued, "He has hardly spoken a word to me since. That was *years* ago. And the one time he spoke to me was to tell me he doesn't want to be my son anymore. I must be a terrible father."

"You also cut him off," she pointed out. "I fought you over that one."

"How could I have done anything else? He spent nearly every night at the tavern."

"But for what reasons?"

Guilt pricked at him as he once again realized his son had been broken, and he stood by and watched. Made it worse, even. He single-handedly drove his son away, but to where? If he wasn't in Ichor Knell, and he no longer had coin to spend, where had he gone?

"And you arranged Cosette's marriage to Oriel," she continued, ever the one to throw fire on the flames. "Without telling him beforehand. You know how much she means to him."

"I get it," he huffed. "I've hardly been an exemplary father figure."

He turned around to face Bridgette, but immediately wished he hadn't when he found the deep worry in her eyes. It had only grown worse over the days, weeks, months, of Luca's absence.

"I suppose you want me to find him."

"He's had enough space," she nodded as she clung to his arms. "At this point, I fear for his safety. What if something happened to him, Lucian?"

Her worries echoed his thoughts perfectly, but they had been mated for nearly a thousand years. They knew each other inside and out.

"I'll find him."

After kissing her goodbye, he materialized into a thousand flakes and allowed the wind to carry him after Luca's scent. At first, it was difficult to locate, but as soon as he reached Ironfell in under a minute, he picked up the faint trace of his son. He had been here. But not for a while, judging by the stale scent. He was about to materialize once more when the scent became stronger, leading him to a town on the outskirts of the large city. A vampire male whistled cheerily as he locked his home behind him and continued down the path.

There it was, unmistakable as it hugged his pinky finger, his skin bulging around the piece of jewelry as if his fingers were too big for it. Anger pushed Lucian forward. He grabbed the vampire's arm and twisted it behind his back until he screeched in pain.

"Where did you get this?" he growled while holding the male's hand in front of his face to view the Dragomir ring.

Judging by the look in the vampire's eyes, he knew exactly who he was.

"H-h-he sold it to me, Your Grace. I swear!"

Lucian grunted in surprise and dropped the male's hand, ignoring the way he nursed his shoulder. His surprise turned to hurt as the information burst a hole straight through his heart. Luca had given up his lineage? His birthright? At first, he'd thought this entire thing was simply a phase of rebellion, but now he realized it was more serious than that. Far more serious.

"I'll buy it back from you. I'll give you twice as much as he sold it for."

The vampire handed it to him so quickly that his anger and hurt disappeared for mere moments. He exchanged the ring for a good sum and held it tightly in an enclosed fist. This was Luca's ring. Whether or not he wanted it, it was his, and Lucian was ready to convince him to return to Ichor Knell. By any cajoling necessary.

"My apologies, Your Grace," the male said before bowing and scurrying away like a mouse fleeing from a bird of prey.

He didn't bother concealing himself from view of the townspeople as he materialized once more and followed Luca's scent. It became stronger and stronger until he reached what appeared to be rolling forests and flat plains. Confusion pricked at him as he continued forward on foot, hesitant footfall after hesitant footfall. What was his son doing in the middle of nowhere?

But then he felt it. A magical barrier rippled through him as he crossed to the other side. The deceiving enchantment dropped, and flat plains turned into high, unforgiving mountains. Luca's scent was strongest here.

"No!" he gasped.

Without further thought for himself, he ran forward, but quickly crashed into something solid and invisible. A second barrier. One with a strong enough enchantment he knew even he couldn't break.

Still, he tried.

He smashed his fists against the barrier again and again, each attempt more desperate than the last. Dwarves had a reputation for killing vampires, and he couldn't help but fear the worst. He punched the invisible wall, and when it held steady, he paced back and forth along the barrier, searching for a crack or a weakness, and when he found none, he continued to slam his fists against the wall.

If the dwarves killed his son, he would rain vengeance upon them like nothing they'd ever seen before—

"Why are you here?" a voice asked behind him, and Lucian spun around to find Luca a mere ten feet away.

"Luca," he sighed in relief. But when he took a step forward, his son took a step backward, causing him to reevaluate the situation.

He looked his son over from top to bottom, noticing how different he appeared since he last saw him. His clothing was odd, a style clearly dwarven and not at all vampiristic. His face was still clean shaven, but his hair was a bit longer than he remembered. And his ears... They were pierced in several different places. His left ear contained a rod-like earring pierced straight through the middle of the ear, and his right ear held three different earrings. He knew dwarves told their personal histories on their ears, but Luca was a vampire, not a dwarf.

His eyes continued downward until he spotted the tattoo on his son's left wrist, but his heartbeat froze completely upon noticing the two rings on his fingers. One was clearly a wedding band, and the other…

"That's a chieftain ring," he gawked, nearly stuttering over his own words.

"And I am a chieftain of Vrork. But I asked you why you are here."

Luca's tone was cold, as if he were speaking to a potential threat rather than his own father. But there was something else in the way he stood, his body turned slightly toward the Mountain. And he kept glancing in that direction, as if he saw something Lucian didn't, something the enchanted barrier hid from him.

It was then when everything finally clicked. Luca had found a mate. That was clearly the reason he hadn't returned to Ichor Knell. But was she truly a dwarf?

In a softer tone, he asked, "Will you allow me to meet her?"

"No." Luca's reply was harsh and biting, before he turned his attention back toward the Mountain as if listening to someone speak, but as hard as Lucian tried, he couldn't hear a thing beyond the barrier. His son's shoulders slumped guiltily as he spoke in a language Lucian hadn't heard in a very long time. He didn't understand Akretti, but Luca clearly did, and he spoke it well.

"I need to ask you to leave," Luca said, switching tongues. His expression turned from hostile to guilt to worry in a matter of seconds as he glanced toward the Mountain again. Something was wrong. Very wrong. Lucian could feel it in the very air. But Luca acted cold toward him. If he asked, he felt sure his son wouldn't say a thing.

"Son, just talk to me," he begged. "Tell me why you sold your Dragomir ring."

"I am no longer a Dragomir. I took Kirsa's name. Now leave."

He stepped backward, dumbfounded as his mind repeated her name again and again. Kirsa? This couldn't possibly be *Kirsa Frey* he spoke about. The chieftain's daughter.

His gaze darted to the ring on Luca's finger, and he shook his head in disbelief. For him to be wearing that ring, he would have to be married to the chieftain. If Kirsa was the chieftain, then her mother was dead.

So much seemed to have happened since he'd last seen his son, but he could hardly make sense of any of it, not when Luca hated him as fiercely as he appeared to. He would never allow him inside Vrork's walls, nor would he allow him to meet his mate and find out what was wrong.

Before he could say anything more, Luca's eyes widened, and he spoke in rushed Akretti as he darted in the direction of the Mountain, but the moment he passed through the barrier, both his body and voice was swallowed up on the other side.

Lucian's worry for his son and his new daughter-in-law flared to life, and it was all he could do to walk away from the dwarven settlement.

Luca clearly would never allow him through, but he knew someone his son *would* allow inside.

# CHAPTER 26

"Kirsa!" Luca gasped when her legs collapsed beneath her. Rocks dug into her palms, but she hardly felt them when compared to the aching pain in her lungs. He reached her side before Gunther and Adrietta, and within moments, she found herself on her feet again. Her breathing was labored, her body weak with fatigue as the Blight continued to spread.

She knew lungs were the second to last to be infected, followed by the heart. After, death took its victim. It had been months since she'd first contracted the Blight, and she knew her time was up any day now. Especially since they hadn't yet managed to find a cure.

"I'm all right, vampire," she said in a weak but teasing tone, though her shaking legs said otherwise. "Finish your conversation with your father."

However, when they both turned their attention back to the barrier, Lucian was gone. His disappearance seemed to ease the tension in Luca's shoulders as he helped her back toward the Mountain. Normally, she would have protested at being treated like a fragile little flower, but even she knew her limits. She shouldn't have followed Luca outside into the increasingly harsh autumn air, but she had never met his father in person, only seen him once in Ironfell.

Despite her reassurances, her lungs seized once more, making it difficult to draw breath. She was hardly aware of her feet leaving the ground before someone placed her on a soft cot she knew belonged to the infirmary.

"It looks to have spread to her lungs," a female voice said moments before gentle hands touched her back and chest. "This will calm the inflammation, but at this point, there is nothing we can do but make her more comfortable."

Someone placed a glass vial to her lips, and she forced herself to drink the foul liquid offered to her. Her wheezing subsided after mere moments, replaced by a merciful calm as if the medicine wrapped her lungs in a cool cloth. She focused on taking several long, deep breaths and sought comfort in a pair of strong, familiar arms.

"Kirsa, please," Luca begged. "I'm close to cracking Arvitash. I know I am. I'd rather lose our two children than to lose them *and* you. Go into stasis."

She glanced up and finally her eyes adjusted enough to make out the worried features of her husband's face. She knew just how much these children meant to him, so for him to ask this of her...

"No," she replied firmly while she touched her growing belly, though her voice came out as barely a whisper. This was such a cruel thing for fate to do. She was nearly six months along, but she wouldn't make it to term. In fact, she probably didn't even have two weeks left before her death.

"Kirsa—"

"This is not up for debate. I will not kill our children just so I might have a chance to live."

He said nothing for the longest time, but only gazed back at her with sadness in his violet eyes as the nurses worked around him. She rested tender fingers against his face and allowed fragile emotions to pass between them through their gazes alone. It wasn't until the nurses finished tending to her when he crawled onto the cot and held her tightly in his arms.

"I love you, Luca," she whispered as she trailed a finger over his soft, dark eyebrows, down his nose, and across each of his lips. "You know that don't you?"

"Yes." His voice sounded hoarse, as if he'd just been swimming in a pool of sand. "Of course, I do, love."

The medicine coursing through her body stirred the drowsiness sleeping deep within her, and she succumbed to its will, comforted in Luca's loving embrace. She wasn't sure how long she slept, but voices dragged her back to the surface until she heard Luca and Elric conversing in the infirmary. Luca's arms still circled her as if he didn't want to let her go until he knew she was awake.

"Lucian Dragomir has returned," Elric said quietly. "He knocked this time rather than tried to bring down the entire Mountain."

"Turn him away. I don't want him here."

"But he brought someone with him. Long black hair. Amethyst eyes."

Luca chuckled against her, which helped ease her out of sleep a bit more. "You just described half my family. It's most likely my mother. As I said, turn them away."

Kirsa managed to open her eyes enough to find Elric shaking his head. "Her name is Cosette."

"Cosette?" Luca gasped, startling her as he shot upright into a sitting position. She clutched onto him as her heart raced at the sudden movement, and it continued to do so even after he murmured a quiet apology. "Are you certain? Was she warm and friendly or quiet and aloof?"

"The second. She wouldn't speak to me."

"That's Cosette then." He blew out a long breath, and Kirsa watched him, wondering what he'd do. She'd support whatever he decided, though she secretly hoped to meet Cosette, his supposedly favorite sibling.

At last, he nodded as he slipped off the cot, leaving a sudden chill where his body had previously kept her warm. "My father is slyer than a fox for bringing her. I'll meet them."

"Let me come," she said as she slipped her fingers around his wrist. "I want to meet your sister."

Luca paused, a look of uncertainty filling his eyes. "Last time you were outside—"

"Then bring them inside. I'll wait in the commons."

"In *here*? Inside the Mountain?" He shook his head, and she found her stubbornness rising within her. "First of all, that's my *father*. Second, Cosette would *never* follow our protocol. I think she'd rather die first."

Her stubbornness would win. She'd see to it. "Then we'll skip protocol for all vampires. They can't carry the Blight anyway and the inspection is a waste of our time."

A small part of her was desperate to meet Luca's family, now her family, if only once before her end. She was willing to bend a few rules, especially when she knew no harm would come to their people.

"You said so yourself that the protocol keeps the dwarves safe."

"From other dwarves, yes. It's up to you, Luca. Allow me to meet them outside or bring them into the commons."

He rolled his eyes at her, but she caught the faint trace of a grin at the corner of his mouth. "You are infuriating, dwarf. But if my father and I get in a fight, this one's on you."

"A vampire fight?" she teased, taking his offered hand as he helped her from the infirmary and into the commons where he situated her on a comfortable sofa. "I think I'll put my money on Cosette."

"Well, she has stopped our fights before."

Nervousness flickered across his eyes. Though, he quickly hid it. The brief emotion only created a pit of anxiety inside her, but likely for a different reason. Would they accept her? What would they think of her round belly? Would they hear the babies' heartbeats as quickly as Luca had?

She watched him disappear down the hallway, his feet making hardly a sound against the stone floor. A chilling quiet filled the room, filled the entire Mountain. Once, Vrork had been filled with far too many dwarves to count, laughter echoing off the walls and the forges billowing to life. And now it was too quiet…too empty…too still. She had no hope for a cure, but she wouldn't kill Luca's hope.

It's what kept him going, and it's what kept him distracted.

Minutes passed of her growing anxiety, and when he still didn't return, she nearly followed after. At least until voices echoed down the hallway. She reflexively reached for a book on the table next to her to keep her hands busy, but her gaze remained fixed on the doorway rather than on the words.

The voices moved closer. And closer. And then three people entered the commons.

Lucian Dragomir looked the same as she remembered in Ironfell, his fangs bared and his black hair brushing his shoulders. And Cosette…

Her jaw nearly dropped upon seeing Luca's sister. She was striking, yet that was an understatement. Her black hair hung in loose curls around her shoulders, her amethyst-colored eyes piercing as she stared at Kirsa curiously. She was far too busy staring back that she hadn't noticed Lucian's attention on her belly until now. He looked shocked, his confidence disappearing as if washed away like sand in the ocean.

In moments, Luca was at her side, helping her to her feet before presenting her to his family members. "Father. Cosette. I'd like you to meet my wife and mate, Kirsa Frey. Kirsa, this is my father, Lucian, and my sister, Cosette."

She reached out for a handshake, but Lucian grasped her wrist instead. It took her aback for a moment before she remembered it was how vampires greeted others. Cosette grasped her wrist next, though much more timidly than her father.

"I'm not sure what to say," Lucian said, his voice choked up as if overcome by emotion. "I have so many questions for you, Kirsa. If you'll allow me to ask them."

When she glanced at Luca, she shot him a questioning look, but he simply shrugged despite the discomfort leaking from every pore in his body. But she had no reason yet to dislike her father-in-law, and she wanted to learn more about him, too.

"As long as I can sit, you can ask however many you want."

"By all means." Much to Luca's apparent annoyance, Lucian guided her back to the sofa, and she cast him a soft smile of gratitude. How could Luca hate him? So far, he was nothing but an attentive gentleman.

Or perhaps he was trying to atone for his past behavior and make amends with Luca.

Lucian pressed his fingers together into a steeple and leaned forward in his chair while watching her intently, and he only spoke when the others were seated. "Forgive my directness on this fragile subject, but I must know what happened to your mother."

The memory of her mother, shredded and bloodied, filled her mind. They were the same images that often haunted her dreams at night.

"She was attacked by a beast the day after our wedding." She reached for Luca's hand and held it tightly. "Luca and I ascended as the new chieftains."

He nodded, his violet eyes seeming to take in more than her words told. "And when are you due? I am shocked children happened so quickly, and twins at that. We've only had one pair of twins in Ichor Knell in centuries. The Covaci twins."

Her grip slackened on her husband's hand as a wave of heartache washed over her, and she lowered her gaze to her lap. She'd always wanted to be a mother, and she knew she should be grateful to have carried the babies for so long, but it hurt knowing she'd never get to hold her children in her arms.

Luca wrapped an arm around her shoulders and whispered uplifting words in her ear in Akretti, which gave her the courage to answer the question.

"I would be due at the beginning of the new year," she said at last as she raised her gaze to meet Lucian's. His eyes already told her he knew her next words before she uttered them. "Unfortunately, I am sick. I will not make it another two weeks."

"Sick with what?"

Again, she glanced at Luca to find his expression hardened, obviously hiding the words he wanted to say. She had protected this secret from other races for a long time, and now she was far too weary and fatigued to keep it any longer. The dwarves would become extinct soon anyway. There was no more reason to hide it from the world.

"We call it the Rotting Blight," she answered tiredly as she slipped off her glove and pulled her sleeve up to reveal the black etchings crawling across her skin. It now covered her entire body, though it left her face unmarred with the exception of a vein of it nearly touching her chin. "It only affects dwarves, and it has been picking us off in batches. There are only two hundred and twelve remaining dwarves, half of what used to remain when I found Luca. He's been working tirelessly to find a cure for us."

"Yet, nothing has worked," Luca cut in, running his fingers through his hair. "We're convinced the ancient dwarves knew of a cure, or at least something that might help, but we can't decipher Arvitash. It's too old to understand."

Everyone grew quiet for a long few moments, and Kirsa risked a glance at Cosette. She hadn't said anything, but the tears swimming in her eyes told stories of her heartache for her brother. If only Kirsa had more time, she'd like the chance to get to know her better.

Lucian broke the silence. "I'm sure you have, or had, talented physicians in Vrork. I'd like to offer ours to aid you."

"No," Luca growled. "Zachariah Degore is *not* stepping foot inside this mountain."

She'd heard the name before, only mentioned once on her first couple of days of Luca's acquaintance. She switched her tongue to Akretti and asked him, "Is this the same Zachariah Degore who stole your beloved Laurel Covaci?"

Instead of answering, he mumbled in Akretti, "I don't want him here."

"And why not? Are you afraid he'll charm his way into my heart as well?"

Luca finally looked at her, and she gave him a teasing grin to let him know she was jesting. But the look on his face told her he thought exactly that. The poor vampire.

"You have nothing to fear, Luca," she said quietly as she touched his knee reassuringly. "But all of our physicians are dead, and we are left with nurses. It doesn't hurt to bring them in for a second look. Perhaps they might have some insight to offer. Or at the very least, they can see if our children are healthy."

Her hand rested on her belly, and bringing his attention to it seemed to soften the hardness in his eyes. Though, she noticed the other two staring at her belly as well despite not understanding their conversation.

"And I thought dwarves were supposed to be the prideful ones," he chuckled with a roll of his eyes before he turned back to his father and switched to his native tongue. "We'd be grateful for your aid."

"Even if I brought Mr. Degore?" Lucian asked with a raise of his eyebrows. "He is a talented physician."

"Just do what you have to do."

Luca's mask slipped for a moment, allowing her to witness his sheer exhaustion, the exhaustion he hid from her. He always remained positive, putting all his energy into being a wonderful and attentive husband while spending almost every waking moment on Arvitash. It broke her to see just how much of a toll this was taking on him.

"I know it's late," Lucian said as he stood, and Kirsa found she had no energy left to stand to see him out, but Luca did it in her place. "Time is clearly of the essence, so I will be going, and I hope to bring physicians first thing in the morning."

"Thank you," Kirsa said, hoping her expression showed the gratitude burning within her. "You are too kind to offer your help."

He said nothing for a moment as if trying to gather his emotions, but then finally he nodded. "For my son and my new daughter-in-law, anything. Cosette, are you ready?"

Cosette glanced from Luca, to her father, and back to Luca, and Kirsa found herself holding a breath. She couldn't help but wonder if the vampire's voice sounded as beautiful as the rest of her.

"Can I stay here?" she asked. Her voice was small and timid, but it did, indeed, hold a striking quality to it. "I've missed you, Luca."

"Stay as long as you want," he nodded. "But won't Oriel be worried?"

The mention of Oriel Covaci seemed to put Luca on edge, like a wolf raising its hackles. It was ironic the way his favorite sister mated with the one person he couldn't stand more than anyone in the world.

"I'll inform him of your stay," Lucian cut in.

They said their goodbyes, and Luca saw his father out, which left Cosette and Kirsa alone in the commons. Her sister-in-law shuffled her feet uncomfortably, craning her neck after Luca as if afraid to speak to a stranger.

Which was why Kirsa broke the silence. "Luca has told me a lot of good things about you."

"Has he?" Cosette frowned as she finally met her gaze. "We parted on bad terms, I thought he'd hate me."

"Quite the opposite, I'd say. I think he missed you as well."

Luca entered the commons right then, interrupting their short conversation. "Well, we didn't get in a fight," he jested, his guard seeming to lower the moment his father left. "I think it's the first time in years."

"It's because Cosette is here," Kirsa jested back, throwing a grin in her direction. "I believe I won a bet."

"Hardly," he snorted. "Besides, there were no stakes to our bet. Tell her, Cosette, how Father was on especially good behavior tonight."

Cosette raised a skeptical eyebrow, and although she still appeared timid around Kirsa, she seemed much less so with Luca in the room. "I think the one with good behavior was you. Your mate must be a good influence on you."

"A good influence, you say?" His grin widened as he held out his tattooed wrist. "I got a tattoo under her *good* influence. I thought Father would burst a vein before the end of the visit."

"You're not just his son anymore. You're the dwarven chieftain, and you are mated. I think he's realized you're no longer his little fledgling."

"I hate it when you call me that."

Finally, this brought a smile to Cosette's face, amplifying her striking qualities. "Which is why I do it."

The effects of the medicine Kirsa had taken hours ago returned at full force, and a wave of exhaustion encompassed her. Nothing got past Luca's attention, and he was by her side immediately.

"I'll take you to bed," he said softly as he picked her up in his arms, and when she normally would have protested, she hadn't the strength. "I'll be back in a few minutes, Cosette."

Once again, the stillness of the Mountain rattled her as they made their way through the housing district before entering the chieftains' quarters. She would have been content to fall asleep right there in Luca's arms, but the soft bed he placed her on was equally nice.

When he tried to pull away, she grabbed a fistful of his shirt and tugged him back to her, capturing his mouth with her own. She breathed out relief at his calming presence. She tugged him even closer and deepened the kiss, which earned her a groan from the back of his throat. For a moment, her troubles and worries melted away.

"I can't leave Cosette alone for long," he whispered against her lips. The passion subdued, yet he still gave her sweet kiss after sweet kiss until she felt as if she were lying blissfully in a meadow of wildflowers. "She gets anxious easily."

"Then send her to bed," she said in an equally hushed tone. Wrapping her arms around his neck, she deepened the kiss once more, and he groaned again, nearly taking the bait.

With what seemed like reluctant restraint, he stopped the kiss and instead pressed his lips against her cheek, her temple, and then her forehead.

"I have to talk to her, Kirsa," he said quietly as if afraid to break the stillness of the room. "We didn't part well last time."

"I know," she sighed. "I'm glad she came."

He smiled and gave her one last kiss to her forehead before leaving the room. In his absence, she allowed her frustration to flare alive. She'd never felt weaker in her life. She'd never give birth to her children. She'd never live to an old age with Luca by her side. Vampire physicians or not, she knew the truth of the situation, and death was inevitable. It was an outcome she could not avoid. No matter which way she turned, doom stared her in the face like a lion preparing to strike.

She pulled her glove from her hand and tossed it to the floor, followed by the second one. The Blight covered her skin like the sickening disease it was. There was no running. No fleeing. No hiding. Death would find her.

And despite her brave front, she was very afraid.

# CHAPTER 27

The moment Luca returned to the commons, he expected to be met with hesitation, timidity, perhaps even resentment, but Cosette rushed into his arms and held on tightly. Although she didn't sob into his chest, he smelled her fresh tears as she hid her face in his shirt.

"I was so worried about you," she sniffed. "You never came home. I know you said you likely wouldn't, but I had hoped you'd change your mind."

He didn't know what to say, so he said nothing. He hadn't planned on returning to Ichor Knell, especially not now when an immense weight rested on his shoulders. Besides, he wanted to spend every waking moment with Kirsa, even if only to sit in the same room together as they worked.

Cosette's tears slowed, and only then did she raise her head to look at him. "You look different than I remember. What do your earrings represent?"

Now *that* was something he was more comfortable talking about. He led her from the room, and they walked arm in arm down the hallway until they entered an even larger room, one they called the greenhouse, filled with plants and flowers of all kinds that thrived without sunlight. The variety was incredible, most of them exotic to Ichor Knell.

As he suspected she would, Cosette marveled at the greenery around them, with the occasional burst of color from a flowering plant.

Pointing to his ardor piercing, he explained, "This traditionally represents love in its strongest form for one's mate. And these three..." He pointed to his other ear. "These are my family. One for Kirsa, the other two for our unborn children."

"How?"

She didn't need to expand on her question for him to understand the meaning. But it was a dwarven secret he'd keep, even from his own sister. "I suppose we just got lucky," he lied with a shrug. "Look at this flower. I thought you'd like it."

He successfully redirected her attention to a plant producing large purple blooms adorned with white stripes and long stigmas that looked frosted over with ice.

"What are they?" she marveled as she reached out a hand, though her fingers hovered reverently over it as if afraid to touch the delicate petals.

"They're called arctic violets. They mainly grow in dark, snowy caverns, but with the right enchantment, we can recreate the conditions here without affecting any of the other plants."

"How?" she asked again, this time inquiring after a different subject.

He shrugged. "Enchantments are still new to me. Kirsa would be able to explain better than I would."

At the mention of Kirsa, his sister's shoulders slumped, and he knew their conversation was about to take a more serious turn.

"You found a mate so quickly after leaving Ichor Knell. You didn't even invite me to the ceremony."

"You didn't invite me to yours, either," he countered. "Me of all people... You'd think you'd at least do that much. Oriel Covaci or not, I should have been invited, Cosette."

Tears swam in her eyes, followed by a faint blush in her cheeks indicating her embarrassment. "It's because it was arranged!"

The defensive retort waiting on the tip of his tongue died as he stared at his flushed sister. He blinked once, twice, as he tried to understand her words. Vampires rarely had arranged unions. "What?"

Now her words came out as a tumbled rush. "Oriel was having trouble finding a mate he wanted to settle down with, and he threw in the towel and asked Nicolae to arrange a union for him. Nicolae chose me, and I had fancied Oriel for so long that I accepted. He didn't know who his mate was until after the ceremony was finished. We ended up falling in love, but it didn't start out that way." She covered her face with her hands when her flush worsened. "I didn't invite you because I thought you'd either tease me relentlessly or you would be so angry as to never speak to me again. I know how you feel about Oriel. I can't say I ever shared the sentiment."

"Huh…"

He ran a hand over his face as he attempted to grasp everything she just mentioned. He'd never known of her secret fancy, and he wished she'd told him long ago. From the beginning, he'd thought the match was strange, but now it made complete sense.

"Now I feel awful for courting Laurel," he said ashamedly. "Should we have become mates, it would have put Oriel out of your reach. But I wish you would have told me. I would have at least tried to understand."

"I didn't want anyone to know the union was arranged. Not even you. But I wouldn't have changed it for anything. I am so happy with Oriel." She ran her long black hair through her fingers and bit her lip. "I only wish I could have seen how happy you were on your union day. You seem to care for Kirsa immensely."

The one person he should have invited, he didn't. Guilt pricked at his conscience, and to give him more time to form a reply, he studied another flower called a shadow blossom. The petals were small, a deep blue, and they only opened after midnight. They grew their largest underneath a full moon.

Finally, he said, "I was prepared to leave Ichor Knell and everyone there behind forever. But seeing you today…" He turned to find red tears shimmering in her eyes, and he realized how much he'd hurt her. "I'm sorry, Cosette."

"No." When she shook her head, a couple of her tears fell free down her cheeks. "It's me who needs to apologize. I was so busy with Oriel and Leif that I neglected you. I didn't realize how much you needed me until you left, how much I needed you. But…" She paused, and this time, she touched a plant with her delicate fingers. "I am realizing you still don't plan on returning. You've made a life here. With Kirsa. And you might be a father if our physicians can stop this disease."

The disease couldn't be stopped, and he knew the physicians couldn't do a single thing about it. They could try, but it was a hopeless case. However, he wouldn't lose hope completely, not while Kirsa was still alive.

"These are my people now. You will always be my dear sister, but this is where I belong."

Cosette embraced him again, and he held her tightly until her tears ebbed. "You will allow me to visit, won't you?" she asked.

He swallowed the emotion building in his throat and nodded against her hair. "As often as you'd like."

They arrived early the next morning before most dwarves finished eating breakfast in the mess hall. As instructed beforehand, Gunther and Adrietta allowed the vampires inside the Mountain, but only in the commons, and this time, Luca and Kirsa aimed to put up a regal front.

Kirsa dressed in clothes of deep burgundy, with a ruby circlet to match, and she wore her hair up to display each of her earrings. Luca wore a similar circlet, though his was crafted of plain gold and embedded with dwarven symbols like "chieftain," "protector," and "leader." His own clothing complimented hers—a deep green the color of the Mountain trees.

She gripped his hand tightly, and he returned the gesture by giving her fingers a gentle squeeze as they walked slowly down the hallway. He cast a worried glance in her direction. Her face looked much paler than it had only a week ago, and despite her careful posture, his ears picked up on her unequal footing while she walked. She just might collapse at any moment, and he wanted to be near enough to catch her should it happen.

They spoke in Akretti to prevent the vampires in the commons from understanding even if they overheard from this distance.

"I'm a bit nervous to be faced with so many other vampires," she admitted, finally meeting his gaze. "If they know what I've done to their kin?"

"It shouldn't be that many," he tried to reassure her. "My father, and perhaps two or three physicians. It's been quiet around here, so perhaps a few more voices might liven it up a bit."

She smiled and gave his hand another squeeze before they entered the commons together, and Luca's own smile faltered as he stopped short.

Of course, he'd expected to be faced with Zachariah Degore. He'd even prepared for it. But what he hadn't been prepared for was finding himself face to face with Laurel Covaci—err, Degore. But instead of a deep, aching sadness filling his chest, he found it blazing with anger. She would dare come here? To his home? Without permission? He never would have allowed her within ten miles of the Mountain.

"Laurel, get out," he growled, and he heard Kirsa take in a breath of surprise.

Zachariah stepped closer to Laurel as if she needed protection. She certainly didn't, not with that barbed tongue of hers.

Laurel held her head high, her blonde curls piled neatly on top of her head while her attire displayed the latest fashion in Ichor Knell. She'd always been one to keep up with fashion, and while he'd found it attractive in the past, it only irked him now, and he wasn't entirely sure why.

"I wanted to see the dwarven kingdom for myself," she said haughtily, a tone he'd quickly learned she used as a defensive mechanism when feeling threatened. "If my mate was given permission to enter, I assumed the invitation was extended to me."

"It wasn't. I want you out. And you too, Oriel." He hadn't noticed Oriel standing beside Lucian until now. "You serve no purpose here."

Oriel was far from haughty like his sister, but his guard was up around Luca at all times, and vice versa. He'd only been kinder to him after mating with Cosette, but they still hated each other.

"My mate is here," Oriel said while glancing around the room, but it was empty of Cosette. She had been so entranced by the dwarven garden that he felt sure she'd spent the night there. "Besides, I brought someone I thought you might like to see."

A small face poked out from behind Oriel's legs, and Luca's heart stumbled in surprise. Brown curly hair. Lively blue eyes. His throat clogged up with emotion as he crouched down and held out his arms. "Leif."

Leif's smile blossomed, and he couldn't help but mimic his smile as the little boy ran straight into his arms and held on tight around his neck. "Uncle Luca! I missed you tons and tons. You always play with me in the gardens, remember? But Mama said you left Ichor Knell for a while. Papa said I can play with you here instead."

"Did he?" He shot Oriel a look that said he won this time around, but he wouldn't be so lucky if he tried it a second time. Turning his attention back to the little boy, he asked, "How old are you now?"

"Six and a quarter," Leif replied proudly. "I'm a good flyer, too. Do you want to see me fly?"

"Perhaps in a little bit," Luca chuckled as he ruffed up the little boy's hair. "Do you want to say hello to your Aunt Kirsa?"

Leif's eyes widened as he turned his head to Kirsa, his jaw dropping slightly as he stared and stared and stared. "You're beautiful."

The entire room burst into laughter, and even Kirsa cracked a smile despite being nervous only a minute before. He smiled softly at his dear mate and took her hand, gently kissing her gloved fingers. He thought the exact same thing of her. She was the most beautiful female he'd ever met, and he made sure to tell her every single day. But not just now when everyone's eyes were on them.

"Thank you for coming," Kirsa said, addressing his father and the two physicians who made the trip, one of them being Zachariah Degore and the other Doctor Enache. He couldn't help but notice how she ignored Laurel's presence entirely. "We have plenty of sick and afflicted. Most of the dwarves affected are in stasis to prolong their lives. Others have chosen to remain out of stasis."

*Like you*, he thought as his mouth turned downward.

"As I understand, Chieftain," Doctor Enache said as he followed them toward the infirmary, "once dwarves contract this disease, it's always a death sentence. How quickly does one die from it?"

As Kirsa explained the intricacies of the Rotting Blight, Luca peeked over at Laurel to find her staring at Kirsa's round belly rather than marveling at the dwarven splendor of the Mountain as everyone else did. Was that a wistful look in her eyes?

She glanced in his direction as if feeling his gaze, and he turned his attention to Leif instead, who was jumping in an attempt to reach the glowing gems on the ceiling. He swept his nephew onto his shoulders, where he laughed gleefully as he dragged his fingers across the gems while they continued forward.

"Are you a dwarf, Uncle Luca?" Leif asked suddenly, and he leaned precariously to the side to look him in the eye. It was all he could do to keep the boy upright on his shoulders.

"No," he chuckled. "I'm still a vampire, but I'm married to a dwarf."

"Married?"

"Mated," he corrected himself. As a young vampire, Leif likely wouldn't understand the terms associated with other races.

"Can I live here with you and Aunt Kirsa?" he asked. "I like all the glowing rocks."

He simply smiled and said nothing more, and thankfully, he didn't have to answer as they approached the infirmary as a large group. Cosette rounded the corner right then, and Luca handed Leif off to her, not wanting him to see what lay behind the door. Sickness and death were nothing a little boy needed to see.

When he felt someone's gaze on him, he turned and was met again by Laurel's curious stare, and he knew her well enough to recognize the look as her trying to figure something out. He had no desire to ask her what it was.

Turning his attention back to his mate, he touched the small of her back and led her into the infirmary, the others, aside from Leif and Cosette, following closely behind. Far too many beds were empty, as the Blight had picked off unit after unit until so little afflicted remained. The healthy now kept their masks on as often as possible, and he hoped it was enough.

"I suppose we have a lot of work ahead of us," Doctor Enache said to Zachariah. Then to Kirsa, he said, "I'll take a look at you first. Then we can—"

"I'd rather you see to my brother before me," she interrupted, leading him to a bed with Tille lying on top in an unconscious state. They'd visited the infirmary often, and while Luca stopped by once or twice a week, he knew Kirsa visited every day.

"As you wish," Doctor Enache said with a nod of his head. "Mr. Degore, see to Chieftain Frey while I work with this patient."

Luca clenched his fists as he attempted to suppress the rage boiling inside him. He didn't want Zachariah anywhere near his mate. Ever. But he was the one who had given him permission to enter the Mountain, so he'd just have to endure it.

Zachariah motioned for her to follow him to a bed with a curtain to give them privacy. Luca followed as well. Zachariah didn't comment, but rather shot nervous glances toward him. The last time he'd confronted the other vampire, it was just before Zachariah and Laurel had started courting. At the time, Luca had been ready to start a brawl to compete for Laurel's attention.

He had never stopped despising Zachariah for so boldly taking Laurel as his own, and now he didn't trust him with Kirsa.

Clearing his throat anxiously, Zachariah turned his attention to Kirsa. "Lucian filled us in on what he'd learned yesterday. The Rotting Blight seems to affect your entire body, but it shows on the skin. May I take a look?"

His mate nodded and pulled off her glove to reveal the black designs covering her arm. Luca clenched his fists tighter as Zachariah placed his hands on her and pushed her sleeve up farther to get a better look. Still, he shook his head with dissatisfaction.

"I need to see how these etchings interact with your internal organs. I will need you to strip to your undergarments."

"Not a chance," Luca growled. "Touch her and die, Degore."

"Luca," Kirsa said quietly as she looked between him and a pale-faced Zachariah before switching to the dwarven tongue. "He's trying to help. Besides, if he already has a mate, he has no interest in me."

"I don't trust him. I don't want him within a mile of you."

She lightly touched his arm, a comforting reminder of her feelings for him when his own felt far too fragile. "You said you'd do anything to find a cure. You will just have to endure this."

He clenched his jaw, loosened it, and then clenched it again as he finally stepped aside for Zachariah to continue. The other male looked even paler than moments before as Kirsa began to strip, though his eyes remained fixed on Luca the entire time. He gave him a fierce warning glare, at least until the other vampire finally turned back to Kirsa.

"I have never seen anything like this," Zachariah mused, his gaze roaming over her skin. "This only affects dwarves?"

"Yes," she nodded.

Zachariah reached out to touch her neck, but Luca slapped his hands away. "Hands off."

"Luca," Kirsa sighed exhaustedly, not bothering to switch languages this time. "I think it's best if you take a walk for a little while. I'll be fine. I promise."

He shook his head stubbornly. "I can't just leave you here."

"Yes, you can. Go. If I see you in the infirmary before the doctors are finished, I will have Gunther personally escort you out."

Frustration filled him to the brink as he turned another glare toward Zachariah. He didn't like having the other vampire here in his home, but as Kirsa had said, this was something he needed to endure.

"Hurt her, and I will kill you, Degore."

Without giving himself any more time to fuel his rage, he tromped out of the infirmary and walked with purposeful strides down the hallway until he found the library. If he couldn't help Kirsa in the infirmary, then he'd find his own way to help her by continuing his work with Arvitash.

He only managed to open a book to a bookmarked page before someone knocked on the doorframe. His spirits rose when he thought it was Cosette or perhaps even Leif, but it immediately deflated once more when he found Laurel instead.

"May I come in?" she asked, her voice full of hesitation.

"Why not?" he muttered under his breath as he focused intently on his work.

She approached slowly from behind until she reached the table he sat at. She didn't sit at the empty chair beside him, but rather stood over his work like an unwanted raincloud. At the moment, he'd prefer exposing himself to sunlight over enduring her presence.

"I thought I could try to help with Arvitash," she said, still hesitant as if there was something else on her mind other than staring at a dead language for hours on end.

He gestured with a flourish to his work spread out over several tables. "By all means. See if any of this makes sense to you. I've been scouring records for months and I keep coming up dry."

She leaned over the table, a look of concentration quickly taking root in her eyes. At over two hundred years old, she was much older than him, and had been involved in scholarly work for much longer as well. If she couldn't figure it out, then it proved no one could.

Silence fell between them as she studied his notes in Akretti, and he sat back to look at the work he'd done already pinned to the walls. He was so close, but he still felt like he was missing something vital, something to connect everything together.

"I notice Akretti is very similar to the Old Language," Laurel finally said. "But Arvitash... It's something else entirely. We have nothing to draw from in our culture. Anything that might have been useful to us now was burned during the religious war in Dracula's and Nicolae's early years."

"I gathered that much already."

"It seems there is nothing you can do but guess."

"I've tried that." He ran his hands through his hair in frustration. "Again and again and again. When I think it starts to make sense, I run into something that proves me wrong entirely. It doesn't follow the same structure or pattern of languages that exist today."

Her fingers drummed thoughtfully on her chin. "Have you tried reading it backward?"

"Yes."

"Downward?"

"I tried that as well."

"What if each symbol is a word rather than a letter?"

He sighed again, seeing failure flash before his eyes. His mate was dying, and as hard as he tried, he couldn't fix it. "Unfortunately, the text is too long for that to be the case."

"Upside down?" she ventured another guess.

A smile pulled on his mouth, surprising him at its appearance. Whenever there was a problem to be solved, Laurel was someone who looked at every angle. Literally.

"It makes even less sense upside down," he chuckled. "Like Akretti, I can tell Arvitash contains dwarven roots. But the language is too ancient. Short of returning to the dangerous ruins to gather more samples, I'm not sure what else I can do. If my current samples are fruitless, why should I risk my life gathering more samples that also prove useless?"

She ran a finger over a page of Arvitash and frowned. "Then let's hope the physicians can come up with something that *does* work."

Her reminder brought a scowl to his face. Zachariah Degore... Couldn't his father have brought Doctor Rosetti instead of Degore?

"I hoped you might aid me, Luca," Laurel said hesitantly after another minute of silence. "I know this is a strange thing to ask of you, and uncomfortable to say the least. But I did the math. I know vampires don't just conceive as easily as you and Kirsa did. You did something to make it happen quickly. I want you to tell me the secret."

Luca's previous scowl deepened as he stood, towering above her, but she didn't flinch away. "You have some nerve to ask me, Laurel."

However, she continued in a rush of words as if knowing convincing him to spill the secret was next to impossible. "I want a child so badly. Adam and Willow have a child and another on the way. Cosette and Oriel adopted Leif. The thought of not having a child of my own for perhaps decades hurts immensely. I'll do anything you ask. Give anything you want. Please, Luca."

He shook his head, his nostrils flaring with anger. This was the last of the bad string of events he could handle for the day. "Like I said, you have some nerve. You estranged me from much of upper-class society. You turned my brother-in-law against me. You painted me as the viper in our courtship. I know I made mistakes, and I am deeply sorry for it, but it's not all on me." He clenched his jaw, continuing even when she flinched at his words. "How long did you string me along while I falsely hoped to become your mate? *Two years*. You hid our courtship like you were ashamed of me. I know I should have ended it officially before I started courting someone else, and that was my folly. But if you think what you did to me was only my fault..." He laughed humorlessly as he gathered up his notes and started toward the doorway. "You have some nerve, Laurel."

As far as he was concerned, she could wait decades to have a child like every other vampire out there. This was not a favor he was willing to grant.

# CHAPTER 28

"We won't mollify our findings," Doctor Enache said in a grave tone as they all gathered in the commons after the assessment. Everyone leaned forward on the edge of their seats as if dreading to hear his next words. "This disease is ghastly. The reversal of such a disease is next to impossible, especially because whatever was stirred up in those ruins is ancient. It's beyond our comprehension. That's not to say we can't try to combat the disease. But my professional opinion is whatever we try won't work."

Kirsa's hopes weren't dashed because she had no hopes left to dash. But she did want to hear more about her unborn children. "And the babies? How do they look?"

At the mention of the children, Luca perked up at the nearby desk where he was working on Arvitash. He often worked near her in case something was to happen.

"Small," Zachariah answered. "As male physicians, we don't often work in midwifery, but we do get an occasional opportunity. They are measuring small, but I assume it's because they're dwarves. Or...half-dwarf?"

*Full dwarf,* she wanted to say, but disclosing the information was unnecessary.

"However," he continued, "they appear to be healthy and unaffected by the disease."

He didn't say what they were all likely thinking—the babies would never survive if Kirsa didn't, and her survival looked impossible. But she knew that already.

Everyone returned to their conversations, and she was distracted as Luca approached her cushioned chair from behind and tipped her head backward to place a gentle kiss on her forehead. Even upside down, he was the most handsome man she had ever seen, his violet eyes entrapping her within their beautiful, tangled web.

"Anything I can get you?" he asked quietly in Akretti. "Water? Something to eat? Medicine?"

"A kiss?" she grinned mischievously.

Luca glanced up uncertainly at their guests, and anyone who might have been looking their way turned their heads. She was suddenly grateful he had learned Akretti, giving them the advantage in a room full of people who didn't understand it.

"There are people in here. My father is sitting less than ten feet away."

"By all means," she continued, her grin widening, "make a scene by taking me in another room to do it. Or you can do it here. No one is watching."

"Do you always get what you want?" he asked with a playful roll of his eyes.

"When it comes to you, yes."

He chuckled before tipping her head back even more and kissing her fully on the lips, his mouth soft and gentle on her own. She smiled against his lips, and her smile continued even when he broke the kiss. Being married, being in love... It was the most incredible experience in her life, and it was the best thing Luca had helped cross off her list. She loved him with her whole entire heart, and she was glad to have captured him all those months ago.

"How did you propose, Luca?" Cosette asked, startling both of them out of their small world of two. Everyone turned in their direction to hear the answer. Although vampires didn't necessarily propose in their culture, or at least choosing a mate didn't always happen like that, being mated to a dwarf would create different expectations.

Both Luca and Kirsa exchanged glances before snorting in amusement. Through his laughter, he said, "You're assuming I was the one to propose? She beat me to it."

"What?" Laurel laughed. "*She* proposed to *you*?"

Although Kirsa tried not to show it, Laurel's presence in Vrork rattled her. Neither she nor Luca had expected her arrival, but what ruffled Kirsa the most was the vampire's beauty. She was, in her opinion, the perfect female. Creamy, flawless skin. Perfectly shaped lips. Bright blue eyes. Shiny blonde hair. She dressed with impeccable taste, and the way she moved was both feminine and graceful. But what bothered her the most was Luca used to court this female and had at one point wanted to become her mate. How could

Kirsa possibly compare to the vampire? Her own chestnut-brown hair was not shiny, she had plenty of imperfections, she was short, and she had an arm made of stone.

As if feeling her change of mood, Luca placed his hand on her shoulder and gave it a gentle squeeze before answering, "I would have you know that *I* took her to the star pool. *I* set the mood. And she swept my line right from under my feet."

"You were taking too long," she grinned as she gathered her bearings once more.

However, she could hardly remember what they had been talking about before she had asked him to marry her, but she did remember everything he said afterward. She would treasure every word for the rest of her life.

"And how did you meet?" Oriel threw out there moments after Leif slid off his lap to wander the room.

Again, they exchanged glances, but this question was not as amusing as the last.

"Umm…next question," Luca said.

"Come on," Zachariah chuckled. "It can't be that bad."

She answered this time, though certainly not with a smile. She was ashamed of how it happened. "It *is* that bad. I believed vampire blood was the answer to our cure. I sought out a vampire in Ironfell and shot him with a dwarven bolt. Our mutual friend, Chloe, the emperor's daughter, made me swear not to hurt him, but Luca volunteered to help anyway. And well, I brought him back here and that was that."

Lucian frowned, finally speaking after remaining silent the entire time. "You weren't courting the emperor's daughter?" he asked Luca.

He shook his head. "No. When you smelled me on her, it must have been when she'd grabbed my hand to tell me to stay away from Kirsa. I obviously didn't heed her warning."

"You never told me that," she said, looking at him in a new light.

He switched tongues. "I thought you were the most beautiful female I'd ever laid my eyes on, and I begged Chloe to introduce me to you. She refused, of course."

A slow blush crept up her face until she was sure her cheeks had turned scarlet. All jealousy she'd felt for Laurel evaporated in a single moment. Thankfully, Leif turned everyone's attention away from her while she recovered.

"What is this, Mama?" Leif asked with his nose pressed to the mirror on the other side of the room, the mirror no one seemed to have noticed until now. Kirsa found herself holding her breath as Cosette crossed the room to observe his findings, but when she stared back at herself, she shrieked in surprise.

She and Luca burst into laughter at Cosette's reaction to seeing her reflection for the first time in her entire life.

"You're right," Luca laughed again. "Watching a vampire's reaction *is* fun."

"Is this a mirror?" Cosette gasped, her hand on the glass. "I can see my reflection."

"What?" Oriel asked, clearly not believing her as he joined them at the mirror. He froze upon seeing the reflections before his hands slowly rose to touch his hair, his face, his chest, as if trying to match himself to the vampire reflecting in the mirror.

"Let me see," Zachariah joined in, followed by Laurel, who approached as if she didn't care, but the way she craned her neck behind the other vampires told volumes of her interest in the mirror.

"Conceited vampires," she muttered as she playfully elbowed Luca in the ribs. "Like I said before, each and every one of you is self-obsessed."

He rolled his eyes at her and playfully nudged her back. "That is false. I haven't looked in the mirror again after the first time."

"I don't believe it for a single second. I caught you admiring yourself in our chambers only yesterday."

"I'm not sure what you're talking about." His grin appeared mischievous, and she knew for a fact he was bluffing.

Doctor Enache was the next to stroll over to the mirror, unhurried unlike the others, which left only Lucian sitting across from them. He seemed to have no interest in the mirror, and for a moment, Kirsa wondered why. Had he already known it was there? A vampire as old as him likely would have noticed it faster than anyone else.

Lucian rested his head against his hand as he looked at her, studied her, and his stare almost convinced her he saw straight through her as well. He commented, "You remind me of a dwarf I once knew a long time ago, Kirsa. He passed through Ichor Knell once and stayed with the Dragomirs for a few weeks. I never did see him again, but he had the strangest name I could never forget. Thrandunli Orchelm. He was secretive and mysterious but—"

"What was that name?" Luca asked with wide eyes, and his father repeated the name.

Luca scrambled back to the desk and carelessly knocked several things to the floor before rushing back to her side as he thrust a pad of parchment into her hands.

"Kirsa, write it down in Akretti, how you think it would be spelled."

It was a strange request, but the crazed look in his eyes told her the last thing she wanted was to deny him. She wrote the name down the way she might write it in her language, but it wasn't a name she'd ever heard before.

She handed it back to him, but after glancing at it, he shook his head and returned the pad to her hands once more. This time, she took more care to sound the name out in her head before hesitantly writing it down a second time. She only barely finished the last letter before he snatched it from her, his eyes widening tenfold.

"By the nine," he muttered as he ran his hands through his hair, and in a flurried motion, he scooped up his Arvitash materials and ran straight into the doorframe in his haste to leave the room, which caused him to drop several papers. He plucked them from the floor and disappeared, leaving no trace of himself behind.

Clutching her hands to her heart, she prayed like she'd never prayed before. She didn't know if Luca had discovered something important, but she hoped with all her heart that he had.

# CHAPTER 29

"By the nine," Luca muttered again as he compared the dwarven name to the death dates Elric had found months prior, a record he'd set aside when he thought it served no use. But as he looked back and forth between Kirsa's writing and the Arvitash death records, he knew it to be true.

He'd found a match.

For a moment, he sat back in his chair, dumbfounded. A low-burning fire crackled softly in the hearth, giving warmth to the room when the weather had taken a frigid turn outside the Mountain. It sizzled and popped, deafening compared to the stupor of his mind.

After all these months of seeking, learning, and beating his head against the wall in frustration from dead end after dead end, he'd found the answer. He'd been looking at the problem the wrong way, treating Arvitash as if the Akretti language had descended from it. But looking at the comparisons now, he realized the ancient dwarven language was a separate entity altogether, completely isolated from other languages in existence today.

When his stupor wore off, he scrambled for ink and a quill, and nearly spilled the bottle on his research in his haste. The number of letters matched. The approximate timeframe he'd gathered from his father about this dwarf matched as well.

Within minutes, he assembled a brand-new alphabet along with its respective numbers, but he didn't stop there. He used his new findings to decipher the Arvitash samples he'd collected from the ruins. He wasn't sure how much time had passed before he pushed his chair back again and found himself staring wide-eyed at a translation that made sense. Although he didn't quite understand the context of every sentence, he didn't need to because it was correct. The translation was perfect.

But one thing was still missing—the cure.

The samples mentioned the Rotting Blight, except they called it the Black Illness. It was deadly. It was binding. But they'd found a solution as far as he understood, one the ancient dwarven chieftain had discovered himself.

"Then why did they all die off in the end?" he wondered aloud as he tapped the end of the quill against his forehead.

Either their cure hadn't worked, or something had hindered its success.

He clenched his jaw as he set his quill down, gathered his translations, and made his way to his and Kirsa's chambers to find it empty. But he wasn't looking for her. Not yet.

His heart pounded with both fear and determination as he dressed himself in leather armor, strapping several knives on his person before he tucked a steel sword into the scabbard on his belt. He thought to grab an extra sword on his way out of his room, and straining his ears to listen for Kirsa, he followed her voice only to find himself in the commons once more. Doctor Enache and Zachariah had already left, but it looked as if everyone else had stayed.

Those in the commons looked up as he entered, and Kirsa scanned him up and down, her eyebrows furrowing in concern.

"Luca, where are you going?" she asked. She attempted to stand, but the moment she tried, she began coughing, her breath coming out as little more than a wheeze. He rushed to her side with a cup of water. Only when her coughing fit died down did he answer.

"I've figured it out," he said as he placed the translations into her lap. "The ancient dwarves called the disease the Black Illness. I believe they found a cure, judging from what I've translated. But I don't have enough information." He took a deep breath and returned her wavering, fearful gaze. "I'm going back into those ruins."

"No!" she cried, almost before he managed to finish his sentence. She grabbed onto his arm with a desperate hold. "The last time was dangerous enough. You could die."

"And if I don't, you will die. Our *children* will die."

He glanced up and cringed when he found everyone watching him, listening to their conversation, and only then did he realize he hadn't thought to switch to Akretti. What were they all still doing here anyway? He suspected Kirsa of actually enjoying their company. The only vampires he cared to be under the Mountain were Cosette and Leif.

"I will accompany you," Oriel volunteered, much to the horror showing on Cosette's face. He'd never allow his brother-in-law to step foot into those ruins, if only to protect his sister from losing her mate.

"Do you even know how to wield a weapon?" he scoffed.

Oriel ignored his barb and reached for the extra sword in Luca's hands. By the way he struggled to attach it around his waist told volumes of his inexperience with weaponry. But something Luca *did* need...

Materialization. To get from here to the ruins quickly. The only two vampires capable of such a feat in this room were his father and Oriel, and quite frankly, he'd choose to nurse his pride for receiving his brother-in-law's help over his father's.

"Luca, don't go," Kirsa begged, tugging on his arm as she struggled to her feet. The action winded her, as she fought for breath to continue her protest. "I would never forgive myself if you got hurt, or worse."

"It's not as if we have any other options, love."

She quieted and averted her gaze as she slowly released his arm. He listened to the way her heart sped up, and he knew there was something she wasn't telling him.

"We do have another option, don't we?" he asked, lifting her chin to meet his gaze.

Biting her lip, she nodded as her uncertainty changed to stubbornness, something he recognized all too well. "I should have told you long ago, but I couldn't bring myself to do it." She switched her language to Akretti, and he knew what she was about to say was a dwarven secret. "Extracting the compounds of your venom was a success. I could use it to grant healing to our people, but it's tied tightly to immortality. If we use it, our people will become immortal. But that's not what dwarves are! We are mortal. We have long lives, but we are still mortal, and to change that would be to change the very fiber of what makes us dwarves."

"Take the elixir," he ordered. "I will not lose you."

Even in her sickly state, she stood taller until the top of her head nearly met his chin. "I choose mortality. If I wanted to become immortal, all I had to do was simply ask you to bite me."

"Please, Kirsa."

"No." It was as if her remaining energy fled from her, and she lowered herself back to her seat while pressing her hand against her head. "My answer is no, and that's final."

Luca snarled and slammed his fist against the table, his strength causing it to crack. He was furious, and the emotion hit him like a surprising flurry, one he hadn't felt in a long time. Not only had she kept this information from him, but she would rather die, she would rather their children die, than become immortal like him.

However, she didn't even flinch, but rather switched back to his native tongue to throw a teasing barb in his direction, likely so everyone else understood it as well.

"I have never seen you so angry, dear. I think I might need to put you down for a nap along with our nephew."

No one laughed. No one smiled. He was still furious.

"If you won't do it," he said as the heat inside him slowly subsided, "then I'm going."

The only indication she gave of her fear was a slight quiver of her chin, but she didn't try to stop him again as he started toward the entrance. Oriel followed him after conversing with Cosette, and Luca stopped short when he heard his father speak in the faintest voice, as if to hide his words from Kirsa. But he still heard them even when she couldn't.

"I can come as well, son."

He turned to face his father, to face his expression that resembled a mix of trepidation and pride. In an equally quiet voice, he answered, "I had hoped you might stay and look after things, and Kirsa, while I'm gone. Heaven knows Cosette can't do it."

Laurel snorted, earning her a questioning glance from Kirsa—who heard none of the conversation—and Cosette's cheeks turned a shade of crimson.

"Be safe," his father said with a nod, and for a moment, the emotion in his eyes took him aback. It had been a very long time since his father had expressed any kind of concern for his well-being. He had no idea how to reply, not in these foreign waters.

"Make sure she doesn't go outside," he finally replied, still quietly, when his head broke the surface of surprise. "The cold outdoor air irritates her lungs. And thank you."

Before he could dwell any longer on his father's seemingly genuine concern, he turned toward the exit with Oriel by his side. Never in his life had he imagined himself working together with Oriel to do anything, and although he still didn't trust the vampire, he'd settle for a temporary truce.

They exited the Mountain, and a chill swept into the air, foretelling the approach of snow on orange-gray clouds. Despite his anger toward his mate for being so stubborn about the way she wanted to live, he was glad she'd get to experience at least one last snowfall. He felt confident about finding what he needed inside the ruins, and he tried hard not to think of what it meant should he fail.

"Ready to show me where the ruins are?" Oriel asked.

"Don't look so complacent." He frowned as he grasped his brother-in-law's arm. "Lowering your guard for a single second could mean your death."

Or at the very least, a lot of pain.

"Thank you for the reminder," Oriel replied dryly, and then they became wisps of silvery flakes, traveling on the chill wind toward a very dangerous, very unnerving destination.

# CHAPTER 30

irsa opened and closed her stone hand, flexing her fingers while staring absently at the fountain of spurting water from Vrork's underground springs. The smell of arctic violets permeated the air, the flower growing in every nook and crevice in the too-empty room. Other than the infirmary, she visited this place often, as it reminded her of her late mother.

The longer she stared at the fountain, the grayer, the bleaker it became. She'd lost everyone she'd ever come to care about, and soon, Tille would likely join the list as well. And now Luca...

She could not believe she'd sent him off the way she had. Without a goodbye. Without a kiss. Without expressing her love for him. There was a chance he might not come back. The ruins were dangerous. They'd claimed Neeva. They'd given Kirsa a deadly disease. And now she feared something awful might happen to her husband.

"He's immortal," she whispered in an attempt to reassure herself.

But dread still clung to her like the smell of Luca woven into her clothing. She pressed her palms into her eyes to ward off the festering ache, but in the darkness of her own mind, she only saw his frustration and anger in the moments before his departure.

"You're a hard dwarf to track down," Lucian said as he entered the cavern. Kirsa lifted her head just enough to roll her eyes from where she sat.

"I doubt it. You forget I'm married to a vampire. There's no hiding from Luca when he locates my scent."

He chuckled and sat next to her on the stone bench, both silent as they watched the fountain continuously spray water. She cast a sidelong glance at him and found her attention drifting to his bared fangs. None of the other vampires she'd met bared their fangs at all times, and she couldn't help but wonder why he did.

"You're really worried about him," he finally said. It wasn't a question but a statement.

"Yes. The horror of those ruins keeps on taking. The last time we braved the journey, I contracted the Blight, and he received a nasty cut to the head that would have killed him should he have been mortal." Her chin quivered, and she tried to hide it by turning her head away, but it was too late. She knew he'd seen it. The children she carried made her far too emotional.

"I'm afraid I misjudged Luca," he said as he leaned forward onto his knees and stared at the fountain more intensely. "I thought he left Ichor Knell in pursuit of his own carnal desires. Drinking, gambling, females… But he was here all the while, serving your people, looking after you, producing my grandchildren. How will he ever forgive me?"

For a long moment, she didn't know how to reply. She knew Luca's feelings toward his father, and up until now, she'd been sure their relationship could never be repaired. But she realized it might be possible after all.

She twisted her wedding band around on her finger as her thoughts drifted to Luca. "When I met him, he was empty. Broken. A shell of the vampire he is now. I've been trying to help him feel again, whether or not he's caught onto my efforts. I hate to send him off angry at me, but it's my last parting gift in case something happens. I don't believe he's felt anger of this magnitude in many years."

Lucian sighed and shook his head sadly. "I never noticed what you seemed to have caught onto so quickly."

Once again, they became silent, and the fountain obligingly filled the silence with its echoing stream of water. Something she'd never admit to anyone, it was nice to have a father again. After her father had passed, the void had felt far too empty. But now, she had another father, one she wanted to get to know better.

"I suppose I need to learn Akretti now, what with dwarves as my kin." He looked at her with a glint of amusement in his eye.

"I'm not sure Luca would appreciate it," she returned with a teasing smile. "I think he likes talking about you behind your back without you understanding him."

"He does that?"

"No," she laughed. "But he'll never get the chance at this rate."

Their conversation was interrupted by ear-splitting warning bells, and her smile immediately fell from her face as horror replaced it. She scrambled to her feet and her legs nearly collapsed from beneath her as her weak body threatened to fail her.

"No!" she gasped.

She tripped in her rush down the hallway, but only managed to scrape her knees against the rough stone floor. It took every effort possible to pick herself up again, but she managed it, if only just barely.

"Please, no," she begged, tears streaming down her face. It was Tille's unit, she just knew it. Their unit had been in stasis longer than any of the others.

Her weak knees gave out again, and just when she thought she wouldn't have the strength to get back to her feet, strong arms picked her up off the floor, and the walls flew by quicker than she'd been able to run. Lucian didn't ask where she needed to go, and she wasn't sure he'd be able to hear her anyway over the deafening panic in her mind.

They reached the infirmary, and he stopped short to set her down, likely because vampires couldn't enter rooms without permission. She burst through the door only for horror to consume her once more. It was truly Tille's unit, each of their bodies convulsing as death squeezed its sharp claws into their bodies. The two nurses ran back and forth between the patients, but their efforts were futile. If Kirsa stood by and did nothing, this would be their end.

"Take them out of stasis!" she ordered between wheezing breaths. "Take them out!"

"Chieftain," one of the nurses protested in her flurry to see to the patients, "they'll likely die if we do that."

"They'll die if we don't. Do it now!"

"But we've never done—"

"Do it!"

The nurse nodded, and one by one, they injected each convulsing dwarf with a clear substance. The seizing became less violent after only a few moments, and little by little, their movements stopped until they lay still, not breathing.

Kirsa pressed her fingers to her lips as the quiet stillness rang in her ears, shock pulsing through her body with each heartbeat. She stared at Tille's unmoving form, and when it seemed like his smile had once danced across his face, it now remained still.

*No. No. No. No. No. Not Tille. Not Tille.*

When looking at her brother became too much for her heart to bear, she turned away from him, her hands shaking where she placed them over her chest. Her entire family. Gone. At the beginning, she'd thought the Blight was cruel. But no. What was cruel was watching each one of them die, one after the other, until only she remained. She couldn't do it. This time, she couldn't handle the loss.

Her knees wobbled, and the room spun around her as if she were trapped in a tidepool.

*Why couldn't you have taken me instead?* she wanted to shout, to cry, to scream to the gods. But her tongue didn't obey her. Her grief, her anger, got swallowed up beyond the four corners of the sky.

"Kirsa?"

At the sound of the small, weak voice, she spun around, her eyes widening in disbelief. The dwarves previously in stasis began stirring, and Tille lifted himself onto one elbow. Before he moved so much as another inch, she flew in his direction and smothered him in her arms, tears trailing down her cheeks as she rocked him back and forth, back and forth.

Like her, the Blight covered his entire body, the black markings even trailing up the right side of his face and into his hairline. He likely had less time than her before his death, but she was relieved to at least spend some time with him, however fleeting, while he was conscious.

"I don't feel so good," he said as he pulled away to look into her eyes before his gaze shifted to the room around them, to the other patients slowly waking, to Lucian still standing just outside the door. He was looking for someone, and she knew exactly who that someone was. "Where's Mother?"

Her tears returned with a vengeance as she pulled Tille closer and held him tight like he might slip away from her at any moment. She ran her fingers through his hair, greasy from not receiving a proper bath in a long time. She looked into his tearful golden eyes, once again resuming their dance of life, though slower this time, like a somber lullaby.

She whispered in his ear, "She's gone, little one. I'm so sorry. It's only us now. But we'll be fine. We still have each other."

Tille's shoulders began shaking, though he made no sound as he wept into her shoulder. She wished she could take his pain away, to shoulder it in his stead. He'd missed so much during his time in stasis, and she couldn't begin to summarize the heartache and pain that accompanied the last year.

Even when Tille ceased crying, he still held tightly onto her as if trying to get used to the idea of their mother's death, all while his gaze scanned the room again and again like he was attempting to re-familiarize himself with being conscious.

Other dwarves exiting stasis called out for their loved ones, and a young female around Tille's age was experiencing a panic attack while a nurse tried unsuccessfully to calm her down.

The second nurse approached Kirsa with bewilderment in her eyes, as if she hadn't believed taking the dwarves out of stasis would work. Kirsa hadn't been sure of it either, but she'd never admit it.

"What should we do now, Chieftain?" the nurse asked as she smoothed down her hair.

"Sound the relief alarm. And notify the dwarves' family members if they have any remaining. I don't know how much time they have left, but it's best if they spend it with loved ones."

Tille looked up at her with his large, golden eyes, slivers of brown tucked away near the pupil. "Am I going to die, Kirsa?"

She caressed her brother's uninfected cheek with her thumb, and somehow, she dug deep within herself to manage a brief smile. "Everything will be fine."

"Why is a vampire here?"

She followed his gaze to the doorway where Lucian still stood with his attention turned outward toward the hall. For a moment, she wondered if he was listening to the happenings of the Mountain.

"Lucian is family," she attempted to explain. "I married a vampire, Luca, and Lucian is my father-in-law."

Her brother didn't answer, but instead stared distrustfully at Lucian from the protection of her arms. Tille had never liked vampires, afraid the "beasts of darkness" would snatch him while he slept.

Placing a grateful kiss on his cheek, she closed her eyes and rested her chin on top of his head. Tille was alive. He was sick. Very sick. But he was alive. And now she prayed for another miracle. Just one more.

For without it, the dwarves would not survive.

# CHAPTER 31

The first time Luca laid eyes on the dwarven ruins, he had been in awe of its splendor, the colors, the architecture, the grandeur, despite the crumbling decay. But as he stared at it now, a feeling of dread rose from the very ground he stood on and upward until it entered his lungs, suffocating him from the inside out. Memories—or rather nightmares—flashed across his vision of the thick darkness, the creatures lurking within its walls, the stale spores floating dangerously in the air.

And as he stared at the high palace-like entrance, the cracked pillars on each side of the ruins, and the chipped, flaking gold, he was reminded of the last time he'd entered the ruins with Kirsa. He should have gone in by himself. If he was unsuccessful at finding a cure, these very ruins would be the thing to kill her.

Especially because she refused to consume the immortal elixir she'd managed to create from his venom.

Fury crawled through him like the very foul creatures lurking within the ruins, and the feeling drove him forward on determined feet. This was for his family. For his future children. For his mate.

They stopped at the entrance, and even now as he stood still, he heard the faint scrambling of the chasotids within. His heart started to race, his palms sweating. At one time, he'd thought iron was the most terrifying thing a vampire should fear. But he'd been wrong.

"Keep your ears peeled," Luca said as he turned to Oriel, finding him studying the ruins cautiously himself. "If I find I'm not able to make it out, I'll at least try to translate any Arvitash I find that might help find a cure, and I want you to hear it when I shout it out."

Oriel shook his head, narrowing his eyes. "Don't think you're going in there by yourself."

At one point, the intimidating look his brother-in-law gave him might have sent him running, especially during the years he'd tried to regain Laurel's favor, but now he had much bigger things to worry about than Oriel.

Luca raised a challenging eyebrow and didn't back down from the warning in Oriel's ice-blue eyes. "Don't tell me you actually care. We both know how you feel about me. Cosette isn't around for you to show your usual half-hearted sliver of feigned concern, so you can drop the act."

He continued to keep his guard up, even as Oriel uncrossed his arms, his own guarded stance falling as his hands lowered to his sides. The display of amity increased his caution tenfold. The vampire had never been kind to him, not even in Luca's earlier years before Laurel.

An eerie hiss followed a scrape on rock within the ruins, making him flinch and instinctively reach for his weapon. However, as his fingers brushed against the cold hilt of his sword, he was reassured by the fact that chasotids never ventured outside their nest, not unless strongly compelled.

Oriel's hand rested on top of his weapon as well, but he didn't seem as concerned about the noise. Likely because he didn't know what the chasotids were capable of.

"There have been few times in my union with Cosette when she was furious with me," Oriel said, his gaze flicking back to him. "I don't think I've ever seen her more upset with me than the night you came by my home, the night you left Ichor Knell. She had every right to be furious. I was never welcoming to you."

This conversation was over. The last thing he wanted was Oriel's pity.

But when he turned and started toward the caved-in entrance, Oriel called after him, "Laurel spoke with me about you. About what happened between you two."

The mention of Laurel halted him in his tracks, though he didn't turn his attention away from the ruins looming above him, the loose stone threatening to crash to the ground at any moment. He felt nothing for Laurel. Not anymore. But everything she had done to him still hurt, the injustice of it all. Not that he wasn't to blame either. The bad blood between them was both of their faults.

"She told me about how unfairly she treated you," Oriel continued, his voice small as the wind carried the sound away from him rather than toward. "She told me she needed to take the majority of the blame, and she regrets slandering your name all because of how upset she was at the time."

Luca was speechless. Had Laurel really set aside her pride and admitted fault to her brother? It seemed so unlike her, and a part of him couldn't believe it.

Oriel continued despite his lack of reply. "I was too quick to believe only her side of the story. Too quick to judge you."

"Yes, well, it seems it's highly contagious as of late," he muttered sarcastically under his breath. Finally, he turned to face Oriel, still suspicious of the apology. "Did she tell you why she spoke to me earlier?"

For a moment, Oriel looked confused, as if he had no idea what he was talking about. "No. Should she have?"

Even more perplexing... Laurel hadn't admitted fault because she was trying to manipulate Luca into letting her in on the dwarven secret of increasing a vampire's fertility. She had done it behind his back, not expecting anything in return.

"I suppose not," he said slowly, still puzzling over the entire situation. But then he reminded himself that every moment he wasted was another moment someone might die, including Kirsa. He needed to get into those ruins. "As I said, I want you to stay out here. Cosette would kill me if something happened to you."

Again, he approached the ruins, only just barely touching one of the fragile pillars when he noticed Oriel following him. He rolled his eyes and finally gestured to the entrance. "By all means. A cat has nine lives and you already used up one of them when you got defanged. After today, you will have seven left."

"Except I'm a bird," Oriel smirked as they both continued forward. "*Your* transformation is closer to a cat."

"I'm not a cat."

"Four legs, small, vertical pupils, retractable claws, can climb trees. Therefore, a cat."

Luca flexed his fingers as his scowl deepened. The other vampire had always been good at getting under his skin. "A fox is not a cat. It's a canine."

"I think I know a cat when I see one. Both Laurel's and Zachariah's transformations are leopards, after all."

"I'm this close to sending you inside by yourself," he growled, to which Oriel chuckled.

The opening in the rock face Luca had created earlier for Kirsa was only large enough to accommodate a dwarf, so instead of trying to squeeze through the narrow slit, they shrank down into their transformations—Luca a fox and Oriel a swallow—and quietly moved forward. The caves were dark, but his vision adjusted after a few moments as his fox eyes helped enhance his already augmented vampire vision. The walls that obviously once held splendor of gold and jewels now only held decay and destruction. Furniture and paintings had all but turned to dust, and where they had once resided on or against the walls were now replaced by giant holes where the chasotids had eaten through solid rock.

*Careful of the floor,* Luca said in a high-pitched noise at the back of his throat only vampires and sometimes other creatures like werewolves could hear. *The chasotids like to leave traps for unsuspecting victims to fall through.*

He remembered the last trap he'd fallen into. His head had ached fiercely for days after the cut he'd received. If he'd been mortal, the fall would have killed him, and he was grateful he'd taken the brunt of it rather than Kirsa who could have died from such an injury.

Oriel swooped through the air and perched on an upper platform of rusted metal as if surveying the area while Luca padded forward on near-silent feet.

*What are we looking for?* Oriel asked in the same high-pitched noise.

*We're looking for the chief, or what remains of the chief. Perhaps where he used to spend most of his time. The library, a study, perhaps. He likely kept records.*

*And what if those records have turned to dust like the rest of these ruins?*

Luca frowned but continued forward nonetheless, jumping over a fallen pillar and ducking through an opening in a pile of rubble. He was surprised at how much easier it was to traverse the ruins without worrying about Kirsa's safety. As a small animal, he was more likely to avoid detection by the chasotids. Still, he kept both ears cocked as he listened to the rumblings within the belly of the ruins. More than one chasotid moved above, slithering through tunnels on their hundred legs or repeatedly bringing their pincers together to sound like chattering teeth. They were too far for immediate concern, but he'd rather keep them in unaware than alert the creatures to their presence.

*I'd rather not think about the possibility,* he finally answered as Oriel followed through the air on quick, slicing wings.

A brush of insect legs on rock made him freeze in his tracks, and he paused, keeping absolutely still while holding his breath as he listened. It sounded as if the creature was in the next room, but he understood enough to know it was likely a series of tunnels the creatures traveled through, ones he couldn't outright see.

The creature skittered past, and it wasn't until the sound moved farther away that he dared to continue forward. Vampires may be immortal, but he was certain getting ripped to shreds just might kill him, too.

*I'll scour ahead,* Oriel said once the danger passed. *I'm sure they're used to birds getting trapped in these ruins. They likely won't see me as much of a threat as they'd see you.*

He begrudgingly nodded his head and watched as Oriel dove down from his perch, his wings cutting sharply through the air as he turned the corner and disappeared from view. A surprising pang of worry entered him as he continued onward, following his brother-in-law's scent while being wary of his surroundings. He'd never outright worried over Oriel's well-being before, not even when he'd gotten defanged by vampire slavers and nearly lost his life. Of course, he'd worried over Cosette and Leif during that time, but never Oriel.

What changed?

*I did,* he realized.

A lot had happened since leaving Ichor Knell and meeting Kirsa. He'd felt so lost for so long, and now that he'd finally found himself again, he realized he'd changed quite a bit.

*Kirsa...*

The mere thought of her quickened his pace, though he cringed at how loud his footsteps sounded against the echoing destruction. They were nearly louder than the water dripping from the ceiling above and splashing drop by drop into a pool near his feet.

Chattering pincers raised his hackles, and he stopped, frozen to the spot as he listened to the danger lurking beneath him this time. Another tunnel only a few feet below. The chattering moved away from him, and only when it disappeared did he dare breathe again.

Moments later, Oriel swooped around the corner, his wing feathers reflecting what little light came from the small cracks in the entrance. At first, Luca tensed as he waited for a chasotid to follow closely behind, but nothing stared back at him but darkness and dripping water.

After perching on a loose brick on the wall, Oriel said, *Most of the ruins are collapsed, likely from the chasotid tunnels. But I found something you might want to see.*

He nodded. *Lead the way.*

Rubble crunched deafeningly loud beneath his feet as he jumped up on crumbling platforms leading into one of the chasotid tunnels. His entire body shivered in distress as the cold, damp earth sank into his skin and straight to his bones. The tunnel reeked of feces and mildew, and it was all he could do to keep himself from transforming back into a vampire if only to be capable of holding a hand to his nose to prevent himself from breathing in the stench.

As he followed Oriel through the winding tunnel, the air thickened with spores, floating lazily across his vision as if it had innocent intent. But he knew what the spores were capable of.

They killed.

He sighed in relief when they finally dropped down into a room, what might have been plush, red carpet at one point now brown and damp, tainted with mildew. Rotting bookshelves lined each wall, and when it might have once been full to the brim with books, those volumes were now piles of soggy remains, having entered their own watery grave many years ago.

When his line of sight was restricted in his fox form, he transformed back into a vampire and squinted against the immediate change of vision. The darkness nearly swallowed him whole, at least until his eyes adjusted enough to find a sliver of light raining down from the rafters above. The fissure was large enough for Oriel to fly through to safety if needed, but as for himself…

"All of these books are ruined," Luca said quietly as he surveyed each bookcase, sifting his finger through the soggy remains. The material turned to mush beneath his touch, the texture slimy between his fingers.

"There has to be something you can use," Oriel replied, his mouth turning into a grimace as he glanced back at the tunnel they had come from. "Otherwise, we'll have to travel through those again."

He continued to search the room, his heart falling more and more with disappointment the longer he looked. It was all useless. Completely useless.

His heart skipped when his gaze passed over a small, rotting desk tucked into the corner of the room. He made sure to approach on quiet feet, only to find a chair that looked to have once been occupied. Only ash remains lingered on the chair as if whoever had been sitting there had been taken by the rot before decaying. An old, rusty pointed object lay on the table beside a stone tablet, a tablet filled with Arvitash.

Every pore in his body screamed at him to snatch the tablet and run, but he couldn't leave the ruins until he found something to help Kirsa and the remaining dwarves.

Carefully, he picked up the tablet and held it beneath the ray of light shooting down from the ceiling to better help him see it. Each page was covered in dust, and only after he blew it away with a gust of breath did he recognize the Arvitash symbols.

He wanted to cry, to leap for joy, just because he could read it. It was a record, a journal of sorts.

*I, Chieftain Galarr, etch my words into this stone far too late. The Black Illness has spread, and even locked away in my study, it has found me as well. I am one of the last to succumb to this disease, and although we sent dwarves out of the temple's reach to multiply and prosper, I fear they, too, will soon come to know the pain of the Black Illness.*

*It is my deepest regret that I was unable to save my people from suffering. The cure was in the blood of the Sleeping Giants, but it takes several decades for them to reach maturity. The creatures are still no larger than my smallest finger, certainly not enough to draw a sufficient amount of blood.*

*We were too late, and the blame is on my own shoulders. I should not have allowed my curiosity and desire for discovery to drive me to the crypts beneath the temple. It awakened a disease far greater than any dwarf can withstand. I now know—*

The words ended there, as if Galarr had succumbed to the Rotting Blight before he could finish his final sentence. Luca's eyes widened and his heart raced as he read and reread the section mentioning the cure.

What were the Sleeping Giants? The last thing he wanted was to venture into giant territory. Even with a group of strong vampires at his backing, they'd either walk away with substantial injuries or not walk away at all.

His ears picked up the sound of chattering pincers, and fear pulsed through his veins as he jumped backward on instinct moments before a chasotid burst through the wall, showering dirt and debris across the room. He lost his balance, the stone tablet flying from his hands as he fell backward onto the ground. The chasotid reacted quickly, darting toward him and lashing out with pincers sharper than an elven blade. Despite rolling out of the way, the pincers still managed to catch him on the side of his head, slicing through the top layer of his skin. Blood trickled from his wound, dripping down his temple and soaking into his shirt.

The creature lashed out again, digging into the flesh of his arm and trapping him against the wall. Its large, beady black eyes held a menacing note, one designed to kill. He struggled against its powerful grip, wishing he was an older vampire, as age gave one more strength. Young as he was, he could hardly fight back against the insectoid.

He cried out as its sharp, centipede-like legs slashed at his side, drawing even more blood from him. It was as if the creature smelled the blood, lusted after it, because it once again raised its legs to attack again.

Oriel charged at the chasotid with his weapon raised, and the creature unlatched its hold on Luca just long enough to look in the other vampire's direction. In its distraction, Luca weakly drew his dagger and sliced off one of its many legs. The chasotid screeched and reeled backward, managing to dodge Oriel's attack and sweep him off his feet with a swing of its mighty black, slimy tail. It didn't notice Luca approach from behind. He smashed his foot against its back, sending it careening into a bookshelf, which toppled on top of the creature.

However, the chasotid was tough enough to withstand the blow.

It shot out from under the bookcase and screeched wildly as it lashed out at Luca once more. He dodged to the side, and the creature crashed into the table, momentarily stunned. He stared wide-eyed at the chasotid getting ready for another strike. It was so large, much larger than him. If only they had entered the ruins when the beasts were sleeping, this would have been much easier.

His eyes widened as the chasotid chattered its long, shiny, menacing pincers.

*Sleeping Giants.*

The words from the tablet echoed in his mind as his gaze ran over the top of the creature's head to the very tail it used to help it stand upright. *The creatures are still no larger than my smallest finger, certainly not enough to draw a sufficient amount of blood.*

"Blazing hills," Luca whispered to himself, now horrified he'd killed one of these monsters in the first place. He turned to Oriel, fresh blood still dripping down his neck. "Go! I have a plan. Meet me outside."

"Are you daft?"

"I said go!"

Oriel glared, but without another word, he transformed into a swallow and shot up through the crack in the rafters, disappearing from view. The chasotid lunged forward, but before it could deliver another blow, Luca rolled out of the way, picked up the stone tablet, and transformed into a fox, the tablet transforming with him. He jumped into the chasotid tunnel and sprinted as fast as his canine legs could carry him.

A smash, followed by a crumbling tunnel wall, alerted him to the pursuing chasotid. Quick, too, judging by the sound of skittering legs getting closer and closer...

He jumped down from the tunnel and into the hallway that had long ago fallen into destruction and decay. The chasotid's pincers chattered as it chased after. Even as fast as Luca ran, the creature was faster. The crack in the entrance seemed so far away as he willed his legs to move as swiftly as they could possibly carry him. Its pincers brushed against his tail only moments before he burst outside into the fresh air of twilight.

The chasotid followed.

It broke through the entire wall, sending shattered pieces of stone flying in every direction. One of those chunks smashed into his back, and he crashed to the ground. He wasn't fast enough to dodge as the chasotid hurtled forward and stood over him, its pincers open as it readied for another attack. He gasped in fright and reached for his dagger, only to find it absent on his belt. He had dropped it, and his sword was pinned beneath a chunk of stone.

He screeched and bared his fangs, preparing to defend himself in the only way he could. The chasotid lurched forward—

—and a gush of blood spurted all over Luca, covering him from head to foot in the tarish-red, sticky substance. Oriel had cut its head off, and the rest of its body lay limp on the ground.

"I didn't realize you knew how to use a sword," Luca gasped as he struggled to his feet, wanting to be as far away from the severed head as possible.

Oriel also breathed hard as he answered, "I don't. But how hard is it to swing one?"

The precious blood was still spilling out onto the ground, and he knew only minutes remained before the substance was gone.

"We need the blood," he said in an ordering tone. "Materialize to your house and grab a pitcher."

With a shake of his head, Oriel said, "By the time I get the pitcher and return, the blood will be useless. It will take too long."

They shared a look, and as if they thought the exact same thing, they grimaced. The odor of the tar-like blood singed his nostrils, making him want to wretch out his insides. His nausea worsened from being covered in the sickening substance.

He continued to grimace as he dropped to his knees, and with his fangs already bared, he sank them into the chasotid's flesh. The first gulp of blood made him want to die as it hit his stomach like a foul acid, burning through him from the stench alone. The taste churned his stomach in ways he didn't know it could churn, and it took every effort not to give into his body's protest to purge the blood.

Oriel, too, sucked up the blood, and he didn't seem to be faring any better. It was only until Luca's stomach was ready to burst when he unlatched his fangs and reeled away from the dead creature, placing his hands on his knees to keep himself from pitching forward from pure disgust.

"I hate you, Luca," Oriel said on unsteady feet, a hand over his mouth as if trying to keep the blood from coming back up.

The blood gurgled unkindly in his stomach, and he forced himself to take several long, deep breaths through his nose to stop himself from retching. "At the moment, I hate myself, too." He gulped in another breath, but it did nothing to dispel the stench from his clothing, his hair, his very throat. "Besides, you insisted on coming. Now get us back."

Oriel didn't need to be told twice. He gripped Luca's arm and they materialized. Moments later, they found themselves running toward the Mountain as fast as their legs could carry them, almost faster than when he'd been running from the chasotid in the ruins.

He burst through the entrance, receiving a startled glance from Gunther before he continued forward, clutching the Arvitash stone tablet in one hand and clamping a hand over his mouth with the other.

"Luca!" Kirsa gasped as they rushed through the commons, and he barely spared a glance in her direction, his eyebrows pulling together in confusion when he found what looked to be a younger male version of herself sitting beside her. *Tille...*

He simply shook his head and held back another wave of nausea, and it wasn't until they burst into the lab when they each found a wooden bowl and purged out their insides. Sweat beaded Luca's blood-crusted brow as he heaved and heaved, and when his stomach was empty of the foul substance, he heaved again.

"That was revolting," Oriel muttered, sliding to the ground with his back against the wall.

Following suit, he dropped down next to him and placed his head between his knees to calm his raging nausea. "I couldn't agree more."

Oriel snorted first, and Luca found himself snorting second, and then they burst into laughter at the absurdity of the situation. Not only had they just agreed on something, but they had gotten out of a literally sticky situation relatively unscathed.

His brother-in-law surprised him by holding out a hand. "Can we start over and be friends?"

Emotion washed over him, and he took a few moments for himself to keep it from showing. When his words failed him, he took Oriel's hand and returned the gesture with a firm shake.

"I would like that," he finally said.

"Now go take a bath. You smell worse than death."

He chuckled and placed his head between his knees. He'd take a bath as soon as he knew he wouldn't dry heave the moment he stood. Besides, he needed to speak to Kirsa immediately. They couldn't waste a single moment.

# CHAPTER 32

Kirsa slammed the lab door open, sheer panic giving her the strength she needed to reach her husband in her fatigued condition. There he was, slumped on the floor near the corner, completely covered in blood.

She hardly paid Oriel any heed as she dropped to Luca's side and placed her hands on his bloodied face. Her panicked words came out in a rush of Akretti.

"Tell me what happened. Are you all right? I was so scared I'd lost you."

Sobs escaped her in earnest, magnified by the blood soaking his clothing, coating his hair, smeared across his skin. She recognized the deeper red chasotid blood, but plenty of it was lighter, and she knew it was his own.

He kissed her palm once, twice, and only when he rubbed his nose against hers did her worry begin to cease. He was alive, and despite the mounds of blood layered on him, her rationale told her he healed fast as a vampire. What mattered was he survived the trip to the ruins, and he came back to her in one piece.

"I'll give you two a moment," Oriel said and quietly slipped out the door, but she hardly spared a glance for him.

"I found something, love." Luca reached for a stone tablet and handed it to her. The engravings in the stone looked familiar, and she recognized the Arvitash script. However, they didn't make any sense at all.

"What does it say?" she whispered, one hand holding tightly to his while her other hand lightly traced the foreign words, each groove in the stone rough against her skin.

As he read the etchings back to her, her eyes widened, hope flaring brighter and brighter in her chest until she could no longer look directly at the inferno.

He did it. He'd found the cure. A vampire of all people. And he had sacrificed so much to find it. Just when she had thought all hope was lost, it returned as a blazing beacon, filling her with a sense of urgency at the thought of Tille, on the very edge of death's grip.

"Thank you," she said quietly. "Thank you so much, Luca. Now all we need is to gather several dwarven soldiers and bring back a chasotid for its blood."

When he grimaced, she thought something pained him, and her hands fluttered uselessly over him. However, he grasped her fingers and held them tightly.

"We brought back some blood. Don't ask how. You don't want to know. It's ready for you to...do whatever it is you do with blood."

She noticed two basins filled with dark red liquid, and an overwhelming sense of gratitude washed over her yet again. She'd never been happier to see blood in all her life. The chasotids of all things! She had never considered that the foul creatures roaming the ruins, the creatures that had killed her sister, would be the very things to offer her people a cure for the Blight.

"I'll get started right away," she said as she struggled to her feet, the energy nearly evading her just when she needed it most. Within moments, Luca was at her side, and before she could protest, he seated her in a chair at her desk. She hated being so weak as to need the help, but she hoped if the blood really was the answer, she wouldn't need help for much longer.

The twins kicked her from within as if they, too, felt the hope surging inside her. She placed her fingers over her belly and took a deep, steadying breath as she cherished the rumbling movement. She swore she'd sit and work in this chair until either exhaustion killed her or the Blight. But she promised herself she'd see this through until the end. Tille's time was approaching quickly, much faster than even her own, and she wouldn't allow him to die if she could help it.

When Luca left to bathe, she turned her intense focus and concentration toward her new task. While the vampire blood she'd harvested again and again had been fruitless, she immediately noticed the small differences the chasotid's blood held. It was compatible with dwarves, and there was no trace of immortality within it.

Hours passed, which quickly turned into days. Luca brought her food and water, and when her shoulders stiffened with fatigue, he rubbed the ache away as she continued her work.

At long last, when she finally finished creating the first batch of elixirs, she pushed away from her desk and stared at a vial of liquid with a slight tint of red to it, a sense of shock overwhelming her. Hundreds upon hundreds of years... That was how much time it had taken to find a cure for the Blight, which she believed stared right back at her.

"You may want to come quick," Adrietta said as she stood in the doorway of the lab. "Tille's heart is beginning to seize."

Panic raced through her as she grabbed a vial from the desk and hobbled down the hallway with Adrietta's help. They burst into Tille's bedroom to find him lying on his cot, his body convulsing as it had days before in the infirmary. Luca knelt at his bedside while tightly holding onto his hand. He looked up at her approach with worry in his eyes, but she didn't spare a moment longer before she strode toward Tille and uncapped the vial. She poured the red-tinted liquid into her brother's mouth and held his jaw closed, forcing him to swallow.

Never in her life had she prayed harder than in those few long moments. Tears blurred her vision as she watched Tille's body continue to convulse, hoping, praying, begging. Her entire family was gone, all except for her brother.

She reached out for Luca's hand and gripped his fingers as hard as her weak muscles allowed. Slowly, Tille's body ceased convulsing until it lay still altogether, just as it had in the infirmary. But instead of her hope evaporating like smoke, she clung to it fiercely, willing it to keep her together.

"He's alive," Luca murmured quietly. "His heart is still beating."

Not quite believing him when Tille lay so still, she placed her hand on her brother's chest and felt a slow but steady rhythm begin to grow and grow, until it felt strong beneath her fingers. She thought her eyes were playing a trick on her when she noticed the black etchings on his face begin to fade, so she wiped the remaining tears only to discover the truth.

The markings from the Rotting Blight withdrew from Tille's skin like shadows in the presence of a blazing fire. They retracted from his face, his neck, his arms, and only when they disappeared completely did his breathing return to a normal rhythm. He didn't wake, but rather lay in peaceful slumber.

"It worked," Kirsa whispered, her fingers trembling as the realization hit her at full force. Tille wasn't going to die. *She* wasn't going to die. Her people would have a second chance to live and prosper, free from the Blight.

She turned rapidly and flung her arms around Luca's neck, clinging tightly to him as she wept into his chest. "It worked," she cried again. "You did it. How can I ever thank you?"

"*We* did it," he amended as he buried his nose in her hair and rocked her back and forth as if wanting to comfort her in her distressing disbelief. "How many more vials do you have? There are other dwarves not too far behind Tille."

Finally, she forced herself to stand, Luca at one elbow and a disbelieving Adrietta at the other. "I have enough. Send all the afflicted to the infirmary. After today, the Blight will no longer pose a threat to our people."

She glanced back at Tille's peaceful face one last time, a smile of gratitude brightening her previously forlorn expression. It was because of Luca that this was possible. He had saved her brother. He had saved them all.

"Where is Kirsa?" his father asked as the vampire physicians finished their patient evaluations, but this time with favorable results. The dwarves were cured, and as far as anyone could tell, they would stay that way.

"Resting," Luca answered in an exhale of relief. He spun his wedding band around on his finger, grateful for the renewed opportunity to live a good, long life with his mate and future children. For so long, he'd thought he'd lose them all. "Healing from the Blight seems to take a lot of energy out of a person."

His father nodded, and for a few moments, they watched the dwarves on the other side of the commons, talking and laughing with the vampires as if they'd been lifelong friends. It was a stark contrast to the way they had treated him when he'd first arrived in Vrork.

Finally, his father turned to him, breaking the silence between them. "I want to apologize for not being the father you needed. I want you to know I'm proud of you and what you've accomplished here. Very proud."

Fierce emotion gripped Luca and squeezed tight, and it was all he could do to keep the tears at bay as he looked away from his father to stare at the chandelier dripping from the ceiling. All his life, he had yearned to hear such words from his father. Now he didn't know what to do with them except give a faint nod.

"Perhaps we'll come visit Ichor Knell someday, once things settle here."

"I hope you do."

They parted ways, and Luca craned his neck in search of a head of blonde hair. He found her with Zachariah, headed toward the exit as if about to leave.

"Laurel," he said, and even on the opposite side of the room, she heard him and turned her head, blue eyes inquisitive. Motioning with his head toward the door, he said, "I want to speak to you alone for a moment."

She said something quietly to Zachariah before standing on her tiptoes to kiss his cheek. Zachariah stared worriedly after her as if Luca might have malicious intent toward her. He didn't blame the other vampire. After all, he was glad Zachariah was leaving soon and would be far away from Kirsa.

Laurel followed him into a hallway lit by glowing purple crystals, casting a soft warmth across her features as he turned to face her. Although he had loved her in the past, after Kirsa, he now knew their love hadn't held a candle to the blazing wildfire he felt for his mate. As painful as their separation had been, he was glad they hadn't stayed together.

Luca produced a vial of clear liquid from his pocket and held it in his palm, watching as her eyes widened as she glanced from the vial to him. She obviously knew what it was.

"Zachariah is even younger than I am," he started hesitantly, second guessing his decision for the dozenth time. "Are you sure he wants children? He doesn't want to wait?"

As for himself, he hadn't had time to consider what it meant to become a father before he discovered Kirsa was pregnant. Although he loved his unborn children with his entire heart, he would have been fine with waiting.

"Zachariah may be young, but he lived almost half his life as a mortal human. Time moves differently for him than it does for us. He wants them, too."

He didn't miss the hopeful lilt in her voice.

Breathing out a gust of air from his lungs, he stared down at the vial in his hands. Memories of his wedding day surfaced of when he had consumed a vial himself. This was an awfully kind thing to do for a male who had stolen the female he once loved right from beneath him. He disliked Zachariah, and he had a feeling he always would.

But Laurel on the other hand... He could never hate her. Besides, she had finally told Oriel the truth. The full truth. And now his relationship with his brother-in-law was on the mend. That had been a kind thing she didn't have to do, but she had done it anyway.

At last, as he made up his mind, he pressed the vial into her hand, watching as tears shimmered in her eyes. She said nothing, but the gratitude in her expression spoke volumes.

"When you are ready, have Zachariah drink this on the peak of your fertility. Every last drop. And don't waste it because I won't give you another."

"Thank you, Luca," she whispered, holding the vial to her heart. "Thank you so much."

She turned to leave, but he called after her, "And one more thing. Tell no one about it. I will not have vampires lining up at my door and expecting the same treatment."

"You can trust me. I will guard your secret with my life."

He watched her leave, the peace of forgiveness finally settling over his heart. He felt so much lighter, as if yet another burden had been lifted from his shoulders. But he didn't dwell on the feeling for long before he strode in the other direction in search of Kirsa. He wanted her to know just how much she meant to him, and he would make sure she knew it every day for the rest of their lives.

# CHAPTER 33

ears shimmered in Chloe's eyes as she first embraced Luca, then Kirsa, and Luca once more. He was immensely glad they were able to visit her in Ironfell. "Do you have to leave already? Stay a few more days. Or weeks."

Kirsa laughed and squeezed their friend's hand, and Luca's gaze darted toward the princess's new human husband who stood by her side. For being strangers when they'd met, they seemed to be happy together.

"We will visit again. Often."

Chloe sniffed and wiped the moisture from her eyes. "I thought I'd never see either of you again. But then I got your first letter and let me tell you how shocked I was to hear about the wedding! Absolutely shocked. I suppose he *was* mooning after you when he first laid eyes on you."

"Mooning?" Luca laughed, crossing his arms. "Give me a little credit. I still managed to retain a few wits about me."

With a shake of her head, Chloe tried to cover her words from his view, but he still saw her mouth, *Completely besotted.*

Kirsa took their daughter Rosalinde's little hand while he reached down and picked up Yvonne and placed her on his shoulders. With one last tearful goodbye, they used a crystal to transport to the one place his mate had longed to visit more than any other.

Ichor Knell—they'd finally made it.

Luca had been nervous all day, all week, all month for this moment, to be faced with the thick and permanent overhanging clouds, the massive black castle he used to live in, and to be surrounded by a sea of vampires instead of a growing hoard of dwarves.

He'd chosen the least conspicuous clothing option for the trip, but he still felt completely out of place amongst the Ichor Knell fashion, a style much more proper and less revealing than dwarven attire. While he wore loose dark blue breeches tucked into brown laced boots and an elbow-length white shirt covered by a brown vest to match, Kirsa had no problem showing skin.

The moment they landed in Ichor Knell, she took off her cloak to show a top that crisscrossed over her chest, revealing plenty of arm, upper chest, and stomach. Of course, he had no problem with the dwarven fashion himself, but he knew vampires would.

But it was the least of his worries.

"You used to live here?" Kirsa gasped, wide-eyed as she took in the scenery displayed before her.

While Vrork had walls inlaid with precious gems and crystals, Ichor Knell grew trees with leaves made of diamonds, sapphires, rubies, and more. While Vrork was enclosed within the Mountain, Ichor Knell was open, covered by clouds that protected vampires from sunlight. Many vampires went about their day, some welding in their shops or selling trinkets at the market. Innumerable people watched them as they passed, taking in the dwarven circlets on their heads, their clothing, and Luca's favorite, his children.

Yvonne, ever the adventurous one at just over a year old, continued to sit on his shoulders while taking everything in with curious eyes. Rosalinde held onto Kirsa's hand while walking slowly at her side, looking like she might duck behind her mother's leg at any moment. They were beautiful twins. Healthy and beautiful with rich black hair and shimmering golden eyes. Yvonne wore two gold earrings in one ear while Rosalinde wore two silver—the one and only thing that made it easier to tell the twins apart when they looked identical.

"This was home," he answered as his gaze traveled up the steps leading to the entrance of the castle. Not only was his family waiting excitedly at the top of the stairs, but Dracula had even made an appearance, likely because he wasn't just Luca anymore, son of Lucian Dragomir, but he and Kirsa were dwarven chieftains. They were the equivalent of royalty, which only made sense to be greeted by vampire royalty.

Dracula's expression exuded caution, as if he wasn't entirely sure how to greet Luca, especially because he saw right through the vampire shah's formidable stance, his overbearing expression, and the fear he often set in people's hearts upon first glance. Dracula was terrifying, yes, but Luca had also spent a lot of time on the training field, sparring with the shah himself.

In the end, the vampire shah said nothing and allowed Lucian to do the talking.

"Welcome to Ichor Knell, Luca, Kirsa," his father said with a smile that revealed his sharp, pointed fangs. "My my, how my grandchildren have grown."

His father stooped down to greet Rosalinde, shy as she partially hid behind Kirsa's leg, and when his mother made a move for Yvonne, Cosette swooped in and took the child from his shoulders, giving her a near bone-crushing embrace.

"Careful there, Cosette," he laughed while following his family into the castle. "You forget vampires are much stronger than dwarves."

"I'm being careful," she argued before kissing the daylights out of Yvonne's face, all while the little girl laughed and unsuccessfully attempted to catch Cosette's lips with her own.

Never one to stay still for long, Yvonne wriggled out of Cosette's arms and when she attempted to run down the hallway, Luca swooped her into his arms and tickled her until she squealed with laughter. He couldn't help but laugh along with her. Aside from marrying Kirsa, having children was the highlight of his life.

His smile fell when he noticed a familiar face across the hallway, a vampire with her curly blonde hair tied behind her back, drooping in large ringlets, not a strand out of place. His gaze drifted to the child she held in her arms, one that couldn't have been more than five months old. The girl wore a light blue dress, and she had short brown hair and large brown eyes to match. Her facial features were gentle, similar to Laurel's, but everything else about the child resembled Zachariah.

When his gaze returned to Laurel, she offered him a soft smile and mouthed, *Thank you.*

He returned the smile and approached with Yvonne surprisingly still in his arms, and he gestured to the child with a dip of his head. "Look at the baby, Yvonne. Isn't she pretty?"

Yvonne's mouth grew into a large, toothy grin as she pointed a finger at the child's forehead, promptly followed by a not-so-gentle open-mouthed kiss. The baby gurgled her protests while both he and Laurel burst into laughter.

"Luca, I'd like you to meet Mariana Degore."

"The first female," he commented, remembering Willow's and Adam's firstborn was a boy, and she had given birth to a second son only recently. Cosette and Oriel had adopted Leif, another male addition to the family. And now Laurel and Zachariah had a female.

Mariana's fangs sprouted without warning, startling him with the unfamiliarity of it. A long time had passed since he'd been around young vampire children.

"I gather the reason you're not used to fangs is because your children don't have any," Laurel said as Yvonne finally managed to wriggle from his arms and ran down the hall in an attempt to explore, only to be snatched up by his mother. "There's not a trace of vampire in them, is there?"

He shook his head and watched his family fawn over the twins, much to Yvonne's exasperation. Kirsa cast occasional glances in their direction, and he knew he needed to end the conversation quickly to avoid upsetting her. "Not a trace," he confirmed, though he'd only admit such a thing to Laurel, as he'd already let her in on a small portion of a dwarven secret.

"How did you do that?"

"Confidential dwarven information."

She lowered her voice. "You will never have vampire children, will you?"

Once again, he shook his head as he finally looked her in the eye. "The survival of the dwarven race depends heavily on *dwarven* reproduction. We cannot produce vampires if we are to make it happen." He shrugged. "But I'm not upset. I will gladly have hundreds of dwarven children if needed."

"Your mate..." she said slowly as she stared at Kirsa, whose gaze once again darted toward them, though she was too far away to hear their conversation. "She's with child again. Just one this time."

A soft smile made an appearance on his face as his hearing sifted through all the noises around them to focus on the one lone heartbeat pattering from within Kirsa's belly. He didn't need to answer Laurel to confirm what she already knew.

"Vampires will begin to get suspicious if you continue to have children at this rate," she warned. "If they haven't already."

"Then let them. They will get nothing from me, and hopefully nothing from you either."

"They won't. I still plan on keeping my promise." Laurel kissed her baby girl and smiled. He was glad to have helped with her small bit of happiness, though it had mostly been Kirsa's doing, as she'd created the serum.

He excused himself and wove around black-haired vampire after black-haired vampire until he forged a path to Kirsa's side, and he didn't care if anyone watched as he planted a kiss of adoration on her cheek. She seemed to relax considerably.

"Ichor Knell is incredible," she said in Akretti as she marveled at the high ceilings, the vampire-styled furniture, and the awe in her eyes increased when she gazed out the window to the cloudy skies. Before Tavian's death, their group of four had once climbed to the tallest point in Ichor Knell, which happened to be on the mountain above the lake, just to see if they could touch those swirling clouds. Of course, the clouds were far too high, and Gavril, who could transform into an eagle, had said flying through the clouds was impossible, as the thickness of them obscured his vision.

"You've hardly seen anything," he chuckled. "I still need to show you the gardens, the lake, the cathedral, and I'm particularly excited about introducing you to a couple of my vampire friends, Skender and Gavril."

She began fidgeting with her earrings, the first display of uncertainty she'd shown since arriving. "Do you think they will like me?"

"I liked you immediately when I met you," he pointed out, yet she still looked uncertain. As much as she'd wanted to visit Ichor Knell, he knew she was nervous about what it entailed.

To take her mind from the worries of meeting new people, particularly vampires, he led her to the window and opened it so she could touch the leaves of a yellow topaz tree nearly scraping against the side of the castle. The topaz reminded him of a vein running through the library walls, glowing with mystery as if the light of the sun reflected through it to make it shine.

"How does it feel to cross the last remaining item off your list?" he asked, running a strand of her hair between his fingers if only for reassurance that she was still by his side, alive, healthy, and completely Blight-free. At times, he could hardly believe she'd survived, especially when nightmares haunted his dreams at night. Oftentimes, he'd find himself grasping for her just to make sure she was still beside him.

Kirsa smiled and turned her head to kiss his palm. "I think I need to make a new list."

"And what will be on your new list?"

She laughed and swatted him playfully. "I will never tell. Good luck stealing it this time, vampire."

He smiled and intertwined his fingers with hers. "I look forward to trying, dwarf."

# ABOUT THE AUTHOR

Sydney Winward is a fantasy and paranormal romance author who dabbles in the occasional historical fiction. She loves building complex worlds filled with magic, strong characters, and emotional stories that can make you laugh and cry.

Sydney is the author of the Sunlight and Shadows Series and the best-selling Bloodborn Series, and when she's not writing, she's reading, thinking about stories, or going on adventures with her children. She lives in Utah with her husband and three amazing kids.

www.sydneywinward.com

www.ingramcontent.com/pod-product-compliance
Lightning Source LLC
Chambersburg PA
CBHW061057210726
48294CB00001B/188